"Officer Silver." The clerk nodded toward the man getting off the elevator. "There he is."

She waited while Agent Paul Falcon passed through security. He was tall with authority in his stride, wearing a tailored business suit. She knew his reputation and what was on his desk. Despite his rank and seniority, he worked cases rather than lead a bureau office. He was as far from bureau politics as a murder cop could get, which made him the man who could help her. He was working on too much caffeine and too little sleep, she thought, noting the coffee mug in his hand and the grim tightness around his eyes. But she'd spent too many days working without sleep herself to find it unusual.

"Agent Falcon, this is Officer Ann Silver."

She stepped aside in the lobby, opened her flight bag and removed two photos. She didn't bother to explain; she simply offered them. He took the photos. His watch looked expensive, and the ring was FBI academy. She'd assumed he was married, yet his left hand was bare.

She saw the flare of heat in his eyes as he recognized the murders. Since the photos were copies of ones in his own files, she assumed they would hit a chord. His gaze shot to hers. She took the punch of annoyance in his eyes because she deserved it. She had set him up for it. She had chosen those two murders for a reason, but the photos themselves were merely cover for her visit. The news she'd come to share wasn't something she planned to write down anywhere.

Praise for *Full Disclosure*

"Weaves a fascinating mystery into a romance . . . [the] ending is as twisty and satisfying as spiral macaroni."

—*Publishers Weekly*

"The characters are strong and the romance is intriguing . . . [Henderson fans] will clamor for this title."

—*Library Journal*

"Be prepared to fall in love with Dee Henderson's writing all over again."

—*CBA Retailers+Resources*

"This is an intriguing story about two detectives dealing with love and trust, as well as murder cases, that will give mystery fans a healthy dose of both romance and suspense."

—*Parkersburg News and Sentinel*

Books by Dee Henderson

FULL DISCLOSURE

DEE HENDERSON

BETHANYHOUSE

a division of Baker Publishing Group
Minneapolis, Minnesota

© 2012 by Dee Henderson

Published by Bethany House Publishers
11400 Hampshire Avenue South
Bloomington, Minnesota 55438
www.bethanyhouse.com

Bethany House Publishers is a division of
Baker Publishing Group, Grand Rapids, Michigan

Printed in the United States of America

ISBN 978-0-7642-3093-6

Library of Congress Cataloging-in-Publication Data for the original edition is on file at the Library of Congress, Washington, DC.

Scripture quotations are from the New Revised Standard Version of the Bible, copyright © 1989, by the Division of Christian Education of the National Council of the Churches of Christ in the United States of America. Used by permission. All rights reserved.

This is a work of fiction. Names, characters, incidents, and dialogues are products of the author's imagination and are not to be construed as real. Any resemblance to actual events or persons, living or dead, is entirely coincidental.

Cover design by Dan Pitts

17 18 19 20 21 22 23   7 6 5 4 3 2 1

Thus says the LORD: Do not let the wise boast in their wisdom, do not let the mighty boast in their might, do not let the wealthy boast in their wealth; but let those who boast boast in this, that they understand and know me, that I am the LORD; I act with steadfast love, justice, and righteousness in the earth, for in these things I delight, says the LORD.

Jeremiah 9:23–24

PART ONE

PAUL FALCON

1

'm pulling into the scene now. There are four dead, but Jackie wasn't hurt. I'll be back in touch, Dad, as soon as I know more." FBI Special Agent Paul Falcon parked behind a Chicago squad car within sight of the blue-and-white restaurant awning with *Falcons* scrolling across the fabric. He shoved the phone back in his pocket. It was just after eleven p.m. and the dark street was bathed in the flashing lights of squad cars. FBI Agent Sam Truebone met him as he cut between the medical examiner's van and the crime-scene van.

"I've seen Jackie, talked to her," Sam said immediately. "Your sister is furious, but fine."

Paul felt the sharp edge of his tension ease off. Being on the other side of town when the shooting occurred had made the drive a slice of private abyss. "Who's got the scene?"

"Lieutenant Sinclair."

Chicago PD had sent one of their top homicide cops. The woman wasn't hard to spot, as she controlled the scene, people flowing to and away from her. Paul headed her direction.

"Hello, Kate."

"Your sister's fine."

"I heard that."

"One of your father's places," she added.

"When is it not?" His father's empire ran to so many corners of the nation, pockets of family business showed up everywhere he turned. "Need some help?"

She smiled at him. Not the one she normally gave him—warm, welcoming, and often amused—this was her cop's smile, cool and assessing, but willing to play nice. "I don't mind working with the Feds when it suits me, and in this case it does. This shooter is one of yours."

"That fits the night this is becoming. Which one?"

"Andrew Waters. We've got him on tape. Rick Ulaw, undercover narcotics cop with the sixteenth precinct, was having dinner with his wife. Waters walked up to the table and shot him twice in the back and once in the head. He then killed three civilians who got in his way. He left the scene in a dark blue sedan. His photo is out to every cop in the state, and newscasts have just put it up. If he's in Chicago, he's ours. If he's slipped out, you can help haul him back so I can bust him."

"You'll have everything we have on him within the hour. And I'll personally take any assignment you want to give me. You want flyers plastered on telephone poles in Mexico, I'm your guy."

"I've already called Marcus and told him I want Quinn on it tonight coordinating the manhunt. Leave Sam with me, and give me Christopher Zun. I like him."

"You'll have them."

She was married to an FBI agent, had the head of the U.S. Marshals as a close friend, and called the Chicago Police her territory. Kate would get whatever she needed to run the case. And he was wise enough to let her have a clear field to do it. If Waters could be run to ground tonight, Kate would get it done. Paul could delegate the work, but he couldn't delegate family. And right now he had family to deal with.

Kate must have been thinking along the same lines. She nodded toward the restaurant. "Go convince your sister to go home. We've got the scene handled. As ugly as this case is, it is also simple. I backtrack to figure out who hired someone to kill a cop, and I chase the shooter into a rathole somewhere."

"Waters has no known family or friends in Chicago, but he's got a connection to the Lacomb crime syndicate, and they work this far north."

"Thanks."

Paul nodded and headed into the restaurant. He knew whom he could trust, and he could trust Sam and Kate. The case and the chase were in good hands.

Waters. The name had actually crossed his mind as a possible suspect when word of the shootings first hit. Paul knew the man's work, and the original report had sounded like his MO. Waters had been hired for nine murders and managed to chalk up a body count of sixteen. Now he was at ten and nineteen. Cops had clipped Waters's car in Virginia, cornered him in Boston, and shot him once in Philadelphia, and no one had ever been able to get a good enough hold on him to snap on cuffs. He'd disappeared into Mexico three years ago, and they had been working a cold case trying to stir him out of the muck. This time cops were on the trail within the hour. They might have him tonight.

The restaurant main dining area showed the chaos of events—chairs overturned, meals abandoned, the violence at table twenty-two. Officer Ulaw's body had been removed as well as two of the civilians. The medical examiner was still working over the waitress who had been shot. Paul could smell the blood and lingering gunpowder, overlaid with the burned smell of overcooked food.

This was absolutely senseless violence. Waters could have shot the detective in the parking lot, or walking into the precinct, or in his car at a stoplight. Waters had chosen to shoot his victim in a crowded restaurant. He liked others to see his violence; he enjoyed killing bystanders who got in his way. They would have to catch him to end this. Waters reveled in killing too much to ever stop. If Kate didn't get him tonight, Paul would on one of the tomorrows. It was a small corner of family truth that a Falcon didn't stop hunting.

Observing the scene, Paul found himself wishing his lady shooter had been hired for this hit instead of Waters—at least then there would have been no bystanders killed. She'd never shot other than her target. She had never killed her victim where the family would see the death or where a child was present. She'd shot thirty people in the head, but treated it as business to be done carefully and precisely. She'd been quiet for nine years. He'd never come close to catching her, but she remained on his mind. And he was still quietly hunting her.

He was the FBI's top murder cop, and hired shooters stayed at the top of his priority list. Tonight he regretted more than ever that he hadn't caught Waters in time. Paul

DEE HENDERSON   15

stepped carefully around the room and moved toward
the voices in the kitchen.

His father would be here by first light, to do what
could be done to help the victims' families, to do what
could be done to help those who had seen this violence.
The Falcon restaurant would reopen, after it had been
gutted, after the image of this tragedy had been erased.

It would reopen with his father at the doors and welcoming the first guests. Paul knew his dad.

And he knew his sister. "Don't throw that, Jackie."

He ducked as a white mixing bowl came sailing toward
him. It hit the door and then the floor and cracked into
pieces.

"You've been hunting this guy for years and you haven't
caught him yet? You let him stay out there and do this to
my guests, my place?"

He ducked another bowl. He'd taught her to throw
as a kid and done a good job. He held up a hand and
pointed a finger at her. She wavered on the third bowl
and set it back on the counter.

"Rough night. Sorry about that."

He was near enough now to simply wrap his arm
around her shoulders and hug her.

"Four dead, Paul. Four." Her voice was muffled against
his shirt.

He rubbed his hand across her hair and let out a harsh
breath. "Glad you weren't one of them."

"Trish worked for me for a year. She's a sweet kid."

"No one is going to rest until this guy's caught. It's
what is left that we can do, and we'll get it done."

"He killed a cop." Her voice trembled. "That's your
table when you come for a meal. It could have been you."

"It wasn't."

He could feel the energy and passion burning out of her. The crime-scene tape marked the area she couldn't enter, but what was within her reach had been scrubbed down and set back to order. The grills and the stoves were glistening clean, the food in process packed away. At least she wasn't running away from it; she was reclaiming the place. The Falcon family would help.

"Let's go home, Jackie. Let me take you home, and tomorrow we'll deal with the rest of this."

She picked up a satchel holding her recipes and personal chef knives, along with the cluttered pad of paper she liked to think of as her business plan. "Can you drive with sirens so we're not crawling home an hour from now?"

"Lights, but not sirens. You were the one who wanted to live out in the suburbs."

"You're on the fourth floor of a building that has no grass. I want better for myself."

He smiled, relieved to hear the normal complaint. He took her out the back way, through the alley and around to his car, managing to bypass the media hunting for a photo and a story. He took his sister home.

———————

Paul walked into Chicago PD headquarters at 4:17 a.m., cleared through security, and found Lieutenant Kate Sinclair in the third-floor command center. The darkened room was crowded with people watching a live video feed on the wall shot from a police helicopter.

Sam walked over and handed him a coffee. "He's on Interstate 74 heading west. Two cops identified Waters and the car at a light just outside Peoria, gave chase. He took a few wild shots, then tried to drive down an embankment to cut away from them and busted up his car. He's running ahead of them now, leaking oil, and they are bringing in cars and boxing him in. State police are going to stop him at Sanders Point."

A flash of bright light tore through the room, turning it into instant daylight.

The helicopter's camera adjusted, and a burning wreck filled the screen—stationary, crumbled, and tossing off flames.

Cop cars that had tracked in behind the fleeing car began pulling into the frame, stopping well back. The pilot in the air had jerked away at the explosion and now panned around an oddly dark area and moved to hover back from the crash site.

"What happened? Back the tape up and toss it on the second screen," Kate ordered.

The crash replayed.

"Doesn't look like he lost control. That was a hundred miles an hour right into a power pole," the cop beside her said.

The tape looped and replayed again. The cop nodded and used his pointer to trace part of the image before and after the crash. "Transformer blew up and took out power to the homes around it. Look at all the lights no longer on."

Sam shifted where he stood to better see the video. "I did not expect this ending."

"I'll take this outcome over a shootout with cops," Paul decided. It was done. Waters died without taking out more cops, and that was its own relief.

Kate, standing in front of the screen, hands shoved into her pockets, watched the cops on the ground now using fire extinguishers to control the blaze. Paul moved forward to join her. "Sorry, Kate. You won't be able to ask who hired him."

"I'll still figure it out." She turned to look at him. "This side of the case is over but for the paperwork. Mind if I keep your guys a few more hours working on the why?"

"No problem. Thanks for doing my job."

She gave a small smile. "You could have rightfully made a fuss about taking over the case. You didn't, so I'd say we're even. Sorry it was your family's place where this happened."

"You can come over and be my guest when it re-opens next month. Anything you need to help find out who paid to have your cop killed, don't hesitate to ask. Wiretaps, warrants, extra coffee for your guys—let me know."

"I'll do that."

He nodded and headed to the door.

"Paul."

He turned back.

"When they offer you the top job, take it."

He smiled. "Now why are you squeezing me like that, beautiful Kate?"

"It's the first time in my memory local cops and FBI haven't wanted to push each other into the Chicago River. I'm getting used to you."

"Have to say I'm beginning to feel the same." She'd married a good friend of his, and he was coming to like this Chicago cop more with each passing year. "Oh, and, Kate?" He held up the cup. "FBI has still got the better coffee."

He left with her laughter following him. The day ahead would be run on two hours of sleep, for he had meetings beginning at seven a.m., but it would be a good day all the same.

———————▼———————

The Chicago FBI office had blast barriers at curbside, and layers of check-in and security to reach the elevators. Having waded through the process a few times in the past, Ann ran an experienced eye around the lobby and chose one of the more seasoned officers working the check-in desk. She offered her badge. "Officer Ann Silver. I'm here to see Agent Paul Falcon."

"Do you have an appointment, ma'am?"

"No."

He didn't recognize the police department on her badge but was polite enough not to say so. "I'll need to check your credentials, ma'am. Do you have a business card with department phone numbers?"

She offered one from her pocket. "Ask for the acting sheriff."

He picked up the phone and made the call.

Her office transferred the call. The phone in her pocket rang.

She pulled her phone out and answered. "Hi, again." She closed the phone with a small smile. "Sorry, couldn't resist."

He leaned against the counter to share the smile. "Small department?"

"You just talked to the entire staff."

"This does present a quandary."

"How about we try this. I came to Chicago to see the Cubs-Cardinals game tonight—I scored third-row seats behind first base. Make a call and ask Agent Falcon to come down to the lobby. Let me show him two photos. If it turns out it's not worth his time, you can keep the tickets to the game."

"You're that sure?"

"I am."

"Which case should I reference?"

"I have no idea what he calls it. Tell him it's regarding the lady shooter he's been hunting for several years."

The desk officer made the call. "He'll come down," he told her, "but it may be a few minutes. You'll find the bench is more comfortable than the chairs."

"Thanks." She settled in to wait, out of habit pulling out a paperback she was reading. She didn't mind the wait. Today was as close to a vacation day as she'd had this year, and if she could pass one more case off her desk, all the better. She planned to head home after the game without much of a voice left and half sick on hot dogs and popcorn, and if she timed it right she'd be at the ballpark early enough to watch batting practice and get an autograph or two.

"Officer Silver." The check-in officer nodded toward the man getting off the south elevator. "There he is."

She got up from the bench and waited while Agent Falcon came through the security barriers. He was a tall man with authority in his stride, wearing a business suit that didn't come off the rack. She had done enough digging to know his reputation and what was on his desk. Despite his rank and seniority, he stayed working cases rather than lead a bureau office. He was as far from the politics of the bureau as a murder cop could get, and that made him the guy who could do something with what she had. He was presently working on too much caffeine and not much sleep, she thought, noting the coffee mug in his hand and the grim tightness around his eyes. She would wonder at why, but she'd spent too many days working without sleep herself to find it unusual.

"Agent Falcon, this is Officer Ann Silver."

She stepped away from others in the lobby, opened her flight bag, and removed two photos. She didn't bother to explain; she simply offered them. He took the photos. His watch looked expensive, and the ring was FBI academy. She had assumed he was married, but his left hand was bare.

She saw the flare of heat in his eyes as he recognized the murders. Since the photos were copies of ones in his own files, she had assumed they would hit a chord. His gaze shot to hers. She took the punch of annoyance in his gaze because she deserved it, because she had set him up for it. She had chosen those two murders out of the thirty the lady had done for a reason, but the photos themselves were merely cover for her visit. The news she had come to share wasn't something she planned to write down anywhere. "I've got the guy who arranged her services in my morgue," she said quietly, simply, and let the words hang in the silence between them. She knew their implications.

He did too. He studied her face, weighing the way she had said it, scanned the badge displayed on her belt, and nodded toward the elevators. "Come up with me."

The check-in officer smiled as he handed her a visitor

pass. She clipped it onto her jacket, followed Agent Falcon to the security scanners, and emptied her pockets into the basket.

"You'll need to check your weapon, ma'am, and pick it up when your business is done," the security officer said.

"No. You can issue me a weapon clearance. Please do so."

"I can't issue a clearance without—"

"I'll vouch for her." The bureau's Midwest counterterrorism chief coming around behind them interrupted. "Give her the weapon clearance. How you doing, Ann?"

"Catching the game tonight."

He was now at the elevator, but he held the door before stepping in. "Yeah? Want company?"

"Lisa beat you out."

"My loss. Call me before you head home. I got your wiretaps approved."

"You couldn't keep that news to yourself until after the game?"

He grinned. "Take good care of her, Falcon. I still owe her for two speeding tickets."

She clipped on the weapon clearance and re-stuffed her belongings into her pockets. She waited until they were alone in the elevator. "His mom is my next-door neighbor," she said, not needing to explain but figuring it didn't hurt to cut politics out of the equation.

Agent Falcon half smiled. "I didn't ask."

"Didn't have to."

She followed him onto the sixth floor and down a long hallway. Paul worked in a decent-sized office, but both chairs across from his desk looked uncomfortable. She chose the one near the wall and dumped her flight bag on the other one. She set her recorder on his desk and clicked it on.

"Four weeks ago there was a wreck on Interstate 72. The driver died. Something was off about the scene, and the patrol officer called me in. Think heavy rain, absent quarter moon, and truckers hauling grain in a steady parade as the barges on the river got jammed up by a damaged lock gate. Not an ideal situation for working a car crash. The car rolled, flipped, smashed, and ended upside down in a bean field. It took out a small metal storage bin, six fence posts, and twenty feet of electric fencing and barbwire. The Angus bull in the field with the downed barbwire was not happy with the flashing cop lights and constant truck traffic, and since he was worth six figures, the bull for a time got as much attention as the wreck, once it was confirmed the driver was dead and that it would take the fire department to cut him out."

She watched Agent Falcon as she talked and gave a half smile as she reached for the pause on the recorder. "Get a drink, pace, make faces at your window, whatever, because I tell long stories, enjoy the telling, and don't plan to repeat myself to whomever else you want to hand this case to later. So I'll tell it my way, record it, and you'll have what I've got. I'm not inclined to fly north again just because I missed a detail you might one day need."

She was enjoying herself, Paul thought, and she was going somewhere interesting with her narrative. She'd delivered her statement in the lobby with exquisite timing. She had the tempo of a good storyteller. She liked telling stories. And he had a feeling she would back up that initial statement with just as exquisite timing. "What can I get you to drink?"

Ann decided she liked Paul's smile and offered a full one of her own. "Caffeine-free Diet Coke if you've got it, hot chocolate if you want me to shut up for a while, lemonade if you're being ornery."

He opened the small refrigerator under his desk and handed her a Diet Coke, no caffeine, pulled a root beer out for himself, and settled back in his office chair.

"Brownie points for it being extra cold." She popped the tab and started the recorder again. "As the patrol officer was a suspicious sort, and I run that way on even my good days, we took enough time to flip a tarp over the car before we dealt with the six-figure and very angry bull. The tarp couldn't do anything for the flood dumping out of the sky, but it kept the volume of water accumulating in the wreck to a minimum.

"The Caldwell County Fire Department arrived to cut open the car frame, the ME removed the body, and everything that wasn't dirt, beans, or grass was hauled onto a flatbed, covered with the tarp again, and taken into evidence for review at a secure and thankfully dry warehouse.

"There is enough video and stills of the scene to count as being there, including a large number of fascinating lightning strikes that washed out otherwise perfectly focused shots. Lightning split three trees that night, and one tree closed a lane of the Interstate shortly after three a.m. I figure we earned the overtime. I doubt the front row of a rock concert would have been any louder than that storm." She paused to take a long drink before continuing.

"The patrol officer didn't like the car crash. It didn't make sense to him. I had the same sense of unease. Why was the guy speeding during bad weather? Unless he had suicidal intentions, his actions made no sense. He wasn't a twenty-something who thought he'd have fun hydroplaning on a wet highway. He didn't have a heart attack and swerve around with chest pain. He simply decided to go a hundred plus on an Interstate, weaving around truckers and running faster than his lights could see in the rain. He was going to crash, and he had to know that. So why was he speeding?"

She let the question hang in the air while she stretched out her legs and crossed her ankles, trying to accommodate her body to the chair that was not very comfortable.

"Truckers on that stretch of Interstate are a friendly bunch in the middle of the night. We've got a string of eyewitnesses to the wreck and its aftermath, most interviews done verbally over the open air of the radio, but real-time enough and varied in detail enough they piece together a mosaic.

"According to two truckers, the sedan pulled onto the Interstate at mile marker thirty-five. The sedan was rolling with traffic until mile marker fifty-two, when he began to speed. By mile marker sixty-five we've got truckers complaining to each other about the idiot speeding around them. A patrol officer hears the chatter, turns around to come back on the Interstate.

"The driver lost control and crashed at mile marker eighty-two. Overlapping radio calls reported the crash to the emergency dispatcher at 10:19 p.m.

"Statements from four truckers confirm a second car stopped to render assistance. A white sedan with

Missouri plates, two guys in jackets and ball caps. All said it looked like the two guys were attempting to assist the driver. We've confirmed the second vehicle was two miles back when the crash occurred.

"The second vehicle was not at the scene when the patrol officer arrived.

"I now have security-camera footage from every truck stop, warehouse, and business that faces the Interstate from mile marker twenty to mile marker one hundred for the night in question. The second car was also speeding, but not excessively. The two cars were never closer than a mile to each other. It wasn't a bump and crash or a high-speed chase. After stopping to render assistance and then departing, the white sedan left the Interstate between mile marker eighty-five and mile marker ninety. The only options along that stretch of highway are back-country roads, which suggests the men were locals who knew the area. Four weeks of poking around should have given me another look at the car if it was local, but it hasn't been spotted again. So it's a mystery."

She wasn't one to like a mystery, even though she spent her workdays solving them, and she frowned a bit as she thought back on the search for the second vehicle. She'd managed to peel back most of the layers of this case, but a few unknowns remained. She glanced up, found Paul watching her. She appreciated a guy who could listen without interrupting. "Because I've got a curious streak to go with my suspicious bent, I backtracked the driver for the day before the crash.

"The dead man entered First National Bank in Dorado Springs, Missouri, at 11:17 a.m. on the day he would die and closed a safe-deposit box. The teller who assisted him with the box stated it was eight by seventeen by two, heavy when he carried it to the privacy booth and empty when he returned it to the safe-deposit box vault. He had rented the same box for thirty-eight years. The security tape has a decent photo and shows him carrying a black briefcase in and out of the bank.

"He ate a late lunch in Jefferson City and carried the briefcase inside with him where he set it on the bench beside him but did not open it. He had roast beef, ate alone, and the waitress remembers a quiet guy who paid cash and left a generous tip. He filled up with gas at the Shell station in Farber. Security cameras show him alone. He pulled onto Interstate 72 at mile marker thirty-five and was dead at mile marker eighty-two." Ann paused, struck again by the sadness of the last day of his life. She could find answers, but not change the tragedy.

"Back to the crash. At dawn, the patrol officer and I walked the bean field and the roadside, compared notes, and then headed to the evidence warehouse where the wreck had dripped mostly dry.

"The first thing recovered from the car was a nice Glock, two full clips, no shots fired. It was taped under the passenger side seat.

"The glove box held an owner's manual, car registration, insurance card, half a roll of quarters, and maps of Ohio, Illinois, Missouri, and Iowa.

"The trunk was crumpled shut, forced open, and found to be empty but for a spare tire, jack, and an extra gallon of windshield wiper fluid, now busted open and splashed around the space.

"A hanging clothes bag in the back seat had one change

of clothes, toiletries, and a pair of dress shoes. Nice stuff, but not new.

"Miscellaneous items recovered from the mud under the car once it was removed from the bean field were a fast-food sack from McDonald's, a windbreaker, and two old pocket day planners, brown and blue covers respectively, from ten and thirteen years before.

"A broken briefcase handle was pulled from the mangled passenger door frame. The clasp had sheared off the case. We still haven't recovered the damaged briefcase itself. It wasn't in the car wreck, and it wasn't in the bean field or thrown out on the roadside.

"Personal effects taken into evidence at the scene were eyeglasses, a nice watch, a plain wedding ring, and a current day planner from his shirt pocket. His wallet had forty-eight dollars in cash, two credit cards, a gas card, driver's license, and a receipt from a bookstore in Missouri for two newspapers. No photographs. No health insurance card. No checkbook.

"He had no phone on him. We went back through the wreck looking for a phone or any signs a phone had been there—a charger, a case—and came up with nothing. Security tapes of him in the twenty-four hours before the crash never show him on a phone." Ann was still surprised she hadn't found a phone.

"We headed from the car wreck to the ME's office. The deceased is a Caucasian male, early to mid-seventies, one sixty, five nine, hazel eyes, in good health, taking no prescriptions. The cause of death is impact injuries.

"His fingerprints are not on file. His DNA gave no match. There has been no missing-person report filed anywhere in the U.S. that matches his description.

"His license is a nice forgery. His credit cards are clones for cards owned by a man in hospice in Oregon. The VIN numbers on the car don't match the registration. The car registration and plates belong to a junked same-make-and-model in Indiana. The gun trace disappears into a police stolen-items report from a gun store robbery six years ago in Nevada.

"The day planner in his pocket reads like gibberish, as did the two day planners recovered from the mud under the car. One from ten years ago, another from thirteen years ago, a current planner in his shirt pocket. Where are the rest of them? I figure the ripped-open and now-missing briefcase had a stack of them.

"Working assumption—he emptied out a bank safe-deposit box, someone knew that, tailed him, planning to acquire the contents of the box. He made the tail, tried to outrun them, failed miserably and crashed. They stopped, confirmed he was dead, retrieved the briefcase and probably a phone, and got as far away from the scene as they could before the patrol officer arrived." She paused and tipped the soda can toward him. "A nice story, since I like to tell them, and a pure guess, but it's a tidy theory."

She couldn't tell if Paul liked her tidy theory or not, but it was a good one just the same. He was turning his pen end to end, his fingers sliding down and turning it a hundred and eighty degrees in a steady twenty-second beat, and he was still carefully listening. She liked a guy who could listen to a story, appreciate its telling, and not interrupt the flow of it. She would know she had him when that pen stopped its graceful path, and what was the point of a good story if she couldn't touch a moment of surprise in its telling? She settled her cold drink back on the coaster and turned the story to the reason she was sitting in his office on, for her, a rare vacation day.

"A day planner written in some kind of code had my attention even in the rain of a stormy night, and it was still holding my attention over the next few days as leads to chase worked themselves into the weeds. My driver remained a mystery, and I was stalled for a name. As the day planner in his pocket began to look like my best chance of identifying him, I started working on the code. Being stubborn along with suspicious, I kept eliminating what it was not, on the assumption I'd eventually find what it was.

"I cracked the code four days ago. He was offsetting his alphabet based on what day of the week the first day of the month came on, reversing his numbers right to left, and swapping first and last digits. It was the same code in all three day planners. He's been a creature of habit through the years.

"The day planners are boring reading on the whole.

"He recorded the price of gas, baseball game scores, the DOW index closing price, and occasionally lunch expenses. Nothing looks like a phone number. There are some appointments—place, time, and initials—including several appointments coming up over the next few months. By the time I transcribed and read the three planners there was a nice tug going on about a few of the notations. Toss out everything trivial and they stand out as unusual.

"Since the only thing I like to do better than tell a story is to remember odd and trivial facts, you'll have to trust me for now that the following quotes are accurate.

"MAY 22, 1999
Call from TM
Called Miss LS
JULY 7, 1999
Saw news YM died
JULY 20, 1999
TM $250,000 deposit cleared
Paid Miss LS $220,000

"And another:
AUGUST 14, 2002
Call from GN
Called Miss LS
OCTOBER 7, 2002
Saw news VR died
OCTOBER 25, 2002
GN $300,000 deposit cleared
Paid Miss LS $270,000

"July 7, 1999, and Saw news YM died, turns out to be a rather unique combination. My search turned up the name Yolanda Meeks. And I landed in the middle of your murder investigation."

His pen stopped moving.

"VR and October 7, 2002, gave me Victor Ryckoff. And there I was again. In your murder investigation."

She waited a beat. She had him.

"So—I know it is thin, but is it enough I can dump this guy and this wreck off my desk and onto yours?"

"I'll take it all."

She grinned. "I knew I'd like you."

He had gone from politely listening to seriously focused, and she could almost see the speed of his thoughts as he ran the prior cases in his mind looking for initials. He'd probably interviewed one of the people who had hired the lady shooter to make a hit. She would not want to be in Falcon's crosshairs when he came hunting with this new information.

"I've got the wrecked car, its contents, his personal effects, the body, a bunch of photos, security disks, and a stack of interviews. You'll need to send someone to pick them up."

"Done. I need to see the day planners as soon as possible."

She opened her flight bag and held up a manila envelope sealed in an evidence bag. "Three day planners and my code-breaking how-to guide, driver's license, car registration and insurance, credit cards and gas card, a still image from the bank security camera of the man before he died, and as an added bonus I tossed in fingerprints and photos of the two who might have acquired the briefcase. I just need a signature for the evidence chain of custody."

He held up the pen. "Got the paperwork?"

She handed it to him.

He signed with a bold, legible signature, printed his name, and added a federal case number beneath it.

She handed him the evidence bag.

"We didn't have her initials," he said. "And the guy in your morgue might be Charles Ash."

"See? You're already making more progress than I did. You can have fun with it, and I can go enjoy a ball game."

"You don't want to stay on the case?"

"Why would I? Assuming my idea of a tail is accurate and someone intentionally took the briefcase and the rest of the day planners, they know by now three day planners are missing. They are going to want them back. I'd just as soon they try to take them from you than from me."

"The wreck was four weeks ago. They likely would have tried by now."

"I'm reasonably sure they have, and failed in the attempts. They tried for the wreck and found it guarded by a very unfriendly police dog, who was keeping a restored Corvette in the same warehouse safe. They tried for the evidence room, but it's a former bank vault. Jesse James tried to rob the bank back in 1871, blew a hole in the building, and still couldn't get it open. They may have tried to hack the department computer system, if you can call a couple connected PCs a network. I'm hoping they made it to the case files, because if they got a copy of the property inventory, it lists three day planners with the notation *destroyed by water, unreadable*."

"Nicely played."

"I wasn't sure, but I was working a hunch even back then. The pictures from the warehouse break-in didn't give me much to work with—two middle-aged white guys, jackets, hats, gloves—but they didn't stay ghosts. They tried a tail on and off for the first couple weeks, but it's hard to tail me in my own backyard. I reversed it back on them a couple times and showed them some very boring countryside and dead ends. Restaurant staff said Southern accent for both of them, which gets interpreted in my stretch of the world as Georgia rather than Texas. I haven't seen them in the last couple weeks. I figured they would send someone representing a loved one of the victim and try to claim the driver's possessions, but there have been no inquiries. I'm still surprised they haven't gone that route.

"They may have concluded the risk is passed, so why stir up trouble by pursuing it further. As far as anyone watching could tell, I worked the case for three days, touched it again briefly in weeks one and two, and haven't done anything on it the last couple weeks. The ME is done and the body will be cremated in three months by the county if a loved one isn't located. The car wreck will go to scrap once the paperwork goes through the bureaucracy. The personal belongings will linger in storage for a year or so depending on when space is needed to be reclaimed. The case is over."

"Who knows about the day planner code and what you figured out?"

"Me. You."

"You've told no one the day planners were in code, told no one you had a puzzle to solve?"

She liked the fact he was a skeptic, and smiled at him. "I recovered the day planners at the scene, including the one from his shirt pocket, and it's my handwriting putting them into evidence. No one else ever opened them. And I'm good at keeping my mouth shut when it suits me.

"I burn my trash—it's the country. My scratched-out attempts to crack the code no longer exist. I'm about six months behind in finishing my reports. I have them transcribed from audiotape so the law clerk has enough work and can keep her job. The tapes for this case and several others are still in the evidence vault in a box I misfiled a decade ago, where I keep all kinds of personal things, including a few nicely autographed baseball cards. When I say it's possible for you to collect and have everything that exists on this case, I'm being literal."

She rose. "You want to get busy with those documents, and I want to get to the game, so I'm going to head out. Why don't we leave it that you'll call me tomorrow when you have arrangements made to pick up the wreck and the rest of it." She clicked off the recorder, ejected the digital card and the tape duplicate, and handed them to him.

He stood up. "Better yet, let me head down with you. We'll stop on three and get an evidence guy scheduled to pick up the wreck and then talk to the ME about transferring the body. I can at least escort you to the lobby before I dive into this." He locked the evidence bag and the tapes in his office safe. "Can you have the rest of it, the security tapes and interviews, packed up and under seal to be picked up tomorrow?"

"I can." She picked up her bag and followed him. Falcon led the way to the elevators and pushed the down button just as the stairway door opened and an agent walked through, scanning a report in his hand.

"Dave," Ann said.

Kate's husband, Dave Sinclair, glanced over and his face lit up with a smile.

"Ann's in the house." Dave slung his arm across her shoulders and hugged her. "I gotta feed you, woman, and bug you with toddler pictures."

"Got them on you?"

He reached for his wallet and dumped out a handful of photos.

"Holly's got her mom's smile." Ann turned one of

the photos toward him. "I told you she was going to love the wrapping paper."

"She's eaten the ear off your fuzzy kitten."

"I figured she would."

"Coming to dinner?"

"Lisa and I are hitting the game."

"Perfect day for it. Come for breakfast then. Kate would love to see you. She's setting you up with her new hire, some guy from Scotland Yard."

"Not this trip, but I'll enjoy dodging her attempt."

"Something interesting bring you our way?"

"Just dumping what I can stretch to be federal." The elevator opened. Ann held the door but didn't step on. "You still need me to ferry the plane to Wichita Saturday?"

"I'd love it if you could," Dave replied. "They gave me a six p.m. slot, and promised a seventy-two-hour turn. They are dropping out the rudder assembly to replace a recalled actuator."

"I've got to be in Salina Monday anyway. Henry Stanton got a new trial."

"How did he manage that?"

"A very fine lawyer. I'll handle the FAA for you, then maybe do a checkout ride south on the loop home."

"It's an enjoyable ride."

She smiled. "It is that. Tell Kate I'll tag her once I link up with Lisa." She stepped onto the elevator. The doors closed. She glanced at Falcon across the elevator. "Sorry about that."

"No problem." Paul pressed the button for floor three. Something special there, he thought. He'd known Dave for too long not to recognize the delight when he had looked up and seen Ann. She had to be nearly family for him to have that relaxed joy show up just on seeing her. It would be easier to ask Dave about that than Ann. "How long have you been flying?"

"I paid for college ferrying planes around. Now it just cuts down on travel time."

"That sounds like serious fun. What did you fly in on today?"

"I took a Cessna with a flaky autopilot into Milwaukee for repairs, and caught a lift south with highway patrol. There's a stranded floatplane on Lake Michigan that needs someone to baby it home. If waters are calm enough in the morning, I may fly that one back."

"You enjoy the air time."

"Like some guys enjoy fast cars."

The doors opened on three. Paul got an evidence guy assigned to head south, and the ME to agree to arrange the transfer of the body by the end of the day. They headed from the third floor down to the lobby. Ann turned in her visitor credentials.

"Enjoy the ball game, Ann."

"I plan to. It's been a pleasure, Falcon."

He watched until she cleared the front doors and caught a cab. He hadn't been expecting to meet someone today, the kind that went on the personal side of the ledger and deserved a second look, and he thought he just might have. *Ann Silver.* He was going to come back to that name before the day was done. Paul pulled out his phone and headed back to the elevators. "Sam, push off sleep for a few more hours. I need everyone to the conference room. We just got a break on our lady shooter."

2

Paul slid his credentials through the security scanner, punched in his code, and entered the secure conference room on the eighth floor that he considered his second office. The walls around the room were old school case boards, filled with photos and reports and timelines, keeping the progress visible to everyone working on his team. And his team had gotten large.

It baffled him how many people he had collected. The early days it had been Paul and Sam, with Rita being the agent Paul pulled along with them through every promotion. She could think on her feet and, more important, put up with Sam, and Paul knew a good thing when he found it. The three of them had worked together on cases, content to stay out of the flow of office politics.

Now he walked in on a mass of humanity. He had fifteen agents assigned to him. Four were seasoned homicide guys, eight were here by request of his boss who wanted him to rub the rough edges off the new guys, and three were here because he'd given in to pleas from experienced guys who otherwise would have been assigned to foreign liaison jobs in the last personnel shuffle.

Get murdered carrying a federal badge and having a security clearance, odds were good he saw the paper on the murder or his guys worked it. He pointed them toward where to start and tossed them out to work the cases, and he played lifeguard if they got into trouble. He didn't have to manage them. Rita handled that for him. She was either their mother, friend, or boss, depending on what she knew was needed.

He scanned the conference room to find Sam and realized the people count had grown even more since he had made his trip down to the lobby. The legal expert who did warrants for the team had appropriated a table for himself, and three interns were clustered around his data expert. He missed the Paul, Sam, and Rita days more every time he walked into the conference room. But for right now, today, he could use them all. He might even need to borrow a few more.

"Rita, case five."

"Really?" Her face lit up and excitement rippled among those in the room. "Case five, coming up, boss." In moments she had boards moving across the walls until the entire room featured one case. Thirty murders, each one displayed in the sequence it had occurred. Tracking down the lady shooter and those who hired her had consumed more man-hours than any other case they had worked, and he had inherited it from the guy before him. Falcon wanted to be the one to close this case.

"Arnett, there is a Diet Coke can on the coaster in my office. Get it to the lab. I need fingerprints for elimination purposes. I'll wait for you before I begin the briefing, so don't get delayed by chatter."

"Two minutes, boss." Arnett headed to the door.

"Listen up, everyone. What you are working on, put it to bed. If you've got calls or interviews scheduled for the next three days, hand them off or push them out. Everyone's in on the first round. We hit a wall, I'll push you back to current assignments."

Around the room, people picked up phones to begin clearing schedules.

Paul set the evidence bag and the audio digital card and tape on the table he used as his desk. He got lunch from the deli tray perched on the half-sized refrigerator. He could feel it now, the relaxed emotions yet intense mental focus that came when a case began to move and there was something interesting to pursue. This was why he was a cop. He had run hundreds of cases over the years, and he never failed to enjoy the detail work and the chase that was at the core of the job.

Arnett returned, and the last phone calls finished. Paul moved to the front of the room.

"I'm going to play a tape, a long tape, and I want it quiet while it plays, no multitasking, everyone doing nothing but listening. Her name is Ann Silver. She's a downstate cop, and she showed up this morning to bring us the best lead we've had on the lady shooter in ten years. She understands exactly what she's got, she's handing it to us, and she doesn't want in on the case. You won't meet many like her during your entire career, so pay attention." He settled into a chair and turned on the tape.

Ann was an even better storyteller the second time

around, when he knew what was coming, and he could see her play it out with that refined sense of timing.

He watched his team as the audio played.

He could tell they didn't know what to think of her. The younger ones around the room were thinking *small-town cop* and beginning to fidget, but the older, more experienced guys were leaning forward, recognizing something in her voice, in the verbal execution of her report, and starting to sense this was more than just a good cop. Sam was leaning back, hands folded across his chest, a small smile on his face. He'd pegged her for what she was, a master class of cop, and was enjoying the story and its telling.

Ann began to elaborate on the day planners, and Paul scanned the room, knowing what was coming.

"July 7, 1999, and Saw news YM died, turns out to be a rather unique combination. My search turned up the name Yolanda Meeks. And I landed in your murder investigation."

He heard a gasp from Rita.

"VR and October 7, 2002, gave me Victor Ryckoff. And there I was again. In your murder investigation."

Christopher couldn't resist getting up to walk to the murder boards, scanning the history.

"So—I know it's thin, but is it enough I can dump this guy and this wreck off my desk and onto yours?"

And then Paul's own voice on the tape.

"I'll take it all."

Jason tried to sneak in a few keystrokes to bring up a file on his console. Paul held up a hand to stop the whispered conversation beginning in the back of the room. No one was fidgeting now. Sam looked happy, and Paul caught his gaze long enough to share the smile. There was reason to be happy. He let the tape play through to conclusion and then clicked it off. Conversations erupted.

Paul smiled as he got to his feet. He picked up the evidence bag and held it up. "Settle down, people. We've obviously got some work to do. Assignments first, then I want to hear what you think.

"William, the initials L.S., T.M., G.N.—check every name anywhere in the case file, people who were interviewed, friends of the victims, every address book, letter, and scrap of paper in evidence. Check it all.

"Kelly, the medical examiner and everything he can tell us about this man. Work the prints, DNA, and photo through everywhere we can touch. This guy might be Charles Ash.

"Peter, the two who were tailing Ann Silver, trying to retrieve the three planners. Who are they, where are they, and are they still a danger to my cop? I want an answer on that today, so use our chits to get others making it their priority too. Who sent these two? Who were they working for? Someone knew the middleman well enough to know he was closing that box, and can give us his name.

"Arnett, forged documents. Who, what, where, when—everything they can tell us. Have we seen documents like them before, who created them, where do they lead us to look next?

"Daniel, those three day planners. Are there any fingerprints that can be recovered other than hers? Then scan the pages, pulling the six dates she gave us first. Use her code how-to guide and throw the decoded pages up on the board as fast as you work through them.

"Christopher, the other notations in the day planners. What do they tell us, where can they lead us?

"Jason, the bank. Did he have an account there as well as a safe-deposit box? Where did they mail his bill for the box fee? And I want the records on that safe-deposit box, every date he signed in for the last thirty-eight years. Signature cards, anything he ever signed or filled out. I want you on a plane today and the president of the bank your new best friend.

"Franklin, talk to the other guys in the sandbox—Treasury, CIA, DEA, other pockets around here—high-value middleman making connections for people. Who are they hunting? Our guy will be doing business with more than just our lady shooter if he's been active this long. We'll share what we have as long as they give us someone inside their loop. I don't want heads bumping. Only one agency is going to go through the door when we find his home, and I want it to be us. We'll share what we find if there are cases overlapping with other agencies. Get Montgomery up to speed; he's going to be our guy working the politics and making that happen.

"Sullivan, the car, its contents, and the other items coming into evidence tomorrow. I want to know what was missed.

"Rita, I need a transcript of that audio, and new boards

started, a timeline on the middleman, and one working the day planners.

"Sam, you and I are going to focus on the murders of Yolanda Meeks and Victor Ryckoff. I'm convinced there is enough here to put names on who paid to have them killed. The initials, the dollar amounts paid, and dates the deposits cleared—we'll find a thread to link old and new.

"I'll want people in the field in forty-eight hours working whatever we find, so rearrange your personal schedules and get freed up to travel. Those of you married, with kids, go home for dinner and stay to put them to bed. You can come back in tonight if you must. Transportation is approved for anything you need while this is hot on the board, so commute on the bureau and maximize your time.

"Any questions?" He scanned the room, and then handed the evidence bag to Daniel. "Okay, assignments are done. Now I want to hear what you are thinking. First impressions, ideas?" To keep it orderly, he nodded at Franklin to start the conversation.

Ann managed to get autographs from two pitchers, share a smile and touch of a glove with a catcher. She was revved when she finally found their seats. "It's going to be a great game." She set her glove on her aisle seat, hoping she left the stadium with a caught foul ball before it was over.

Lisa handed her a hot dog. "I started without you."

"Excellent. How's your world? How's Quinn?"

"I'm good. He's wonderful. Yours?"

"I'm great." They slid past the fact they were both working murder cases, for they were ignoring it to get this day off. Lisa, a forensic pathologist covering small towns out West, was often the only trained crime-scene investigator available when tragedy happened. She had worked in Chicago before marrying and moving west, so this was a homecoming.

Ann grinned at Lisa and nudged the new ball cap her friend was wearing. "Looks cute on you."

"Team spirit and all."

Ann flagged down a vendor bringing around soft drinks. "I missed lunch, so thanks for the hot dog. Oh, here's Kate on the phone. Pull it out of my pocket. She wants to ask you about that picture you just emailed her—some fuzzy animal?"

Lisa grinned and tugged out the phone. "Hey, Kate. Why did you call Ann? Oh, okay. Hold on." She looked at Ann. "Dave's birthday—is it okay for Kate to give him a pet when it's probably going to turn into being her pet? I found her this adorable cat that has a coat so soft it's like cashmere."

"Absolutely." Kate's old tomboy of a cat had died two months ago and everyone knew she had been secretly attached to the crabby animal, chiefly because it had been a gift from Dave. She needed another cat. She wouldn't get one for herself, but saying it was a gift to Dave, that would work.

"Ann agrees, Kate."

"Tell her to buy a nice negligee too, or re-box the one from last year."

Lisa laughed and passed it on. "Kate says they already have one adorable daughter," Lisa relayed back to Ann, "and our suggestions are going to insure they have another."

"Holly deserves a sister." Ann dug out cash to pay for the drinks.

The stands were almost filled, the weather was beautiful, and talking was going to require something more like shouting once the game began. Ann leaned back in her seat and propped her feet up while she ate and listened to Lisa's side of the conversation with Kate. This was going to be a perfect day.

Lisa reached over and slid the phone back in Ann's pocket. "She left the decision late this year—his birthday is Sunday."

"She was nervous about what to get, so she couldn't make up her mind. She knew one of us would help out. I was going to suggest a vacation without Holly. I want a chance to baby-sit."

"I'd love to have her for a week. Quinn is talking about kids. I want to practice first."

Ann smiled at the idea. "He'll talk you into it."

"I'll let him." Lisa waved her drink at the stadium. "I'm so glad you said let's get away and meet up for a ball game. I'm hundreds of miles away, and work can't find me for this twenty-four-hour block of time. I needed this break."

"I did too. I'm sitting here remembering the last perfect day we spent together. Beach. Two fine guys. You had Quinn and I had brought Ted. Those icy drinks with the cherries—and I got a sunburn on my nose." Ann smiled at the memory.

Lisa dug in her pocket and pulled out a small bottle

of suntan lotion. "Quinn stuffed it there when I left the hotel room."

"Are you enjoying being married as much as I think you are?" Ann accepted the bottle, rubbed some on her face, and handed it back.

"More. But life isn't the same without an occasional girl's day out thrown into the mix."

"I've got a question for you, about a guy I met," Ann remarked, pleased at the casual tone of her question, even though there was nothing casual about what she had been mulling over during the cab ride to the stadium.

Lisa looked over, surprised. "Yeah?"

"I think you met him once. Paul Falcon."

Lisa turned to fully face her and grinned. "I hear story. Come on, give."

"Just wondering what you know about him. Single? Divorced? Bad table manners?" Ann asked tongue-in-cheek, for she already knew some of the answers.

Lisa laughed. "I have indeed met Paul Falcon. He was one of the first to brave a dinner I fixed as a new wife entertaining company. Quinn invited him over— they were working on a case together. Paul survived the meal. I admit I probed, for I was nervous, he was in my line of sight, and I kept him talking. He's single, East Coast educated, bureau straight out of college, and won points from me by asking about the kittens that kept appearing in the dining room without implying they should be elsewhere, and more points from Quinn for being sincerely interested in the art collection around our home. I remember thinking smooth, relaxed, polished, sincere, and something really solid and nice under the good manners and expensive suit. Quinn introduced him

as Paul Falcon, a good cop. That told me a lot even before
the man ever said a word."

Ann thought that over. "I got the impression of authority, expensive suit, nice smile, and good at listening.
The last point being what caught my attention. I told
a really good story today, and he didn't interrupt me
once."

Lisa beamed. "He's a keeper."

The stadium came to life as the game was called to
order, with introduction of the teams and the playing
of the national anthem. Ann added an expert whistle
to the crowd's roar of approval as her favorite players
were named.

"Going to see him again?" Lisa asked, leaning close
to Ann to be heard.

"Doubt it. I handed off the case. But I like knowing
who I'm dealing with if I do."

Ann clapped and whistled again as the Cubs' pitcher
took a few practice throws and the umpire took his stance
behind home plate. She settled into her seat for a memorable afternoon.

The first pitch was tipped foul, and Ann scrambled
up and darted onto the stairs along with two hundred
equally enthusiastic fans, all hoping to snatch the first
possible ball. She saw a young man snag it fifteen rows
farther back. She slid back into her seat and put down
the glove to reach for her drink. "This is going to be a
great game, Lisa!"

Lisa laughed and thought there was no better en-
tertainment than Ann at a ball game. The next pitch,
and Lisa saved the drink Ann was going to spill as she
signaled her disagreement with the umpire. Seats behind

the first-base line had cost Quinn a pretty penny, and Lisa wished she could capture this priceless moment to share with her husband later. When she whispered her thanks tonight and followed it with a kiss, Quinn would smile as a husband would, glad their afternoon had been a good time. He'd be genuinely happy she was happy. And he wouldn't truly understand. This was Ann. This was her friend. And this was another memory of a perfect day together.

Lisa spotted a vendor with popcorn and caught his attention, then dug cash out of her pocket. She was going to make sure that by the time this game was over, Ann was well fed, tired, smiling, and hoarse. It's what friends did for each other. She grinned as she stuffed a bag of popcorn into Ann's hand. "I could invite Paul Falcon to dinner, and just happen to invite you too," Lisa offered. It was another thing friends did. They meddled.

Ann smiled but shook her head. "Ask me again in about six months, and I might take you up on it. There's too much on my desk right now." The first hit of the game streaked down the first-base line, and bodies in a ballet of motion sprinted for the ball and raced to cover the base. Safe. Ann absorbed the joy of it, leaned over and with one arm hugged her friend. "Tell Quinn thanks from me too."

In the midst of launching his determined hunt for the middleman, Paul hadn't forgotten the other more personal question today had raised. When he saw Dave's office light still on at seven p.m., Paul backtracked. Dave had his feet up on the second chair and a report open in his lap. Paul leaned against the doorpost. "Tell me about Ann Silver."

Startled, Dave looked up and blinked twice, mentally shifting gears. "A good friend. She worked eighty-three murders last year, and she needs a vacation. If she passed something off to us, I hope you took it."

"I did. I didn't place her as being a homicide cop."

"She's the MHI."

"Ann?"

Dave smiled. "Top flight cop. Easy to hang out with. Knows more about murder than anyone I've ever worked with outside of you. And not an ambitious bone in her body, which is why everyone keeps voting her into the role."

Falcon wasn't sure what to do with the information.

The Midwest homicide investigator was voted into the position by the 214 active homicide cops in eight Midwest states. Any of the cops could call and ask the MHI to come in on a case. What made the position unique was the MHI worked for the cop who made the call—and never filed a piece of paper on the case. The MHI just helped out when asked. It was one of the most trusted and under-the-radar positions in the region.

And that person was Ann Silver. She would be carrying credentials from at least eight state police departments as well as have a security clearance level higher than most FBI field agents. And yet she had stayed with small-town cop and no title, beginning with check-in downstairs through leaving the building.

Dave shuffled through the rest of the report and dropped it on his desk. "Surprised?"

"Some."

"She doesn't like to advertise. The cops who vote her into the position know who she is. If she had her way, no one else would even know the role exists," Dave remarked. "Ann's also the acting sheriff for her grandparents' hometown this year while they dissolve the township and move policing over to the county. The stories she can tell about candy thefts, drunk drivers, truant teenagers, and lost pets—she's enjoying it. I frankly was surprised to see she took the time to come north, but I'm glad she did. Her work load is pretty heavy."

"She flies to relax."

"I asked one time how many hours in the air she's logged, and it was over sixteen thousand."

"She seeing anybody?" Paul asked casually enough he was pleased at the tone, but there was nothing casual about the question he'd carried in the back of his mind for the better part of a day.

Dave studied him. "Why are you asking?"

"Ann Silver dropped into a seat in my office today, wandered around through a good story, and cracked open a case that has given me five thousand hours of grief. She knew what she had, and she gave it away. How many ladies like that cross a guy's path in a career? I already know she's special. You just added a deeper layer to it. I'd like an answer to my question if you'll trust me with the information."

"I don't know that I want to answer it. I just don't know. She's a good friend, and more than that she's family to Kate and me."

Paul could feel the protective wall going up. He'd never seen it happen before. "Dave, give me a break here. Ann Silver caught my interest. She's your friend. I'm asking."

"You said you didn't want to date a cop. You've been real clear on that."

"You know I'm not looking for just a date. You know I have in mind something more and have been for quite a while."

"You've been out with most of the friends Kate and I know, and you're still looking. I'm not inclined to add Ann to that list."

"What do you want from me?"

"Are we friends?"

Paul crossed his arms. "You know we are. So why are you raking me over the coals for no crime?"

"Just hear me out. Your father is larger than life. You're the eldest son, the prince in waiting for the king to die. The Falcon empire and Falcon family responsibilities will fall to you one day soon. And it's messing up your head. You think you need to be married before you become head of the family. And you're a cop. You can barely reconcile the two roles. Now you're looking for a wife who can also bridge the two worlds. I'm not interested in putting Ann in the middle of that tug-of-war."

"I'm not aiming to get married because of my family."

"I don't believe you."

"Believe what you want. I'm hoping to get married because I'm tired of being alone when I get home. I'd like a wife to share my life with. I'd like some kids running around. And it's time. I don't plan to be the single guy coming to dinner when I'm fifty. I'm also smart enough to consider what being my wife is going to mean for the lady I choose. I want a marriage to survive me becoming head of the Falcon family, not end up scrambled in a mess when she realizes what she got herself into." A marriage that could survive was at the top of his list. "You want to look me in the eye and tell me Ann Silver couldn't handle the Falcons?"

Dave thought about it, then laughed. "It's the Falcons I'd be worried about. You have no idea who you're asking about, Paul."

"So trust me and give me an answer. Is she seeing anybody?"

"You said you didn't want to date a cop," Dave said again, aggravated. He reached for his office keys and phone. "Let's go for a walk."

Paul had known Dave long enough to not break the silence as Dave sorted out what he wanted to say. The night was turning past dusk and the rush hour had ended, leaving the sidewalks half empty. Dave waited until they were walking along Spring Avenue before he broke the silence.

"Ann is my wife's best friend. Ann would say Kate's best friend is Lisa or Rachel, but that's Ann. Create a list with someone at the top, and Ann will put someone else in that role. She does it instinctively. She's comfortable in the background and prefers it," Dave began, then paused.

"You'd be good together," Dave said abruptly. "I know you both. You would be good together. So I'll answer your question, I won't dissuade the interest, but I'm going to make incredibly sure you don't blow this up in my face. Ann trusts me, she trusts Kate, and I'm crossing a lot of lines having this conversation. This isn't one of my other friends. This is Ann."

Paul heard the sharp edge just under the warning. This was going to cost him a friendship if he didn't handle this carefully. He found himself oddly relieved to hear it. Ann had a claim here. And he began to glimpse the truth of just how significant a lady he had met today. "I won't hurt her, Dave."

"You'll try not to," Dave agreed. "If I'm going to expect you to not make a hash of it, there's a lot you need to know. I can't unpack Ann Silver in a couple sound bites. She's . . . where do I even start? There's a reason I don't do this, Falcon. Not with Ann."

"Just tell me about her," Paul said before Dave could change his mind. "She doesn't live here. Be a friend and help me out. It would take months for me to learn what you could simply tell me. Be *her* friend and tell me what I need to know."

"You'll need the help," Dave agreed, "because Ann is the most private person I know. She is like this buried mine shaft with so many passages you don't realize what's there until you happen to fall into a new one. I know her well, and I'll lay money I still don't know all the turns she's got tucked away. I'll tell you enough of her background you won't have to flounder around trying to figure it out, but I don't know how you'll avoid some of the rapids. With Ann, you're suddenly in a turn you weren't expecting to be there.

"She's not seeing anyone. To be fair to the question, Ann's gone out with lots of guys, and always parts friendly in a month or two. She dated the former VP's Secret Service guy for a few years, and I thought it would be the one that lasted. He's a good guy, the kind you'd want a friend to marry. She trusts him—you can see it when they're together. But even though she still pulls him along for holidays when he's at loose ends, it's another of those relationships she's closed off and keeps as a friend. She doesn't let a guy stick. I don't know why."

Paul stopped walking. He wanted to make sure he understood what Dave had just said. "She dates for short periods of time, keeps the friendship, but never gets serious?"

"It's different than that, but yeah, that's the pattern." Dave thought about it and then shook his head. "I'm probably getting it wrong." He started walking again. "The problem is she's nice. Everyone asks Ann out. She's good company, Paul. She's the kind of lady that makes you glad you shifted your calendar to spend the evening with her. She gets asked out a lot. She's too polite to say no."

It didn't explain why she hadn't settled down. It did suggest she had had plenty of opportunities to get serious about a relationship if she wanted to do so, and hadn't taken that step. Paul wondered at the reason, or reasons, and wondered if he'd be one of the many with whom she parted friendly in a month or two. "What's her background?"

"She'll be forty in June, grew up poor in south Chicago, spent her summers with her grandparents on a farm in central Illinois. No brothers or sisters. Never engaged. Her parents and grandparents have now passed away. She's been a cop since she was twenty-six. She started out in Chicago in robbery and fraud, moved to major crimes, then to homicide. She worked directly for Howard Benson for eight years. He'd toss Ann into a case or a task force ahead of him and let her sort out what was really there. He put a deep well of experience under her belt, and when he retired, cops started calling her directly. Urban, rural, state, federal—she fits in wherever she finds herself and makes a contribution without stepping on toes. They all like working with her. She was voted in as the MHI five years ago, and they have done that unanimously every year since. I haven't met a homicide cop in the Midwest who doesn't have something nice to say about her. She's made for the job.

"She's learned to leave the cop at the door and turn it off—the job and the weight of it—and be somewhere else for an hour or two. When she was in her twenties I didn't think she'd be able to do it, in her early thirties it was getting bad, but she's doing it now, managing the images that come home with her. They're there, behind her eyes, but it's not pain bleeding out of her the way it did for a season. As MHI she gets called when a case is stressing out and getting on top of another cop, so it's the worst of the cases she's living with now. Grace is there now, and sacrifice. She's seen so much of it she's willing to deal with more of it just so someone else doesn't have to. She's coping, and she's making a point to cope."

Dave's somber mood lightened and he laughed. "She's a truly awful cook. Ann doesn't like to keep house, garden, putter, cook, remember vehicle repairs, or go shopping, so she has people she trusts do most of what she calls the stuff of living.

"I buy her a new pair of tennis shoes for her birthday every year because she needs them. Ann walks—her hands in her jacket pockets and a pad of paper tucked in her back jeans pocket and no particular destination. She's off somewhere with that dog of hers. She's not one for crowds, or concerts, or fancy places, or collecting things. She wants a sunset and a dog, a cold drink and a book."

Paul had been listening intently. "It sounds like she knows what she wants in life."

"She knows what she likes. She's busy, and she stays busy. She's an experienced pilot, she holds a computer-engineering degree, she built a fabulous rare coin business, she traded during the last bear market and remodeled her current place with cash, and every seven years or so she picks a new direction and something else appears in her life. She's carrying around art books recently. Her version of relaxing is to be doing something that isn't a murder case."

Paul understood perfectly that search for a diversion. It took an intense focus on other things when off the job to balance the weight of working homicide. "I can relate to that way of relaxing."

"Ann takes it to an art form. She's a writer. She won't tell you. Not many know. She's published fifteen books now. She thinks about the book while she flies. She'll have thought through her book on yellow legal pads of paper and hours of flying, and it's there when she sits down to put it into story form. She's written Kate and my story, Lisa and Quinn's, turned them enough into fiction they don't jump out to friends as ours, but the heart of them is ours. All fifteen are that way—fiction, but people Ann knows well, who have stories she's heard and seen and understood. They are good, solid books and optimistic, which is quite a statement for a murder cop to make. The flying, the writing, the hobbies that turn into businesses, that's how she dumps the weight of the job. It keeps her able to be a good cop."

Paul remembered her in his office, telling the story of the crash. She was indeed a storyteller. "You've got her books?"

"I can loan you a set," Dave offered.

"Keep going," Paul said. "While you're willing to cross the line and talk about her, what else?"

"She doesn't carry stress with her, Falcon. Memories of blood and murder, that's there in spades. But not stress. Hang out with her for a few days, and it doesn't seem like she's that busy. She puts her feet up and tells stories, pokes at puzzles, buys things that look cheap to her, and sells things that look expensive. She watches the weather like it was breathing to decide when to fly, and writes down notes when she has an idea, reads whatever is handy, and pushes murder cases along, cracking them like peanut shells to find what's inside. She just keeps all these balls floating around. It adds up over the years to being a lot of stuff she's accomplished. But the odd thing is, of everyone I know, she's the only one who does not have a list of goals or timelines or a plan for her life."

"She doesn't waste her life. She just lives it."

"Exactly."

Paul liked what he was hearing about her. He looked at his friend. He understood the matchmaking sales job he was getting from Dave. Nothing but the good points, and laid on thick. Paul could read between the lines. Dave might not like to talk about Ann, but once he decided to, he was determined to make the point Ann was worth a guy's time. Dave had never taken a strong position one way or another about who Paul was going out with among Dave and Kate's friends. Ann was a different matter. Paul thought Dave was acting quite a bit like the older brother Ann didn't have.

Dave paused in his walk. "It seems odd to me that Ann isn't married. She's good at relationships, in a way that cuts out the fluff and leaves the substance. The things that matter to you are on her radar screen. You part ways with her in better shape than you arrived. And it goes both ways. She shows up with her life, not some plastic-wrapped version of what she thinks you should see. She's quiet, she's private, but she's authentic.

"Ann once told me no one can sustain more than a handful of good friendships over a lifetime. She's intentionally and carefully choosing hers. She's never told me a number, but I think she considers thirty to forty her personal limit. She's watching people to see who is a good fit, because she's going to try to keep them as her friends for a lifetime.

"I don't know if it's the job that has her wanting to stay unattached, or if it's her history. She's a good cop, she likes to write, she invests time in her friends and the interests she enjoys. She'd have to give up something to make room for a serious relationship, and she's probably decided it's not worth the cost. It may be that simple. Ann can be that practical. You'll have to give her a reason to want something more," Dave said. "No one has ever made that sale with her. You are the one guy I think could, but I honestly don't know what the answer is going to be."

"Okay, I'm going to ask. Has she ever slept with a guy?"

Dave stopped.

Falcon stopped.

"No." Dave shoved his hands in his pockets and blew out a breath. "And don't ask me when or why she bothered to tell me that fact. It's rather a point of pride with her that she's not been stupid in such matters. She's got too much self-respect for one thing, and some lines that she lets no one cross."

"So she's got some common sense then, to go along with those high standards. She's solitary, Dave, and marriage is a two-person life. She's good at being single. Why risk something good for something that might not be?"

"Speaking as the married guy, I was doing fine with single until Kate walked into my life. There's more to living than what Ann has settled for. That's what bothers me. I agree with my wife on this one. It would be a travesty if Ann stayed single all her life. I don't want to see that happen. So I'll meddle like I'm doing tonight and risk the consequences."

"Have you told Ann that?"

"On occasion. She'll give this wise smile and gentle thanks, and she'll even agree to meet the guy Kate's decided to introduce her to and do it with grace, even have a sincerely good time, and yet no one ultimately changes her mind."

"She made a decision and closed a door."

"Then someone better find the key."

They both pondered that reality while they turned back toward the office.

"I appreciate you being willing to meddle," Paul said. "You've made the sale that she's near perfection. Care to tell me her flaws?"

Dave laughed. "She's got them. There are a couple obvious ones. She hates to multitask. She doesn't like to drive at night. She can be persistent, bordering on stubborn. It's hard to shake her off the course of action she's decided on. Oh, and my favorite—she has the patience of a sea turtle. She can outwait just about anything. Drives me nuts. I think she waits because she knows someone else will eventually go deal with the matter, and she won't need to. She doesn't burn energy on stuff she doesn't have to."

Paul thought about what Dave had offered, smiled, then asked, "Is she a morning lark or a night owl?"

"Night. She'll spend her evenings with friends, then go back to work. Ann has worked from ten at night to two in the morning for as long as I've known her. Cop work, or personal work, or just a book she wants to read. It's her four-hour block of uninterrupted time. She calls it her piece of sanity. I wouldn't have said she's an introvert if I didn't know about that four-hour window of time. But that's the real Ann. No people around and time to think."

"The stories should have told you that," Paul replied. "She lives inside her mind, solving puzzles, writing books, thinking about people and watching what they do. She's likely a very strong introvert, and people wear her out. That's why she's careful not to make a mistake by choosing the wrong friend. It's too costly."

"So you think you can figure her out?"

"No one figures out a woman like Ann; you just hope to get the center of it right before you make a fool of yourself. She's interesting. I like interesting."

"You're going to call her."

"She dropped a case on my desk that is going to have me busier than she is for the next few weeks. For now, I'll take those books she wrote. The rest I'll think about for a bit. You walked a mile of leather off my shoes tonight to make sure I knew she would be worth my time. So let me mull it over. Whatever I decide, I'll be careful, Dave. I give you my word on that."

"You'll like her novels."

"Likely. She convinced me this afternoon she can tell a good story. It's a bombshell of a case she dropped in my lap. The guy in her morgue was the middleman for my lady shooter. And Treasury is falling all over themselves because he might also be the middleman for their currency thief. The thief has hit Federal Reserve currency shipments and stolen more than fifty million over the last decade. I don't know who is busier tonight, my team or the guys over at Secret Service. There may be enough in the current day planner this guy was carrying to locate their thief. I'm convinced there is enough in the older day planners to put a name on my lady shooter, and at least two of the people who hired her."

Dave stopped walking. "That's the 'just dumping what I can stretch to be federal' case she mentioned in passing?"

"Your girl likes understatements."

Dave started to say something, stopped, and then just laughed. "That's Ann. Falcon, you want to know who Ann is, you just saw it. That is quintessential Ann."

3

Paul didn't often bookend a day with family business, but when he walked back through the doors of Falcons just after eleven p.m. he thought the day reflected his priorities. He'd started with family, handled the job, sliced out an hour for a personal interest, and returned to end the day with family. He turned on lights as he walked through to the main dining room. The crime scene had been released, and during the course of the day everything in the dining area had been carried out in preparation for a remodeling job. Paul placed a call. "I'm here now, Dad. The carpet is gone, and the contractor has the three half-wall changes marked out."

"Kevin took what happened personally. He called at dawn and offered to step in with a full crew, and I wisely said thanks. Jackie wants to come in at first light and oversee the work."

"She'll drive the contractor nuts, but it will be okay. She needs to be able to walk around this place without flinching when a tray gets dropped. It no longer looks like a crime scene."

"Take photos for the board and share them with the family. They need to see as well as hear that restoration has begun."

"I will. How are arrangements coming for the victims' families?"

"I've gotten in touch with friends of the families to confirm a visit would be accepted, and I'll be making brief visits tomorrow to pay our respects. From there, it depends on how we can best help each family. They died in our restaurant. We'll help however is needed."

"We will." This was personal. The restaurant bore the Falcon name. They wouldn't be forgetting the victims' families. "I've got a case that needs my attention, but I'll free up whatever time you need. Let me know how else I can help."

"You got Jackie home, made her smile, and made it possible for her to sleep without a nightmare. You did what was most important, son. The rest is simply putting the pieces back together."

"You got my message about Kate?"

"I spoke to the mayor this afternoon and conveyed the family's appreciation for the way the Chicago Police Department responded to the shooting and handled its aftermath. Kate runs a case with care and speed and has this family's thanks. It will filter down to her boss."

"Thanks." Paul shut off the lights on his way out. "How's Mom?"

"She was braced for hearing you were the one that had trouble, not Jackie. So she's hovering a bit, and Jackie is indulging her. This will ripple a few more days, but it will heal. Head home, Paul. I know it has been a very long day. The family survived. I'm glad you were near."

"Wish I had been closer. I'll talk to you tomorrow, Dad."

"The prince waiting for the king to die"—Dave's words still lingered like a bit of grit in the back of Paul's mind as he stacked a bacon sandwich together for breakfast. The fact he would one day be head of the Falcon family was a heavy responsibility that often felt like a burden even as it was also a great trust. Even though he was adopted, his father was honoring him as the eldest son. He headed to his home office, sandwich on a plate and coffee in the other hand. It was six a.m. and the extra hour of sleep had helped with the fatigue, but it left him feeling like he was running late.

His phone beeped, and he saw a voice message from Kate sent from her office number. He listened to it as he logged on to his computer and made a note to follow up with her on his way in to work. He glanced again at the time and reached for the phone. Kate at work, Dave at home—he had a question to ask.

Dave answered on the fifth ring. "Tell me you're not calling me this early."

"Kate just left me a voice mail from her office phone, so I know you've got Holly duty this morning. Your daughter is up at five a.m. whether you like it or not."

Dave was silent trying to come up with an answer and gave up with a sigh. "I really dislike the fact you're a detective. What do you need, Falcon?"

"What's the biggest mistake people make with Ann?"

"Seriously? You called now to ask me that?"

"You're the one that went from not going to tell me

about her, to trying to be a matchmaker. If I've got a question, I'm going to ask it," Paul replied, smiling. "So what is it? The biggest mistake people make with Ann?"

"Calling her at five a.m. She's a night owl."

"You already told me that."

"Well, she's not as forgiving as I am," Dave replied. "I'll give you it's a good question." He was quiet for a bit, then said, "People think they have time to win her over, to gain her trust. The truth is Ann's efficient and decisive, and she's acutely paying attention from the point she meets you until she makes a decision about you. She wants to know if you keep your word. She wants to know how you treat your current friends. People think she keeps an open mind about them. Actually she doesn't.

"Once she's seen who you are, once she's made a decision about you, the door closes. She'll be just as friendly, cordial, polite, and helpful as before, but once she's made a decision about you, it's final. You're either on her list of potential friends, or you're not. It's the small stuff that is the most telling to her. If you tell someone you will do something, do you remember what you said, and do it? Do you remember who your friends are and create space for them in your life? If you don't create that space for current friends, you don't need another one. If you can't remember and keep your word, you can't be trusted. It's a brutal standard, but if you want a chance with her, you have to pass that character test."

"Thanks. That will be useful."

"I sure hope I'm not making a mistake encouraging this interest. I'm dropping Holly off at my sister's on the way in to work. You can call me until seven if you've got another question."

"I haven't made the decision to call Ann yet."

"You're not an idiot. I'm hanging up now. Holly wants her breakfast."

Paul set his phone back on the desk. He thought about Dave's answer. Ann was a very cautious woman if those were her personal lines. He wouldn't have seen that answer coming.

He set aside the conversation to come back to at a later time and turned his attention to family business. He logged into the private email system the Falcon family maintained and brought up the secure family website. His dad believed those old enough to press a button on a camera could keep the rest of the family updated on what was happening in their lives. The photo book was filled with pictures of family meals, school outings, and pets doing funny things. Paul uploaded photos from the restaurant, confirming the rebuild was under way, read over Jackie's post about what had occurred, appreciating her ability to finesse the seriousness of what had happened with the reassurance she was okay, then took time to read over his mom's shoulder from her chat two days before with his niece Celia, who apparently now had a new boyfriend.

Despite the tragedy, life went on, and Paul made a conscious point of trying to come up with normal things to post. He sent brief personal notes to his brothers, ribbed Joseph about his new haircut, asked Harper how his busted finger was healing, made an impassioned plea for Boone to find him another one of Scott Hickory's seascapes, and sent slightly longer notes to his sisters. He sought advice from Marie about birthday gifts for his nieces, and sent Jackie his grandfather's peanut-brittle recipe and bargained for a tin of it for his team. He asked his mom about her friend Linda, and forwarded to his dad a cartoon link he knew would get a laugh.

It meant something to be a Falcon, if only because a group of people knew the real you and would laugh at your jokes and take you down a peg if your ego got inflated. His dad worked the phone and the emails for three or more hours a day, discussing business, reviewing ideas, and keeping in touch with grandkids. The Falcon world revolved around him.

It was a good family, sprawling in its interests. There were pockets of animal care, art-quality paints, electrical work, boat manufacturing, magazines, restaurants, and numerous bakeries and food distributors. His father bought when a business was in trouble, got it back on its feet, and sold it—then moved on to the next opportunity. Paul thought at times being a Falcon made business part of how you looked at the world, for only a few of them had veered off into law enforcement or the military as their chosen path as he had done.

His dad had posted three messages before the shooting had taken precedence, and Paul took time to consider his answers as he ate the sandwich. Five to seven a.m. had been for family business ever since he was a young man in high school. Paul replied and posed a few more questions. His brothers ran the day-to-day operations of the businesses now, but all sought their father's perspective.

When the time came that his father died, controlling interest in all of this would pass to him as the eldest son. Paul was still surprised his brothers saw that as a good thing—that majority control would pass to him. They meant it. They loved him, appreciated him, and didn't want the top job. The business empire and the Falcon family would rest on him. His responsibility would be to see that it stayed stable and passed safely into the hands of the next generation.

He loved them all. And he wasn't going to let them down.

Satisfied the family overall was content and quiet, Paul logged off.

He wasn't looking to get married because of his family, but he was certainly keeping them in mind as he looked for a wife. It was a family without a history of divorce. He didn't intend to be the first. Common sense told him if he wanted a good marriage, it began with a wise decision on who to date. He wanted someone who could share what he had, who he was, and what was inevitably coming as his future. He wanted a partner in every sense of the word.

He had avoided dating a cop. Two of them with schedules like his, burdens like his, it could crack even a good marriage. But maybe that was worth reconsidering. Ann Silver was interesting.

A cop who worked murder cases—on the face of it he almost liked the idea. She'd be someone who could talk about work and know which questions to ask, how to care about the cases. He could share his life with a murder cop. But for his family—he had hoped for something other than a cop, for a softer person than a cop would often have to be.

Dave had laid out a biography of Ann Silver that spoke of a fully alive and wise woman doing a tough job with grace. She wasn't a small-town cop, that was for certain.

Paul turned the idea around and looked at it from the other direction. The husband of a cop. They'd live with the constant undercurrent that one of them might not come home that night. The amount of traveling she did, the number of cases she worked, the odds she would be killed on the job or in transit to one were slightly higher than the odds it would be him.

He returned to the kitchen to fix a second sandwich and get another cup of coffee. If they had children, the risks of the job were going to be an issue for both of them. He drank some of the coffee and pondered that problem and weighed again if he wanted to open the door to consider dating a cop. There was nothing simple about this decision. He didn't plan to mess with her heart, or with his, by starting something that didn't make sense. He didn't have time for it now, for a misstep that could cost him months.

Ann was a night owl. He was a morning lark. Of everything that needed to mesh, he'd never thought through a way around that basic difference. He wasn't inclined to make a pro-and-con list when he tried to get to know a lady, but he'd have the things that had to be mulled over and sorted out in his mind. Schedules for them would be more than just a casual matter. A night owl and the current MHI—he couldn't conceive of a schedule more difficult to finesse.

"God, I'd like to ask you a couple questions." He licked Miracle Whip off his thumb and added lettuce to his BLT. "You know the subject that has been on my mind for several years—the idea of getting married. Even in yesterday's chaos, it managed to get an hour of my attention, so I don't need to tell you how big a matter this is becoming. I'm not that lonely, and I'm close to being too busy, but I want something more. I want to share this life you've given me with someone, and have a wife to care for, kids and pets to run around here, with the inevitable stuff cluttering the counters. I want someone else in my life, the messy disarray that is sharing life with another person, and I don't know how to find that right lady.

"What do you think of Ann Silver? Am I going to regret going that direction? And how am I going to consider her when she's not even within a hundred miles of here? I don't know where she lives, but it's somewhere so far south she flies rather than drives to Chicago." Paul thought about that and laughed at himself. He lived in the midst of a major city, and his attention was caught by someone who didn't even live here. It wouldn't be so funny if it weren't his personal knot to finesse. "My parents are growing older each day, and I want them to meet and love my wife. I want to get married."

He was tired of waiting and hoping the lady would show up one day. He'd been deliberately looking for the last few years, systematically looking at the single friends of his friends. If he hadn't ruled out considering a cop, Dave probably would have mentioned Ann years ago. Paul refilled his coffee. He and Ann proved it was possible for two people to slip past each other, even with close mutual friends in common. She lived out of town, and Paul might have been escorting someone else when he stopped in at Dave and Kate's occasional gatherings—however close they had come to meeting over the years, they hadn't been introduced.

Paul took the sandwich with him into the den where he had left his Bible the night before. He settled in to read and to listen. If there was a good marriage to be found, God would be involved in making it happen.

He wanted a wife who understood this bond and affection he felt toward God. While still in foster care, long before he'd met George and Karen Falcon, he'd met Jesus. This relationship with God was the one thing he had chosen for himself. The more time he spent with Him, the more he wished to spend, for it was the place he felt most at home. He wanted to share his family, job, and faith with his wife. He needed to find a lady who loved God with the same passion he did. He rubbed his eyes briefly. The list of what he hoped for just kept getting longer.

Paul detoured on his way into work to see Kate Sinclair. He walked into Chicago PD headquarters just before eight a.m., cleared through security, and headed to her office on the fifth floor. Her phone message could have been answered with a return call, but he preferred to do it in person.

Kate's office walls were covered with commendations and awards, large blown-up photos of the Chicago skyline, and finger-painting artwork by her daughter Holly. The desk and shelves were gleaming mahogany, buried under stacks waiting for Kate's attention.

She wasn't in her office, but Ann Silver was sitting on Kate's couch. Paul felt a rush of pleasure at the sight of her, a similar unexpected delight that Dave must have felt when he realized she was in town. He paused at the door rather than step into the office, content to watch her for a moment before she realized he was present. She was reading.

She was sitting on the couch, legs stretched out, tennis shoes crossed at her ankles. The floor around her was piled with open binders and printouts. She was working with no sleep and too much caffeine, he thought, judging by the lined-up empty soda cans, and he felt a tug of sympathy for the devotion this job of solving murders inspired. It was tough on a personal life—even the idea of having a personal life—with the hours the job demanded. At least she had thought of food and was eating, as she had a fork in the same hand as her pen. She was writing herself a note in the margins of what she was reading.

He thought of all the things he could say, queries on the ball game, a comment about the case she had brought him, a compliment that would veer this to a personal conversation. He pushed them all aside and simply smiled. "Good morning, Ann."

She looked up. Surprise shifted to a quick, warm welcome. "Morning, Paul." She glanced at the clock to check the time. "Kate will be back soon."

"She called you," he guessed.

Ann shook her head. "Quinn told me a cop was dead, but not until after the ball game was over. I gave him some grief about that delay, and to Kate too for not calling me. I volunteered." She gestured toward the photos on the board of the Falcon restaurant after the shooting. "Sorry I didn't know before what had been in your day. How's your sister doing?"

"Coping."

Ann tugged over her flight bag and pulled out a book. She considered it, then held it out. "For Jackie. She'll have time on her hands while the restaurant is reconstructed. She'll like it."

"Thanks."

Kate came in drinking coffee.

Ann tilted her head and looked pointedly at Kate and then the coffee. "That better be decaf."

Kate smiled, amused. "Nag, nag, nag." She pushed aside paper and took a seat on the couch next to Ann. She tugged open the lid of the second carryout carton Ann had brought in, then hurriedly shifted to reach for napkins because the carton was still hot. "Pepper steak for breakfast?"

"We both missed dinner and the chef was being kind." Ann tore the plastic wrapper off another fork and offered it. "Eat."

Kate took the fork and carefully took a few bites. "This is good. The fried rice needs more soy sauce."

Ann tugged a packet from under a stack of papers and passed it over.

"Thanks. What can I do for you, Paul?"

He grinned. "Invite me to dinner."

Ann glanced in sacks and tipped one his way. He took the offered egg roll and two napkins with a thanks and returned to Kate's question. "You called me, Kate." The egg roll was wonderful, stuffed with pork and pieces of shrimp.

Kate tried to remember why she'd called.

"Kelser," Ann prompted.

"Oh, yeah. We stumbled into a guy who mentioned he knew about a murder in New Jersey. The note is there on the desk—half sheet, blue paper. He just moved to Chicago and was trying to be helpful. Maybe it's something or maybe it's not."

Paul retrieved the note. "I'll check it out. How's it going?"

Kate shook her head and looked at Ann. "Tell me you have something."

"I have something."

Kate leaned her head against Ann's shoulder. "Don't try to make me laugh, Annabelle. I've been up for thirty hours."

Ann winced at the name, and moved Kate's coffee out of her reach. "One idea. You're looking for someone Officer Ulaw arrested, testified against, put in jail, within the last five years, sentenced to at least ten years, who has a cell mate with East Coast crime-family connections."

Kate sat up. "Yeah?"

"If it is not that, I've got nothing."

"How did you get there?"

Ann offered her legal pad of paper. "Officer Ulaw hasn't arrested anyone at the top of the food chain," she said, pointing to the list of names she'd sketched in. "He's been making cases against the mid-level guys and the distributors. It is someone who works in Chicago, lives here, is from here, who wanted Officer Ulaw dead.

"He hired an East Coast shooter. Why? We've got enough shooters for hire around Chicago it's not necessary to go elsewhere. And why did he bother to even hire someone? Why didn't he kill Officer Ulaw himself? It's cheaper to do it himself. More satisfying. He's crossed the line to be willing to kill a cop. So why hire someone? Only answer I can come up with, it's because he had to, and he didn't have access to hire someone from Chicago."

"Interesting," Kate said, studying the logic chain.

"Yeah, well I'm brain dead, because that's all I've got.

The rest of the ideas are trash." Ann held out the cup. "This coffee is awful."

"You don't like coffee."

"Reminds me why. Tell someone to look for a name, and then stretch out on the couch for a few hours. I'm going to make a trip south. I'll be back tomorrow if this goes nowhere."

"You shouldn't fly when you're this tired."

"I've got a sweetheart who asked if he could give me a lift home. Virgil Hale."

"That old codger still alive?"

"He's sixty, and you like him."

"Hard not to like someone who blows stuff up for a living. I'll let you know if this goes anywhere."

Ann dropped a kiss on Kate's head in place of a hug and picked up her flight bag. "Call Holly when you get up. She'll perk you up better than the coffee."

"Always does. Paul, walk Ann out of the building so no one intercepts her, or she'll still be here four hours from now."

He wiped his hands on the napkins and stepped to the door. "Sure."

Paul walked with Ann toward the elevator. She stopped several times to exchange brief greetings with people, to ask about families, to remember birthdays, to share a laugh.

"You used to work here."

"My office was next to Kate's."

The elevator doors opened and it was empty. When they had stepped on, Ann leaned against the back wall of the elevator and sighed. She closed her eyes. "Excuse me while I catnap." She reluctantly opened her eyes when the elevator stopped at the lobby and the doors opened. She pushed herself away from the wall.

"Let me give you a lift to the airport."

"No need. Virgil is over at the ATF office, hanging around until I'm ready to go."

"You've been busy."

"Normally am."

"I got told you're the MHI."

She half smiled. "I probably should have mentioned that."

"I don't mind the surprise of it—it makes you more interesting."

She gave him a look that was considering, and made it a full smile. "Do me a favor and tell Dave to come kidnap Kate in a few hours." The cop waiting at the curb lifted a hand in greeting, and Ann headed his direction. "See you around, Paul."

"You can count on it."

When he reached the FBI headquarters, Paul bypassed his own office to avoid getting pulled into whatever had landed on his desk overnight and headed upstairs. His boss had the best coffee in the building, and used it as a subtle incentive for his direct reports to find an excuse to stop by in the morning and give him brief updates. Paul liked to oblige. His boss ran the Chicago office and the Midwest region. The boss of his boss was the director of the FBI. It made for a short reporting chain.

Paul walked into Suite 906, not surprised at the calm. Efficient and quiet defined how his boss liked to do business. "Good morning, Margaret. I need five minutes of Arthur's time."

She checked the board. "He's finishing a call, then he's yours."

"Thanks." Paul poured himself coffee and picked up the morning paper. He had scanned the sports headlines when Margaret indicated the call was finished.

Paul walked into his boss's office. "Morning, Arthur." His boss was a practical, common-sense cop with deep family ties. Paul liked the man both personally and as a boss. If he had a mentor in the bureau, it was Arthur.

"You're smiling. I'm going to like this."

"We have a good lead on the lady shooter." Paul settled into a chair and updated his boss on the wreck and the day planners. "Ann Silver showed up in my office yesterday to hand me the case, so it arrived as a gift."

"Ann was in town? Sorry I missed her."

"You know her?"

"She handled the Delford matter for me. Nice lady."

"So I'm finding out."

"So what's your plan on this? Anything you need me to clear away for you?"

"We find his name and where he lived, this gets interesting. He didn't know he would be dead, and he will have left some interesting materials behind. I can use some help keeping this orderly between us and Treasury. They want him too."

His boss smiled. "I'll be glad to handle it. Keep me posted. And good hunting."

"Thank you, sir."

4

The one thing Paul particularly liked about chasing paid shooters was the money trail. Financial footprints were the FBI's bread-and-butter expertise, something tangible to follow. Just having amounts paid for two of the thirty murders was a useful new fact.

Around the room his team was busy. They didn't need him. The car wreck had arrived, the ME had the body, there were computers running facial comparisons through databases, and they were data mining to answer interesting questions. It was Monday, they'd had the case since Thursday, and before the day was out, maybe two, they would have a name for the middleman and a location where he lived. So Paul sat and thought about the lady shooter and kept his attention on the end goal.

Paul knew the woman through her work. She had murdered thirty people, a single gunshot from a distance, all head shots. She left a calling card of sorts at the perch where she took her shot. She wanted to claim the kill, a résumé of sorts for more work, and a warning to others she was out there.

A partial distant image from a security camera from murder nineteen gave them a woman about five-foot-six, slender, shoulder-length hair. Until that murder, they had been working under the assumption their shooter was a man, though not discounting the fact it could be a woman.

The calling card was a small crystal cube, smooth on all sides, white as a sugar cube. They were a novelty item from the late 1800s made as a promotional item for a gaming company. They had shipped as a box with fifty cubes. Nothing there they could trace.

His lady shooter now had a partial name, Miss L.S. If it wasn't an assumed name and courtesy title, his lady shooter was single, and while Paul had figured that, it was useful to have it confirmed. The first letter L wasn't the most popular for a woman's name: Laura, Linda, Lisa, Lois, Louise. They were creating a master list of possibilities from census data. The search of the case file had come up dry so far, but the initials would be useful when they located the middleman's home and could search his records.

The day planners gave him a price for murders twenty-five and twenty-nine. His lady shooter had made a lot more money over her career than Paul had thought a month ago. The idea she had retired after the thirtieth murder was becoming a more interesting idea to consider. They had speculated she was either dead or in jail as reasons she had stopped, for she would have been in her forties at the time of the last shooting they could be certain was hers. They watched for shootings where there was no calling card left, but over the years had found no case which stayed open. It looked like she had stopped after thirty kills.

Sam took the seat beside him.

"Do you think Flint Meeks could have afforded to pay two hundred fifty thousand to kill his wife?" Paul asked, voicing the question he had been mulling around.

Sam considered it. "No. Maybe a hundred fifty thousand, but not that additional hundred."

"So he's off the likely list. Who on our suspect list could afford this hit?"

"Not many. Three, maybe four."

"That's what I was thinking. The price bothers me. Why this much? If you have a casual hatred, 'I wish this lady was dead,' you might pay five figures to have her killed. But two hundred fifty thousand? That was a significant amount thirteen years ago. Instead of a hit, we have a high-priced assassination. There's got to be something about the murdered wife we don't know."

Paul looked to the board for murder twenty-nine. "The same problem exists for the Victor Ryckoff murder. The price for the hit doesn't make sense, given what we know about the victim. We're missing something. I've reread the two bios, but I'm not picking up what it might be."

"I'll tug Peter in, and we'll build out the timeline of their lives. If we can't account for a few years, maybe that will give us a place to focus on."

"Good. Something is there, Sam."

"Boss, we've got something," Rita called, excited. She rolled her chair between tables to switch databases she was searching while Paul walked over with Sam to join her.

"Two good ideas are intersecting," Rita said. "This guy's been dead going on five weeks now. No one has reported him missing, but lots of people are beginning to feel the fact he is dead. He hasn't paid any bills. His electric bill, gas bill, water bill, phone bill, cable bill. He's going to go late and then delinquent on everything at the same time. He lives *somewhere*.

"Facial recognition started generating matches overnight. I've got sixteen drivers' licenses with different names, different addresses, across different states, but all are his picture. Buried under all these aliases is his real name and address. Only one of the addresses stopped paying bills five weeks ago. Our middleman has a tentative name, Gordon Whitcliff, and he lives in Reston, West Virginia."

"Nice job, Rita." Paul turned to scan the room. "Listen up, people. Rita has a name and address." A collective cheer went up at the news. Paul smiled. "Let's see if it holds. Arnett, Daniel, Sullivan, any activity on Whitcliff's credit cards, phones, or bank accounts since the day of the crash?

"Christopher, we need a local cop to make a check of the property. Send him the picture of our guy and have him show it to the neighbors. Is the photo the man they know as their neighbor?

"Kelly, give me a fast bio. Married? Ever? Have kids?"

Paul paced the front of the conference room as the first answers filtered in from around the room.

"Two phone numbers in his name. No calls out on either one since the day of the crash."

"Boss, his finances are dead quiet. A few checks cleared, but all were written before the date of the crash."

"He's drawing Social Security. No wife or dependents are listed. Never filed a joint tax return. Nobody but him holds a driver's license with that address. He's seventy-four years old. I can't find a marriage license or divorce decree for that name, but it's not conclusive since records that far back would be on paper."

"I can't find any credit cards issued in his name. There's a gas card with no activity on it in the last month."

"Paul, I'm on the phone with the police officer at the address. Neighbors on both sides confirm the photo is Gordon Whitcliff. According to one neighbor, Gordon has lived in that house for at least thirty-five years. They thought he was away on business. He had asked a neighbor to collect his newspaper and mail, hadn't indicated how long he would be gone."

"Okay, people. I'm satisfied," Paul said. "We've got our middleman.

"Christopher, see about getting the property secured until we arrive. We'll be there before dark.

"William, find Whitcliff's dentist and get us X-rays for the ME to use in comparison. We'll bring back a toothbrush and hairbrush for a DNA match as well.

"I need volunteers for a road trip to West Virginia." So many hands lifted he had to smile. "If you want to go, I'll make room for you—just don't expect to get much sleep once we're there. Close down what you're working on, then go home, pack, and be back here by three. I want us to be in the air by four.

"Sullivan, I expect he's got at least one safe-deposit box under his real name. See if you can find it.

"Kelly, rip apart his phone records and identify anyone he has ever called. Any names with initials L.S., T.M., G.N., call me and start diving deep on who they are.

"Peter, his financials. Tax returns. Bank accounts. Any sizeable deposits and payouts, I want to know where they originated from and went to.

"Arnett, I need to know what other properties, if any, he owns.

"Sam, open a feed with Treasury and keep them copied on the phone and financial records. The recent flow of calls and cash may intersect with their currency thief. I'll leave you to run things here.

"Any questions?" Paul scanned his team. "Okay. It's solid progress. You are one step away from making your boss a very happy man. Now I just need a name for Miss L.S."

Paul put in a quick call to Arthur, then headed down two flights of stairs and stopped at his office to sign the paperwork and get the travel department busy making arrangements. A box on his guest chair was from Dave. Ann's books. Paul took the box with him and went home to pack.

———————▼———————

"That's the house, sir. The brick ranch with the flagpole and petunias along the sidewalk."

Paul had been expecting something different. His middleman had lived all this time tucked in the center of a subdivision. The dusk of late evening showed there were still people out walking dogs, and kids riding bikes.

The officer in the patrol car stationed at the street came to meet them.

"Thanks for staying, Officer Marson. No one has been inside?"

"No, sir. Not since we received your call and secured the premises. The neighbor on the west, Mr. Olson, had a key to the property, as he took the mail inside each afternoon. I took the liberty." He held out the key.

Paul walked to the house and unlocked the front door.

It was a neat, tidy house—that was Paul's first impression as he stepped inside. The drapery on the windows were heavy fabric, formal, the floors hardwood. Furniture in the rooms he could see from the door was sparse, and there was no clutter on any surface. The interior was hot and smelled a bit musty. The air-conditioning must have been left off or set high.

"Jason, I want photos of everything before we start. Walk through the place with video and also get me stills of his desk, anyplace he likely handled his mail.

"Rick, bring in those boxes and make a call to get more delivered.

"Christopher, take the attic and garage. Franklin and Rita, the home office. Larry and Kim, the bedrooms. Sidney, the kitchen and commons areas. I want a careful and thorough search of this home. He had reasons to hide items of value where they would be difficult to find. So until we locate a document trove and a very large hidden cache of money, I will assume we haven't looked hard enough.

"Anything that is paper, look through it, then put it in a box and set it in the dining room. We'll take it all back with us. Keep a close eye out for anything that suggests he has another property—photos, insurance paperwork on a different address, contact numbers for repair people in another town—anything suggesting this isn't his only residence and that we need to be searching somewhere else as well."

His team spread out. Paul walked through to see the layout, then went outside to see the backyard, finally coming around through the garage. The man had lived here a very long time, and he hadn't planned on not coming back. He would have taken precautions when he traveled, but he wouldn't have removed things from the house. It wasn't as big a property as he had feared, and his middleman had lived a contained life, by the look of what was here. They could find what was here. It might just take a day or two.

To give his team time to work, he walked out to speak with the officer and discuss security for the next few days. Twenty minutes later, Paul returned to the house, and went back to the room serving as the home office.

Franklin was sitting at the rolltop desk looking through drawers. He glanced over and held up papers. "He's a record keeper, and neat. I just pulled the last four months of phone bills from a folder marked Phone Bill. We've got two address books filled with names and numbers. Rita is checking them. And we've found taping equipment on the phones. There will be recordings of his phone calls—his own version of insurance—somewhere around. Probably a safe since I'm not finding anything so far in the office but blank tapes. The paperwork in these files is current to this calendar year, nothing before that. There are more records somewhere. He has no computer that I can find, and there are no cables suggesting a laptop is used here, no printer, no backup power strip, nothing suggesting Internet service. He may have stayed old school and simply not used one."

"I already like this guy. Rita?"

"Dining room, boss."

Paul found her at the table, making lists of names from the address books.

"So far I've got a Linda Surette, Lisa Simkins, and Laura Saranoff for Miss L.S. Arnett is checking them out. I'll run the books for T.M. or G.N. next."

Kim came into the dining room with a gallon Ziploc bag full of matchbooks from different restaurants. "There's a safe in the master bedroom closet, no attempt to hide it, but it will have to be drilled out to open it. Do you want me to make a call?"

"Very big safe?"

"Six by eight. The kind you tuck in jewelry to keep it from the casual burglar."

"We'll wait to make the call until he can do his job without getting in our way."

"Boss, I've got a gold mine."

Paul followed the voice back to the second bedroom. A four-drawer file cabinet stood in the closet, and beside it six stacked white banker boxes. Larry had one box on the floor and another with the lid off.

"Old bank records. He kept everything in date order back to 1982. A quick scan shows the two hundred fifty thousand deposit in July 1999, and the three hundred thousand deposit in August 2002. Assuming they all went through the same middleman, I can give you the amount the lady shooter was paid for each of the thirty murders."

Paul handed him the pad of paper from his pocket. "Good news. The file cabinet?"

"Old tax returns. At least thirty years. Insurance and warranty information. One drawer looks like personal history, playbill to a Broadway show from twenty years ago, old photos in a shoebox, that kind of thing. We're going to want to take all of this."

"I'll get you more boxes to empty that file cabinet."

Christopher came down the hall to join them. "The attic is empty. There is no sign anyone's been up there in the last five years. But I did find a safe in the utility room. It's behind the water heater and behind the clipboard hanging on the wall that lists where fuses go in the electric panel. Pure fluke I found it. The light in the attic wouldn't come on, and I was checking the fuse box. I don't think we get the safe open without finding the combination. We would have to move the water heater to get enough access to drill it open."

"Boss. I need a hand in here—master bedroom."

Paul followed Christopher down the hall to see what Kim had found.

She had moved the bed, and the rug beneath it. "There may be a cache here. The floor is soft, dead center of the room, and the boards don't feel linked into the rest of the hardwood floor. About two boards wide and four feet long." She was rocking one of the boards, and it shifted a fraction higher than the rest of the floor.

It took five minutes of careful work and they got the first board to lift out. They easily lifted out the second board.

"What do you think? Thirty thousand, maybe forty? I don't know dimensions for hundred-dollar bills."

"Is it real?" Kim picked up a packet. "It doesn't look like it has been in circulation. You think it might be some of the stolen cash?"

"What better way to pay your bills than with stolen money? Both of you count it, agree on the amount, then get it sealed and on its way to the Treasury guys to check out the serial numbers," Paul said.

"This is one task I won't mind."

Paul left them to it and returned to the dining room to see how Rita was doing with the names. They had found the kind of document stash and cash that could break a case wide open.

Paul brought in pizza and gathered his team together at the dining room table. He snagged two pieces from the second box before he took a chair. "Eat while it's hot and listen. I'll run through my list, then you let me know what I've missed." He scanned his notepad.

"He made it easy on us. There were records, and a lot of them, all neatly organized.

"We need to drill out two safes, and move the water heater to get to the one. There could be something very interesting in that one. Jason, make some calls and make that happen.

"We're still missing the phone tapes. Rick, I want you to head to the bank when it opens. Sullivan found one safe-deposit box in this guy's name. Let's see if he kept the tapes there.

"Daniel, Larry, we need the old bank records and phone records scanned tonight and distributed to Treasury and others in the sandbox. It will take you a few hours, so get a pot of coffee. Get them scanned and distributed, and then you can sleep in.

"Kim, make arrangements for secure transport. I want all the paper we've found shipped to Chicago. We can go through the records there in a more organized fashion.

"Local PD is going to provide security here for the night." The pizza was making him thirsty, and he glanced toward the kitchen. "Didn't we shove a case of soda in the freezer to fast-chill about three hours ago?"

Kim dropped her pizza and shoved back her chair to dart into the kitchen. "We did." She returned carrying a case of soda. "They haven't gone to ice, but they are close." She passed the soda cans around.

"Thanks." Paul drank half of his, appreciating the icy coldness, before looking back to his list. "Almost done. Rita, I want you to interview the neighbors tomorrow. Where did he shop, eat lunch, and go for coffee? What was his routine? Then find any security cameras in those areas, and let's see if anything is still available going back more than five weeks. I'd love to have six months' worth of time to see who visited him.

"Franklin, Christopher, Sidney, work the address book, have Peter generate a quick profile on those who live locally, and go interview those that don't have a criminal record. How long were they friends, did they ever travel together, what did he do for a living, did he have family in the area? Anything useful you can get that will give us a picture of the guy. Those with a criminal connection, I want us to look at more carefully before we show up for an interview."

He reached the end of his list, and finished his slice of pizza. "We have rooms at the Hyatt over on Juniper

Street, and Wilson volunteered to shuttle us around. If we push, we can wrap this up in a couple of days. Anything else?"

He looked around the table at the group and smiled. "You're too tired to think if you can't come up with something I missed. Get squared away for tomorrow, then let's head on to the hotel."

Paul tugged out his folded list and scanned what was not crossed off. It had been a good three days. "We're still missing the phone tapes. I want a final search of the house for another safe—floors, walls, and stairs."

"On it, boss." Those waiting for their next instructions dispersed to the search.

Franklin slid a document box into the van. "That's the last one."

"Do me a favor and open desk drawers and file cabinets just to make sure nothing got overlooked."

"Will do."

Paul's phone rang. He glanced at the caller ID. "Hello, Kate."

"Ann was right."

"Yeah?" Paul felt a smile forming. Good for her.

"Eric Lorell, doing twenty-five years for murder, paid Andrew Waters to kill Officer Ulaw. We've got the money transfer traced back. The lawyer for Lorell's cell mate helped him make the arrangements. Eric just smiled when we put it to him that we knew, didn't waste time with an argument. He gave us a written confession. He'll move to death row, but I'm afraid it's not much justice."

"It's what's possible."

"Yeah. Glad it's done, wish it was a better result," Kate said. "What Ann gave me went somewhere. I hear what she gave you is going somewhere too."

"It is. Where is Ann today?"

"Missouri, I think."

"She doesn't stay put for very long, does she?"

"A day or two occasionally. I hear you and Dave had a conversation about her the other night."

"You don't need to play matchmaker too."

"Moi?" Kate laughed. "Have you called her yet?"

"Thinking about it."

"You should, you know. You'll like her."

"I'm sure I will." Paul smiled. "I appreciate the update. Anything else?"

"That was my excuse to call. Safe travel home, Paul."

"Thanks, Kate."

Paul slid his phone back in his pocket.

Ann was in Missouri. Given he was in West Virginia, the travel was relative. Ann was good at her job. He tucked away that fact and looked back at the house. So was he. He had a lady shooter to catch. The two safes and bank box had produced false IDs, valuable gold and silver coins, and several thousand in foreign currency. They didn't have a name for the lady shooter yet, but they had paper to work. It was time to get back to Chicago.

———◆———

The plane trip back to headquarters was quieter than the trip out. His team was listening to music, sleeping, quietly chatting. The immediate work was done, and they deserved the break.

Paul clicked on the overhead seat light and pulled over his travel bag.

Dave's box had been a stack of books with a note: *Ann's published works. Read the O'Malleys in order.*

Before he had packed, he'd spread them out on the table and reviewed the titles. The covers weren't his style, and they were romantic suspense, which wasn't his preferred category either. There were three military novels in the mix. She wrote under a pseudonym, but he had expected that.

After some checking on the O'Malley series titles, Paul had stuffed three into his bag. Now he selected the first book and opened to the first chapter.

Kate O'Malley had been in the dungeon since dawn.

He'd found Dave and Kate's story, if he wasn't missing the mark.

He looked out the window and considered waiting for another time to read it. He didn't feel like getting disappointed, and he figured that was what was going to happen. Ann was a friend of Dave's, and friendship made for a lot of allowances about what was good writing.

What did you decide to write, Ann, when you sat down to tell Dave and Kate's story?

He settled in to read. He began to hear Ann's voice in the telling, and then the story took over.

Three hours later, the flight attendant's voice announced they were landing soon. He rolled his shoulders to work out the tension. Ann had crashed a plane in her story. He had not seen that coming. She had worked at least one plane crash in real life to have caught the details she did. And right now he was about to land. He felt like chuckling at his serious wish that fiction didn't come true.

She had his attention, and she did not let go. He needed to read all her books. The more he read, the more convinced he was that he had best make the time.

Who are you, Ann? And where did this storytelling gift come from?

5

Ann Silver landed at the airport in Alton, Kentucky, early Wednesday morning, and by nine o'clock was walking into the Alton Police Department. It wasn't the first time she had routed from one MHI call to the next, and it wouldn't be the last. Missouri had been raining and cool, while Kentucky was sunny and warm. She'd picked up a bagel and cream cheese for breakfast at the airport, found her sunglasses, and borrowed a car. If not for the weather, the day could have been a repeat of her prior one.

"Thanks for coming, Ann."

"Glad to help, Ben."

She set down a hot chocolate for him, perched on the edge of the desk, and blew on hers to cool it. The murder board behind him was filled with photos and notes, and she scanned out of habit.

"Her name is Elizabeth Verone," Ben told her. "Fifty-two, divorced ten years, no children, a hairdresser for thirty years. She was shot in her home on May twenty-first.

I'd rather you make your own judgment on the rest of it. The murder book is current as of last night, and I had a duplicate made for you."

"Let me read what you've got and get up to speed. I'm sorry for this, and the loss. It's always bad when it is someone you know."

"She was a pain in this department's collective side with her fountain of collected gossip about crime tidbits she heard while cutting people's hair, but she was our nuisance, someone killed her, and the days are running off the calendar. We need this one solved and off the board." He looked at the photos a final time, shook his head, then turned and pulled together what she would need. He handed her a thick binder and a set of the photographs. "Want me to find you a desk?"

"No need. I'll find a quiet place to read, then find you and talk it through."

Having worked for the department before, she took the route most cops took when they needed a break, and she headed to the roof. If she was going to think murder, she would do it while she also got some sun.

It took four hours to get through the weight of it, and she rubbed her eyes as she let her mind drift for a bit. This victim didn't have family issues to tug. Family was states away with solid alibis, and that eliminated the easy answer for where to look. Their victim had told the police about enough crimes, real and imagined, that if Ann picked a file at random out of the history of this town, there would be a link of some tenuous nature to the lady who had died. No wonder the cops were hitting their heads against the wall trying to get this case to give ground. Many people would have strong emotions about this woman, and more than a few might prefer her to be dead. So who had acted?

They hadn't found the shooter.

She mulled that fact around in the back of her mind while she let her thoughts sort out what was here. The cops knew their town, knew who to question, who to suspect as possible shooters, and they had done a solid job of doing that. The interviews were extensive, comments were cross-checked, and alibis had held.

The cops hadn't found a viable suspect for the shooting.

Ann stopped on that thought again and let herself ponder the fact for a good few minutes, stepping back through the river of information the investigation had uncovered and mentally following the flow of it, looking at how the case had unfolded. The cops should have found their shooter.

And that told her something.

She looked one last time at the photos of the murder scene, then closed the murder book and went back downstairs.

She brought in roast beef sandwiches for the cops working the shift, the meal a habit when she was a guest in their house. She settled in to share Ben's desk and enjoy a really good sandwich.

"You got through it all?"

She nodded around a bite. "Fat murder book, good investigation, and you're right. It's going cold."

His partner, Greg Ornell, waved toward the murder board with his spoon from one of the coleslaw sides that came along with the sandwich. "It's like this perfect crime. Shoot her, no one sees you, everyone we talk to maybe had a reason to want her out of the way—it's too many needles. We're finding the needles in the haystack, but there are just too many needles."

Ben nodded. "Too many people got rubbed the wrong way over thirty years of her life. A shooting is a cold way to end it. Someone thought about this for a long time, then got triggered somehow and said, Today I'm going to do it, and did it. She's lived here her entire life, Ann. There's too much here, and yet not enough of the right things. We don't have the evidence that can focus us in on where to look."

"Then we work through it, and we look for what might narrow it in. Do you have a preference for how you want to do this?"

"I'd like you to tell me the story of it, Ann," Greg suggested. "Let me see it fresh, and maybe I can spot where I can tug next."

Ben concurred.

Ann finished her sandwich and got herself a new drink. Since she was better off in motion, she moved to the murder board. "Okay. Story first."

Ann knew it would not be polished or smooth as she spun it out, but it would be useful, as all reviews were, to hear again the story and its mystery to be solved.

"My name is Elizabeth Verone. I'm a tidy woman, with a generous laugh. I love to gossip and pass on what I hear and ask you what you know. I'm a woman of routine, same breakfast of a morning, same route to work, same station where I've cut hair for thirty-two years. I keep cards of useful people with handwritten numbers tucked along my mirror. I get business for people, and I'm proud of that networking I do for folks. You need a plumber, I've got a name of a good one. I'm a broker of information, that's how I see myself, rather than a gossip. I want to help you out. You come and sit in my chair to get your hair shaped and styled, and I consider you one of my people. I want to know your troubles and your news, and I want to know what's going on in your friends' lives too.

"Nothing stays confidential for long if I know it. My pleasures in life are to know information about you, and share information with you.

"It's cool on Monday morning, and I stop to find a sweater before I go to work. The car needs gas, so I stop to put in five dollars, then I stop at Parker's Bakery for coffee and a donut and mention to him that Janet's daughter got a scholarship to art school and isn't that a grand thing?

"I open the shop a few minutes early. Amy wants her hair trimmed and to talk about her boy getting in trouble with Henry's boy Lou last weekend. Paula is next and wants her hair colored, and I nudge her into talking about what real estate has sold recently, and if there are any new homes coming up for sale.

"I have two perms and then a lull, so I sit with Jenny and Karen by the dryers, and we read through the new magazines for this month. The talk turns to men. Nathan is back in town and that runs for ten minutes of reminiscing. Jeffery stayed overnight with Melinda, if the parked car was any clue. I mope about how I haven't been on a date in ages and want a decent dinner out and movie, just to have a nice change of pace in my day.

"I lock the shop door at five p.m. I've been on my feet most of the day and I'm tired, so I take myself straight home. I putter in the kitchen and fix myself a cheese-burger and salad. I eat alone while I go through the day's mail. I trade off grocery shopping with my neighbor and we rotate the weeks each of us will shop. Since this is her week, I dump the store flyer into the trash with the other junk mail.

"I start a load of laundry, towels and other whites. While they run through, I go out back and water the six new roses I planted this year around my patio.

"I decide I should mow at least by the garage so I won't have to do it all on Saturday. I get out the mower and do the stretch alongside the garage and in front of the flower bed. I need to bag the grass but don't like to do the job, so I half rake at the tall grass and pile it by the dead stump and call it done. I put the mower and the rake away and I close the garage door. I come inside and drop my headphones and iPod on the dining room table.

"Someone has been in my kitchen. There are groceries on the counter and ice cream ready to go into the freezer. I call out for my neighbor Susan DeMarko, thinking she came over while I was mowing. I hear water running in the guest bathroom. So I walk into the kitchen and open the refrigerator to finish putting the groceries away.

"The window shatters and I'm shot.

"Head shot kills me instantly and I drop right where I'm standing. The refrigerator door swings back and stops at my shoulder. The pickle jar in my hand shatters and splatters pickle juice over the lower cabinet doors.

"My friend hears the shot, hears me fall, comes into the kitchen, sees the blood, and starts screaming. She goes flying out the front door shouting for her husband, who comes running. He calls the cops while the wife screams hysterical that Elizabeth is dead, someone shot Elizabeth. No one enters the house until the cops arrive."

Ann looked over the pictures on the board and wondered again at the horror of it. A nice neighborhood, not rich but not poor, quiet of crime, and a woman shot in the head without warning. A few more cops had joined them now, and she scanned faces to confirm she had the latest facts right. "There are no other sniper-type shootings anywhere in the surrounding states, no local shootings since this one. It wasn't a random thing where she's the first victim of many." Nods around confirmed it.

Ann returned to the story, thinking about the why of it. "All right, it was me, Elizabeth Verone. Someone wanted me dead. Does someone want my gossiping to stop? I knew about real estate, who was sleeping with whom, and who came and went from the town. That's just what I happened to learn about today. Add up a year of days, and I know a lot of bits and pieces of news that might mean something if I put together the details.

"I know something someone doesn't want me to say. I talk about everything I know, so you're going to have to kill me to shut me up. Maybe I've already talked, and you are paying the price for it. Maybe I've shattered our world with my gossip, and you hate me with everything that's in you. I know something you don't want me to tell, or I've said something already and hurt you bad, and you've decided you're going to be the one to shut me up forever." She paused to drink while she switched roles to the one who had come to kill.

"I came with a rifle to the back of your house planning to kill you. I came during the daylight hours rather than at night, so I stay in the woods to avoid being seen by neighbors. I don't want you to see me in case I miss.

"You're outside in your yard. So why don't I shoot you when you mow, when your back is turned as you walk back and forth and your attention is on the ground in front of you?

"I don't shoot you in your backyard because I'm in a perch quietly tucked away and already zeroed in on your kitchen window. I know I won't miss that shot, so I'm just waiting for you to appear in the window at the kitchen sink. My nice little target and right there in my rifle sights.

"So why didn't you shoot me while I was fixing myself dinner? I was in the kitchen for quite some time. You hadn't set up behind my house yet? You weren't there before I got home from work? You came in afterwards? You shot me in the side of the head as I looked in the open refrigerator. You didn't want to see my face when you killed me?"

Ann closed her eyes and put herself into the mind of the shooter. "I was looking for just the right opportunity to kill you. I didn't kill you in the backyard. I waited for you to go back inside. I shot you through the kitchen window when you opened the refrigerator to put away the groceries. Was I really planning to kill the neighbor who came over with the groceries, and I shot you by mistake?"

Greg pointed at her and interrupted—"That's interesting. That is interesting, Ann. The neighbor was the intended target, not Elizabeth." He pivoted toward Ben, and his partner was already nodding.

"Why shoot your wife in your own home? Quite a mess to clean up and it's a crime scene for a long while. Shoot Susan next door. Nice solid alibi. I want my wife dead, and I know exactly where she will be five minutes from now. Guy was right there on the scene when the cops roll up.

"His wife goes out the door carrying the groceries over to Elizabeth's. He's got to get his rifle, get around the back of the house to the woods, get lined up for a shot in the kitchen window, and take that shot while Susan is still in the kitchen with the groceries. A rifle with high-powered scope, all you're going to see in the scope at that distance is brown hair and a lot of it. They're both brunettes. The shot could have been meant for either brunette in the house. Run it that way, Ann. See where it goes."

She mentally reoriented what she knew about the crime as she nodded. "My name is Kevin DeMarko and I'm an angry man. I've been married to a woman I've grown to hate, and I want her gone. Divorce means alimony and maybe it comes out I'm sleeping with someone else. I kill my wife and get away with it, problem solved.

"My wife goes out the door carrying groceries to the neighbor. Murder is on my mind, and I see the opportunity in an instant—see all the potential of it. The one person in the county most people would love to see gone is the gossipy lady next door who is into everyone's business. Kill my wife over there and everyone will assume the shooter made a mistake and the person who was supposed to have been shot is the hairdresser.

"Susan goes out the door with the groceries, and I'm up from the table and running to take advantage of my opportunity. I grab my rifle and go through the backyard. I glimpse my wife at the window unloading the groceries. I find a spot where I can brace and steady a shot. I'm breathing hard and anxious to get it done. I have to wait while Elizabeth pushes the mower around to the garage so when she hears the shot she won't turn this direction and see me in the trees. I hear the garage door going down, I see brunette hair enter my rifle scope, and bam, my wife is shot in the back of the head and goes down. I run back to my home and ditch the rifle somewhere fast, shove it into the gutter extension or bury it in the stack of two-by-four scraps in the garage. I get into the house. And I hear screaming."

Ann stopped, looked at the murder-board picture of the husband at the scene. "You hear screaming. Only it's your wife screaming that your neighbor is dead, rather than your neighbor screaming that your wife is dead. And you have really screwed up your life.

"You call 9-1-1 while your wife stands there sobbing. You have an alibi of sorts as you were home and you came running when your wife screamed—you've been standing there on the driveway with her while the cops arrive. You get through the first search, the second search, without them finding the rifle. You get to the night when you can move it to a safer place, and another day when you can dispose of it. Get that far, you know you're okay on the murder. It doesn't point towards you. But you have really screwed up your life.

"You still have the wife in your house. You have cops crawling over your neighbor's property and, by extension, seeing what's going on at yours. There is going to be no chance of getting rid of the wife now without the cops noticing and without suspicion falling on you for both murders. You can't get a divorce very soon either because cops might wonder if you hated your wife that much a few days before as well. And to top it off, the value of your home just dropped by at least twenty percent because a murder happened next door. You have really screwed up your life."

Ann stopped, and looked at Ben. She'd about convinced herself it was true just by telling the story.

He nodded. "It plays that way, and it is doable. It's even oddly plausible." Ben looked at the cops who had accumulated around them to listen to the story. "Listen up, guys. We need chapter and verse on the husband. We need to know if he owns a rifle. We need to know if there was trouble in that house. We need to figure out if he's our guy and do it fast. The wife is still in that house. Let's get it done."

Cops started dividing up assignments between them.

Ben got to his feet to come over and join her. "Thanks, Ann. I always do enjoy your stories."

"We'll see if this is a rabbit hole or if it's a gold mine." Ann nodded to the murder board. "You'd have to convince a jury he really wanted his wife dead, and even if you put the rifle in his hands, they're going to wonder—well, if he wanted his wife dead, wouldn't he have at least shot his wife? I think you are going to have to get a confession on the murder if you want to close this case. A random shooting of a neighbor, and he has an alibi of sorts? The DA won't know what to do with it."

"We can at least put the fear of God into him that we're looking at him, and keep the wife alive. He was there. That's the nice thing about it. He's the only other person who was right there—neighbor, wife, and husband. The victim, the intended victim, and the murderer. It would have been easier to see that as a possibility if our lady hadn't been the talkative sort and so easily seen as the intended victim. You want to stick around and see where this goes?"

"You've got this one covered. I'll head home. If this turns out to be a rabbit hole, call me, and I'll come back. I'll be surprised if our first idea turns out to be the right one, but the story has got that ring of possibility to it."

"I think it's going to turn out to be on the money. I'll let you know either way. Safe flying, Ann."

"Thanks, Ben."

Ann headed back to the airport. She would file a report in her log that noted who called her and the location. The two lines would be the only record of the day. And that was a good thing. Maybe she had helped, maybe it was a rabbit hole. Time would tell. But it was what she could do—read, listen, talk it through, and help find a new idea to work.

If her phone stayed quiet for a few more hours, she would have a leisurely flight home, a long walk with her dog, and a chance to sleep in her own bed. She might even make it home in time to take the evening patrol. She placed a call to the Medora Police Department and left a message for Marissa that she was heading back. If she was fortunate, she would get four days, maybe five, before the next MHI call came in. She liked being sheriff, taking her turn on patrol, answering calls to settle neighbor disputes, arresting those who deserved it, warning those who were skirting the line. The job of sheriff would end when the county took over policing, but until that day came, it was a job Ann could do and enjoy. No one had been murdered in Medora in twenty-three years. It would be good to get back home.

6

Paul was pleased with the case progress. His team was surging through the paperwork they'd brought back from the middleman's home five days ago. With help from other agencies, they were linking receipts and phone calls and bank records and reconstructing his business dealings. It was good, solid forensic work, turning documents and other written pieces into a functional picture of the man. There was a web around the middleman now—names, faces, places.

Gordon Whitcliff had his fingers in a lot of crime, made connections for a lot of people. He was the go-to guy for those who fenced stolen goods, were known to run car-theft rings, along with a few suspected of being black-market art dealers, two crime families on the East Coast, a banker convicted of fraud five years before, and then there were the big connections to the currency thief and the lady shooter. The middleman's records were yielding good evidence for all kinds of lawbreaking. Paul had his team passing on the data to other agencies as fast as they found it. The only piece of it they were going to keep for themselves was the lady shooter.

Over the last five days he had also carved out time to read three more of Ann's books, grabbing hours when he got home, and waking himself up with extra coffee of a morning.

Paul stopped on the fifth floor after lunch. Dave was on his office phone, twisting a page ripped out of a thick report into a fine-looking funnel while he listened. Paul figured an interruption would be doing the man a favor. He tapped on the door, and Dave motioned him in, then promptly announced to those on the call he had to go— he had a guest. He hung up. "I swear they were talking just to talk. Thanks for the save."

"Glad to help." Paul offered one of the breadsticks from the sack he carried, for he had done Italian for lunch. "Ann writes religious books."

Dave dealt with the report by dropping it in the trash. "She's religious."

"Something you forgot to mention." Paul settled into an office chair.

"I would never have considered you a good match for her if you weren't a solid Christian. Guys that treat their faith as an afterthought don't have a chance with her."

"The books were just unexpected." He hadn't thought he had it in him to be surprised after everything Dave had told him. Ann had surprised him. She was weaving God into her stories as seamlessly as the romance and suspense. If a certain character didn't believe in God, that fact was as interesting to her as if a character did. "I could see you and Kate in *The Negotiator*. She did a nice job on your story."

"We think so."

"Marcus and Shari—I'm still getting my mind around the fact Ann knows the head of the U.S. Marshals and the Virginia congresswoman well enough to write their story. And I've had dinner with Quinn and Lisa—their story was like a photograph of them together. Are the other O'Malley stories like that—true at the core?"

"Yes. We asked Ann to write the O'Malley stories. We wanted to capture who Jennifer was to us. How many have you read?"

"Four. I think Ann's misplaced as a cop. She should be writing for a living."

"She doesn't want the weight of it. She writes for herself and her friends. They just happen to be good reads."

"What about the military novels?" Paul asked.

"Real people, friends of Ann, and written by request. They're fiction like the O'Malleys, but built around what is true. I've met the navy pilot that is Grace. I've heard rumors about the woman awarded the CIA Intelligence Star. I know Joe and his wife met up with Ann for a winter trip to Canada. Ann's circle of friends extends in a lot of different directions, and I am constantly surprised by who they turn out to be.

"You get used to it," Dave continued. "Ann is private about her friends. It's not that she doesn't want to share them, or thinks you wouldn't be interested. She just keeps confidences. She gives people privacy. And she doesn't trade on the fact she knows someone. Ann will introduce her friends to each other if they are in the same room, but she wouldn't think to mention them otherwise."

"Ann protects her friends."

"Yes. To her, it's what a friend does."

Paul thought about what that said about Ann. She'd be someone his dad could trust. She kept what she knew to herself. But she'd also be hard to get to know if she decided not to share her life. There wouldn't be many clues to what was even out there to know. He'd have to get her to the point that she trusted him, and somehow figure out how to make that happen sooner versus later. "Is she working on a book right now?"

"The signs are there that she is," Dave replied. "She'll fly with a passenger more often when she's between books. I don't have a clue whose story she is writing. Kate thinks it's a friend with a background in art. It's as good a guess as any since Ann's been carrying art books with her the last couple years. I know Ann made a special trip to see Quinn a few months back, and followed it with a trip to New York. She borrowed my bulletproof vest for the trip. Never a good sign. So she's researching something significant. Those were personal trips, not work related to her MHI role. When Ann has a book to the point she wants first readers, she'll call and ask if there's time to give her some feedback on it. That's always a nice request."

"Do you happen to know when she is coming through town next?"

"She's planning to do a turn at the airport next Saturday night, in and out, probably never leave the airport grounds. You thinking of going to see her?"

"'Thinking about it' being the accurate phrase." He was still mulling over the approach he wanted to take with her, and it was best to plan it out before he made the first move on the board.

"Did you see my birthday gift from Kate?" Dave dug out a photo. "She got me a cat."

Paul looked at it and laughed. "What's the name?"

"Carmine, for today. It keeps changing. It's a big soft fuzzy thing and purrs like an engine is going."

"You already love it."

"I do. Kate got it for herself, but we're both pretending she didn't." Dave returned the photo to his pocket. "I've got a strong-willed, beautiful wife, an adorable little girl, and now a fuzzy cat. There are worse things in life. But I'm going to sneak a dog into the picture as Kate's birthday present. Something big enough to tower over the cat and guard the kid."

Paul laughed. "You love being married."

"Best thing that ever happens to a guy." Dave's phone interrupted. He glanced at the number. "I need to take this. I'll get you the time Ann's flight is due in."

"Thanks."

Dave reached for the phone, and Paul headed upstairs.

He entered the secure conference room where boxes taken from the middleman's home now lined one wall, documents filling most of the table. They were continuing to build his world and write his biography. Paul took a seat and scanned the boards.

They had five possible names for Miss L.S. All had been eliminated. Phone number and bank account were still flagged as open.

"Sullivan, where are we at with the phone numbers?"

"We know the middleman called her. We have his old phone bills that overlap the last few murders. Jason has one number that repeats—might be the lady shooter. He can't find a name to attach to it. Records simply don't

exist back that far. The number today is a business, and
the number has been changed between one business and
another over the last several years. I'm helping him look,
but we're running out of where to tug."

"Was there better luck with her bank account?" They
knew the middleman had paid the lady shooter with a
bank transfer rather than a check, and that all payments
had been made to the same account.

"The bank failed during the savings and loan crisis.
We've been able to determine the account was closed
shortly after the thirtieth murder. The address we've
been able to tie to the account is a city dump."

Paul looked at the boards, made a decision. "People,
listen up." He got to his feet. "I like what's on the boards.
You're making good progress. You've been pushing and
it's appreciated. But we're heading into the middle game,
where forward momentum is going to get tougher. I need
your best on this for the next few days, so I'm stepping
on the brake. Shut it down for now, and get out of here
by no later than five o'clock. Enjoy an evening catching
up on your personal lives. We'll hit it fresh tomorrow."

Paul took his own advice and turned off the lights in
his office shortly after six p.m. He took the stairs to the
lobby. It was a comfortable night and he thought about
making a visit to the gym. He got to the shooting range
once a week and to the gym four or five days a week if
possible. He could feel the stiffness that set in with too
many days moving paper.

He was approaching his car and digging out his keys
when his phone rang. He pulled the phone out of his
pocket. "Yes, Sam."

"Treasury guys just picked up their currency thief."

"I owe you five. I figured it would take them another week."

"You want to go over for the interview? You can tell they were in a good mood because they offered to let us sit in."

Paul unlocked his car and weighed the pros and cons of the offer. "Ask them for a tape. I'd rather watch it at our leisure. We go over, we're going to one day have to return the courtesy."

"True. You want me to let the others know?"

"Sure, spread the word. They've earned something to celebrate tonight."

Paul thoughtfully closed the phone. The news changed his plans. There was a possibility here he could use. He worked it through as he drove and started making calls when he got home. The gym would have to wait.

———————▼———————

Ann unlocked the motel room door and pushed it open with her foot. She found the light switch. It was a twelve-room, privately owned motel along Interstate 80 in Chappell, Nebraska, and that made it one of the more significant businesses in town. The soft blue walls, floral rose bedspread, and bright white towels on the vanity were basic and familiar. She stayed in motels like this more nights than not when she traveled. Her bag went on the bed, along with the murder book she had picked up from Elliot Reeve to review tonight. She'd managed four days at home before this call came in, and she was glad she had caught up on her sleep. The coming days promised to be anything but restful.

A thermos sat on the round table by the window. She

opened it, sniffed, and found hot chocolate. The note beside it was tugged from a standard pad of paper, but it was addressed to her.

> Ann, please call me. Type www and the following numbers and it will be secure video. Two a.m. is fine, whenever you get in. Paul Falcon

She made the connection while she shrugged off her rain slicker. She'd forgotten how much of a punch the man conveyed as his image appeared on the screen. He was in a short-sleeve shirt rather than suit and tie, and he looked tired. He also looked like a guy who wore authority as a second skin, even off the job. That was his home behind him. There had been nice art in his FBI office, but nothing like the painting that was visible over his shoulder. Since he was sitting someplace he could answer an Internet call, she assumed it was his home office. The picture finished stabilizing, and the audio frame went from red to green.

"Falcon? Something wrong?"

He looked over as her image appeared on his end of the video link and smiled. "Hello, Ann." He laid down the document he held and turned fully toward the screen. "Just news I thought you should hear. The guy in your morgue was the middleman for my lady shooter. He was also the middleman for the Treasury Department's currency thief who's hit Federal Reserve shipments and stolen more than fifty million over the last decade. Treasury picked up their thief today and recovered about fifteen million in cash and have leads on a good portion of the rest."

"Nice." She dumped her jacket on the back of a chair and dropped down into a seat that had been plush a decade ago and now was closer to a fabric-covered frame.

"It wouldn't have happened without you working the wreck until it gave up its secrets. I thought it deserved at least hot chocolate. Treasury will have their own thanks, I'm sure, once they finish their happy dance celebration over getting their guy."

She smiled at his description. "The hot chocolate will be fully appreciated."

"We've also identified the two guys who were tailing you looking for the other day planners. They are freelancers who worked for the thief. The tail wasn't coming at you because of the lady shooter."

"That closes an open question for me. The other day planners?"

"Burned, unfortunately. They found the damaged briefcase and remnants of the day planners. On better news, the middleman is Gordon Whitcliff. We've located his home, and now have his phone records and bank records. We don't have a name for the lady shooter yet, but we've got a lot of material to review. I'm hopeful."

"I wish you good hunting."

"I tracked you down to a small town in Nebraska. Working a case?"

She felt her smile fade. "A sixteen-year-old girl got shot in the back, probably by another teenager. I'm helping sort through it."

"I'm sorry for it, Ann. For the family and for you."

"I could feel the grief just walking through town tonight. No matter the answer at the bottom of this, the tragedy has devastated this small town. The officer who called has a girl the same age. I'm glad he pulled me in. He needs a sounding board that isn't someone who lives here." She nodded back to the thermos. "That was nicely timed; I've got some reading to do."

"I won't keep you then, as you've got work and still need some sleep. Thanks for the call back, Ann."

"'Night, Paul."

She closed the link, puzzled that he'd made it such a brief call. Then she tasted the chocolate, and was glad he had left her to enjoy it uninterrupted. "Thanks for arranging this. I was a bit chilled," she murmured softly. She retrieved the murder book. The death had been violent, near the girl's home, and the dad had called it in. She drank the rest of the hot chocolate in the thermos as she read, and pondered what she found there.

Paul saved the conference video with Ann to his personal files, then played it back. He pressed pause when she turned toward the screen with a smile. He hit the print button. A photo of her scanned to the image printer. It was raining there, for her hair was curling and damp around her face. She was dressed tonight as she had been when she came through Chicago, a comfortable shirt and jeans, with a jacket covering her side arm. She had expressive eyes, that was what he had noticed that first day when she sat in his office and told him the story. He paused the video again as she spoke of the case that had sent her to Nebraska. Those pretty eyes were blue and, tonight, sad. The murder of a young girl wasn't going to easily be put away, even when it was solved. He'd heard it in her voice, the weight of it, and could see it in her face, the pain of it. It bothered him in a way that he couldn't explain, that she was in a hotel room tonight with a murder book and alone. "She could use your help, God. To find the truth and clear the innocent, to name the guilty, but more, to just get through this."

He played the video through again, then closed down his work and left the home office to turn in for the night.

He was still mulling over the call when he stopped, struck by a thought. Ann hadn't really been alone in that motel room. If the books she wrote were any indication of what her relationship with God was like, she knew God intimately. She hadn't been alone. And quick behind it came another truth. God knew her. The inside Ann where she thought about people and books and pieced together murder cases. God knew Ann like no one else did. Paul wondered what it would be like to know her that well. What he knew so far interested him, and it looked like it barely skimmed the surface.

7

Paul could feel the hooks and jabs he landed on the heavy bag rippling back into his body rather than forcing Sam to lean into the bag to hold it steady. Years ago it would be Sam with his eyes narrowed and sweating, trying to take the assault. Now Sam was practically taking a nap on the other side of the bag. Paul attacked it until his blood was pounding and his breath coming in gasps. He was getting old, and the case was getting cold. He could feel the lady shooter case slipping back into a block of ice and couldn't figure out a way to heat it up again. She was "Miss L.S." and still as much a vapor as before.

The lady shooter was a careful planner. She tailed her quarry to decide where to make the kill. Maybe there was a witness out there. Maybe someone who had hired her, and knew she was out there, had seen her trailing her victim as she planned the murder. Maybe someone remembered seeing her and could describe her. Maybe.

And he knew he was grasping at straws.

Paul tossed a final jab at the bag and stepped away. He leaned over, his gloved hands on his knees, and lowered his head to get his breath back.

Sam let the bag go and shook his head. "You want to go for a run next?"

Paul looked up at his friend, shook his head. Trust Sam to rub it in. He couldn't get a breath deep enough to answer. "It's going cold, Sam," he gasped out.

Sam hugged the bag and considered Paul's statement. "Our problem is the fact the case never fully got hot. We profiled her as working alone, arranging her own travel, doing her own surveillance and planning for the murder, using the same weapon. Now we know she dealt with the same middleman for every one of the murders, and he handled the client and the money. He's dead. And we're cold. There are no more ways in."

Sam stepped back and tossed a couple of open-handed hits at the bag. "The only way forward now is if she generates it. If she makes a mistake, or makes a new move. Maybe someone finds the weapon. Maybe she commits a new murder. Maybe she tries to blackmail one of the people who hired her. But short of her walking into an FBI office and confessing, there may not be another thread that can reach her if she stays quiet and keeps her head down."

Paul knew Sam was right all the way down the line. It was possible she'd never be found. The thought burned. They had been working the paper they had brought back from the middleman's home for two weeks now, and the case was stalling out.

"Want to hit the bag some more?" Sam asked, considering him.

Paul waved him toward it, took a few more shots.

Paul blocked the sunlight coming across the monitor with his hand while scanning messages which had come in overnight. He mentally sorted what he could push off and what he would prioritize in on his list. He had learned early in his career that the first half hour at his desk was about the only slot he could expect to control—the job was simply too responsive to events. There were a lot of other cases climbing up to demand his attention.

Sam tapped on the door, held up a tape. "You want to watch it here or upstairs?"

"Here. I heard it's long."

Sam settled into one of the guest chairs. "Four hours plus. Lincoln said we'd find it worth the time."

Paul pulled out an orange juice from the refrigerator and passed it over, then got one for himself. He popped the tape into the machine and pressed play. "Let's see what the currency thief has to say."

The Treasury guys were thorough, that was clear within the first thirty minutes. Paul listened to the interview and forced his mind to stay focused on it so he wouldn't have to listen to it again. An hour into the tape, he sat up straighter. The thief was talking, his voice low but clear.

"He would call you; say he had work if you wanted it. If you said yes, he would play you the tape of what the buyer wanted. The tape was his insurance that the buyer would honor the terms of the deal. You did the job; he paid you and gave you the tape. Now it was your insurance in case the buyer ever tried to put the crime back on you. You had proof he had paid to have it done. I liked it. No one could welsh on you, and they had equal risk. It kept things quiet. He was always professional about business.

"So was I. I never took a job where I didn't already have a buyer for the currency, and someone else paying all the expenses for a big crew and a lot of planning. I'd take thirty percent as my payment. Washing the cash was someone else's problem. My job was to steal it clean and neat, and in big enough quantities that made the job worth the effort."

The interview concluded at four hours twenty-two minutes.

"I wonder if Miss L.S. kept her tapes," Sam pondered.

"We find her, we can ask her." Paul ejected the tape. "The suspect, in his own voice, giving the name of who to kill and the price he would pay. Thirty murders, lined up in a neat row. That's a set of tapes I would love to have."

"They're a death sentence for our lady shooter if their existence becomes known. Thirty people, with motive to kill her who already have demonstrated they have substantial financial means and the will. What are the odds this thief's interview gets leaked? Or the fact the middleman had taping equipment on his phones gets leaked?"

"It will eventually leak because it is news. The question is, do we have our lady shooter before then."

"She's going to have to want to be found. We're running on fumes here."

Paul had grown philosophical about it over the last few days. "We know the price she was paid for each murder, the initials L.S., T.M., and G.N., and the name of the middleman. It's more than we knew last month. We'll have to make it enough. The individual murders will give us something, or we'll have another idea. We always do."

Paul wished he had a way to conjure up the tapes the lady shooter had pocketed for the thirty murders. Knowing good solid evidence was out there that he couldn't access bugged him. He walked into his home, planning for a ball game and a pizza, and the phone started ringing. For a brief moment Paul considered ignoring it. He answered in the kitchen and quietly set his briefcase on the counter as he listened to the news. "Thanks for the heads up, Lincoln."

Paul stood motionless for a minute, phone in hand. The Treasury Department was about to give Ann an award for the capture of the currency thief. A large award. The bits of information he knew about Ann said he should warn her it was coming. It was well deserved, she had earned it, but she wouldn't see it as a good thing if it came as a surprise.

He needed to alert her, in person if that was possible. They would find her and call her tomorrow with the news. So he had to get to her tonight. Where was she? Still in Nebraska? He hoped she was on the ground right now. If she was in the air, by the time she got on the ground to answer a call, he might not have time to tell her in person. This was one conversation he didn't want to have over the phone, even a video conference call.

He balanced the receiver on his shoulder as he checked

his cash and pulled out fixings for a sandwich he could eat on the road. "Dave, can you find Ann for me, where she's at now and for the next twelve hours? And can you do it without telling her I'm the one asking?"

------------◆------------

Dave had found her in Davenport, Iowa. It was shortly after ten p.m. when Paul walked into the Hyatt Hotel, headed to the reservation desk, and showed his ID. "I need Ann Silver's room number."

"May I see that ID again, please? Yes, we were told to expect you, Mr. Falcon. There's a note for you." He retrieved it and passed it across.

Paul opened it, read it, and nodded his thanks to the desk clerk. He headed outside.

He walked across the hotel parking lot to the empty mall parking lot and started scanning the moonlit darkness.

"Falcon, over here."

He spotted the motion and moved to join her. Ann Silver was sitting in a folding chair with a pair of binoculars, a book, and a sandwich all laid out on a foldout tray beside her. There was also a second chair.

"Not the place I expected to find you," Paul said.

"I like to stargaze at night. It's my way to decompress."

He wondered if she also had a rule about guys and hotel rooms that was part of this but didn't mind the results. They could talk without interruption or chance of being overheard out on this massive piece of empty asphalt.

He held up what he carried. "I brought the hot chocolate."

Ann smiled. "I like this visit already."

He handed her one of the two mugs, opened the thermos, and poured for them both before he sat down.

"What was so important you had Dave tracking me down tonight? Don't tell me you were just in the area."

"A four-hour drive put me in the area. Dave was to keep quiet the fact it was me asking."

"I asked Kate. She said Paul." Ann shrugged. "A puzzle, but I figured you would tell me why. I thought you would be calling, not arriving. The note at the desk was just in case. As was the chair. There's a problem with the lady shooter case?"

He settled back and set the thermos on the pavement beside him. "Nothing beyond an upcoming budget fight on my part. I spent the day filling out travel requisitions for one hundred twenty-three interviews in sixty-four cities. We know how much the lady shooter was paid for each murder. It lets us narrow down the suspect list in each murder to just a few names. We're going to go re-interview, see if anyone reacts to a photo of the middleman and the amount of the hit. It won't get us to the lady shooter directly, but it will close individual murders and maybe give us new information to pursue."

"A good plan."

"Costly. Sam thinks I'll get about ten approved a month, I'm betting about twenty-five, and then things begin to stall. It's an important case, but it's a cold case. If we close the individual murders, if we catch the lady shooter, and we do it this month or it takes until next year, it isn't going to make a lot of difference when it has been on our board for twenty-two years. So I spent my day on paperwork hoping to be persuasive."

"I much prefer my job. No paperwork is one of the job mandates, and travel approval is looking at the sky to see what the weather is like."

He smiled. "You do have the better of it." He studied her and felt his smile fade. She looked exhausted, the lines around her eyes deep, and the smile there by effort. She had brought a sandwich out with her, but had yet to eat. "You're not in Nebraska tonight," he said. "There was resolution to the case you were helping with, the teenage girl?"

She looked away to the horizon, where the lights of the town hid the stars of the sky. "Her father shot her in the back because she wanted to go with a boy he didn't approve of." The words were said with the calmness of a cop, but he saw the truth in her face. This one was still sitting raw on her emotions. "There was sexual abuse in the home that had been going on for a while. The boyfriend knew and wanted to get her away from it. We were looking for the boy since he had disappeared that night, but if he hadn't eventually had the courage to stop running and let the cops talk to him, I'm not sure we would have put it together."

She looked back at him. "She was good at hiding her secrets—no diary, no confidences shared with a girlfriend, no mother to see the signs. We might have had ideas, but we wouldn't have been able to prove it. That fact both-ers me a lot. The father wasn't an easy man to see as a molester or a murderer. Most of the town still doesn't believe it." She shook her head and turned her attention to the mug of hot chocolate. "But you didn't travel four hours to ask me that. Why did you come?"

"Not a good transition, I'm afraid, Ann. Let me sit and watch the stars for a minute and grieve the fact she had that father."

"It takes me a few days longer than it once did to put it in a box and leave it behind." She took the lid off the tin beside her flight bag. "Want a brownie? I find lots of chocolate helps."

He considered the contents of the tin with some regret. "Dave says you're a lousy cook." He was still tempted to risk it. Maybe she couldn't ruin chocolate. He glanced at her. "Yes, I asked him about you. He's your friend. He would know the inside scoop."

The admission had been the right thing to offer. He saw her blink, and then she laughed. "I am a *terrible* cook, so it's a good thing I didn't make the brownies."

"Then bless my heart, I am partial to chocolate." He chose the biggest brownie in the tin, and was pleased when she selected another for herself. He took a bite and sighed. "These are excellent."

She sampled hers. "They are indeed." She snapped the lid back on. "If you can't cook, know who can."

"It should be a golden rule." He licked his thumb of icing. "I've got parents, three brothers, two sisters, six cousins, and a bunch of in-laws, nieces and nephews—there are at least thirty-four of us. You want the scoop on me, nobody spills it like family."

"Thanks for the heads up. How's Jackie doing?"

"She's done better than I thought possible, getting past what happened. Falcons will reopen in just a few weeks, with a new interior look to the place."

"I'm glad."

He watched the stars and let nearly five minutes pass in silence. She didn't break it.

Paul finished his brownie, then turned to her. "Treasury wants to give you a reward for the capture of the currency thief. There was a bounty for information leading to the arrest, and you're the one who cracked the day planner that directly led to his capture. Treasury is going to call you tomorrow. There's a half-a-million-dollar award with your name on it."

She didn't say anything, and her expression didn't tell him much. He had expected surprise, shock, joy—anything but this stillness.

"You've earned it," he said quietly. "He stole more than fifty million, and he was still active. Treasury won't lose more cash. They recovered a good amount of what was taken, and they'll be able to round up the crew that helped him and the people who hired him to execute the thefts. All of that is worth the reward."

"I agree it is news. And I appreciate you tracking me down to tell me before I got surprised by it tomorrow."

She was quiet for a full minute, and then she sighed. "Let me make a call."

She picked up her mug and stepped away.

She returned in less than five minutes. "I declined the award. Any more hot chocolate in that thermos?"

He poured her another mug. "You declined it. You don't want the money?"

"I want a lot of things. I don't want award money for doing my job. Would you?"

He thought about it, shook his head.

"So, it's declined."

She finished the last of her brownie and companionably offered the last one in the tin to him.

She stored the tin away and then gestured to the sky. "You know much about stars? I fly at night and love the sky, but I never know what I'm looking at. I'm trying to figure out this star map." She clicked on a flashlight to show him the book she had open.

Paul looked at the map, then at the sky, then at her. She'd just turned down half a million dollars and had spent less than ten minutes on the matter. She didn't even dwell on it; she just made a decision and was already moving on as if the news hadn't made even a small dent in her evening.

She glanced at him. "What?"

"You puzzle me, Ann."

"I puzzle myself at times." She shrugged and pointed. "Do you think that might be this star cluster? If I kind of squint and ignore everything that doesn't fit, it might be a match."

He laughed. "That's true about most things. We need an astronomer. You know one?"

"No. Best I can do, I probably know someone, who knows someone, who knows one."

"So close the book and just enjoy the view. Your evening will end better. You can study another night."

She looked at him and closed the book. "You've got a four-hour drive ahead of you, and work in the morning. You should get on the road."

"I should get going," he agreed. He offered the thermos. "There's one more mugful."

"Thanks."

"It's been a pleasure, Ann."

He headed back toward the hotel parking lot. "Oh, and Ann?"

"Yeah, Falcon?"

"Next time you turn down half a million, can I have a witness?"

Paul shared the elevator with Sam the next morning and gladly accepted the extra coffee he had picked up.

"Late night, boss?"

Paul rolled his eyes, and Sam laughed.

"I'm going to be late starting the morning update. Warn people for me. I'll give you a heads up on when."

"Will do."

Paul stopped off at his office before heading upstairs to the conference room. A tall stack of travel requests sat on his chair. If they were back in a day, he'd made a mistake and the entire lot had been rejected. He picked up the stack and scanned the top one. Approved. He looked deeper into the pile. It was approved. He flipped to the back and found it approved.

He stepped to the door. "Rita."

"Yes, boss?"

"Count these. I submitted a hundred twenty-three."

She took the stack and started counting in sets of ten. "One hundred twenty-three. All your travel requests were approved in less than a day. What's going on?"

"That's what I'm wondering. See if you can get an answer from whoever you normally work with in budgeting."

He sorted the travel requests into order by murder

while she worked the phone and the computer, moving through the finance department budget screens.

"Paul," she called over, "according to Shelly, your budget line has the dollars, so the travel requests went right through the system without needing anyone else to allocate money and sign off."

"The team doesn't have this large of a budget."

"Apparently someone changed the budget line, because you do now. I've got the screen up. These travel requests are approved and cash is reserved against them. You've still got a sizeable unallocated amount of cash in your budget line. A partial year of funding is still there."

"Can you find out who changed the budget line?"

"Maybe. Hold on."

Paul suddenly had a pretty good idea where it was going to lead. How had Ann Silver managed to move her award money to his FBI budget line overnight? He'd told her about the award at ten o'clock last night. She had declined it. And now his account had a lot of cash. He didn't believe in coincidences.

"Boss, you're going to want to see this."

Rita turned the screen and pointed to the authorization on the transfer.

He closed the door to his office before he made the call.

"Ann, it's Paul."

"Hey, Paul. Be fast. I'm about to be in the air." He could hear the engines being throttled back.

"When I got to the office this morning I found all my travel requests had been approved because my budget line had been fully funded. I was wondering if I might have you to thank for that."

"I thought the money should do some good."

"It was a very nice thing to do, Ann."

"But . . ."

"I just wondered if you knew the Treasury secretary had personally moved the award money."

"Gannett probably asked him to." The airplane engines revved. "Sorry, Paul, I'm cleared, gotta go. I'll be on the ground in about ten hours, give or take. Catch me then if you need to."

She dropped off the call.

Gannett. That would be former Vice President Jim Gannett. Ann called him last night to decline the award?

Paul found himself down one of the deep tunnels Dave had mentioned that defined Ann. He didn't know if he was impressed or stunned as the emotions flowed through him. He could almost get his mind around her reason for declining the award and her generous act of sending it to him. And he could understand that kind of influence—his father did it as a matter of course. But he hadn't seen this coming, that Ann had this kind of influence and connections. *Who are you, Ann Silver?*

He looked at the time. Ten hours. He had no idea where she was heading. He tried to decide if he wanted to have the next conversation on the phone or in person. At a minimum he wanted her someplace she could make a secure conference call, and he could see her as they talked. So late tonight, when there would be some time for an uninterrupted conversation.

Paul set aside the puzzle because there was nothing he could do to get answers at the moment. He called Sam to get the team together and headed upstairs with the stack of travel forms. Those who enjoyed traveling and collecting airline mileage points were going to be able to choose their own destinations for the next couple of months. For the first time since this began, Paul began to feel real hope that at least some of the murders on the board could be cleared.

8

At home that evening, Paul set his watch alarm for ten p.m. to call Ann and then fixed himself a meal. He debated picking up a file of Falcon business to work on but felt too restless to concentrate. The box of books Dave had sent over was almost empty. Paul picked up another of Ann's novels, choosing one of the military ones. He took it with him into the den and settled into a comfortable chair with the White Sox game muted on the TV. He opened to chapter one.

Shelton, North Dakota

There was a bounty on Darcy St. James's life, and in the world where she had once worked, having someone come after her was still more likely than not.

He read the first sentence and had to smile. Ann could grab your attention. This story was going somewhere. He settled in to see where she was going to take him.

The disquiet started in his gut after the first fifty

pages, then turned into a baffled sense of confusion the further he read. When he finished the story, he checked the front of the book to see when the book had been published.

Dave had said all the books were based on people Ann knew, friends of hers, and had been written by request.

In the books he had read so far, the first name of the character matched the first name of the real person. The last names had been changed, and the descriptions were a bit different, but if you knew the connection was there, you could see it. Dave and Kate, characters in a book, were based on Dave and Kate in real life. Lisa and Quinn were based on the Lisa and Quinn in real life. If that pattern held, the Darcy St. James in this book was based on a lady with the first name Darcy.

Paul had an inkling he knew who the actual person was, but this time her true first name was not Darcy.

He turned to chapter thirty and scanned the pages again, pulling out the passages that had him wondering and debating and baffled that what he was thinking might be the case.

Shelton, North Dakota

It was good to be home. Darcy leaned against the triple-rail fence she had painted the day before and watched as Sam and Tom tried to figure out what to do with the evergreen that threatened to collapse onto her garage. She was glad it was them and not her.

She watched the tree sway and heard the sharp cracks as wood gave way. The tree came down on the garage roof. There were only so many miracles two SEALs could work. Cutting out a tall dead evergreen safely apparently wasn't one of them.

"Gabe, let me call you back in about ten minutes, okay?"

"Sure."

"Thanks." She hung up the phone and headed over to join the guys.

She stopped beside Sam and folded her arms across her chest to match the way he stood just looking at the tree. She tilted her head, studying the way the tree had crashed. They had done a great job. The crown line of the roof had been broken.

"We decided you needed a new garage," Sam remarked.

"That's a good idea because as it turns out I do."

Ignoring the time, Paul reached over, picked up the phone, and placed a secure call. His brother Boone answered.

"I would like your wife to take a call. Could you arrange that?"

"About?"

"Ann Silver."

His brother said nothing, then softly sighed. "How?"

Paul relaxed for the first time since he had begun to sense something was there. His sister-in-law was former CIA, awarded the Intelligence Star for Valor, and one of the most treasured people in the family. The book was different from her . . . except it rang true to her in real life. And not all of it was fiction. "I've heard the story about the evergreen a few times, and I park in front of that new garage every time I visit."

"Ann was visiting the day we tried to drop the tree. She howled with laughter, right along with my wife."

"It would have been a sight to behold. It is, in the book retelling."

"How'd you stumble on to the novel?"

"Dave loaned me a whole set of them. Ann Silver had dropped by my office to tell me a story and hand me a case."

"Sounds like Ann." Paul could hear his brother's voice soften as he smiled. "There are reasons we didn't tell you about the book."

"No harm, no foul. I know there were reasons. But I need to have a conversation with your wife."

"She won't tell you much. And she'll tell Ann whatever you say."

"I expected as much. I need an hour of her time. Let me know when's convenient."

"I'll call and be back with you in a minute."

Paul hung up the phone.

Ann had captured his sister-in-law so well on paper he could see the real person in the fiction. He marked the page and closed the book. What was he going to do with a woman who wrote this kind of special fiction and did it in her spare time?

He pondered that question while he waited for his brother to call back. Vicky Falcon, formerly Vicky Bassett, had retired from the CIA after a long career overseas. She'd retired to marry Boone. Her career was still so classified that even with his security clearance, what he could see about her in documents was only a mostly blacked-out page.

How had Ann become a writer of biographies wrapped

in fiction about cops and soldiers and spies? How did she know the former VP? There was something so large sitting just behind what he could see that he could feel its shape and sense its form.

The phone rang.

"Vicky will call you in twenty minutes," Boone told him. "She can't spare an hour right now, but she can in a couple of days when she gets back home."

"Thanks, Boone."

"Can I ask a question?"

"Sure."

"What did you think of Ann, the day she dropped by your office to tell you a story?"

Paul smiled. "I thought she was, well, cute."

"Ann?"

"You had to be there. I thought she was cute. I thought she was enjoying herself. And then I thought—*she's caught my shooter.*"

Boone laughed.

"Ann being cute got dropped in the flurry of action as the lady shooter case turned red hot, but I'm circling back around to rectify that."

"Good luck with that. I'm just not sure Ann's a quarry that can be caught."

"I'm wondering about that too."

⎯⎯⎯⎯▼⎯⎯⎯⎯

Twenty minutes later, the phone rang. Vicky prided herself on being prompt. Paul was smiling as he answered. "Hello, Darcy St. James."

"Hello, Paul." He could hear the answering smile in her voice.

"How did you choose the name?"

"The name is Ann's doing, and I fell in love with it, just reading the opening page."

"She captured your heart on paper, along with your love for my brother."

"That she did now, didn't she? She has a nice touch with a word."

Paul thought about where to start and how to convince Vicky to help him. "I am trying very hard to get to know her, and planning how to help her get to know me."

"Boone called me back to mention you were smitten with her."

"I said I thought she was cute."

She laughed. "Same thing to my way of thinking. She caught your eye and caught your attention."

"She did, Vicky."

"And you are starting with your deeply ingrained habit of information collecting before you make the first move."

"I like to know where I am heading before I start. You should admire that, Vicky. I believe it was your entire advice to me on dating."

She laughed. "Indeed it was."

"So help me avoid a few blunders with Ann. You've got information I need, and I'm of a mind to ask for help. You have to admit, I found the right source to ask."

Vicky was quiet a moment. "We have an agreement, Ann and I, that curiosity is good for a guy," she finally said. "She and I are good friends, Paul. We plan to grow old together and reminisce about stories and be friends for a good long time. So I'm inclined to leave you in the dark for the sake of friendship. But I like the idea of you and Ann together. So ask your questions, and I will answer maybe one or two, then defer the rest to a longer conversation at another time."

"You're not making this easy."

"Ann's worth the effort."

"Something happened today I need to ask you about, Vicky. The Treasury Department offered a half-a-million-dollar bounty for information leading to the capture of a currency thief. They wanted to give the award to Ann, and she turned them down. Instead, Ann had the money moved to my FBI budget line so I could use it to help catch my lady shooter."

"What a lovely thing for her to do." He could hear the pleasure in Vicky's voice. "Ann wouldn't have wanted the award for herself, Paul. And if she accepted the cash on behalf of her department, the town would have reversed their plan to transfer policing to the county, and that would have been in the long term a disadvantage to the safety of the residents. So she sent the cash where it could do some good. That would be Ann's logic. You didn't know she was going to do it?"

"No. She probably wanted it to be a pleasant surprise, and it was. Then I learned the Treasury secretary was the one who did the transfer. I can sort of get my mind around the reason she gave the gift, and I can understand that kind of influence, but I just didn't see it coming, Vicky. That Ann has that kind of influence.

"She doesn't come across as who she really is," he said after a pause. "She's the MHI and she never said a word. She knows spies and soldiers and U.S. Marshals, has written books about them. She's friends with the VP. A good enough friend the VP doesn't think twice about calling the Treasury secretary late at night to do her a favor."

"Paul—she's just Ann. She introduces herself as a cop, because that's who she is. She's also an author, has good friends, some of whom would make people do a double take, and was voted in as the MHI. But why would she mention those things? To try to impress you? She'd be annoyed if they mattered to you. They don't change who she is."

"You know it's not that simple."

"I know it's not that simple. But Ann would like it to be."

"How did she get to know the VP? How did her world become what it is? Something big is back there. I can all but feel it. Who is she, Vicky?"

She hesitated. "She's one of the VP six," she finally replied. "After he lost the presidential election, Jim Gannett retired to Illinois. His résumé reads intelligence community—FBI director, U.S. attorney general, vice president, presidential candidate. He was working on his autobiography and he wanted to include some of his cases from when he was the state attorney general. Ann got assigned to find them and keep him happy. Not being an idiot, Gannett soon figured out she was a good writer.

"The next thing I know, they're doing a background check on Ann. It goes so deep even I'm wondering what she's done, and suddenly she's on the VP six list—the six people he reads into the original classified material that form the basis for his book. She's a twenty-something cop, and she's helping ghostwrite the VP's autobiography in her spare time.

"He's releasing it in three volumes, and from what

I've read of the first two they're actually not half bad. He's had an interesting life. The third one is due out this year or the next. There are maybe fifteen people in total who know she's helping on the book, Paul, so be careful with that information."

"I will, Vicky."

"She's the one who's kept it quiet. The VP wanted to put Ann's name on the cover as coauthor, wanted to carve off a percentage of royalties for her, and she turned him down. She said it would kill her chance to learn to be a good author if people knew her name before she had enough written to have learned to write well. She's listed, unnamed, in the front of the books on the ac-knowledgments page as the writer who made his words crisp and smooth and flowing, and he thanks her for her assistance. That's classic Ann, even decades ago. She doesn't accept the spotlight even when it is earned."

"I'm learning that," Paul said. "So she's met some of her friends through her work on his autobiography."

"I think it's more like the VP introduces her to people occasionally. Paul, the VP was the one who introduced me to Ann. I've never told anyone that before. That day changed my life and hers in more ways than I can say. I ended up with a really good friend. There's not much I wouldn't do for Ann, or that she wouldn't do for me. Don't mess this up, okay? Ann matters."

"I'll be careful," Paul reassured. He knew his time on this call was running out. "Has she ever been in love, Vicky?"

"Twice. Both times broke her heart. Both were before she became a cop."

"Can you tell me something about her you think I should know?"

Vicky hesitated. "I will tell you of one thing you must know. And I'm only doing so because I know of no other way to protect her. She dreams, Paul, terrible dreams, of writing and watching blood drip on the page—so dark a dream that I wonder at times how she can keep on writing. She wakes to a gunshot."

Paul closed his eyes. Everyone had secrets. It was one of the reasons he was going to her friends first, so he didn't stumble around blind to what was there.

"How long has she been having that nightmare?"

"I've known her for nine years."

"And she works from ten p.m. to two a.m. every night, to avoid the dream."

"That is Ann too."

"What happened?"

"I only know what she's told me, and she's told me precious little."

"I don't know what to do with the information, Vicky."

"You will. When it most matters, you'll have figured it out.

"She's got a good heart, Paul. She'll give you a chance, but she'll stay cautious until she's made a decision. She will like to know your story. Who you are and where you come from. She will like to meet your family, for seeing how you are with them will tell her more about you than anything you could say. She's quiet waters, with a lot underneath you don't see. But she's fair, and she'll be inclined to like you. She likes cops as a rule."

"Thanks for that."

He could hear a hum in the background and the sound of muted voices. "I should have asked when this call began where you are tonight."

"Over the Pacific Ocean in a vast airliner lazily circling as the night sky fills with stars. We'll climb to high altitude at midnight and begin taking pictures of the Pella comet as the debris trail crosses into the atmosphere. And while we are there enjoying the view, we might take a couple thousand close-up photos of the satellite that popped up in stationary orbit unannounced a month ago."

"I thought you were going to stay retired, Vicky."

"I brought the coffee," she replied with a laugh. "Seriously, there are enough satellite geeks on board wanting to decipher the new toy in the sky and who put it there, that the boss needed an adult to come along so someone remembered to take pictures of the comet. Pretty gnarly mess, going on a trip to take pictures of a comet and not take pictures of the comet."

"Would you bring me one of the better ones? Ann likes to stargaze."

"Gladly. It's a fun job tonight, Paul, so don't worry about me. I'll call you when I get home, and we'll have a longer conversation."

"Thanks, Vicky."

Paul stood at his office window, watching the moon rise and the occasional plane trail across the night sky, waiting for the ten o'clock alarm. When it signaled, he shut it off and returned to his desk.

He knew the number by heart but still looked it up

in the case file before he dialed. Ann answered on the third ring.

"Ann, it's Paul."

"Just a sec, Paul, I'll bring up video."

He looked to his screen and her image appeared, flickered, and smoothed out. She offered a quick smile in greeting, and he smiled back. He put down his phone and switched over to the secure conference call. "You remembered the code."

"Numbers tend to stick for some reason."

He wasn't sure what was on the wall behind her, but he realized with some interest he might be seeing where she lived. "You're home?"

"Just got in." She turned the screen and camera to show him the room. Lamps on tables lit the room, and he saw a dark burgundy couch, two wingback chairs, tables stacked with books, and what looked like an easel at the edge of the camera's view. The wall opposite the couch looked like his conference room walls, scattered with photos and timelines and colored marker notes. As she turned the camera back, it passed over something moving, and a dark mass of hair wiped out the lower inch of the monitor's view. A dog, a big, massive dog.

"It looks like a comfortable place to work on a murder."

She glanced over her shoulder at the cluttered wall and turned back to him with a smile. "That one's a book rather than the job."

"You build your books, then, like you do your cases."

"Something like that."

"Where's home?"

"A place about six miles north of Medora."

"Is that your dog pushing at you? I can see part of an ear."

"I promised him a walk. I'm not supposed to sit down."

Ann tilted the camera and he got a screen full of dog face looking back at him.

"This is Midnight. I just call him Black."

Paul laughed. "He's handsome and beautiful and very big."

"His feet are like dinner plates."

"I always wanted a dog. They just don't deserve city buildings and elevators and lots of asphalt."

"Live downtown?"

Paul nodded. "One of those old brick buildings that survived the Chicago fire. My family has owned the fourth floor for the last eighty years. It used to be my grandfather's home."

"I like the art behind you."

"Yeah?"

He slid out of the way so she could better see the canvas. "It's one of several of hers I've collected. I like the way she handles her blues. I could send you a print if you like. I've got a connection that can get her lithographs."

"Pocket that idea until you need a favor."

"Feels like I already got one, Ann. I am going to enjoy spending your money. I'm sending teams out to sixty-four cities without any bureaucratic delays. So thank you again. When the roses arrive, you're going to put them on your desk and enjoy them."

She smiled at the news. "I'll find a place for them."

"It was a very nice thing to do."

"I gather I caused you some problems with how it was done."

"You caused curiosity on the part of a lot of people over what had happened and why. Rumors were flying that I had an in with the Treasury secretary. The budget office personnel were in a tizzy as they had never seen his name on a budget transfer before. And I didn't really have answers to give them. Ann, what did you do?"

"Called a friend." She shrugged. "It was going to get messy if I didn't do something, because the award was there, and it's a good reason to have a press conference and announce they caught the currency thief, and I'd get my arm twisted to be there and accept the award—I had to do something to cut it off before it went that far.

"I called a friend at the Department of Justice and said the award would be a problem for me, and since the money could solve a problem for you, I asked if it could be transferred. She said yes. I said thank you. That's all I did. She's a lawyer and actually likes paperwork. I thought she would talk to the director of the award program, figure out the right paperwork, and get it to the right person. It obviously turned out to be more than that."

"Can you ask her what she did?"

Ann hesitated, and then nodded. "Since I made such a mess of the gift . . . hold on."

She picked up her phone, pushed her dog to move him over, and disappeared from video to make a call.

She looked relieved when she returned.

"She talked to the director of the award program. He said no problem, but it was complicated because it was one government agency to another. So she called her fiancé and explained the problem. He talked to his boss. His boss made two calls. The Treasury secretary said okay, the FBI director said okay, and the Treasury secretary sent the award money to your budget line. It took twenty minutes. It was done before I finished that second mug of hot chocolate you brought." Ann smiled. "That's what a friend does. They make an intolerable problem go away for you. A press conference is an intolerable problem for me. So she said yes and handled it."

"Who's her fiancé?"

"Reece Lion. He's Secret Service, the lead agent for the former VP. I introduced them. He wouldn't have thought twice about helping her out, and the VP is a nice guy. He used to be the FBI director back when the lady shooter first began killing, so making a couple of calls to arrange the money transfer would have been something he'd appreciate doing. It took twenty minutes, my call to my friend, to transfer of the funds. It wasn't that big a deal."

Paul could tell she really believed it wasn't that big a deal. "Ann, answer me this. Are you surprised the Treasury secretary was personally involved in fulfilling your request?"

She looked perplexed. "No. I needed the person who could move the money between departments, and that turned out to be the Treasury secretary. My request passed along a line of friends until someone had the ability to solve the matter, and they did."

"Help me understand, Ann. Is the former VP one of your friends?"

She hesitated, then nodded.

"So you could have called the former VP. You have his number."

She reluctantly confirmed it. "I have his number."

"You called your friend at Justice."

"I thought it was going to be one call to the award director and paperwork, Paul. Of course I called her. I hate paperwork. I could have called the VP, but why would I? If you go higher than you need to, you're only doing it to show someone else that you can. It's unnecessary, wastes your friend's time, and shows your own poor judgment. The fact this request ended up at the VP shows how bureaucratic the government is. My name was on the award money. I should have been able to send it anywhere I wanted and gotten a thank-you instead of someone saying we can't take it without approval."

Paul started to smile. "I see why Dave said you could manage the Falcons just fine."

"What?"

"For another time."

"I'm sorry for this mess. I thought it would be a pleasant surprise, having the budget delays dealt with, that's why I didn't tell you what I was going to do when I declined the award money. It was intended to be a pleasant surprise. It's probably the last one I try to do for a few months. No wonder I hate surprises myself."

"The thought was nice, the outcome is appreciated, and I learned a whole lot about you, so it didn't turn out that bad. What color of roses do you prefer?"

"Pink," she replied without hesitation.

"Are you going to be home for a few days?"

"I'm normally home. The phone rings with a case, I'm not home anymore. I don't mind the unpredictable schedule. I get to spend a lot of time flying. A neighbor watches my place when I'm away."

"You like the job."

"Love it, as a rule. I just wish there were fewer homicides to work."

"Email me your address, and I'll have a nice bouquet arriving tomorrow."

"Send it to the sheriff's office here in town, if you don't mind. The job's over at the end of the month when the county takes over policing, but there's enough packing of case files and evidence in storage to be transferred to the county that I'm spending most of my time there."

"I'll do that then. Oh, one other thing . . . another piece of information I should mention. My brother Boone is married to Vicky Bassett."

He saw brief intense surprise cross her face and relaxed when he saw it. She hadn't known the connection. "When you came to Chicago you didn't realize who I was?"

"I obviously recognized the Falcon name. I figured you were related indirectly, second cousins or something. You don't look like your brother."

"I'm the adopted oldest, and Boone's next to the youngest. I've read Vicky's story. You write a nice book."

"Thanks."

He was fascinated to see the start of a blush.

"She asked me to write the book because she couldn't tell her family what had happened during the years she was gone. It was her story, but it was fiction. She was in Asia, not Europe, during those years. Did she tell you about the book? I thought I had her identity camouflaged pretty well."

"I recognized the evergreen falling on the garage."

"I debated back and forth putting that in the book. I

was there when it happened and it was so sidesplitting funny, I just couldn't resist."

"I could see it just as you described. You've got a good friend in Vicky, Ann. I'm glad you two know each other."

"So am I."

"I'm surprised we haven't bumped into each other in her kitchen, swiping a piece of apple pie."

"She does make a really good pie."

Paul wanted to end the conversation on a smile and this felt like a good point. "I won't keep you any longer. Have a good night, Ann."

"'Night, Paul."

Without referencing the reason he had gone, Paul posted pictures to his family the next morning from his late-night trip. "I watched someone turn down half a million dollars this week. I wish I could tell you that entire story. It was quite a trip."

"Him or her?" his father emailed back.

What was his dad doing up this early? "Her."

"Nice. Coming to dinner this weekend?"

"Planning to."

"Bring her to dinner."

"Maybe someday." Paul wisely redirected the conversation. "How's Mom?"

The roses were gorgeous. Ann smiled as she placed them on her desk, where everyone who came through the sheriff's office would see them. She anticipated her first *Who's your beau?* question would come before noon. She loved the small-town interest. She fingered one of the rose petals. She would say they were a thank-you gift. That was true enough, and kind of Paul. She had wondered how he would take the gift of funds and he'd surprised her by accepting them without much of a fuss. The lady shooter needed caught, and she needed to avoid a press conference. She was comfortable that her decision to decline the award had been the right one.

Paul Falcon was an interesting guy. She should have listened better in the past when Dave had talked about his friend. They had for years overlapped friends, but not in schedules or she would have met him some time ago. She'd had in the back of her mind that he was seeing Gina Lewis, and hadn't paid much attention when that had changed.

Paul wasn't seeing anyone now, she knew. Kate's antenna had been quivering at the idea of Paul and Ann getting together—Kate had already made a pitch for Ann to fly north for dinner.

Ann picked up another packing box and turned her attention to her desk drawers. She had pleaded off with too much work, and it was true enough. But she'd ducked Kate's invitation because she was still uncertain if she wanted to follow it. She sensed an interest on Paul's part, but a casual one. The roses were an interesting choice of a thank-you, and hard to read. A guy sent a lady roses, it was some degree of personal. And she felt just a bit of interest in return. But patience defined how she treated guys and possible situations, and she wasn't inclined to do more than wait and enjoy the roses.

She liked his personality. He had driven hours to deliver a message, tracked her down in Nebraska with hot

chocolate, asked thoughtful questions about her work.
There was a lot to enjoy. He put effort into people, and
she admired that trait. He'd make a good friend. If Paul
was interested in pursuing matters, he would let her
know. Ann stepped around her dog and got the roll of
tape. She paused to smell the nearest rose again and
smiled at the gift.

Paul studied his calendar, thinking through options.
Most of his team would be traveling for the next two
months conducting interviews. A skeleton staff left behind could handle the other active cases on the board.
He had seven experienced guys in the group, who were
fully able to run their cases without assistance. He was
wise enough to let them. He had a lot to supervise but
not too much pressing on his day-to-day. It would get
intense again if one of the lady shooter interviews turned
up something.

If he wanted to get away for a few days, sometime
during the next two months would be his best chance.
It looked like his personal schedule opened up in about
two weeks. He went to find Sam. He'd take a few days
at the end of the month. Ann was worth pursuing, and
it was time.

PART TWO

ANN SILVER

9

Paul navigated the country roads, the numbers marking the fields and the crossroads beginning to make sense the more of them he read. He looked again at the photo he held, then at the house up ahead, and knew he had reached his destination. He pulled in behind a blue pickup truck and parked. He picked up the gift he had brought along with the sack Joe had sent, leaving his personal bags in the car.

The mother of the FBI regional counterterrorism director stepped out on her porch. "Welcome, Paul. You made good time."

"I appreciate you letting me visit, Mrs. Rawlins."

"Neva, please. My son calls, says he's sending a guest, I am too curious to say no. Then I hear it's about Ann Silver and I know I have to meet you. You'll stay, at least for a week."

"A weekend, Neva. It's all I can—"

"You can't court someone in a weekend," she replied, a twinkle in her eyes.

"Ann doesn't know I'm coming. A weekend will do for a surprise. A week would be an intrusion." He stepped inside with her. "The gift with the bow would be my thanks, and the sack would be from your son. He had ideas about glassware and crystal and told me to take care on the delivery."

"Leave the sack for me on the kitchen table, and I'll see if he found me the right pattern to match my mother's collection. You'll join me for lunch?"

"I was thinking if you would direct me, I would see Ann first, then we would both join you for dinner?"

Neva laughed and nodded. "She's not much of a cook, so it might be wise. You'll likely find her at the sheriff's office. She calls if she's had an MHI request, lets me know she'll be away, so I'm certain she's still in town."

She stepped back out on the porch with him. "The center of town and her office would be five miles west on the road you came in on, just stay to the right when the road splits off." She pointed toward the trees in the distance. "And that would be her property from the trees and for the next half a mile."

"I'll call you if we'll be later than five." He smiled. "Or if for some reason it will be just me."

"I'm glad for the company, but you didn't come to see me. Dinner's going to be my leftover roast beef for sandwiches, corn on the cob, and pie, and doesn't need a particular time. I'll expect you when I see you. And I'm partial to the late news and a movie, so you'll not bother me by making it a late evening."

"Thanks." Paul left the porch, stopped, and came back to lean against the base post of the porch railing.

"Would you have any advice for me, knowing Ann as well as you do?"

She looked surprised by the question, but paused to think about it, and nodded.

"One piece of good advice about Ann. When it's silent and you make a remark and she looks startled that you interrupted her, just repeat the remark or question and don't take offense. She's busy in her mind. The quieter she is, the more likely she's listening to dialog, or watching a scene unfold, or having an internal conversation. She goes somewhere else as easily as I breathe. Bothers people who don't know her well. She's just listening to a few things the rest of us don't hear, sometimes misses the first of what you say."

Intrigued, for it was unexpected, he thought about it and could see it. "How do you know when her mind is quiet?" he asked, curious.

"She'll grab one of those yellow legal pads that go everywhere with her and write it all down longhand. Sometimes the characters go quiet for a bit after that. There are days there is nothing in particular on her mind, and others where she is so busy creating she can't write it down fast enough. You can tell with just a bit of noticing what kind of day it is. When she goes to get a drink and stands with her hand on the soda can for a minute or two before she remembers to open it, you can bet someone you can't see interrupted her."

"You like her books."

"I do. She was writing stories here on my porch when she was a young girl, and I knew she'd have a future at it. She writes for the love of it, rather than thinking of it as work."

"That's going to be very helpful. Thanks, Neva."

Paul drove toward town thinking about Ann.

The cop part of her life he would easily understand—what she saw, what mattered, the crime scene and the people involved. He'd share that slice of her life easily, even have something to contribute. The writing would take much more effort to understand. What he'd just heard was going to be very useful advice. He hadn't stopped to think about how she wrote. Would have assumed it was like any job, there when you sat to work on it, and out of mind the rest of the time. But writing would be more about puzzling out questions, he decided, a lot more of her subconscious figuring out the details and then playing it out, than sitting to just write. She would create the stories one piece at a time and weave it together on the page. He wondered if she would be willing to share that part of her life with him, and hoped she would.

The population listed on the Welcome to Medora sign was three thousand twenty-six. He found a center square with benches, grass, a pretty fountain, and two statues honoring soldiers from the town. The square was surrounded by restaurants and businesses spreading out a few blocks. He could see open fields down the road.

He used the flag and the post office as a guide and found the sheriff's office beside it, a real estate office on the other side. He parked near the front door, next to a county police vehicle and a light tan vehicle that had police lights and radio antennas but no location markings.

The doors were glass, heavy, with hours listed as eight a.m. to six p.m., and a phone number stenciled beneath. He stepped inside.

The office was an open room with three desks and a long counter. A hall disappeared back into the building. From the items on the table and the bulletin board inside the door, it also served as the town's lost and found, and the hub for community announcements. The pink roses on the far desk still looked reasonably alive. Ann's desk. A phone, a monitor, a stapler, but not a single piece of paper or personal picture. She had already packed for the move.

The woman at the nearest desk was town police, the guy talking with her was county police. They were discussing a burglary, based on the snatch of conversation Paul heard before the woman looked over. He was recognized instantly as a stranger, for they both focused on him and slightly turned. He turned the badge on his pocket toward them, knowing he'd raise questions for why he was wearing a side arm under the suit jacket.

"I'm looking for Ann Silver."

The massive dog lying by her desk rose to his feet.

He made a guess and held out his hand. "Hey, Midnight."

The lady stood, her curiosity obvious. "May I ask who's looking to find her?"

"Paul Falcon with the FBI."

"Bad wreck, driver died?"

"That's me."

"She was glad to have that off her desk. Midnight, go find Ann."

The dog ambled away down the hall.

"He saves us shouting for each other."

She glanced at the roses on the other desk and back at him, but before she could ask, the front door opened behind him. A young man pushed a flat cart inside with a stack of boxes and a tower of tape rolls. "Where d'ya want these, Marissa?"

"Straight on back to the end of the hall."

"Packing day. We're moving policing to the county, effective Monday morning," she said to Paul.

"What's going to happen with this building? It's a nice location."

"A community center. We'll fill it with tables, games, and have a place for the young and old to mingle."

Midnight came back and flopped into a heap on the floor by the counter, Ann trailing in a few steps after him. She had rubber bands around her wrist, along with a roll of tape worn like a bracelet. She stopped when she saw him. "Falcon." The idea of it processed, and she smiled. "You're a long way from Chicago."

"I heard you needed a hand to help pack."

She leaned against the counter. "A nice story with a bit of fiction in it, I'm thinking. I pack fine—what I dislike is the carrying." She considered him and dug keys out of her pocket. "You'll need these. The moving van out back is heading to the county building. The red truck is mine. You have to relock the van padlock every time you come back inside. What do you like to drink?"

"Root beer, diet orange soda, tea-no-sugar, in that order."

"Marissa, why don't you go buy a case of his root beer and a bag of ice. He's my roses. When I wear him out hauling boxes, you can rescue the leftovers."

"He's your roses?"

"He'll want them back after I have him help clear out the vault."

Marissa laughed. "I'll forward phones to you and be back in ten."

Ann pushed away from the counter. "This way, Falcon."

She headed down the hall. "Your conscience bothering you about the money?" she asked quietly. "I'll take the help, but you shouldn't mind the gift. The only response needed is 'thank you.'"

"Not the money. I've got a year of vacation time accumulated, and you're moving. I show up when friends move. Family too, but for them I tend to bring several guys and expect to be doing the packing as well as the carrying."

"In that case—how long can I keep you?"

"I'm staying with Mrs. Rawlins for the weekend."

"Nice. Think five star bed-and-breakfast. Don't pass up her cinnamon rolls or her cherry pie."

She pointed to the closed, door-sized bank vault. "Evidence vault. We've been hauling out for a week, and it still looks stuffed. And my personal nemesis"—she stepped through an open door and gestured—"years of case files. I'm shredding what I can if the person is dead, if the statute of limitations has passed. The rest go to county. I've got five years left to sort."

"Why don't you have half the town crowding in here to help you?"

"Three reasons. I promised the town council if they agreed to move policing to the county, I'd protect the privacy of those who'd had encounters with the law over the years and manage the move myself. Second, we don't have to be out on any particular day—it's my own imposed deadline. I'd just like to get the job done.

And third, Nita Stans is also moving this weekend, and she's the sweetest lady in town. If you show up here, you get sent to help her. My contribution to her hour of need. Along with a side agreement between her and me that no one gets to see the fact her late husband got arrested for driving the mayor's car into the town fountain as a youth."

"Everyone probably knows the story."

"Not a question. But it still embarrasses her."

Midnight trailed in after them. Ann ruffled his ears and absorbed his weight as the dog leaned into her. "If Midnight gets in your way, just tell him to go away. He'll move a few feet."

"He's a calmer dog than I would have figured."

She grinned. "Deceptive. He conserves his energy for what's important."

"These boxes are ready to go?"

"Those are heading for the county, and that box of pictures—that goes with me."

"Return to shredding and sorting. I'll start carrying."

He stacked three boxes high and disappeared.

By the time she was down to two years to sort, Paul had cleared the room of boxes ready to go to the county.

He brought back two glasses of ice, took a seat on a rolling chair, and split a root beer with her. "Finish the drink, then you can open the vault for me and give me an overview of what is ready to carry."

"You are trying to impress me by doing it all in one day."

"I was thinking one afternoon."

Ann touched her glass to his. "Appreciate it. Marissa and I flipped for who would be on duty today, and I cheated on the coin toss. Used a mis-stamped coin to make sure she got the duty. I couldn't handle the last day of calls. I'm going to miss this place, right down to the flag that gets stolen and the candy that gets lifted and the kids speeding around the square on rainy nights. We've had four burglaries, six domestic calls, a dozen public intoxications, and four times that in nuisance vandalism, noise, and sidewalk disputes in the last few months. The worst of it was an aggravated assault with two guilty parties, and a fire that was probably deliberate. Not a single murder. It feels so normal, and I haven't had normal in a long time."

"Might have been easier if you'd chosen to be an accountant, or used that engineering degree."

She lifted one eyebrow.

"Dave," he confirmed.

"I designed chips for a telecommunication firm for a while. Logic puzzles, tests that could check if you were right or wrong, and I was good at it. I was knocking down solutions to problems and watching my chips go into production. It was good for a summer or two, but I found the desk and design software and a square office with walls as draining as anything I had ever done. I could do the work, but as useful as the work was, it would have a limited lifespan. Two years, five, and my chip would be obsolete and replaced with someone else's design or a new one of my own. I decided I'd rather do my puzzle solving on something more interesting that might matter more."

She finished her drink. "Let me show you the vault."

She set the combination and spun the door lock to ease back six inches of balanced steel door. The shelves were neatly arranged to push back and forth, and only one aisle could exist at any one time. Boxes were uniform and in three sizes—small, medium, and large. "Anything in a box sealed with red tape has already been documented and is ready to go to county. I've got just a portion of a shelf still to review."

"Your personal box is safely set aside so I won't accidentally load it?"

"It is."

"Do I need to close the vault between each trip?"

"I'll lock the front door and ask the dog to maintain vigil in the hall. It will do. Most of the valuable items in evidence were moved by Brink's last week."

───────◆───────

"That's the last one." Paul slid the box into the moving van.

Ann pulled down the door and set the padlock. "All right, Kevin. Sign the paperwork, and it is now the county's evidence and files."

She took the signed document and handed him the keys.

"Greg's going to drive," Kevin told her, "and Bob and I will escort just to make sure there's no road accident. Want me to call when it is settled into its new vault?"

"It's your problem now but, yes, give me a call."

She watched the van pull out. "Thanks, Paul. I didn't think it would be done today."

"My pleasure." He held out the keys to her truck. "You've got a decent load of personal effects."

"I'm a pack rat on occasion. I'm not planning to unload the truck today. I'll just park it in the garage."

"An hour, it can be unloaded, and you'll be done. Invite me home, Ann."

He was amused to see her mentally debate it with herself.

"I'm the first drive past Neva's. Follow me."

Ann's crushed-rock driveway took three leisurely turns as it moved through an avenue of trees. Paul tried to imagine clearing snow in winter for this length of driveway. The house was set in an open patch of land, a two-story and classic country, with a new addition of a double-bay garage.

She opened the garage door and parked the truck outside near it. A car that from the radio antennas and lights was a police issue was in the far bay. He parked far enough to one side to not block either vehicle.

Her dog bounded out of her truck and disappeared around the house.

"The boxes with red tape can be stored in the garage. There should be room on the shelves with a little rearranging. The boxes with yellow tape go inside, first door on the left."

The dog returned with a ball and considered Paul. "Throw it as far as you possibly can out in the field. He gets offended if you give him a little kid toss."

Paul hefted the ball, considered the weight, and threw the ball from home plate into the deep outfield. The dog looked at the sailing ball, looked at him, and took off with a joyous bark.

Ann smiled. "You just made his day." She passed him with the box of pictures and disappeared inside.

Paul turned on lights in the garage and began shifting boxes to make space for the new items. He saw Christmas decorations and several boxes marked Party Supplies. Paul started unloading the red-taped boxes.

When Paul was done, he started carrying the yellow-taped ones inside. The dog returned, maneuvered around him, and disappeared into the house. Ann came to help him, and between them they got the last of the boxes. Paul locked the truck and followed her inside.

The doorways were wide and the ceilings high. "The house doesn't look like what I expected." Even the hallway was cheery, with soft-toned walls and rich cherrywood.

"I've had most of this level gutted and rebuilt," Ann commented. "The upstairs is closed with rooms full of what would now be antiques. It looks very much as it did when my grandparents lived here. Come on through to the living room."

It was the room he had seen on the video, with its couch and wingback chairs, and a large table serving as a desk with three monitors letting her do her work and research at the same time. There was an easel set up by the north windows.

"It's not an office, but I use it as such."

"It's a comfortable room, Ann."

The photos on her wall-long murder board were a jarring contrast to an otherwise peaceful setting. He walked across to study, understand, what she was working on. The timeline ran for more than two years. He stopped at the photo of an airline crash, looked at the next photos and saw the house fire, and smiled. "These are the O'Malley books."

"I'm working on a background piece on Jennifer."

"Really?"

"It's not going to be a book, or even a story with a spine; it's just my notes from when I was building the series. I'm doing the days when Jennifer and Tom met. Tom's going to be at the gathering this fall, and I wanted to give him the piece as a gift."

"I'd love to read it. They were a solid set of books."

"Thanks."

"What's it like, being asked to write a book about your friends? Does it make you nervous, wondering if you'll get it right?"

"It did at first, and then I realized the request was really a gift. When friends ask if I would write their story, what they are really doing is saying, I trust you, ask what you want to ask. For the months of working on a book, I could ask any question, ask about any event in their life, and they would spend hours giving me the inside history on what they were doing, thinking, and wishing might happen. It's intense, for both sides. It's why the stories ring so close to who the person is, even though I'm wrapping it all in fiction. The books turn out to be them at every level I can figure out how to capture in words."

He stopped by the third book in the series on the timeline, Lisa and Quinn's story, looking at the photos on the board and her written notes. "When you chose the themes for the books—that Lisa's struggle would be about the resurrection and the case would be buried victims—were you choosing those because that was her question, her case, in real life, or because it gives you the best vehicle to present your friend?"

"Real life is busier and more complicated for both of them than what the novel presented. Lisa's a forensic pathologist in real life, and she's that in the book. She came to believe in God as an adult, and that happened because of conversations she had with Jennifer. Quinn is a U.S. Marshal. They married and now live on his ranch out West. How they fell in love is almost word for word what I heard from them as they reminisced. So it's real life. But the case itself was my creation, the topic of the resurrection my choice of where to focus. I try very hard to find the heart of the matter, the key thing that if you understand this about the two of them, you will know who they really are. That's what people notice the most when they read the books. The fact it rings true to who they are."

"I've had dinner with them," Paul said, nodding, "and you really did get their story right. It was a good series."

"That's what I hoped when I wrote the six books. We're a close group. I got the people right; I got the people to be real. So the series worked."

"The group works because you're part of it. You're the eighth O'Malley. You might not be in the books by name, but it is your voice threading through all the stories."

She looked thoughtful. "I hadn't thought about it that way," she said, then smiled, "but yes, I am the eighth O'Malley. It's a lovely compliment."

He lingered another minute studying the board, then turned back to her. "So this is what you do in your spare time."

"I get bored watching TV."

He laughed.

Her dog walked into the room carrying his dish,

paced over, and dropped it on her foot. She affection-
ately shoved him back. "Black, that's just rude." She
scooped up the bowl. "Excuse me while I feed my family.
He thinks it's possible to forget him."

Paul and the dog trailed her into the kitchen, where
she pulled open a pantry door and chose a can of dog
food. She dumped two cups of dry food and the contents
of the can into the dish and set it on the dog-bone-shaped
mat by the patio door. The dog planted two massive
paws on either side of the bowl to keep it from moving
and ate so fast he practically inhaled it.

Paul leaned against the counter to watch him. "How
old is he?"

"Six, probably," she replied, watching the dog with
obvious affection. "Someone left him at the gas station
and drove off when he was about two. They no doubt
knew from the size of the feet he wasn't done growing
yet."

She opened the refrigerator. "I've got Coke and Pepsi
and one ice tea."

"I'll take the tea."

She handed it over and opened a Diet Coke for herself.
"The dinner hour was a couple of hours ago. You must
be very hungry."

"I'd say you must be the same. Neva invited you to
join us for dinner. Roast beef sandwiches, she said, and
I remember pie being mentioned. I gave her a heads up
once I saw what needed done, and suggested we'd be
done about eight p.m. We've beaten that handily."

"If I stop in, it will be a couple hours of conversation
before I can escape. I've got a few things around here
that have to be done tonight. And before you ask, I've

got lunch plans for tomorrow already scheduled. I'll be free after about one o'clock."

"Then I'll take some of your time after one o'clock. We'll take a walk and let the dog wander. I plan to head home around four and be back in Chicago at a decent time."

Her phone rang. She walked over to pick it up. "This is Ann." She found a pen and wrote a note on a yellow legal pad. "Yes. I'm on my way." She hung up the phone and stuffed the note in her pocket. "Somebody just drove himself into Larry Jenkins's pond. Not a heart attack, as the guy is floundering around in the water yelling at the cows. Probably a tourist and drunk since only those who don't know the road miss that curve in such a spectacular fashion." She found her keys. "I need to go."

"Last days as sheriff."

"If it is a DUI, I'm dumping him off on county—it's their road." The dog was now licking his empty bowl and pushing it around the kitchen floor. "Black, I've got to go. Find your bed."

The dog howled but disappeared down the hall. She laughed. "Now he'll sulk."

Paul walked outside with her.

She backed her car out of the garage and did a swift three-point turn. The garage door closed. She lowered her window as she paused beside his car. "Tomorrow you'll have to tell me the real reason you came."

"Didn't buy my packing story?"

"Not entirely. If something comes up to disrupt to-morrow, my thanks for today. It was nice."

"You're welcome, Ann."

She flipped on the lights and headed out to do the job.

Paul watched her car disappear and slid into his own. For the day it might have been, he was pleased with what it had turned out to be. The look at her place would have been worth the trip alone. She hadn't expected company, so he had seen it as she had left it this morning.

Coupons on the refrigerator, mail piled on the table she used as a desk, the dishwasher run but not emptied, stacks of legal pads and notes on the table by the couch, an old towel balled up on the fireplace hearth next to a dog brush, an easel and drop cloth tucked in the corner of the room. She was painting in a semiserious way. What he hadn't seen was just as interesting: no food wrappers, newspapers, glass on a coaster, kicked-off socks or shoes, signs of a shopping trip. The only thing that had surprised him to see was the two guitars. She lived with stuff out and visible, but neat in its own way.

10

Paul took his time on the short drive from Neva's back to Ann's on Sunday to look around. He understood why Dave said Ann liked to walk. The countryside was beautiful. Paul parked where he had the day before, walked up the front sidewalk to Ann's porch and rang the bell. The breeze rippled hanging pots of flowers and two wind chimes. With no sounds of traffic, or sounds of crowds, it was as different from his home as it could be. There wasn't silence—too many birds were singing, and the trees were rubbing branches in the wind—but it was nature's sounds.

The front door opened, and Ann pushed open the screen door. "Hi, Paul. Come on in." She was wearing jeans and an army shirt, with white socks on her feet. She was towel-drying her hair.

"It looks like you didn't get much sleep."

"I'm an absolute idiot for ever wanting to wear a badge." She walked back toward the living room.

"Bad night?"

She snorted. She stepped over the dog, who didn't so much as lift his head to acknowledge company, and sat down on the couch which, by the look of the tweezers and Band-Aids and the about empty quart of orange juice on the coffee table, was where she had been stationed when he knocked.

He settled into a chair with a smile. "Tell it. You'll enjoy the telling, and I'll enjoy the listening."

She drank the rest of the orange juice and waved the carton at him. "Pond guy. I convince him the cows aren't going to charge at him, get him out of the pond. He's obviously drunk, so we end up at the hospital getting his wrist X-rayed. I hand him off to county on the DUI while my best tow-truck guy figures out how to yank the car out of the water. Larry calls me back. Seems there are now babies floating in his pond. Swears he's not joking. So I'm back out to the pond, and he's right. There are baby dolls floating in his pond. The guy was hauling display-quality baby dolls for his company and states he 'tossed them out of the car to save them.' I rescue twenty-two lifelike baby dolls worth several thousand from the pond. His company now wants to sue him for property damage.

"So I'm leaving the office having finished the paper-work on pond guy, and dispatch calls. Someone cut the locks on the Petersons' chicken coop doors, and there are now one hundred forty-six chickens wandering around on the railroad tracks that border his property. Black and I are good at flushing birds, there were nine of us to walk the line, and it still took three hours. Think very unco-operative birds, brambles and sticker bushes, and grass as sharp as a razor blade. A miserable night all around.

"From there I went and arrested the Gibson twins, seeing as how they wrote their names and the date on the chicken-coop door. They were drunk too, both of them, and laughing. Their birthday is tomorrow. Since today was their last day to be charged as juveniles, and they hadn't done anything worthy of note this year, they thought chickens and a train would be a memorable birthday present to themselves. Their dad went to have a talk with Peterson and pay for the damages. I believe the boys are going to be mucking out that chicken coop for the summer or volunteering for the army, whichever they find least onerous." She ran her hand through her still-damp hair.

"My job as sheriff," she said, "is ending with drunks, dolls, and chickens. No one is ever going to believe this story. I went to church from there and stayed awake on too much coffee, and I don't particularly like coffee. I'm going to have to pass on a walk, and I'm going to be a pretty lousy hostess and let you fend for yourself. There's now root beer on the bottom shelf of the refrigerator, so help yourself." She nudged her dog with her socked foot. "Black might move sometime next month. I put salve and Band-Aids on his big paws and gave him the rest of a cheeseburger. He's done for the day."

Paul leaned over to pick up one of the wounded paws, and the dog opened one eye to look at him. "You did a nice job on the first aid."

"Lots of practice. He'll lick them off when the paws stop hurting."

"You had lunch to go with that coffee?"

"Coleslaw and fried chicken from one of the best cooks in the county. She's got grandson troubles."

"Neva served steak, twice-baked potatoes, fresh green beans, and dream-whip-topped pumpkin pie."

"I'm officially jealous." She pulled over a throw pillow and dropped back on the couch.

Paul headed to the kitchen and came back with two sodas. She accepted hers, and he settled into a comfortable chair. She was struggling not to yawn, and he smiled just watching her. She was adorable. "You have to admit, your days are not boring."

"What are yours like?"

"I've got a conference room maybe twice this big, with walls that look very similar to your board there. A bunch of active cases and a lot of people to keep busy. I haven't had to wade into a fistfight or haul in a drunk or even had a decent car chase in more than . . . what, ten years? Five, for sure. It's paper, and interviews, and more paper, and eventually a lead you can follow that goes somewhere. It's way too much time inside office walls."

"Lady shooter, thirty murders, that's got to tug at the interest."

"It's a nice rush to solve a tough case. But it's process work—phone records, bank records, travel records, interviews, surveillance to locate a guy, wiretaps to listen in. It's being smart to see the details and figure out where to look, and careful to build a case that can get through court. What the job is not is dispatch calling to report a problem, with me expected to go out and solve it. I'd trade you for a few days. You get to be sheriff of your town. It's a kid's dream job."

"I used to walk the square as a young girl, sit on that bench outside the post office, and write stories about the cops who came and went from the police station I now call mine. It was always exciting, being a cop, and there was always some big wrong to make right. That's why I said yes when they asked. I remembered the childhood dream."

"I wanted to be the guy who caught the guys on the FBI's Ten Most Wanted list," Paul remarked, following her childhood dream with his own. "It was an incredible idea to a young boy, that you could catch one of the most wanted guys in the world, and you'd get on the news with the capture, and then they would put another name and photo on the list and make it ten names again, and you could go do it again. It was like permanent job security. You always had ten people you were to chase, and you got paid to chase them."

She laughed. "We were idealists."

"We were kids."

She considered him. "I don't know that I would like your level of being a cop. It's more going after organizations or particularly bad people. Being MHI is more the mid-level of crimes, the guy who kills his wife, the employee who shoots his boss, the random shooting at a school. They are tough puzzles since I don't get called unless an experienced cop wants some help, but they are generally understandable crimes." She ran her foot lightly over Midnight's back.

"I typically come into the investigation late," she went on, "so the MHI calls are mainly process work for me, not unlike your typical day. A murder book. Someone who died. Someone who's hoping to get away with it. Lots of interviews, photos, and lab reports. Lots of alibis and gathered facts. Two questions you ask as the MHI. Why are the cops stuck? And who lied to the cops? There tends to be a way to help if I can answer one of those questions. And I'm willing to admit I am better at the murder cases than I am at being sheriff. You have to react as sheriff, but you also have to anticipate. My predecessor was much better at anticipating than I am. He would have seen the Gibson twins doing something like the chicken coop a month before they'd even thought of it."

"The policing shift to county is for financial reasons?"

"When you factor in the insurance, liability, facilities, and vehicles, the town can get two officers assigned by the county and spend about half what they do now to have Marissa and me on the job. This change saves money and gives the town a community center. It's a good trade-off."

"Is Marissa going to shift over to work for the county police?"

"They've offered, but I don't think she's decided yet. She's getting married in a few months."

Ann set aside her soda, moved from the couch to the floor, and reached for the dog brush. Midnight rumbled a sigh of pleasure as she started brushing tangles out of his thick coat. "Why don't you tell me why you really came?"

Paul smiled. "You're interesting, Ann. You tell nice stories, write good books, and have a reputation I admire among your friends. According to Dave, you're not seeing anyone in particular. And I'm looking."

She brushed Midnight for a while, then looked over at him. "You came all this way to ask me on a date."

"Nothing as common as a date. We're going to start a romance."

She took it as a charming punch. The brush paused, but her eyes barely flickered from his. "Not shy, are you?"

She blushed easily, he was intrigued to see. "I'd just be wasting time."

"Breathtaking directness aside, I don't move at your speed."

"I didn't figure you did. Just setting the stage. You might be slow to catch the drift of things, and I'm of a mind to speed up that part of the matter."

"Quick enough when a Falcon is circling."

He laughed.

She smiled at him, just a bit more shy than before, and then focused on the dog, who had lifted his head to see what was amusing. Paul waited to see if she wanted to say something, but she stayed quiet. "So what are you thinking?" he asked.

"I'm thinking I'd say yes to a date, if you take some care in what you offer."

"What constitutes a good date?"

"I'm partial to a movie. I love to get lost in someone else's story. And I'm for walking and talking and a vendor hot dog over a fancy place to eat."

"I'm going to like dating you. Do you want to set the day and place, or do you want to leave it as the next time we're within fifty miles of each other, we'll call and see if there are a couple hours that can be freed up for a movie?"

"I figured a friend would have already warned you." She tossed him her pocket calendar. "Take a look."

He found one date in the rest of the year with an entry, and it was for Midnight to get his three-year rabies shot. "You keep a clear calendar."

"I don't like juggling life around things I have to do. I'll share a movie and enjoy it; just don't ask me now to say when or where."

"You don't plan vacations, or trips, or meeting up with a friend?"

"I know it sounds stupid, but no, I don't. I show up when weather works in my favor, and close my eyes while I pay more for hotel rooms. I factor in what's available when I get somewhere. It's worth it. I find life is a lot less stressful."

She started with the brush again. "That ball game with Lisa. We agreed it would be fun to go to a game together. Quinn had tickets for that particular one. We both snuck away from work and had a wonderful time. But I didn't plan it. I'd call it a wish and a want too.

"No one called urgently needing me. The day was open. But I didn't book a hotel room. I didn't sort out a plane for that morning. I just called around the night before, found what my options were, went to Milwaukee at dawn, caught a ride back to Chicago, dropped a case off with you, took a cab to the game, and had a wonderful time with Lisa. I didn't plan it. I just did it."

"Ann, you planned it, you just didn't plan it in advance. You wanted to go to a ball game with Lisa. You did. If it had been raining, I bet you would have made a road trip of it and gone to Chicago the night before. It was a nice day to fly, so you flew up early enough you could make a side trip and hand me a case. You are good at knowing what you want and flowing your life around those wants. How about this. You put on your want-to-do list, Go to a movie with Paul, and we'll see how soon it happens."

"I can do that."

"I'm not interested in rushing you as that would not be in my best interest or in yours. But I do want to get somewhere, and I'm not inclined to leave the destination to chance. I want you to learn to trust me, and for that you need to know who I am. I was thinking on the way down that one place I could start opening doors for you is to start with you seeing my career. How high is your security clearance?"

She looked uncomfortable.

"That high?"

"Vicky says I've got a security clearance higher than God, but she's exaggerating a bit."

"Then when I ask them to clear you to see my file, they won't redact much. You've read a lot of police reports. You can draw your own conclusions from the details."

"I'm not comfortable with that, Paul."

"I know. But you need to know what is there. I've been shot twice, Ann, and while I'd like to talk with you about those events, I'd rather you know the background from the official file before I do." She'd been brushing the dog's coat rather than looking at him, but she stilled at the news. He gave it a moment, then changed the subject. "How much do you know of the Falcon family?"

"Enough to have a sense of its breadth. I know I frequently bump into stuff with your name on it. You have a division that does aeronautical parts. And those tie latches I used in the truck are yours. My vet has a shelf of your pet vitamins."

"That sounds about like the Falcon empire—a little bit of stuff everywhere. It's a big family, with a lot of interests, and when my father passes away, the weight of it will fall to me. I'm a cop. I plan to retire a cop. But I'm one day destined to be head of an interesting family. I'd like you to meet them in small doses. I'll take you to lunch at Falcons when you're in Chicago and introduce you to my sister Jackie. And maybe next time you are visiting Vicky, you can ask my brother some questions about me."

"You want me to be curious."

"Yes, I do. Get to know me, Ann. Then you can decide what you think about me."

"Is that why you've been asking my friends so many questions?"

"I started asking questions the day you dropped by my office, told me a story, and handed me a case. Then I read several of your books, and I asked more questions. I'm a deliberate guy. I didn't come here to ask you out before I'd concluded the risks were worth it."

"I'm not thinking about settling down."

"I know. That's one of the risks. This wasn't done to pry, Ann. Think of it more as insurance. I didn't want to waste your time or mine. Your friends know you well, and if they'd waved me off, I would have listened. They uniformly did the opposite."

"I think you've heard a lot about me from friends, but you haven't really met me. I'm going to surprise you in a whole lot of ways."

He smiled. "I know you will. I'm looking forward to it." He looked at the time, then back at her. "Come to the door and say goodbye, and I'll leave you your afternoon so you can stretch out on that couch and get a nap."

She accepted his hand, and he pulled her to her feet. She walked with him to the door.

He took a final study of her and smiled. "We're going to enjoy the coming weeks."

"Maybe."

"You'll change that qualifier soon."

"Your confidence is interesting."

"So is your amusement. Get that nap, Ann. I'll call you."

───────◆───────

Paul drove home to Chicago, well satisfied with the trip. She hadn't rebuffed his interest. He'd chosen to give her direct and she'd responded by meeting him partway with casual friendly. She wasn't wary about starting a new relationship.

So—friendly. He would bet it was going to be nearly impossible to get her off of friendly to something more personal and intimate. She wouldn't move further until she decided to trust him and she would need to know a great deal more about him to reach that point. The job would be simple enough to open up for her. The family would take some time to introduce her without overwhelming her. She needed to get to know him, and he was inclined to open a few doors and help her do just that. It was a plan, and he could make progress with it.

He liked the amusement that touched her face and words. She wasn't a serious woman, not about the day-to-day of life. He liked her home and what it said about her, the books and the dog and the good, comfortable room where she chose to work and live. He liked the conversation and the relaxed way she approached his interest.

"What should I have noticed that didn't catch my

attention?" He let the question to God sit out there as he reflected on the weekend. It was interesting that she hadn't changed anything about the house between Saturday and Sunday. She hadn't felt the need to straighten up things. She'd been dressed as casually as the day before. She hadn't arranged food to set out for a guest—he'd been grateful for that, knowing he'd have to try what she made to be polite—but she had arranged to have a case of his root beer waiting in the refrigerator. He'd taken the first soda from the case, which hadn't been there the night before.

Dating was always a give-and-take. He showed his best side, so did she, and it took time to get past that effort to get to know the real person. The long-term future of the relationship depended on the ability to clearly see the other person and figure out if they were a good fit together. She hadn't changed because he had expressed an interest. She was going to let him meet the real her. That was the most interesting fact Sunday told him.

11

Ann got home Monday just after six p.m. and found a chocolate bar taped to her front door at eye level. She opened the screen door and rescued the chocolate bar. It was wrapped in a piece of blue paper.

What does it feel like no longer being Sheriff? If it's a bad day, I hear chocolate helps. Paul

It feels like someone took away my special badge, she thought with a smile. She gave him points for the note, and taking the time to arrange it. She wondered who Paul had helping him out on the gift, and assumed it was Neva. She carried in her mail and, after a quick glance at what was there, left it on her desk to deal with later. The evening was unscheduled and nothing had to have her attention. "What do you say we go for a long walk, Black?"

The dog disappeared into the bedroom and reappeared with his Frisbee.

"Oh, one of those walks, huh?" She laughed and took the Frisbee. "You want to run yourself into exhaustion, I'll help you out."

She slid the candy bar in her shirt pocket and pulled a piece of jerky from the canister for Black as she wasn't going to share the chocolate. Out of habit she tucked a notepad and pen in her back pocket and then headed out the front door. "Let's go, boy."

The sun was still bright, the sky clear, and the sunset still some time ahead. She set out at a good pace down the country road as Black roamed ahead of her.

"His note asked an interesting question." She liked to talk to God as she walked, and she settled into the conversation knowing she had a lot she wanted to discuss. "I'm glad I'm no longer the sheriff. I've been carrying the weight of it with me ever since I accepted the badge. The duties belong to others now, and I'm breathing easier for it. As much as I loved being sheriff, it's good to have it done."

She spotted a chipmunk searching the ground near a fence post and paused to watch him, knowing as soon as Black spotted the animal he'd disappear back into the heavy grass.

"What are you thinking, Lovely? Time is mine now, outside of MHI calls, and I can take those anywhere. I could travel to see friends, or I could stay put and work on a story—for that matter I could work on a story anywhere. I just need a pad of paper and some quiet. Do you have a preference for where I am? I don't know that I have a particular preference, other than a desire to catch up on some sleep."

She tossed the Frisbee for Black, and he raced ahead of

her to grab it. Home sounded good. Sleeping in. Finishing Jennifer's story. She could pick up a paintbrush and finish the painting on the easel. She retrieved the Frisbee from Black, ruffled his ears.

Tonight she wanted to walk to the river and watch the sunset. God probably had something planned for the coming months, He normally did, but she was content to wait and see what came. Paul was interesting. A romance. She smiled just remembering the way he had phrased it. She rather liked this cop, and the way he handled himself. Kate liked him and that told her a lot about him. Kate had a good read on people.

She knew Paul's brother Boone, and one of his cousins, Luke Falcon. She'd written a book about Vicky and Boone. She'd also done a book about Luke and Caroline, and it was only a matter of time before Paul picked up that book and realized it. She remembered meeting his parents at Vicky's wedding.

"Where might this be going? I'm interested. I'll enjoy a movie with him. But he very clearly laid the ground. He's the first guy I've met who is intentionally looking to be married. I'm not. I haven't thought about getting married in a serious way in years. I certainly wasn't planning to open that question this year. I'll like the friendship; I'm just feeling lost on the rest of it. This came out of left field on me. I don't have my bearings, so I need you to keep the road straight for me. The last thing I want to do is mess up what could be a very good year with a relationship mess."

The fact she was worrying about it already was depressing. It was her first day of freedom and should be enjoyed. She pushed the problem on to God's list and off hers. Guys were always a dilemma, and she'd given up thinking she could figure out relationships with the ease she could do murder cases. She dug the chocolate bar out of her pocket and offered the jerky to Black.

The first bite had her looking at the chocolate bar and straightening out the wrapper. Paul had really good taste in chocolate. She broke off another piece and wondered if one of his family's companies had made it.

Black stepped in her path and angled for her to share. She laughed and ruffled his fur. "I'll find you something special for dinner when we get home." She offered the Frisbee to distract him and gave it a smooth toss. She finished the chocolate as the river came into view.

By the time they looped around and came back home, they had wandered almost five miles. It was the nicest walk Ann could remember in months.

Paul called just after nine p.m. Ann paused what she was writing to answer the video call. The image stabilized and the audio bar turned green. He was in his kitchen. She could see the corner of a spice rack and part of a counter where a cutting board was in use. Something leafy and green. His smile had her answering in kind.

"I was hoping I would catch you at home. How did you like the chocolate?"

"The English language doesn't have a rich enough word for how good it was."

"Thought you might like it. I was afraid it would melt on you, or attract ants."

"Neva was your courier?"

"Yes."

"She probably taped it to my door five minutes before I arrived home. She has more people to clue her in on where I am than my parents ever did. She would have considered the chocolate a proper gift."

"So she told me. Last day go okay?"

"The mayor brought a cake, and most of the town stopped by at one point or another, so they could tour the famous evidence vault that Jesse James tried to break into. I had to promise the town council that I would have the vault door permanently removed so no kid could lock another kid in once the building is the community center. What are you fixing?"

He tipped the bowl to show her the diced vegetables. "My sister's version of a salad. She's had too much time on her hands this last month. She went shopping and restocked my refrigerator as if I cook for two dozen. Since I can't stand to see fresh stuff go bad, I'm eating a lot of vegetables. But the zucchini she can have back, and the eggplant."

"It's late for dinner. Long day at the office?"

"Falcons reopened today and most of my family is at the restaurant. I stopped by for a couple hours this evening to greet guests and confirm all was well. Somehow I managed to leave with dessert and not a meal. I just tossed a steak on the grill to go with the salad."

"What's for dessert?"

"Jackie's hot blueberry dish. It's exceptional. She loved the book, by the way. Remind me to get it back to you."

"Pass it on to another reader. It's what I do with books I like."

"I'll do that. I've been meaning to ask you something.

Tell me about flying. Who taught you? Why do you like it?"

It was a topic close to her heart, so she settled more comfortably into the chair to enjoy the conversation. "My neighbor taught me to fly. He owned a small Cessna for his business. I started going up with him when I was fourteen, taking lessons when I was sixteen. I got my license as soon as I was old enough to apply, and I've accumulated more ratings on more types of aircraft over the years.

"I love being in the air, higher than the clouds when the sun sets and the colors ripple out. It's my place. There aren't crowds, and cars, and places to be in a hurry that keep you from enjoying the view. In the air there is just open space and a scene spread out before you."

"It sounds peaceful, Ann."

"It is. I love the Great Plains from the air, where the land below is winding rivers and miles of open grazing land and neatly planted fields. I don't like flying over busy cities. I don't like deserts and high mountains unless it is absolutely necessary. And I hate flying over extended bodies of water. If I've got one fear as a pilot, it's having to ditch in water. Give me a good floatplane if I'm going to be flying around water."

He started to ask her something, then stopped.

"What?"

"There's no polite way to put this question, it just is. Have you ever crashed?"

She laughed. "I've had landing-gear problems, icing problems, bad fuel, fouled oil lines, once had parts explode in an engine. But I've never actually crashed. I've had to glide a few times, had a few hard landings. There have been some white-knuckle moments when I've had only a few moments to figure out a problem. It comes with the number of hours in the air. I dread landings most, when the winds have a mind of their own, and the calm becomes a hand reaching out to grab you and toss the plane around."

"You scare me."

She just smiled.

"Do you ferry planes for particular companies or people?"

"Not by plan, but I've flown for enough years around the Midwest, people keep me in mind. Every airport has a guy who is a matchmaker, putting together planes and pilots. It's typically the refuel guy, as he'll know what planes are on the ground or are coming through. If I want to head somewhere, I'll check in at the airports and see if there's a plane needing to go my direction. I know where the private airstrips are, where repair work is done, where hangar space rotates for public charters. Planes are forever not where their owners would like them to be. I can find a plane easily and can often put a couple ferries together to get to my final destination. If I'm stumped and I need to be somewhere, I have a long list of names I can call to borrow a plane on short notice. The average small plane only flies one to three times a week. That's a lot of hangar time." She paused. "I can almost smell that steak from here. I'm going to let you go so you can eat dinner while it is hot."

"I wish you were here to join me. Do you think Black knows what I've got on this plate?"

She glanced down at her dog, who had maneuvered in to see what he was doing. "He knows the word *steak*."

Paul laughed. "Sorry, fella. Good night, Ann."

"'Night, Paul."

———————▼———————

Ann spent three days in Kansas on an MHI call, then stopped at Neva's on the way home. She shared a piece of pie and town gossip and some laughter, gathered up Black, and headed to her house. She found a note taped to her front door.

Ann, call me when you get home. Paul

A second note below from her neighbor simply had a big smiley face. She was dating. That's what it felt like more than anything else. There was a relationship under way. Neva had tactfully not asked a single question about him while they shared the pie, but it had been there in the twinkle in her eyes. Paul wasn't being conventional, calling and leaving her voice-mail messages. He was arranging to leave her actual notes to enjoy when she finally got home. She liked it.

Black disappeared down the hall, and a squeak erupted from his rubber duck. Then his spinner whistled. She heard dog feet on the floor race toward the kitchen. The talking bird started talking. She smiled. Used to the routine, she still enjoyed it. Black had to do a count of his toys to make sure they were all where he had left them. She dumped her travel bag on her bed and unpacked. She waited for the bear to growl, and when it did she leaned out into the hall and saw Black carrying the bear with him toward the living room. Still his favorite. She tossed laundry in the washer, then repacked so the bag was ready to go again at a moment's notice.

"Comfortable, Black?"

His tail smacked the floor. He had the bear in a stranglehold in his paws, chewing on an arm. She got a cold soda and connected the video link to Paul. "Calling, as requested."

His smile warmed her heart. "It's good to see you, Ann. How was the trip?"

"I'm not going to mention the case, as it took the whole flight back to even start to forget it. The flight itself was interesting. A lot of crosswinds, and the thermals were ugly. Hot summer air can be some of the most challenging for flying. On the bright side, the scenery was gorgeous."

"I'll just say I'm glad you're safely home. How's Midnight?"

She turned the camera so he could see. "Say hi, Black."

The dog paused his enthusiastic chewing long enough for a single bark.

"He looks happy to see you home."

"Neva spoils him. What about you? How's your day been?"

"Paperwork—reading over interview transcripts." He held up the pages in his hand. "It came home with me. The team has done forty-six out of the one hundred twenty-three interviews, and so far nothing solid is showing up. We're not getting the reaction to the middleman photo or the amounts that I had hoped. Ten of the thirty murders are now officially cold again."

"Ouch. I'll let you get back to your reading."

"Ann, leave the video on, and we can share the evening.

Go get a book to read, find a show to watch, work on a story, whatever you want to do with your evening. Just spend the time with me. We don't have to say anything to enjoy each other's company."

"It's a nice thought, but—"

"You have plans for the evening? Company coming over? You want me to go away and are too polite to say so?"

"I talk to myself. Or more accurately, I talk to the dog."

He grinned. "Will you get embarrassed if I say that's endearing?"

She smiled. "I don't want to feel on display in my own home, so no, let's end the call."

"You have to trust me sometime, Ann. Why not start with what you tell your dog when you think no one else is listening? How about I promise, unless you say, Paul, I'll ignore what you are saying?"

"Don't try to be so reasonable. I'm likely going to read a book. That's exciting."

He held up the pages in his hand.

"Point taken."

"Share your evening with me. I'll enjoy your company."

"We'll try it. But I reserve the right to change my mind without notice."

"Not a problem. Don't even need to explain. Thanks."

Paul finished another interview and added it to the stack he'd read. He glanced over at the screen. Ann was stretched out on the couch, pillow and book propped on her stomach, reading. Midnight had moved to sprawl beside her and use the couch as a backrest. Paul saw Ann turn the page, then reach down and rub her fingers through Midnight's thick coat. He could almost hear the dog's sigh. Paul smiled.

A phone rang. He glanced at his, then realized it was Ann's. She picked up her phone, and a moment later the audio bar on the screen turned orange as she put the video call on mute. She disappeared for twenty minutes. When she returned, she plugged the cellphone in to charge the battery and hit the button to turn on the audio. "How's it going?"

"It's not." He set aside the pages. "Talk to me for a bit, Ann. I need a break from this."

"Sure." She settled into a comfortable chair.

"You picked up a book tonight. Is that a normal evening?"

"Pretty much, when I'm unwinding and just want to relax."

"What do you like to read?"

"Popular fiction—mysteries, adventures, romances—well-drawn characters with an interesting story. I enjoy a good biography, but generally stay away from history. I read a lot of experts on food, finance, birds, baseball, politics. I like the *New Yorker* profile pieces. What?" She stopped because he was smiling at her.

"Everything. You read everything."

"I don't often read the side panels of cereal boxes, the sports page, or the magazines in the spin rack at the grocery store. But, okay, other than that, I read just about everything. What was the last book you read?"

He shifted stacks on his desk and held one up. "Andy

Stanley's book, *The Best Question Ever: A Revolutionary Approach to Decision Making.*"

"Oh, I read that one. Good choice. *What is the wise thing to do?* And the answer to that question for right now is to ask you to change the subject."

"New topic then." He waited. "Your question," he offered.

She thought about it and studied him thoughtfully. "Can I ask you a tough personal question?"

"Sure."

"You said you were adopted."

"Yes. My parents were killed in a wreck when I was four. I remember the smell of my mother's perfume. I remember in a vague way my father's laugh. But I don't remember much else about them."

"There was no family to take you in?"

"No. A distant cousin who lived in Japan was my last living relative. I stayed with a foster family for a couple years, then moved to a larger group home near my school. George and Karen Falcon adopted me when I was nine."

"Does it bother you to talk about it?"

"I don't talk about it much, but it's relevant and important. What do you want to know?"

"What was it like to be adopted, to have your world as you knew it so radically change?"

"It's a good question. I knew them, George and Karen Falcon, in the casual way a kid knows adults. They supported the group home through their family charity. They would stop by to speak with the administrator, or be at the head table to share a meal, and I'd see the lady sometimes around the home. She'd be involved with the girls, and they would be giggling.

"I was out on the jungle gym one afternoon, done playing basketball, hanging upside down, thinking about how to get out of school the next day. The music teacher was going to assign roles for the school play, and I didn't want to get selected for a part. George walked out to the playground and talked with me for a few minutes.

"He asked if I liked living at the home, liked where I went to school, and I kind of shrugged that it was okay. I didn't have much to compare it to. I had a comfortable bed, good food, and kids to play with. It was a good kind of place to be, and I was, for a nine-year-old boy, attached to it in a way. There were adults you had to listen to and rules to follow, and while there wasn't any real sense of family, it was a place I could function and feel like I could be myself. I thought of it as boarding school, and tried to pretend my family was still alive but just far away. I had learned to cope with being on my own."

Paul reached for his soda. "George returned a few more times that month, enough I knew his name, enough to realize out of all the kids around, he was making a point to find me and chat for a few minutes. There were a couple of weeks where I could feel the emotion setting in, the worry that I had done something wrong to get the attention, the opposite realization I was coming to depend on him stopping by for a few words, that no one had ever done that before, searching to find me. I was eager to see him, and also scared by that, just wondering what was going on.

"One Saturday the administrator had errands to run, and that morning during breakfast my name was drawn out of the hat. I could go along for the day trip if I wanted to. I went with him to the store, the bank, and the post office. Then the administrator said he had a visit to make, and he could either drop me back at the home or I could go along if I could sit quietly through a meal while he talked business. I went with him. We had dinner at George and Karen's house.

"It's a massive home, and I was in awe. I was sitting between Boone and Jackie with Harper across from me, having a cheeseburger and fries, in the house of this man I liked. His kids were all younger than me, and I liked them and was laughing with them, and it felt like a normal evening where dinnertime was a table of kids. I played basketball in the driveway after dinner, teaching Jackie how to dribble the ball, and showing Boone and Harper how to make a free throw. The evening was over, and I was putting the ball away when George came over and put his hand on my shoulder and said it was nice I had come, and would I mind if he asked me to come over again?

"It became a regular thing, dinner at George and Karen's. They took me out for ice cream after the school play. They stopped by when they were going to go swimming to see if I wanted to come along. I had known them about six months when George asked if I wanted to be part of a family again or if I felt old enough I would rather not be adopted.

"I wasn't expecting the question, because it wasn't something I thought about much. The younger kids got adopted, especially the girls, but no one had ever suggested I would be one of them. My life had been the home, the adults who ran the place. I hadn't thought of being adopted, I had parents who were dead, but I said I did miss having a family and that I didn't like the fact I was alone.

"George knelt down to my height, held out his hand, and he said, 'If you would like to be part of my family, I would like to be your father. You would be my son, just the same as Harper and Boone. You would have a sister in Jackie, and if Karen has more babies, you'll have even more family to care about. You can be one of us if you want to be.'

"I remember trying not to cry when I said I would. We shook hands on it. I went to live with them the next week, and the adoption went through later that year.

"I remember the first thing George bought me was a phone, and he put everyone's numbers in it, his and Karen's, and all the aunts and uncles and cousins. And he gave it to me and said, 'This is your family. You should love them, and fight with them, and laugh with them, and spend your life talking with them.' That phone used to ring all the time. It was an embarrassment of riches, how many relatives I had that made a point to call and get to know me.

"He's never really said why he adopted me, when he had kids of his own and knew more were likely. He never said why he chose me, knowing I would be the oldest of his kids. George accepted me as his son, as his eldest son, and has never wavered from that decision.

"I know George thought it all out. Harper said once that he had been asked, did he want to be the eldest son or did he want me as a brother? And he'd said he desperately wanted me as a brother." Paul stopped, finding it difficult to finish the memory.

"They loved you," Ann said softly. "By choice. By decision. George loved you the same as he did his other two sons. Harper loved you like his brother Boone. Nothing says we have to limit who we love as family to just those who share our blood."

"I know. But it still feels weird to me, knowing I got chosen like that. There wasn't anything special about that nine-year-old boy. I was polite enough, and reasonably smart, and I liked people, but I was just one of a thousand boys just like me who didn't have parents. There was no reason for him to adopt me. He already had kids.

"He tried to explain it once. He wanted me to have a father, and when he thought about it over the weeks that went by, he realized he wanted to be that father. He asked me to be his son because he wanted to be my father, no other reason than that."

"Some things in life are a mystery. Love is one of them," she said. "You thrive being part of a large family with lots of relations."

"I do. I don't have the right words for it, but family makes me complete. Having this as an important part of life, having family around to care about and share life with, fills in part of who I am that nothing else ever could."

He was quiet for a moment, then looked over at her and gave a rueful smile. "And here I'm talking about big families and going from none to many, while you're in the opposite situation, having gone from many to none. I'm sorry for being tactless about that. Does it bother you enormously to be alone, Ann? To have no family left? Are you surviving that?"

"It's not the same when it comes as an adult as when

it happens as a child. I shared years of life with my parents and grandparents. I don't feel like they are missing from my life as much as they are just not here. They've been gone a long time, but I still feel like they could walk through the door any day. So I don't grieve like I once did. I had a good place in life as a child, a sense of who I was as their daughter and granddaughter. It's not that I like being without family or would choose it; it is simply what it is."

"Did you feel lonely as an only child?"

"I've never been alone, not in the sense of having no one to relate to. I had my parents, my grandparents, my neighbors, friends my age. And then I had books. Even as a young girl, I loved books. In my imagination I was there on those adventures. And even as a young girl, my stories were starting to appear, with characters as rich as real friends to me. And then somewhere about the age of ten, I fell in love with God, and got to start talking with someone who loved me. It's hard to be lonely when you are never alone."

"We share that, Ann. I met God when I was six. I think that's one of the reasons why I coped okay with being at the group home. I had already chosen God, and He was there. I didn't feel totally alone. Even today, it's the relationship that sits at the center of all others."

"You and I have had it easier because of that. Could I ask one last question about the Falcons?"

"Sure."

"What's your mom like?"

"She loves to laugh. She's kind. She's disorganized in a messy kind of way, and all the family kind of keeps her together and helps her find what she's misplaced.

You want her waffles when you visit and her big chunk chocolate cookies. She loves people and kids, and she's an optimist about everything. She created a weekly cartoon strip for years."

"Really?"

"It was syndicated nationwide and better than *Peanuts*, in my humble opinion."

"Tell me you've got copies of her strips I can see."

"I do, and I'll share."

Black started barking and took off. Ann looked toward the patio door and then back at Paul. "You mind if I go deal with this? It's probably my prowling raccoon."

"Go."

She opened the lockbox and retrieved her side arm. "Just in case it's not the raccoon. Black, don't chase." She glanced at Paul. "He'll chase, so this will take a few minutes."

She disappeared from the room.

Paul got up and stretched, and since she would be a few minutes he transferred the video to the den, and then went to find another soda. He caught the end of a ball game while keeping an eye on the screen for Ann's return. Forty minutes passed, and he was beginning to get uneasy. He heard a door kick open, and Ann appeared, carrying Black. She put him down on the couch and grabbed for his legs to keep him from getting up. "Just stay put, you big doofus. Stay."

"What happened?"

"My raccoon was three raccoons, and Black promptly chased himself in circles and crashed into a tree. He's wobbling." She sank down on the floor beside the couch, breathing hard and keeping a firm hand on the dog to keep him from moving. Black licked her face. She wiped at it, too tired for more than token protest. "Yeah, I know. Next time we let them get into the trash, buddy. It's easier on both of us."

"Three of them."

Ann laughed. "It was a wonderful sight, up until the collision. I'm going to have to bring in my hanging flowers and redo again where I keep my trash. One of the joys of living in the country. They'll be back now that they've found it."

"Will Black be okay?"

"Give him an hour and he'll be fine. I think he's nearsighted. It's not the first accident he's had." She ruffled the dog's ears and reached over him to get her book. "Give me a few minutes to catch my breath." She stretched out, using the couch as a backrest and found her page in the book.

"Sure." Paul watched her and had to smile.

He ended his night with the late evening news. Black had gone to sleep on the couch, one of his paws draped over Ann's shoulder. She was still reading. He wondered if she was going to finish the book tonight. "Ann, I'm going to turn in for the night."

She looked up from the book. "I'm a night owl. I should have warned you."

"Dave already did. Thanks for the evening."

"You're welcome."

"Admit it, I'm decent company."

Amusement lit her face. "I'm getting used to you. Good night, Paul."

"Good night, Ann."

He closed the link. He'd asked her to be curious. Of

everything he had expected, it hadn't been a question about his adoption. She hadn't landed on that question by chance. She'd been thinking about him, and who he was. She had asked a deep question that would tell her a lot about him. He turned in, thoughtful, mulling over that fact, and pleased with the evening.

PART THREE

LINDA SMYTHE

12

Paul was growing used to the eye strain from reading endless reports. He pulled out a cold root beer and thought about heading to the shooting range for a couple of hours. He wondered how Ann was spending her day. Probably not at her desk, unless it was by choice.

Rita tapped on his door and offered a blue-and-white-striped mailer. "This just came by courier for you. Security opened it since media can't pass through the scanner."

He was the boss—it wouldn't do for him to groan. "Thanks." He accepted the package, wondering who would be sending mail by hand-delivered courier. He waved at the piles in front of him. "You could take a stack of this if you like."

She laughed. "Who do you think put most of it on your desk? Sam just got back. You want to talk about the Yates shooting?"

"Ten minutes and I'll find you both. I still think it's the brother. I listened to the audio of the interview on the drive in, and something is definitely off with his answers."

Paul tipped the package she had brought and slid out two small audiotapes and a number-ten envelope. He opened the letter and pulled out a light green sheet of paper.

"Rita!"

She came back.

"Get Sam. And we'll need evidence bags."

He picked up the desk phone and punched the direct line to building security. "This is Paul Falcon. The package just delivered by DMD Couriers to my attention. I need the person who brought it in identified, the video of him—anything you can give me."

He carefully set the sheet of paper down and kept it from folding closed with the edge of his coaster and the stapler. He took photos of the letter with his phone camera. He encrypted the images with a ten-digit code.

Rita came back with gloves and evidence bags. "What is it?"

Paul stepped away from his desk and waved her in so she could read it for herself. "Bag the courier package, the two tapes, the envelope, the letter. Everything gets hand-walked through for fingerprints, and none of it leaves our sight. Top guy only sees that letter; this stays highly classified. We can't afford even a whisper of a leak on this."

Paul read the letter through for a second time, using his photo of it.

Sam stepped into the office. Paul turned his phone and let Sam read the letter on the screen.

Sam nearly dropped part of his sandwich. "This isn't a forgery."

"There are two tapes in the package."

Agent Falcon—

I understand you are looking for me. I offer two tapes in good faith to prove my identity.

My offer—I want a deal in place in case you ever catch me. I will send you four more tapes if you agree to take the federal death penalty off the table for the thirty murders you now believe I have committed.

Send two signed copies of the deal agreement to the address below. I will send the four tapes and a signed agreement back to you.

L.S.

She wanted the reply mailed to an address in St. Charles, Missouri.

Rita gathered up the evidence bags. "I'm heading downstairs to rush all this through prints."

"I'm going with you," Sam said, adding his sandwich to the stacks on Paul's desk. "Soon as they're done checking the tapes, I'll have audio duplicate a set."

Paul picked up his phone. "Meet me upstairs. I'm activating the small war room and tight security. We tripped into her. She heard about an interview. Who did we talk to, and who did they then talk to?"

"Maybe we have her prints."

"Wouldn't that be a rush? Go. Bribe with whatever you have to so that's the next thing worked."

Paul called his boss, then headed upstairs. The building security chief came off the elevator as Paul started to open the stairway door. He stopped to see what the man had.

"DMD Couriers, five packages dropped off. This is the photo of the delivery guy. He's a regular to this building. His route ends in twenty minutes, and DMD Couriers will hold him at their office until you've spoken with him. Trouble?"

"Yes. If any more deliveries come for my attention, hold the delivery guy and call me."

"Will do."

Paul took the stairs up. He entered the small room just off the secure conference room they normally used and personally reset the access codes. His boss arrived. Paul punched in the encryption code and offered his cellphone and the photo of the letter.

Arthur read it. "The director is going to love this. What's the plan?"

"We need to put a reply in the mail within seventy-two hours, with a thought-out plan for tracking the package and catching her when she picks it up. We wait longer than that, we risk her disappearing. During those seventy-two hours we need to figure out how we tripped into her, follow where these two tapes can take us, trace the package she sent, and hope we get fingerprints somewhere along the line so we know who we're chasing.

"We catch her, this gets simple. We open the door for a deal, she's got twenty-eight more tapes. She can whittle the terms of the deal in her favor a few tapes at a time. We open that door, there's no way to predict how far it is going to go. So it ends up being a conversation for the director's level. It's a tactical problem, to game what she might do and how to proceed, to figure out what the attorney general can live with. That would be your kind of problem, sir."

"Tomorrow morning, ten a.m., my office. I'll have the decision-makers in the room. We keep it to ten whoever sees this letter, or we're going to lose control of this."

"You, me, Sam, Rita, the director, the U.S. attorney general, that gets us to six. Chief of the lab trying for prints, a good audio guy, makes eight."

"We'll use Thomas Gates from legal to write the deal agreement. That gets us to nine."

"I'd like to discuss it with the MHI. If we need someone with clout to open a door for us, she can get us a conversation with Vice President Gannett. He's got an interest in this case."

Arthur nodded. "Granted. That's ten. What else do you need?"

"The questions are easy; speed is the problem."

"I'll be near a phone if you need me or if there is news."

"Thank you, sir."

His boss headed out.

Paul's phone rang. "Yes, Sam."

"Six sets of prints on the package, three of them are going to be our people, one the courier, figure another at the DMD offices, so there's a chance. The prints are being run now. The audiotapes show no prints. Rita's staying with the letter and envelope. I'm going to walk the tapes to the audio lab and stand over him while copies are made, then put the original tapes in your office safe. You need the delivery package upstairs?"

"I can work off photos. Send them to Franklin."

"Sending them now."

Paul moved into the large conference room. Six teams were in the field doing interviews, so it was down to a skeleton crew, and the room looked almost empty. He'd have to decide which ones in the field should be on a plane tonight to get them back here.

"People, I need your attention." Agents turned toward him. "For the next several days there are going to be code-level assignments going out. This is the kind of case that will be on your résumé thirty years from now. It's going to be urgent and come in waves. And you're going to have to work with less than normal information about what's going on. Give me your best, and as fast as you can."

He looked to Franklin. "Sam just sent you a picture of a package from DMD Couriers. I need you lights and siren to their office. When did the package arrive at DMD Couriers, who brought it in, who accepted the package, and what do they remember about who brought it in? I need security-camera footage for as far back in time as they have it. The courier who delivered it here will be at their office in twenty minutes. I need everything he knows about the package, and ask everyone if they will give us elimination prints. Kelly, go with him, and work on how the delivery was paid for. Was anything signed? Is there an account number that can be traced? I need the handwriting.

"Peter, there are six sets of prints on the package. They are being run now. Monitor the progress. I need names and faces for those prints. Then focus on the return address on the package. Is it real? The middle of a lake? Tell me everything that can be known about the address where this package originated.

"Christopher, I have an address in St. Charles, Missouri. I need everything about the address that can be known short of doing a drive-by to take pictures of it. Then I need a list of the lady shooter interviews on a board, listed by date and time." Paul handed over a Post-it note with the address where she wanted the reply sent.

"If you hit a problem, find or call me. Tag me with results as soon as you have them. I'll tell you all later why you are now having fun."

Sam was now in the doorway of the war room. Paul joined him and closed the door behind them.

"This *is* fun, boss," Sam said. "My heart's got some adrenaline going."

"Tell me about it." Paul grabbed a marker and started making a list for himself on the board. Package, tapes, prints, letter reply, lawyers she chose, address to send agreements, how to track the reply to her. "Have any problem with me bringing in Ann?"

"None. She thinks in puzzles, and we've got one. Want to hear the tapes now?"

"Yes, but it will be faster if we wait for Rita. The package is under way. What else are you thinking?"

"The currency thief kept the tapes the middleman gave him. So we have the middleman's voice to use as a comparison. We can establish these tapes are legit if we get a match on the middleman's voice."

"Can you get Treasury to offer a couple of the audio files without telling them why we want them?"

"I can be persuasive."

"Get the tapes," Paul agreed. "I'm still working on the fact we got her attention. An interview? The middleman investigation? She knew the middleman for years, so maybe she knew him well enough to know where he lived. A trip wire related to his home makes sense. A neighbor. The FBI shows up at the middleman's home, the lady shooter hears about it. 'If you ever see cops at my uncle's home, call me and I'll give you five thousand dollars.' Maybe we were the ones who tripped into her."

"Do we suspend the interviews while we focus on this?"

"At a minimum we turn around and re-interview everyone we just talked to." Paul was grateful he had Ann's cash to work with. He wouldn't have to waste time making a case for funding. This had to happen fast, and it could get expensive. "Anyone within a four-hour flight, see if you can get them back tonight. We'll regroup for a day and send them out again. I don't want to run shorthanded here until we get our arms around this."

Sam reached for the phone.

Paul thought about the list on the board and added another one. Why did she make contact now? Something changed. Something had to have changed for the lady shooter to be looking for a deal.

Paul headed back into the main conference room to hear the updates.

"Boss, the return address is nonsense. There's no such street," Peter said. "And the six sets of prints on the package—I've got names and photos, and they are all employees, either here or the couriers'."

"I've got something on the address in St. Charles, Missouri," Christopher offered. "It's a house in a nice subdivision on the west side of town. I've got photos from a real-estate sale last year—it's a three-bedroom, two-bath ranch. The homeowner is a Mr. Lewis Graves.

His DMV photo just generated a match with a high school science teacher."

Paul was surprised. He would be astonished if the lady shooter had that homeowner helping her. Why that address? A plus, though, that surveillance would be easier in a subdivision than with a busy downtown street. They would be able to see who came and went. He had to assume someone would be sent to get the package, who would then take it to the lady shooter. "Do what you can to tell me more about Lewis Graves without alerting him that you're looking. Stay with public records."

"Will do."

"Boss, I've got Franklin on the phone," Jason said. "According to DMD Couriers, they picked up the package at the Hyatt Hotel on Thomas Avenue, in the guest business office. It's entirely automated. You set the package on the receiving tray, it takes the weight and your destination address, and gives you the price. You pay and it spits out the address label to put on your package. You drop it in the outgoing mailbox. The machine tells the office there is a package waiting for pickup and a courier stops by to get it. Franklin is on the way to the Hyatt to get security footage on the one who dropped off the package."

"Good. Tell him we also want the area checked for prints."

"Boss." Rita was in the doorway of the war room.

He moved to join her. "What do we have, Rita?"

She closed the door behind them, pointing at Sam to put down the phone. A smile danced on her face. "We've got her fingerprints." She opened a folder and took out a piece of paper. "Linda Smythe. Miss L.S. is

Linda Smythe of Boston, Massachusetts. She is fifty-three years old now. Her prints were the only ones on the letter and the envelope. We have an old photo." She placed it on the table. "In 1981 she was charged with assault, pled it down to misdemeanor battery, and did thirty days in county jail. There is nothing in the last twenty-five years to give a current address. The address listed in the old report is now a parking lot."

"A name, photo, fingerprints—we've got someone to chase." Paul wrapped an arm around Rita's shoulders. "Sam, the whole team comes back. Tell them to return first class, sleep on the plane, and be ready to work when they arrive."

"Will do."

"Who else knows?"

"The three of us," Rita answered, looking between the two. "Once the lab chief confirmed prints were present, he gave me an encrypted file with the prints, and returned the letter and envelope. They are now in your safe. I ran the prints on the classified system myself and got the match."

"I'll tell the boss, but otherwise we keep the name to ourselves for a few hours. We've got two tapes from her, and there are twenty-eight more out there. We'll have to figure out how to pursue the investigation without sending her back into the shadows—" Paul stopped abruptly.

"What?"

"She didn't leave her prints on the letter and envelope by accident. She *gave* us her prints. She thinks she is well covered. She doesn't think that name and photo will lead to her. Or she gave us prints that are not hers to redirect us and keep us busy elsewhere."

"So a wild goose chase."

Paul nodded. "She's after a deal, the tapes are real, but the prints may be a way to stall us while letters go back and forth. She doesn't want to get caught until she's got the best deal she can arrange, and she's got twenty-eight tapes to work with to get that best deal."

"More like cat and mouse then. She wants the deals from us while we are busy trying to catch her."

"Yes. We work the prints and the photo, but we keep in mind it may not be her. What's helpful, though, is the prints are on both the envelope and letter. If the prints are a plant, we still know the lady shooter handed the pieces of paper to this Linda Smythe, so she is our lady shooter or she recently met our lady shooter.

"Rita, stay on the prints. See if they lead anywhere else, another name, an open case elsewhere, then age the photo and check it against DMV records and passports. Sam, focus on the bio. Let's find out about Linda Smythe, and if she has family out there and if any of them are still alive."

"What is upstairs going to decide about the offer?"

"The boss will have decision-makers in his office tomorrow morning, ten o'clock, to figure it out. Sam, I also need you to start gaming out how we use the reply to catch her. We have the address where it is to be delivered, and it's a house in a subdivision owned by a high school science teacher. She's not going to pick it up herself. We stake out the address and follow whoever picks up the reply. What options give us the best chance to catch her without scaring her off and sending her back into the shadows?"

"It's not as easy as it sounds. She sees us or believes

we're on to her, she simply won't pick up the reply. She writes and says send it again to a new address, and we repeat the chase until she gets the pages without us getting her."

"Whatever she has planned, you can be sure this is not going to be easy. I'll go up and tell the boss the name. When I get back we'll listen to those two tapes."

Paul returned in twenty minutes, pulled out a chair beside Rita at the table in the war room. "Let's hear the tapes."

Sam's fingers gave a short drum roll on the table and then he pressed play. Static began the tape and then faint voices. A man's came to the fore.

"I don't do oblique references. You want my help, you need to state clearly what you want, why, and what you're going to pay."

"I want you to kill my wife, Yolanda Meeks. I'll pay you two hundred fifty thousand. She's a liability to me, and it needs to be done this week."

"You understand when I make a call, that you cannot change your mind? If you fail to pay as agreed, you will yourself be killed by the shooter."

"I understand the deal, just get it done fast."

The tape went back to static. Sam put in the second tape.

"You want my help, you need to state clearly what you want, why, and what you're going to pay."

"I want you to kill my brother, Victor Ryckoff. I'll

pay you three hundred thousand after you've done the job. He's pushing into my business for the last time."

"You understand when I make a call, that you cannot change your mind? If you fail to pay as agreed, you will yourself be killed by the shooter."

"I understand the terms."

Another round of static. Sam removed the tape. "It sounds like he's reading from a script."

"He probably is. He's got down when he wants to start and stop the tape, and he's careful about what he wants on that recording," Paul commented. "Flint Meeks killed his wife, Yolanda Meeks, and Tony Ryckoff killed his brother, Victor Ryckoff. The initials don't match the day-planner entries."

"Nicknames," Rita guessed. "Tin Man. Our aluminum company executive Flint Meeks is Tin Man, TM, and Tony Ryckoff wrote a newsletter called the Gold Nugget, that's the GN."

"No names on the tapes, just voices. We need a voice match, that it really was them on that call, not just someone saying 'my wife, my brother.'"

"We use Nathan Scholes," Rita suggested. "He's good and he can keep his mouth shut. Lock him in a room, swear him to silence, give him the tapes, tell him what we need. People post birthday parties, family videos, these guys give speeches, maybe there is a public audio file he can work with to match their voices."

Paul agreed. "Take him the tapes."

"How do you want to handle investigating Flint Meeks and Tony Ryckoff? If they hired a murder, they've likely committed a few more felonies over the years. Can we start guys digging into their current lives without saying why we are looking?"

"I'll think on that overnight. It might be better to wait until we have as many tapes as we are going to get from the lady shooter before we start using any of the information. I don't want to tip our hand early and give these guys a warning. They believe they have gotten away with the crime. I'd like them to stay confident they are in the clear until the day we put handcuffs on them." Paul could finally feel the calmness settling in that this was going somewhere. "Let's dig in and see how far we can get today. The boss offered to buy dinner."

Paul glanced at the time when he got home and saw the clock had moved past midnight. He punched in Ann's number for a secure video call. He would have called from work, but it felt more personal calling from home. He was taking Vicky's word for it that Ann worked ten p.m. to two a.m. most days, as well as Dave's comment that she was a night owl.

"You're having a late night, Falcon."

The fact she was smiling gave him some hope she was going to be forgiving about the interruption. "You look wide awake."

She held up a book. "Another hour or so to go. I'd like to know how it ends. Something wrong?" She tilted her head. "No, something right. You look pleased. So . . . how was your day?"

"Long and profitable. We caught a break in the lady shooter case." Paul saw her instant smile and matched it with one of his own.

"That must feel really good to say."

"It is." He picked up his phone and decrypted the image of the letter. He held it up without comment. She read it, smiled, and read it again. "Which tapes did she send you?"

The single question she started with told him he was right to bring her in on the case. "Twenty-five and twenty-nine."

"She knew which day planners you had. She's been watching all the way back to the middleman's death."

"I think so. Her name may be Linda Smythe, fifty-three, from Boston, Massachusetts. Or the prints may be a misdirect."

He watched her think it through.

"She's not one to make a mistake like that," she said. "If they are her prints, it's because she wants you to know something about her. She's going to work very hard to get a good deal in exchange for those tapes."

"Agreed."

"She's a planner. You won't catch her retrieving a package, not when her fallback is to walk away and tell the lawyer to resend it. But you'll have to try, and you'll have some fun making the chase. In past cases she's shown no indication she'll harm a bystander, and she isn't likely to start now. Someone will pick up the package, and her plan will simply be an attempt to elude you in taking the handoff."

"That's my read of it too. There's a chance now, a real chance, to catch the lady shooter, with the evidence to convict those who hired her."

"Tapes of the murder for hires. I'm glad for you, Paul. I hope you get all thirty tapes."

"I have a feeling this is going to unfold as a lot of hurry up and wait, and last for several weeks. Notice I said weeks, and I'm impatient at that thought when the case has been on the boards for years. I have a feeling patience isn't going to be my strong suit this time around. I'm hoping I can kill some of that waiting time with you."

"I'll enjoy watching the FBI work. It will be nice being a spectator to a case for a change." She studied him. "Could I meddle for a moment?"

"Sure."

"Remember to get some rest during the times this case does sprint. I'll like you better when this is over."

"I will. You can keep me honest."

"Good. Because I'm about to hang up on you so you can go get some sleep."

He laughed. "Good night, Ann."

She was smiling as she dropped the link. So was he.

13

Paul entered Suite 906 just before ten a.m. Margaret offered a mug of coffee and nodded toward Arthur's office. "Go right in."

Paul walked into his boss's office. "Good morning, Arthur." He hesitated. "Director."

"Paul." The director of the FBI crossed to shake hands. Edward Baine was career FBI, politically accustomed to turf wars, and underneath the polish was still a sharp cop with good instincts for people and problems. Paul liked the man. "I believe you know Tori Scott from the U.S. Attorney's Office."

Paul took her hand. "I do. It's a pleasure, Tori." She had been a guest along with her husband at his father's dinner table many times.

"Let's take a seat and we'll get started," Arthur directed. Paul took a seat beside his boss. "Give us the highlights of where you're at, Paul."

"The audiotapes are as advertised. She sent us tapes for murders twenty-five and twenty-nine. We've confirmed the voice print of the middleman and the two speakers on the tapes. Flint Meeks paid to kill his wife, Yolanda, and Tony Ryckoff paid to kill his brother, Victor.

"There are prints on the letter and the envelope which may be the lady shooter, or they may be a distraction to keep us occupied. For reasons only she understands, she may want to let us know who she is.

"The prints are for a lady named Linda Smythe, now fifty-three, from Boston, Massachusetts. It fits with her first three murders, as that was her home territory. We have a bio for her through age twenty. She grew up in a violent and abusive home. Drunken father. Mentally ill mother. Numerous domestic calls, aggravated assault, drunk and disorderly. She was removed from the home twice. The mother died when Linda was ten, the father when she was seventeen. It could be her real bio, as it's the kind of background that could lead to a hired shooter. We haven't generated a match for the photo in DMV, or passport records yet, but we're working on it. The big question is her letter, and the decision on what to do."

"Tori," the director said, "you had an interesting perspective on this case that you shared on the flight here. I'd like to start the discussion there."

"Thank you, sir. It seems best to keep an eye on the larger picture of what is possible when we decide what to do." The woman shifted to sit forward. "Paul, you made her nervous with your investigation, she broke nine years of silence, and she contacted you. She is likely already regretting sending that envelope. She's confirmed to you she's still alive, and she has something you really want—tapes of the murder contracts. By her actions she intensifies the hunt to find her, she's no longer a ghost, and she's got to be on edge about that. If we reply with anything other than the offer she made in her letter, we give her an excuse to walk away. So we stay cautious with this first decision. Her letter is not a negotiation. She wants us to take or reject her offer."

Tori sat back and folded her hands over a crossed knee. "With four more tapes, you have solid proof on six murders. And by continuing the interaction with her, you rapidly improve your ability to catch her. In my opinion, that is worth taking the federal death penalty off the table. We still have the state death penalty in play on some of the murders. We use the first reply to show we will work with her, we convince her to keep talking with you, and we have that back-and-forth of mail to help find her.

"The more tapes you can get in your possession, the more your position improves relative to what she has to offer. She has the bulk of the tapes. When you have more than half of the tapes, the balance shifts and you can risk offering a different deal from what she wants. When her demands get too high, you counter with a smaller deal for a single tape, you try to drag out the communications, or you say no to her offer, ask her to suggest something else and see if she will offer a counter proposal. But you can't risk that move unless you are prepared for her to break off contact and disappear." She looked at the director. "I don't think we are ready for her to disappear. So we stay with what she's requesting for now. Speaking personally, I want those thirty tapes. It's worth a great deal to get them."

The director nodded. "I like commonsense plans, and I just heard one. We ignore the offer, we turn it down, and we lose access to tapes that are valuable and a chance to catch her. So we take the deal as offered and play this round out." He looked at Paul. "You've been thinking this through. What else is on your mind?"

"We have a timing problem. We have to keep quiet the fact the lady shooter has made contact and is giving us tapes. If we tip our hand, the people who hired the hits will disappear. Or they will find and kill the lady shooter before she gives us all the tapes she's going to provide. So we need to wait and make all the arrests at the same time."

Paul looked to Tori. "We have the tape with their voices contracting for the murder, the middleman records of what the lady shooter was paid, and—if we can catch her and she'll cooperate—the lady shooter's testimony. It's enough for an arrest. I don't know if that will be enough for a conviction. The two men we now know about have solid reputations, and these are old murders." Paul looked over at the director. "We'll have to do the aggressive investigations of the murders *after* the arrests are made. And we'll have up to thirty murders to investigate at the same time. It's going to take a lot of agents. I just don't see a way around that problem. We start making arrests before all the tapes are in, too many things can spin out of our control."

"The priority for now is acquiring the tapes and capturing her," the director decided. "Do whatever you can without jeopardizing that goal."

"I appreciate that. A minor but critical point: we can't afford a mistake like those tapes accidentally going through security downstairs and getting erased, so we need a different drop-off place for her to return the agreement and tapes. I suggest we use Zane's address. I want to read him in on what is going on. He can alert me when a package arrives and can hand-deliver the tapes here."

Arthur winced at the name of Paul's predecessor, but nodded. "Agreed."

The director smiled, well aware of the complex history. "He'll be useful. Paul, run this out in time to the endgame. How would this ideally unfold?"

"There is a back-and-forth of letters while the thirty tapes come in. We identify who is on each tape. Once we have all the tapes, or all the tapes we judge we are likely to get, we rapidly scale up in personnel.

"Forty-eight hours before we make arrests, we lock a task force of lawyers in a room, lay out what we have for each case, and we decide in advance what kind of deal we will be willing to offer to each person.

"We make the thirty arrests as rapidly as possible. We serve warrants for financial records, phone records. We do the thirty interviews immediately and put the deals on the table. Twenty-four hours in we assess where we are at—who is going to take the deal, who is going to stay quiet, what information we've been able to gather in the field, and what needs pursued next. We hold a press conference announcing the arrests.

"We start interviews in the field related to each murder. These people got away with hiring a murder, and odds are good at least a couple of them have made remarks to a friend or family member they are going to regret having said.

"Each murder gets assigned a legal team and a lead prosecutor. There are thirty arraignments. We hand off the murder cases to the attorney general and keep the lady shooter as our focus if we haven't caught her.

"We have one extra point working in our favor. The odds are good these people have committed at least one other major felony since they hired a murder, so while we focus on the investigation, we also get as aggressive as we can within the scope of the warrants and the inquiries to see what else is out there that might be easier to prosecute."

The director nodded. "Let's hope it goes that smoothly. We'll need a room large enough to handle at least a hundred lawyers, and we'll need better than a hundred sixty agents available when this case moves to arrests, warrants, and interviews. I'll work on those preparations. Keep us updated on where the tapes lead, and let me know if there is anything else you need. We'll reassemble this group when there is another letter from her to decide how to answer."

"Yes, sir."

Paul looked to Arthur, who nodded and got to his feet, indicating the meeting was concluded. "Catch her, Paul."

------------▼------------

Paul returned to the small war room where Sam and Rita were working. He wrote down Tori Scott's direct number on the contact board. "That went smoother than I expected. We'll have an agreement drafted today as the lady shooter's letter specified."

He turned to face the two. "I made a few decisions last night. This is going to play out over weeks, if not months, with a lot of urgent moments and then a lot of waiting, and it's only going to be us working the case, so we divide and conquer. Rita, I'm giving you the tapes. Become best friends with Nathan Scholes. Identify the voices. Put a name on the person who paid for the murder. Prove the tapes are authentic. I need an audio match for each voice that will hold up in court.

"Sam, your priority is catching the lady shooter. We are sending signed copies of the agreement. She has to receive and sign those documents. We don't want her to abandon the package, we don't want to spook her and send her back in hiding. But within those boundaries, figure out how to use the reply package to catch her. As a cover story, someone is leaking classified information, and the package is being followed to locate who is receiving the information. Recruit whoever you want to use from here or a field office, and don't skimp on field expenses. Arrange whatever gives you an edge in catching her.

"I'll handle her letters and the agreements, and I'll work on building the murder cases once we have the names." He looked at his watch. "I'm going up to talk with Thomas Gates as this agreement gets written, and then I'm going to go tell Zane I drafted him for another job. Let's meet back here later this afternoon."

Paul pulled out a chair at the table. "Okay, Sam, I'm back and I'm all yours. Talk me through your plan for catching her while she retrieves the package."

Sam reversed the video on his screen. He told Paul he had sent a local FBI agent to drive through the neighborhood in a van and now had a good video of the area to go along with the street maps and the satellite photos.

Sam paused to point out a house. "I'll be here. There is a good view of the front door and mailbox. I will see anyone who takes the package and be able to get good photographs. If it looks like a middle-aged lady, we'll take her down right there. If it is someone she's sent, we'll settle in to trail them to her."

Sam turned around the street map. "There's only one road leading out of the subdivision, and it has a stop-light. I will call ahead when the package is taken, and they will flip that light to hold at red and not turn green. Those assigned to tail the individual will pick him up as he leaves the subdivision. If the individual leaves the subdivision on foot, we will have teams at all corners of the subdivision to pick up the surveillance. We want to spot the handoff of the papers. We'll have six teams in the area to trade off coverage as he moves.

"We are going to mail the documents overnight mail via the post office. It will be big and blue and be put into the mailbox. If we tried another delivery service, the package gets left between the screen door and the front door, and we can't see it. I want eyes on the package at all times, and I can see it if it's in the mailbox."

Sam paused a moment, then said, "It's possible the homeowner is involved in this. So we have a plan for that contingency. We'll be watching the homeowner. We'll have a team on his car at the school, and we'll know when he leaves for home. If she hasn't taken the package before he gets home, we'll assume he's involved. We'll have a warrant to monitor his home phone and the cell-phone we know about, but the concern is he's carrying a burner phone. So when he gets his mail, we will jam the cell towers so he has to call her on the house line.

If he calls someone, we'll follow where that call leads us. If he doesn't do anything, we will wait and tail him whenever he leaves the house.

"My guess, she'll step in and take the package from his mailbox. But since she doesn't know when the reply will arrive, she has to have someone in the neighborhood watching for it to arrive, or she has someone checking the mail every day. We're going to have a problem being stationed around the neighborhood and not being seen. The biggest risk is she spots us and abandons the pickup. If there's no activity after forty-eight hours, she well may have decided to walk away. At that point we will step in and interview the homeowner."

"It's a good plan. You're using agents from the local office?"

"Yes. They think we're investigating someone leaking classified documents. Are you sure you don't want to be there, boss? It's going to be an interesting chase."

"If something goes wrong, she's going to be contacting us again. It's better if I'm here. You pick her up, and we'll celebrate together when you get back."

"I'll head out just as soon as you have the document."

"I'll be back with it signed in about two hours."

The next morning, Paul set up a series of monitors and audio feeds in the war room, with the names Sam, Rita, and Ann labeled on the feeds. He would spend much of the next few weeks in this secure room, reading, listening to updates, working problems, and he might as well be organized and comfortable while he did so. Rita would focus on the tapes, Sam on catching the lady shooter, and he'd work on answers to the questions sketched out on the board.

"Sam, audio check."

"You're loud and clear, boss. Five minutes and I'll have a feed for you of the mailbox I'm watching."

"I've got a monitor open for it."

"Rita."

She was in the audio lab downstairs and looked over to wave at the camera. "Boss, you should see the tools Nathan has in here. He can make me sing on perfect pitch."

"Enjoy it." Paul knew Rita and Nathan had set up the original taping equipment the middleman had on his phones in order to test out what could be used as additional authentication for the tapes.

Paul tried a secure call to Ann. Her picture appeared, stabilized. "Hi, gorgeous."

She glanced over and grinned. "You're being kind."

She was home. He could see her living room behind her. "What are you doing?"

"Working on a story."

"Mind if I leave you up on the monitor? This is the war room just off the conference room. I'm in monitor mode. The reply gets delivered today, and Sam is running the op to try and catch her."

"No problem. When it gets busy there, just mute me out so I don't have to try and follow your conference-room chatter. I'll wave if I want you to toss audio back on."

"Will do. Good story?"

"Ask me in a few hours."

"I'll do that."

He muted her screen as he saw a mailbox appear on the far screen. "I'm getting your feed, Sam."

The package had been sitting in the mailbox for the last two hours, and nothing approached the mailbox except a sparrow looking for somewhere to land. Paul was watching the same video as Sam. "I hate this waiting."

Ann paused what she was typing to glance over. She pointed to the plate on his table. "Eat. From your personnel file I would have thought you were an expert at stakeouts."

"I'm remembering now why I enjoy leaving fieldwork to others. You've started reading my file?"

"I have."

He reached for the sandwich. She didn't volunteer anything else about what she'd read or what she thought. He wanted to start a conversation, but while her hands were on the keyboard he was trying to keep his remarks to her at a minimum. He forced his attention back to Sam. "Sam, how are you doing?"

Sam put a hand into the mailbox video feed to wave. "I'm having to get up and pace to keep my legs from going to sleep. She's good at this, boss. She didn't show up five minutes after the mail arrived when we were most ready to react."

"I hear you." The afternoon was wearing on.

Paul finished the sandwich. He picked up an interview only to put it back down, and then simply took a few more minutes to watch Ann. She had been typing at a good clip ever since he had put her up on the monitor this morning. She paused occasionally to scroll back in the text to read a few pages, often stopping entirely just to look at the screen and think. This was Ann writing, and he would really like to know what she was working on.

He felt something as he watched her that didn't easily get defined. Enjoyment certainly. Fascination. And something a lot more tender.

"Boss."

"Yes, Sam." Paul put his finger on the printout to mark his place and looked to the monitor, expecting to see someone heading for the mailbox, but there was no movement on the video.

"The homeowner is on his way from school. No one's picked up the package yet. We have to assume he's somehow involved in this. We're getting ready to jam the cell towers once he retrieves his mail."

"At least it gets interesting if he's someone who knows who she is, rather than just a random bystander whose mailbox she's using. Let me know when you can."

"Will do."

Rita joined him in the war room. Paul read the audio report she handed him. The tapes would hold up in court.

"He's home, boss," Sam said.

Paul watched the car pulling into the garage and waited for the homeowner to open the front door and retrieve his mail from the front porch mailbox. Twenty minutes passed. The front door stayed closed; the package stayed where it was.

"Well, this is unexpected," Rita finally said.

Paul slid her one of the quarters he had been walking

through his fingers as he killed time. "Welcome to an afternoon of adrenaline-filled stillness."

Forty minutes later, the front door opened.

"He just retrieved the mail," Sam told his team. "Larry, jam the towers. Let's force him to the house line if he makes a call."

Paul watched the front door close and waited for word from Sam there was a call being intercepted. The garage door stayed closed, the front door too. Paul gave it an hour. "Sam?"

"This is not good. He's made no calls. He's not preparing to leave. My guys are reporting he's in the kitchen fixing dinner."

"Wonderful. Did anyone see what he did with the mail?"

"No. He didn't have it in his hands when he entered the kitchen, and we didn't see him go upstairs. We don't have good angles on the rest of the house. Boss, we need to release the jam on the cell towers."

"Agreed. And watch for someone to approach the house once it grows dark. He's waiting for someone or some particular time."

"We're adjusting for that now."

"What are you thinking, Rita?"

"She knows we would be watching the address. He isn't making any move to take the package to her. So she asked him to repackage it and mail it to another address?"

"Maybe. Or she thought through what we would do and is countering it. We were the ones eager to see her take the package, and she's countering with a long delay and patience, waiting to throw us off our game. She's doing a good job of it." Paul leaned back in his chair and picked up his quarter. "We've got no choice but to watch and wait."

"Boss?"

"We're still here, Sam."

"It looks like he's turning in for the night. He hasn't done anything, gone anywhere, hasn't made a call. He just got the package, and he's apparently waiting."

"We do the same. Settle in, Sam, but rotate guys to keep fresh eyes on the house. She shows up at three a.m. and he's left the back door open for her, this could happen fast."

"Will do. Go home, boss. I'll call you if there's anything. You too, Rita."

Rita covered a yawn, and gave an apologetic smile. "That sounds like good advice."

Paul glanced at the monitor where Ann was still working. She'd ducked out for half an hour to fix herself a sandwich, then left for about an hour to walk Black, but otherwise she'd been writing the entire day. It looked like her concentration was fully engaged and she was still going strong. "I'll stay around a bit longer."

Rita got up, glanced at the screen for Ann, and smiled at Paul. "You have to admire her ability to work. She makes me tired just watching her."

"It's the first time I've seen her working on a story beyond just yellow legal pads and handwritten notes. It's been instructive."

Rita picked up a marker and added a note to the board. "I underestimated our lady shooter. She knows how to create an opening. I don't know her plan, but I'm beginning to appreciate what it might be. We're getting distracted and fragmented, and he's just sitting there. Our homeowner leaves, does he take the package with him or leave it behind in his house? A few days from now when he goes to school, does he take the package with him or leave it behind in his house? Another few hours or few days of this, she catches us at a shift change, she arranges a distraction, she might be able to walk up to the house and walk out with the package."

Paul nodded. "We learned something about her today. We learned she has patience. We're going to have to have more than she does if we are going to catch her. Head home, Rita. I'll see you tomorrow."

"'Night, boss."

Paul waited until Rita left, then waved at Ann. She clicked on the audio. "Hi." He had pulled her out of a train of thought, and she visibly shifted gears to focus on him.

"Our teacher took his mail inside and didn't call anyone, didn't go anywhere. He fixed himself dinner, watched some TV, and just turned in for the night. No one has picked up the package. Apparently it's just sitting there."

"You have to admire her plan. She just freezes everything you set up to catch her."

"What do you think?"

"One of you will blink first. You don't want it to be you. You wait."

"My thoughts too. She's good."

"I hear admiration in your voice."

"We would have caught her years ago if she wasn't

this good at staying in the shadows. I can admire her tactics even as I try to outthink her."

"She's had time to plan, and that time has put all this in her favor. I'd guess something simple. He mails it on to her. If he dumps a few hundred letters into several mailboxes on his way to school Monday morning, what are you going to do?"

"Cross that bridge when it arrives."

She smiled. "She wants the document. She doesn't want you to trail it to her. She'll get what she wants. You should head home, Paul. Lack of sleep isn't going to help this."

"Soon. Are you about ready to call it a night?"

"I've got a bit more to do."

"I'll let you get back to it."

"Thanks for the update." She was already reading what was on her screen.

He had always understood and appreciated the difference between a night owl and a morning lark, but he was beginning to physically feel it now. She was wide awake, and he could feel fatigue beginning to grip his muscles. He got up to get himself a cold soda.

He wanted to know what Ann was like during what she considered the best hours of her day, and while he hadn't realized there would be an opportunity today, it was here and he wanted to know. He settled in to watch Ann, wishing he was at home in a more comfortable chair.

She finally stopped writing shortly after one a.m. She saved the work and stretched. Then she yawned and popped her jaw and wilted as the energy that was left in her ran out. She reached for her soda and glanced at the can a second time when she realized it was empty.

"Having read your books, I somehow had a picture in my mind of what writing was like. I didn't expect it to be easy, but I didn't think it was this intense for every step forward."

"Being a cop is work. This is something I just love to do."

"I've enjoyed watching you. So . . . you read my personnel file."

She rested her chin in her hands and grinned. "I did. Want to hear what I thought?"

"Been curious about that all day."

"I thought you might be. I've got one word for you, Paul, and it's *wow*. You've been holding out on me, buddy. You were a hotshot in your newbie agent days. Out there putting bravery into actions."

He felt his face get warm and was glad she'd waited until they were alone to have the conversation. "I was too green to realize the idiot I was being. I got shot twice for that enthusiasm."

"Even though you had told me those episodes were there, they stunned me on the first read-through. But given you survived, I managed to find a glimmer of humor on the third read-through—if you're going to get shot, at least you have interesting stories to tell. First through the door after a murder suspect, and he's waiting by the door to shoot the first cop who enters? I'd say you got lucky to just get shot in the shoulder. Second hit—I don't know how you avoid that one either. A teenager on a stairwell landing pulls the trigger on a shotgun when you come to question his father in a murder. Those kind of volatile encounters are going to happen if you're a cop long enough."

"The hospital stays were something I never want to repeat."

"I wondered occasionally why you aren't married already, but now that I see the file, it's a little more obvious. You were all over the nation that first decade. You were never somewhere long enough to have a really serious relationship."

"That, and I didn't want a wife to temper my do-whatever-needs-done attitude. A wife means being home occasionally, not taking outsized risks."

"Still feel that way?"

"Time at home still feels like a must. The outsized risks—that more depends on my wife. The line gets drawn in a lot of ways. And what was a risk when I was a newbie is probably not as much of a risk now. At least I want to think experience helps with judgment. What are you smiling at?"

"I've got friends who think a close-quarters gunfight, outnumbered two to one, is a routine day at the office. It's relative."

"I'd probably flinch if I knew some of the places, circumstances, and times you fly."

"You would, and you'd have reason to. I can get a plane into some marginal places if it has to be done. I don't go looking for the chance to prove it, but I get volunteered occasionally by a friend." She leaned back in her chair. "So . . . change of subject. You didn't have a girlfriend in high school, college, that you thought might be the true love of your life?"

"I made a point of having good friends, but not as far as having one lady who thought I was her future." He hesitated.

"You aren't going to ask me."

"Not sure I want to know the answer."

She smiled. "I got close twice in my twenties. Edged toward falling in love with two good guys—enough to meet their families and spend a lot of time together for a couple years. In both cases, somewhere in those last days before I got offered a ring, I stepped back. One had a tense relationship with his mom that raised a red flag, and the other could slip into moody for no reason I could figure out. The only hint for who they would be fifty years in the future was the subtle stuff I could see about who they were then. I probably was too cautious—they were and are nice men. In both cases I finally decided I didn't want to live with either one of them for the rest of my life. Then I decided I wanted to be a cop, and that kind of changed my priorities. It was hard enough building a relationship with a guy when my true love was writing, trying to figure out how to tell a story. Add cop to that mix and I had bigger priorities than wanting to be a wife and manage a home and talk about having kids."

Her remark generated several more questions he wanted to ask her, but it was growing very late. He tucked them away for another day.

She closed down her files. "Would you call me if something happens tonight? I'm curious."

"I will."

"Then I'll say good night, Paul."

"Thanks for today, Ann."

"I enjoyed it too. You're kind of cute when you are trying to figure out how to kill time."

"Cute?"

She chuckled and dropped the link.

Paul checked in from home at five a.m. with the agents still watching the house, and again at seven a.m. When he called from his office for an update at nine, a tired-sounding Sam answered the call.

"Where're we at?"

"Still quiet. He's retrieved his Saturday newspaper and otherwise hasn't done a thing. No phone calls on the numbers we have. He's got to make a move soon. Teams just rotated here, so there are fresh eyes watching the house. We've got it covered."

"Sorry I'm not there to take a shift."

"It's not so bad. Our host believes in feeding guests, and the coffee is good. I've had worse stakeouts. She says she likes the excitement. I'll call you when something happens, if it ever does. Miss L.S. could have spotted us and simply abandoned the package."

"Stay optimistic. She didn't know when it was going to arrive. Maybe she's the one who missed a connection, or intentionally planned a delay to try and throw us off."

"If she planned with this in mind, it's working. We're going numb watching for something to happen. If it goes another night, I'm going to need to bring in new guys to spell us for a shift."

"Whatever you need."

"I decided about an hour ago that we've finally met a worthy opponent. I'm still wondering why she chose this teacher."

"We'll get that answer eventually. Hang in there, Sam."

Paul hung up and thought about calling Ann, but didn't have anything to tell her that was different than where they were last night. And hopefully she was still sleeping. He got up and went for more coffee.

Paul's phone rang just after eleven a.m. He saw the caller ID and grabbed for it. "Yes, Zane."

"The four tapes just arrived by courier along with the signed agreement."

"You're kidding."

"It's an original document, even an ink stain where the pen bled."

"We never saw her retrieve the package. Any further letter from her?"

"No. Just the four tapes and the document."

"Can you bring them in, Zane?"

"I'm already on the way."

"Take them to Rita when you arrive."

"Will do, Paul."

Sam grabbed his cellphone and answered after the first ring. "Yes, Paul."

"Zane just called. The four tapes and a signed agreement just arrived."

"How?" Sam was shocked. "The teacher hasn't gone out since he took in the mail, and no one has arrived to see him."

"Good question, but she got it."

"Hold on. I'm going to go knock on his door."

Sam walked across to the house they had been watching and rapped on the door, thinking with every step that there were few things in life more frustrating than getting conned. The teacher answered, a cup of coffee in his hand and a puzzled look on his face.

"Mr. Lewis Graves?"

"Yes."

Sam held up his credentials and badge. "I'm FBI Agent Sam Truebone. I need to ask you a question about a piece of mail you received on Friday."

Mr. Graves stepped back and waved him inside, looking perplexed. "What's this about?"

"You received a blue-and-white overnight mailer."

"Yes, the school where I teach sent retirement plan options." He nodded toward the rolltop desk in the next room. The mailer was sitting atop a stack of papers.

"That was the only overnight mailer you received?"

"Yes. What—?"

"We're tracking down a package that was misdirected. It would be helpful if I could have the mailer those documents came in."

"Sure." He retrieved it and passed it over.

Sam looked at a woman's handwriting on the shipping label. He had been the one to write the label for the package they had mailed. "Thank you, sir. I appreciate the help. I won't keep you longer." He stepped outside and pulled out his phone as he walked to his car. "Paul, she switched out the packages. We've been watching an overnight mailer that was school district materials. Where she made the exchange is an interesting question. She's got someone helping her at the post office branch?"

"That's the likely spot. Regardless of how she did it, she's not going to use this same method again. Come on back. We'll let one of the local guys see what they can find at the post office. Let's you and I focus on what the tapes can give us."

Paul called Arthur.

"Interesting," his boss remarked. "She got to the package in transit. It tells us something more about her. If her plan is to intercept the packages we send her, she's going to have to group the tapes. She can only have a handful of these arrangements planned out. So she can't let this string out in a lot of back-and-forth offers. Three, four, maybe five exchanges at most."

"There wasn't another offer in this package."

"Even more interesting. She's giving us time to see how valuable the four tapes are before she makes another offer. That's smart."

"She's planned the details of this, just like she did with her shootings."

"She's going to be a challenge, which means it will be all the sweeter when you do catch her, Paul. We've got six tapes now, and that is progress. Keep me posted."

"Will do, Arthur."

Paul watched Rita neatly write a fifth name on the board. They had six tapes. They had found five voice matches and names. By end of the day she likely would have found a name for the last tape. "Nice work, Rita."

They knew some names of those who had hired a murder. Six out of thirty tapes in hand. He wanted the next tapes and the full truth.

"When do you think we will hear from her again?" Rita wondered.

"A day, maybe two," Sam guessed. "She'll want to get the best deal secured as fast as she can, in case we catch her during one of these exchanges. What's your prediction, Rita?"

"She's patient, she's a planner. Not acting too fast keeps us off-balance. So I'd guess we'll hear from her within a week."

"Boss?"

"A month," Paul replied. "She will want to make very sure there are no leads from this exchange that can be traced back to where she is. She's going to freeze us so we're icy cold before we hear from her again. That's what I would do. I'm afraid that's what she is going to do."

Sam winced. "She's going to drive us crazy."

"I see a lot of time at the gym and at the firing range in our future. The waiting is going to be miserable. Rita, I'm putting you on mail watch. Packages, envelopes, deliveries, anything that might be from her, you have my permission to check for prints and open."

"Done." She considered him. "What does Ann think, boss?"

"That we'll catch her."

Sam grinned. "I knew I liked her."

14

Sluggers Corner across the street from the gym was a popular stop-off for law-enforcement officers, both local and federal. Paul settled on a stool to watch the last of a ball game and ordered a diet soda to go with peanuts from the basket. The Reuben and the roast beef sandwiches were good, but he was thinking he'd fix a stacked cheeseburger when he finally got home. Ann was in Iowa, and there was no particular reason for him to call it an early evening. Two weeks without word from their lady shooter, and there wasn't even work in his briefcase to think about. He'd finish the game here.

"Buy me one of those."

Paul glanced over to see Ann sliding onto the stool beside him, and grinned, delighted to have her with him. He wondered why she'd been walking in the rain. "You're wet." Paul ordered her drink and tugged open his gym bag for a clean towel.

"It's raining." She took the towel, shrugged off her jacket, and wiped her face. Too many cops in the room noticed the side arm, didn't recognize her, and didn't see a badge. Paul held up his.

"Sorry."

"You could turn and say 'MHI.'"

"I'd end up talking shop. Tonight, I came to find you." She accepted the drink with a thanks and picked up a handful of peanuts.

"Are we on for a movie?"

She took a deep swallow of the drink, then a deep breath, and turned to face him. "That was my hope, but I got a call. I'm on my way to Ohio as soon as this weather front clears. I'll likely be there awhile."

He saw it then in her face, and heard it in her voice, and his smile faded. "Something bad."

"Kind of regret I'm the MHI." She nursed the soda and shook it off. "Sorry, tougher for the cop on the other end of the call than for me. I'll know more when I get there. I've got a couple of hours before I want to be in the air. I'll be following the front, and the winds get whippy."

"I can provide dinner if you haven't eaten."

"I'll take you up on that."

"Did you drive?"

"Walked over from seeing Kate."

"I'll bring the car around and pick you up at the door. Let's find a quieter place."

"I don't mind the rain. Lead the way to your car."

He reached for his gym bag and held the door for her.

A few tough days coming at her and she already looked tired. Paul thought through the evening's options and turned the car toward his place. "I've been practicing at making a really good hot chocolate."

She turned her head against the headrest to smile at him. "Sounds wonderful."

"I'll fix us cheeseburgers and fries, and you can flip through my photos and get to know my family. I can give you a laugh or two with some stories I can share."

"Thank you." She closed her eyes. "I was looking forward to the movie."

He reached over and took hold of her hand. She turned hers palm up to interlace her fingers with his.

"My brother Joseph wants to buy a candy business. He sent samples."

She smiled. "I hear a family bribe."

"Great caramels. The current owner has tried to expand too fast and has too much debt, but the product is good and the employees love the company. We'll need to find new markets quickly to stabilize the operation at the production levels they need in order to make the expansion carry itself. It's several hundred thousand more than the Falcon family would normally invest in a business, and the size of the acquisition brings more risk than I'm comfortable with." Paul shook his head.

"What are you going to do?"

"I don't know. I'm talking to God. Looking for an idea. It's hard to mitigate the risk. The business doesn't yet have strong brand value, an intangible asset as best. The production plant is new, but it wouldn't find a buyer at what was spent to build it. The cash we invest would all be at risk. The debt holders need to be willing to take equity in the company, let us buy them out over time as sales build to match the production that is possible. Hope this isn't boring you." He glanced over at her.

She shook her head. "No, sounds nice, and different

than what I've got on my plate today. Writing's a business too, and planes have expenses. You're on familiar terrain with me. What are you thinking you might decide?"

"Joseph is good at execution, he's confident in his abilities, and he could probably pull off the increase in sales in time to meet the debt payments, but part of my job is to protect him from himself. Dad needs to talk to the current debt holders. If there's a deal where they want to work with us, the family could step in as buyer. Otherwise we need to think more about this one."

"Will Joseph agree with you?"

"He wouldn't be asking if he didn't want to listen to advice. Dad is the final opinion whenever we can't reach consensus."

"That will be you in the future."

"One day. I'm in no hurry for it to arrive. Dad plans to live a very long time, and that sounds ideal to me."

He pulled into his long-term parking space. "We walk from here half a block." He reluctantly released her hand and came around to open the door for her.

"Do you like living in this neighborhood?"

"I do. It's in the center of the city, but it's still a neigh-borhood."

He led her through the doors of an architecturally beautiful old brick building, across the lobby, and to the elevators. It took a key to select his floor. "I think I mentioned my family has owned the fourth floor for decades. When my grandfather lived here, I loved to visit. When the choice for me was staying on the East Coast or moving to Chicago, it was this place that made the difference."

"Will you stay in Chicago when you take over leadership of the Falcon family?"

"I took a job with the FBI so I could work wherever the situation needs me to be when that time comes. Jackie loves Chicago and will stay here. Marie likes New York. My father splits his time between here and New York. Harper is comfortable in Boston, Boone in Colorado and Texas, and Joseph has never settled. The cousins are settled on the East Coast."

The elevator stopped and opened into an entryway with a marble floor. Facing the elevator was a large statue of a horse and rider, straight out of the Old West. Ann grinned. "This is unexpected."

"I promised my grandfather it could remain in its place of honor. The rest of the apartment has been redone in more my style, but he loved the Old West." He hung up her jacket and then his on a coatrack.

"With a grandfather like that, you had to love being a boy visiting here."

"I did. Okay, living room is to the left, kitchen and dining room to the right, den and office straight ahead, and down the hall four bedrooms. Why don't you wander around and see the place while I start some dinner?"

"I'd like that."

He was at home in the kitchen and enjoyed the idea of fixing her a meal. He put Jackie's apple cobbler in the oven to warm and turned his attention to cheeseburgers and fries. Comfort foods were a good fit for an evening like this. Ann wandered into the kitchen twenty-five minutes later and slid onto a barstool. "I like your home. You have a nice collection of art."

He slid a mug of hot chocolate over to her, along

with a bag of miniature marshmallows. "There isn't a yard, so I'm inside when I'm home. There isn't much of a view except other buildings from this floor, so I keep art I like around to have something to see and enjoy. It's my way to relax. I wander galleries when I've got a few hours of free time on a weekend."

He turned the hamburgers and added cheese.

"You don't have much clutter. It makes me feel a bit uncomfortable."

He laughed. "You can relax about that. The idea of living in a cluttered place doesn't bother me. I just learned to be neat as a very young man, when I didn't have much stuff and even less room, and I never changed the habit. You're creative and visual, what you're working on is out and seen. I'm not so visual. I don't forget something once I close a drawer. And this is a big place; there's a place for everything with empty drawers left over."

He folded paper towels and scooped the fries from the hot oil to drain. "I'm comfortable with this space even though it's much too large for me. It's designed and intended for kids and pets and family and guests. I rattle around here, but I love it. I host a dinner gathering of friends every month or two—Sam and Rita from work, family friends. Family stop by frequently, stay overnight when they want. I watch a lot of sports, I do paperwork on family matters, and I enjoy fixing an occasional meal. It's a good life, for what Chicago can be."

"It suits you."

He slid a loaded plate in front of her. "A cheeseburger and fries are best eaten hot. Get started while I finish up."

She reached for the ketchup. "No debate from me. I missed lunch." She settled in to enjoy the meal.

He fixed his plate and slid onto the stool beside her. "I'm glad you came, Ann."

"What did you put in this?"

"It is Jackie's secret. I'm not allowed to tell."

"It's a gourmet cheeseburger."

He laughed. "I'm good for a meal anytime you want to stop by."

"No offense, but I think I need to get to know Jackie."

"Her apple cobbler is warming in the oven."

"You're killing me here." She leaned over against his shoulder and paused long enough to close her eyes. "Thanks. I really needed this."

He dropped a kiss on her hair. "My pleasure."

She returned to her French fries. "Why did Jackie become a chef?"

"A food-expert businesswoman."

She laughed. "Her words? I love her already."

"She runs a kitchen like she's on a battleship bridge. I don't know how her chefs survive working with her, but they adore her. They've gone with her to start six restaurants now. They get the concept flourishing, train their replacements to meet their standards, and then go on to the next challenge. It lets them take a few months off between restaurants every three or four years."

He spun the monitor around and flipped open its protective cover. He tabbed over to the folder where he kept family photos. "We've got a private and secure family website where everyone posts pictures and messages, and we keep up with each other's lives. But my favorite pictures over the years I drop into here." He stopped on one he'd snapped of Jackie in a restaurant kitchen and pointed her out among the myriad of busy staff. "Jackie."

"In the midst of all that commotion, she's calmly focused on getting a cupcake perfectly iced."

"A birthday cupcake." He flipped to the next photo.

Ann laughed. "She's a thrower?"

"Her version of a pineapple-upside-down cake flopped. To her credit, she cleans up her own messes. She's tame everywhere but her kitchen, where occasionally emotions get the best of her."

"You love her."

"Yes. Every year for my birthday and also for my other birthday—the day the adoption became final—she makes me a white cake with chocolate icing and sprinkles."

He turned photos and stopped on a picture from last summer. "My brothers—Harper, Boone, and Joseph." The memory was a good one. They were sitting on the beach as the sun went down, sunburned, windburned, tired, and content. He clicked on one more photo. "My sister Marie."

"You haven't mentioned her."

"Because she prefers I don't brag on her too much. You're like her in some ways. She hates the limelight and any attention. Marie likes to understand how a business works. How something gets done. How something gets made. She'll wander around an enterprise asking questions and being curious and come back with what is going on and how it can be changed to make it faster and more consistent, which in turn leads to better service and better quality. She's the family's secret special sauce for making a business profitable.

"She's married now, lives in New York. Her husband worked for my father, and fell in love with her. You see them together and you think 'perfect couple.' She is so happy with him, and he loves her beyond any description."

"Marcus and Shari are like that. A perfect fit."

Paul got up to get the apple cobbler. "The family is getting together next weekend. If you're back from Ohio, you should come with me and meet them in person."

"You know they are going to get ideas if you bring me along."

He smiled. "Falcons aren't slow about the obvious. I figure they'll be a plus in my column for what you think about me."

"They no doubt will be."

He placed a bowl of the apple cobbler with a scoop of vanilla ice cream in front of her and handed her a spoon. "Enjoy."

She did.

He cleared the remains of their dinner, watching her turn reflective and into her own thoughts. He'd caught her glance at the clock. "Going to be okay for a flight tonight? It's a long trip."

"I'm a night owl. The trip won't be a problem." She took her time on the last of the cobbler. "She is brilliant with food."

She brought over her bowl and slid it in the dishwasher. "Thanks for tonight."

He settled his arms around her and gave her a comfortable hug. She leaned against him. "Glad you came and found me," he said, relieved when she relaxed in his arms, and content with the moment and the memory tonight would be for them both. "Come on. I'll drop you off at the airport."

"I can take a cab."

"You could. I'd rather have that time."

It was a forty-minute trip, and he let her have the silence. He drove through the private side of the airport and to the hangar she pointed out. "Call me when you land?"

"Sure."

He took her hand to pause her. "If it gets on top of you, call me."

She studied his face and nodded. "I will."

He released her and watched her stride toward the flight line. He could have asked where in Ohio, could have asked who had called. But some of what she did was, by her own definition, private. She'd help who had called, and he'd do what he could to help her when she got home.

Paul watched the news, and it didn't take Ann telling him for him to realize she was working the murder of a cop by another cop. He knew how difficult the days would be for her, but as much as he thought about her, he chose not to call. She'd have her head down doing the job, and sometimes it took that focus to simply survive a difficult case. He waited for the call saying she was finally home. The video call came five days later. "I'm glad you're home, Ann," he said, sharing a smile with her.

"So am I."

She looked exhausted, but he kept that opinion to himself. "How's Black?"

She rolled her eyes. "You want to borrow him for a few days? He's sulking, as only he can. He's not talking to me anymore, and I even brought him presents." She looked toward the hallway. "Four presents!"

Black howled back.

"I'm going to be paying for this trip for a long time. My dog-sitting friends have two young boys who adore Black. He's had his photo taken wearing their football helmet, created two masterpiece paw paintings, and had his tail braided with ribbons." She found the photos and held them up so he could see.

Paul laughed at the images. That poor dog.

"Black could put a paw on each boy and hold them in place just by looking at them, so I don't think he particularly minded the boys. I think the real problem was the four kittens that followed him everywhere, thinking he was their mom. Black actively dislikes cats, even small ones, and there wasn't a thing he could do about them. He's not happy with me. He ignored dinner. I'm going to try ice cream next, as that is a decent bribe."

"Let me know how that goes."

"Will do."

"You must be really tired. Why don't you fix yourself some hot chocolate and go stretch out. I'll be around."

"I think I'd better. Even for me it was a long few days."

⬇

Paul returned to the den with a bowl of popcorn and a cold drink. He looked over at the screen and was relieved to see Ann stretched out on the couch, her writing pad now on the coffee table. She was either thinking with her eyes closed or she had finally slipped into sleep.

He found a ball game to watch. He was nearly as tired as she was. The hurry-up-and-wait of the case was grinding him down.

The ball game finally ended with a pop-up caught in center field. Paul glanced again at the monitor.

Ann was still sleeping, but it wasn't a calm sleep. He watched as a nightmare rolled across her face, and saw restless movements as her body fought to get out of the dream. He couldn't use the video connection to wake her up—she'd muted the audio and hadn't turned it back on when she'd finished an earlier phone call. He reached for his phone to call and wake her, began to dial. She jerked awake, breathing hard. He slowly put his phone back down. She was deathly pale. She sat up and reached for the balled-up towel and held it against her mouth, trying to stop herself from being sick.

Black, worried, crowded in beside her. She took a deep breath and another and ran a shaky hand through her hair. Black tried to get up on her lap, and she reassured him with a kiss on his head. She got to her feet, but she was unsteady. She disappeared toward the kitchen.

What was she dreaming that put such panic on her face?

Ten minutes later she returned bundled up in a white sweater and sank into one of the tall wingback chairs. She reached for the television remote and flipped through channels, eventually stopping on an old movie. She needed the sleep, but he knew from what he had seen that she wouldn't be sleeping again for several hours.

He could call her and have her un-mute the video for a conversation, but invading her privacy right now risked having her pull away. She was fighting to get her mind settled. He felt slightly sick himself, having seen how bad it was. Vicky's words warning him about the nightmare had just taken substance.

On a hunch, Paul saved and replayed the video, wondering all the time if this was too personal, too private. But he cared too deeply to ignore what he had seen. He moved to slow motion at the point just before Ann jerked awake. And then he saw it. The flinch and sharp pain that coursed through her body in the instant before she awoke. A gunshot. Vicky had said Ann woke to the sound of a gunshot. He replayed that moment and knew it was even worse than that. She woke to the *pain* of a gunshot. Her mind was reliving it.

Paul waited until their conversation had turned quiet the next night before he brought it up. "You had a bad dream last night. What are you dreaming about, Ann?"

She glanced over to catch his gaze for a moment, and he could see the wince as she realized what he had seen, but then she sighed and shrugged as she looked away. "Being a cop brings with it some bad dreams. It's a fact of life for me. I quit my job, maybe I dream less. But since I'm not willing to do that, I live with the dreams."

"How often do they come?"

"Often enough I simply assume I will have one."

"I'm sorry for that."

"So am I. I've learned to cope with it. Change the subject, Paul."

He knew when a subject was a serious hurt, and this

was one. She lived with a dream that left her sick when she woke up. There was something big behind that, more than just work-related events that kept aggravating the memory. He tucked it away to come back to later, and changed the subject.

15

The sun had turned the day hot in a way that made the air shimmer, and sweat had Paul's shirt sticking to his back. He wished he'd thought to wear white today rather than blue, for even the perception of being cooler would be welcome.

Sam peered at the target sheet he was holding. "That last round is on the line. It caught an edge of white."

Paul finished picking up the ejected casings and glanced again at the target sheet. "You're seeing things, Sam." They'd been shooting competitive for two hours and were still tied, the count drifting back and forth two points on either side, neither man able to knock the other out by the required five points. "You want to challenge?"

Sam held the target sheet up to the sunlight. "Yeah. I'm challenging." He dug another twenty out of his pocket, and Paul held up his hand to signal the shooting judge to come over for a ruling. He'd taken eighty dollars off Sam today and would love to make it an even hundred.

FULL DISCLOSURE

His phone rang. Paul dug it out of his pocket. When he saw the caller was Rita, he caught Sam's shoulder and held the phone so they could both hear without putting the call on speaker. "Yes, Rita."

"Boss, there's a letter from her in today's mail. I recognize the colored stationery she's using. I can see it through the envelope."

"Open it, Rita, and see what she's offering."

"Hold on."

Sam pointed the shooting judge to the target sheet they were debating. The man pulled out his jeweler's eyepiece and studied the shot. "Clean inside."

Paul grinned and pocketed Sam's twenty bucks.

"It's the same light green stationery, and the response goes to a street address in Indiana. She's offering four tapes—high-profile names—in exchange for serving her time in a prison in the state of Wisconsin."

"Who does she know in Wisconsin?" Sam asked, surprised. "Do you remember anything in the file about Wisconsin? I don't."

"I don't either," Rita said.

"Run everything for prints, Rita. Sam and I are on the way." Paul pocketed his phone.

"I was beginning to think she'd disappeared," Sam said, digging the car keys out of his pocket as they headed to the parking lot. "You said it would be a month, and it was, almost to the day. I hope she doesn't hold to that pattern or it's going to be a long year."

"It's an asymmetrical deal—four high-profile tapes in return for a location. It suggests someone important to her lives in Wisconsin."

"Has to be," Sam agreed. "The difference for her serving time in one state versus another would be marginal based on the climate in the state, but the federal prisons themselves don't differ much in their routines. Maybe someone important to her would visit her in prison in Wisconsin? Or is it something else entirely—someone within the prison system she's bribed to make her life easy once she's inside?"

Paul opened the passenger door. "Our lady shooter just tipped her hand, if we can figure out what Wisconsin means."

"'High profile.' Those are interesting words."

"At least the next few days are not going to be boring."

"Wisconsin is a peculiar request," Ann agreed, pulling out the chair at the hotel table to take a seat and finish her dinner. "I'm saying that while ignoring the fact I'm currently in the state of Wisconsin. Four high-profile names in return for a prison in this state is simply odd."

Paul added a legal pad of notes to the stack of papers destined for his briefcase, then glanced back to the video. "I've been over the case file, and nothing—not a murder she did, not even a middleman phone call—went to the state of Wisconsin. I couldn't even find that state in anything related to one of the victims."

"She could be simply tossing out a red herring. Here, Agent Falcon, go spin your wheels with this little gem for a while."

"I'd be inclined to believe that except for the fact she's giving up four tapes with high-profile names to get this agreement." He'd been working the problem with Rita and Sam all day and there was nothing to be found.

"The director decided we'll take the deal, but continue to worry about it because it doesn't make sense. Miss L.S. wants this reply to be sent to an address in Indiana. It's in a subdivision again. But I'm sure she's going to throw something new at us."

"She doesn't want to get caught. That's the one thing you can count on about her."

"Such has been my day. What are you up to, Ann?"

"Someone murdered a college student and left his body in a stolen car at a rest stop just outside Madison. It's an absolute puzzle. The primary is stumped and so am I, so I'm hoping for some inspiration by reread-ing everything tonight." She held up a three-ring binder murder book.

"Looks like some light reading."

"I've worked this case before, and we focused on a teaching assistant from the college, but that idea turned cold. When my cop called, I thought, this time I need to look at the family. I think it was his mom who came and shot him, not someone from the college, not a stranger. Don't ask me why that is sitting out there as an idea, but it is."

"You picked up something before, and it is just now jelling in your mind."

"Probably. Anyway, that's my evening."

"Wish I was there to help you."

"Wish I could explain Wisconsin for you. If you like I can ask around among the state police guys up here. Maybe there's something odd about federal prisons in Wisconsin."

"It wouldn't hurt, as I've got nothing now. Don't work too late, Ann."

"I won't. Thanks for calling, Paul. I appreciate hearing the news."

After she dropped the link, Paul closed his. She had looked somewhat more rested, focused on the job. He wondered a bit about the murder case she was on, but there was not much he could offer without being there. He picked up his briefcase and took himself home. The idea of going home to an empty place grew less appealing every day.

Two days later in the small war room, Paul looked again at the dark monitor with Ann's name on it. He wished he could make her appear on the screen, if only for a few minutes to see how she was doing. He looked toward the video Sam had set up, watching a second attempt play out to catch the lady shooter. This mailbox had a daisy painted on the top curve of the box.

"I'm back, boss."

"Any problems?"

"None," Sam replied. "The postman looked at the address, sorted the big trays in the back of his vehicle, showed me the other mail going to the house, and added our package to the stack. He's a twenty-year veteran of the post office and a former marine. The reply is safe with him. The only thing that caught my attention was the number of blue-and-white overnight mailers in the bins. I asked, and he said some company had done an overnight prize envelope to every address in the neighborhood. Being a suspicious sort, I'm wondering if those originated with her."

"I wouldn't be surprised. She'll have something planned, Sam."

"I'll try to be ready."

"Boss."

"Right here, Sam." Paul pushed through the door and into the war room, looked over at the monitor, and saw mail was now in the daisy mailbox.

"The postman just delivered the mail and our package wasn't part of it."

"It isn't simply folded over?"

"It isn't there. I'm backing up the video to get a closer look at what he had for the address. A lot of letters, one magazine, one of those prize envelopes, but no blue-and-white package from us. The four corners were marked with a bold red line from a felt-tip pen so I could spot the mailer no matter how it was carried. I'll get back to you. I'm going to go check it out and find the carrier."

Paul also backed up the video. Sam was right. The package he had given the courier wasn't in the delivered mail.

Sam returned in thirty minutes. "She got it out of the delivery van. The lock has been jimmied. The carrier parks in the same place every day, in the shade in the curve of the road, so his walk on the route is equal distance from the truck both ways. It's out of direct sight to any of the homes, and traffic is light. She could do it without being seen. We'll dust for prints and talk to everyone we had watching the neighborhood, but I doubt we get lucky. She's slippery, boss, and she's good at this, or more likely, she's paid good help."

"We never thought it would be easy. Make some inquiries, then come on home, Sam. There will be plenty to do when the four tapes arrive."

"Will do, boss."

Paul quickly muted the baseball game and leaned over to accept the incoming video call from Ann.

"I'm home, Paul." Black stood up and planted his front feet on her desk so he could see what Ann was holding. "Down, you beautiful beast, I'm not sharing." She backed up and the dog came with her.

Paul laughed. "You're not going to win that conversation."

"It's bologna and cheese—you'd think it's a steak or something."

The dog's ears perked up.

"No, I don't have any of that word that shall not be mentioned for you to share." Laughing, she backed into a chair. She let Black have the last bite of her sandwich and rubbed his furry head.

"Did Wisconsin get solved?"

"Maybe pushed a little further along. The primary is going to take another look at the brother. Something odd is going on with the case, but whatever it is, it's not obvious to either of us. I expect I'll go back in a few days if this idea goes dry." She found Black's ball and sent it rolling down the hall with the dog in corner-crashing pursuit. "How are things going for you?"

"She's got the agreement. We're still waiting on the four tapes to arrive."

"So you're watching a ball game. I'm proud of you. You're not working."

"And I'm shopping for birthday presents. I could use some help."

"Sure."

"The first is for Kelly." He clicked through pictures, found one of the group at the last family picnic, and slid it into the video portion of the screen for Ann. "She's the one with the pink shirt and shoes. She is fifteen, exuberant, outgoing, loves dogs, and talks about being a vet." He held up a catalog with two circled ideas. "So tell me—which of these do you prefer?"

"The red bag. Very useful."

"Good call. Birthday two is Emily." He studied the photo. "Sitting on the picnic table, holding her two-year-old brother. Emily is thirteen, a touch shy, loves babies and dolls, and has a good eye for fashion. She sketches clothes."

"A nice set of pastel pencils. She'd love them."

He wrote it down. "Thanks. Got plans for your evening?"

"None." She picked up her glass and settled more comfortably into her favorite chair. "I might dig out a jigsaw puzzle later if I get really bored."

"Then I've got a question for you. Something I've wondered at. Who do you talk to, Ann, when you've had a really bad day?"

"Where did that question come from? Shari, Kate, Rachel, Vicky, whichever one I happen to talk with first, all of them before I'm done. I don't have that many bad days. Bad cases, sure. But personal bad days—that's when Black about gets hit by a car, or I get violently sick from something I ate. I can roll with the odd flat tire, a water-heater problem, and the ants that got into the kitchen."

"You got ants in your kitchen?"

"A couple of months ago. The worst part was Black deciding he could help by licking them up. They started running all over him and got into his eyes and nose and ears, and he went howling on me and frantically wild. I had to tackle him and put the hose in his face to wash out his eyes and mouth and nose and ears and then give him a bath on top of it. He didn't speak to me for days afterwards, and he'd walk out of any room I entered."

"Steak bribed him back?"

"The second one. The first one he actually looked at me, looked at the steak I'd cut up for him, and I could almost hear him say, I'm still upset with you, and then he turned and walked away." She laughed. "Midnight and I have had our moments."

She tipped her near-empty glass toward him. "New question."

He thought about it as he studied her, then smiled. "An observation and a question. Most people are constantly interacting—texting, emails, phone calls, visits. You aren't. Numerous shared evenings now, and it's a pattern. Is there a reason you are so solitary, Ann? Your days flow by without seeing people unless they come into your circle."

"I've spent some evenings with you."

"Set us aside, and think about it. I'm curious, Ann."

"Hold on, I'm going to get a refill." She came back in a minute and settled in the chair she favored. "I don't easily give up a day or evening alone to fill it with people.

The MHI requests always eventually come, so I guess I treat every day I'm home as a vacation. I tend to keep my vacations people-free. I like to sleep in, read, write, walk with Black, and just have time to think. Fill my time up and there isn't time for that. Book ideas are born in those quiet days, after I'm still enough for long enough that my subconscious can begin to lay out something interesting. I can't think deeply if I'm interrupted every few hours. I like the solitude."

"Do you feel like you need more of it than you have now?"

"If I had a month of solitude, I'd love it—I'd make good progress on a book. But life's a pretty good balance right now, I have to say. I'm somewhere on an MHI case most of the time. I'm often seeing friends or talking with them. I'm just not planning when it happens. I enjoy people, I enjoy a good conversation and doing something together, but I don't require it in my week. I do need several hours of quiet."

"I'm much more people-involved," Paul offered, "even though I can do without the crowds. I need those interactions to feel like I know what's going on. If I don't talk to someone for a few weeks, it feels wrong."

"You're wired to be head of the family, head of your team. You'll be good at it. You need the day-to-day. I guess I don't."

Her phone rang. She looked over at it, then gave him an amused smile. "Want to guess? MHI or friend?"

"Hope it's not MHI."

She answered the phone. "This is Ann."

She started writing, and he knew she was about to be leaving.

When she hung up the phone, she folded the note. "Sorry, Paul. I need to get Black dropped off and get out of here. Nevada. A bit out of my normal territory, but a cop I know needs an opinion before he proceeds, and he wouldn't be asking if it wasn't bothering him. This one's a personal favor. Just for the record, I used to date him."

"I appreciate you telling me that. How often do MHI calls come in on top of each other?"

"Most of the time they overlap while I'm in the field, and I fly from one case to the next. This is the first time this year I'm arriving and leaving home on the same day." Ann opened the lockbox and retrieved her side arm, tucked credentials in her pocket, then picked up her go-bag. "Black, want to go for a ride?"

The dog looked like he wanted to protest, then picked up his bear and headed toward the hall.

Ann watched him walk away. "This is going to be fun."

Paul smiled, knowing Black was going to give her fits, depending on where she dropped him off. "Safe flying, Ann."

She laughed. "Always. Good night, Paul." She dropped the link.

He closed down his. She was flying late, but he wasn't worried about the hour or the distance she was going. She did this routinely, and he'd rather have her in the air than on a highway for that amount of time.

The more conversations Paul had with her, the more intriguing she became. She was unlike anyone he had ever met before. Content for the most part just to be. Maybe that was the core of it. She wasn't out wanting more than life was already giving her.

He considered finishing the ball game, then shut off

the television. He'd call it a night. He found, not for the first time, that he was more relaxed after being in her company than anything else he did.

———————▼———————

Two days later, Paul shifted in his office chair, reading through emails, sending replies, and trying to pretend impatience wasn't crawling up his spine. His phone rang, he saw the caller ID, and grabbed for it. "Yes, Zane."

"Four tapes marked High Profile have arrived by courier, along with a signed copy of the agreement."

"We mail it, it never arrives, and yet she has it. You've got to admire her arrangements."

"I've already talked to Rita. I'll have them in her hands within the hour."

"Thanks, Zane."

———————▼———————

Paul entered Suite 906 shortly after six o'clock the next morning. For the first time in his memory he had arrived before Margaret. He passed her desk and walked back to his boss's office. "Good morning, Arthur."

"Morning, Paul. Grab some coffee. I'll get the director on a conference call, even if I have to bump him off another one."

"Appreciate it, sir." He poured himself a mug of coffee and took a seat across from Arthur's desk. Paul had brought no notes, for he wasn't going to forget the information Rita had given him. He needed the coffee since he'd been at the office until two a.m.

"Hello, Paul." The director's voice came clearly through the speakerphone.

"Director." A year ago, Paul would have felt at least the edge of nerves at being on a conference call with the FBI's director, but time had changed matters. He was relaxed and tired enough he was fighting to keep from yawning.

"I understand four tapes have arrived. She said they were high profile. Was she stretching that or are they as advertised?"

Paul gave a slight smile, appreciating both the question and the answer he had. "Rita's good at her job. She had them matched in less than a day. One is a former governor, another a mob boss, and two are high-ranking officials in the State Department."

Arthur stopped what he was about to say to look over.

"The mob boss is Daylor Globe," Paul added.

"The two at State?" the director asked.

"William Fisher and Jack Chase."

"I've met Fisher and heard of Chase. Those names alone would draw a press firestorm. She has—what, twenty tapes left?"

"Yes, sir."

"Makes you wonder what else she has. Thanks for the update."

"We'll be in touch, Director." Arthur ended the call. "Daylor Globe. He's been so careful I thought I'd never see that name on an arrest warrant. When this began, I had hopes the tapes would be worth something to us, but I never imaged this. It's going to be more than nice making these arrests."

"Very. If she's got tapes like this, we want them all."

"Do whatever you have to, Paul, to clamp down on security for this case. We can't afford word leaking out that the lady shooter has been in touch or that these tapes exist."

"I've been thinking on it, Arthur. It was a month between the tapes and this last letter. If she stays with that pattern, this could take six months to a year before the thirty tapes are in our hands, before we can turn the corner to ramp up personnel and go make arrests. Security for that length of time is going to be a problem.

"No one involved is the type to say a careless word out of place, but the pattern of people coming and going is a concern. Sam, Rita, and I are spending time in the secure war room; the director and Tori Scott have been in town. You can put together something is happening by watching the people involved.

"I'm going to work on some way to divert attention from what's going on. Vacation time thrown in the mix, a different case that we focus on, or something that involves the three of us that can serve as a cover. I need a way to push the tapes into the background if someone is curious about what we're doing."

"Agreed," Arthur said. "Your primary task is to work the letters and tapes when they arrive, and create a smoke screen for the rest of the time. Success is getting to the day of arrests without news of this case getting out. You'll figure it out. Let me know what I can do to help."

"Thank you, sir."

Paul was glad Ann was back home from Nevada. He enjoyed his evenings a lot more when she was part of them. She was now stretched out on her couch with a pad of paper, working longhand on a story. His relationship with her was unlike any he'd ever imagined. Her stillness was immense. And he found himself a bit jealous of an unknown cop in Nevada who had once dated her. He found that fact a bit disconcerting. Both the fact and his attitude.

Ann glanced up from her pad of paper. She smiled. "What? You've got that look that says I'm a puzzle to you again."

"You are, but I like figuring out puzzles. I'm just thinking."

"About?"

"You're quiet, Ann. The more time I spend with you, the more I realize that."

"I thought that was pretty obvious."

"I'm curious. Are you as quiet inside your mind too? When you're with friends you trust, do you have a lot you want to say? Or is your mind as still and quiet as you often are?"

"What a wonderful question." She tilted her head, sat up, and set aside the pad of paper. "I'm pretty quiet. Even when I'm not tired, the real me is pretty quiet inside. With people I'm not shy, not timid, but I am quiet. I listen. I hear what's being said. If it's someone I trust, I'll return confidences in kind. When someone risks with me, I'll risk back. But I rarely initiate, even when it's comfortable, safe surroundings and a group of friends. In tennis terms, I prefer to return rather than serve."

"Why is that?"

"I don't like being in the spotlight, even when it's with friends. I am most comfortable one-on-one, when the topics are going where someone else wants to direct them."

She hesitated. "No, let me modify that. I am comfortable talking with God. I initiate conversations with Him all the time, on easy topics, hard topics, what's going on, and with the emotions I want to express in full color. If you really want to know, the Ann inside speaks freely and often only to God."

"You're safe with God."

"I am. So that's where I thrive. It's not that I hide with my friends. There are very few subjects, if any, I haven't shared with at least one friend. I trust friends with my secrets. I talk about what matters to me all the time. But there are large chunks of who I am, of what I think about and talk about, that reside only between myself and God. I don't think that will ever change."

"How have you learned to trust God like that, Ann?"

She shrugged. "I'm God's daughter. He's possessive of me. I like that fact, that certainty, that God chose me and considers me His. So I give God me. When I have something to say, when I want to talk, He's listening. When I need a friend, He's there. When I need something, God's got it covered. God and I are good together. We've got a relationship."

"Would you ever let someone else know you like that? Well, at least in the neighborhood of like that?"

"I don't know. I can show you glimpses of who I am, the inside Ann, but it's not an easy request. Lovely knows me."

"Lovely?"

Paul saw her visibly wince. She got quiet and busy, standing up and picking up her bowl and drinking glass. She looked shaken.

"Ann?"

She shook her head and disappeared into the kitchen. *Lovely knows me.*

Who was Lovely? What had just happened?

He heard a phone ring. She came back in the room, on the phone. "It's Kate," she told him. "I'm going to be a few minutes." She muted the conference call audio.

He watched her as the phone call with Kate went on and turned long. He hesitated, then picked up the phone himself. He called Vicky.

"Can I ask you a question about Ann, an important question, but one that might feel like you're crossing a line?"

"Try me."

"Has she ever mentioned Lovely to you? It's a person's name."

"Last name, first name?"

"She just said Lovely."

"I'm sorry, no. What's going on, Paul?"

"She said something I don't think she meant to say, and I just landed down one of those deep tunnels Dave mentioned. I'll figure it out. Thanks for taking the question, Vicky."

"Wish I could have been more helpful."

Paul hung up the phone and watched Ann, her attention still focused on Kate's call. He'd never seen that set of expressions on her face before, an almost raw grief.

He picked up the phone again and called Dave. "Is something serious going on? I'm watching Ann and Kate have a very long and very serious conversation."

"An old case Kate and Ann worked together has resurfaced. Two murdered kids. The dad just got a new trial. The surviving sibling just hung herself with a suicide note saying they were going to let the monster out, and she didn't want to be around when it happened."

Paul closed his eyes. "I appreciate the info, Dave."

Ann's call with Kate lasted almost an hour. He saw her open the lockbox and withdraw her service weapon. She added a jacket over her shirt and then pushed a pad of paper in her back pocket. She turned the audio back on. "Sorry, Paul. I need to call it a night. I'm going for a long walk with Black." Her voice was clear, her face shadowed by grief.

"Dave told me. I'm sorry, Ann."

"It happens, way more often than I'd like, I'm afraid. I'll talk to you tomorrow."

"Tomorrow," he agreed.

Paul called Ann as soon as he was home. She answered the video with an absent-sounding, "Hold on, still typing." She hit keys to save her work and looked his way. She smiled. "Hi."

"Have you had dinner yet?"

"A late lunch. I got some writing done and hadn't paused to think food."

"Go find something and I'll do the same. We'll share dinner together."

"Sure."

He returned in just under thirty minutes and set a plate of spaghetti and meatballs on the desk, along with a side plate of toasted French bread. She was reading over what she had written that afternoon.

"What did you find?"

She tipped her bowl. "A carryout from Neva's. She saved me some of her chili-mac casserole."

"Looks good. Before I forget—I met my mother for lunch. She mentioned I should say hi. She remembers you from Boone and Vicky's wedding. Looking back, I'm surprised I didn't meet you that day."

"I was only able to put in a brief appearance. Vicky needed me to handle something for her that came up at the last minute."

"What are the odds you'll ever tell me what that was?"

"Some secrets are best left unsaid. I was glad to do it. I'm not much for wedding receptions anyway. I love the cake and punch, but then I like to say my congratulations and call it a day."

"I'll bet you look good in your finery."

"The next wedding in your family, you can tell me what you think."

He finished his spaghetti and picked up one of the last pieces of bread. "Who's Lovely?"

She froze on him.

"I know it was a slip of the tongue, Ann. You never intended to say it. But it was an incredibly important-to-you remark. 'Lovely knows me.' Who's Lovely?"

She shook her head and took her bowl and disappeared into her kitchen. When she came back, she settled in one of the wingback chairs with a pudding cup. He knew she wanted him to change the subject, but if he stepped back from this he was likely to never get an answer. "Trust me, Ann."

She shook her head.

"Someone from the secret side of your life?"

She leaned her head back against the chair and studied

him through eyes calm and serious and a bit sad. "Are we going to be allowed to keep secrets? If this relationship goes somewhere permanent? Security-clearance secrets aside, as they have their own lines, will there be secrets or are you expecting there to be none?"

It was such a difficult answer to put into words. He wanted to give her room, needed to give her room, and yet he also knew there was something profound he had to convey. "Secrets tend to be the things that have hurt us the most, the events that have changed us the most. Will you wonder for the rest of your life, if he knew this about me, he wouldn't love me anymore? I would rather know everything important about my wife before I'm married so that when I say 'I do,' she knows there's no secret that could change how much I love her. I want to be able to give that certainty to a marriage." He watched her for a moment, trying to read her reaction.

"You need to be able to trust me, Ann. I'm not saying trust me now, tonight—not until you're comfortable with what you know about me, who I am, and decide you *can* trust me. But when you reach that point, I wish you'd see those secrets as something you could share with me. I wish you could trust me enough there didn't need to be secrets. I won't hurt you. I promise you, I won't hurt you."

"Would you want to know the secrets if they would rip apart and end the relationship?"

"Could they?"

"Yes."

"Have you shared them before, and that's what happened?"

"Would you want to know?"

What an awful choice she gave him. "Yes, I would want to know. You assume the truth would end the relationship. I would assume they would make the relationship stronger, to have the truth shared and known."

She thought about what he had said and finally nodded. "We've got a friendship, Paul, a good one, but not one that is ready for what you are asking. And I don't know if I agree with you. Sometimes the past should stay the past for everyone's sake."

"You've got some big secrets." Her smile was so sad it made him wonder what crossed her mind, but she didn't answer. "Okay. Do you want to watch a movie tonight? We could find something on television to watch together."

"We could do that."

"You choose while I take these dishes back to the kitchen and find myself some dessert. That pudding looks good."

"Tapioca."

"Yeah? I haven't had that in ages."

"I'd share if I could."

"One day we'll be in the same place, and I'll remind you what you offered." He came back with a bowl of ice cream. She had chosen an action movie. They put it on pause partway through so they could both make popcorn. Paul watched the movie, and he watched Ann, wondering what she was hiding that scared her so bad she couldn't imagine sharing the secret with him.

Ann had trouble sleeping. It was rare to be awake for more than a few minutes after she wrapped her arm around a pillow and closed her eyes. She knew the reason. *Paul*. More and more, her quiet time alone at night was filled with thoughts of him.

She had fully expected to enjoy time in his company, for she liked cops, liked the practical personalities that tended to gravitate to the job. He was a comfortable man to be with. She had wanted the friendship, and Paul had granted her that, and more. He'd pulled her into his life like no other guy ever had. She liked him. She trusted him. She just wasn't sure she wanted to trust him with her secrets. Or could.

They were reaching the point every relationship did after a few months, where the reality began to settle in for what this would become over time. A good friendship, or would it find the strength to become something more? She didn't know what she wanted.

She had ducked this question in the past, and time after time said no when the path had turned this direction. She had dated nice guys, but only with Reece had she considered the next question, and even with him the right answer had been no. She was comfortable being single, content. She hadn't expected to have this choice before her this year.

If she didn't trust Paul with her secrets, their relationship would stay a friendship. She knew that. Paul wouldn't push. But life inevitably would. She'd have to make the decision.

"What am I going to do, Lovely?" she whispered.

She wanted, needed, more time. She didn't know what the right decision would be. She didn't want to get hurt, and she didn't want to hurt Paul.

Maybe she wouldn't need to make the decision. There

were two of them in this relationship. He might decide first to leave it a friendship, and then she wouldn't have to make the decision. He was a careful man. He had asked questions of her friends before initially coming to see her. He had been asking her questions, thinking about her to understand her, in a way no other guy had. His questions would inevitably get closer to the subjects that were heart matters. He was a family man, and eventually would ask her about children, would want to understand her dreams for the future. She would trust him enough to give him full answers. She could do that for him. She could give him complete answers to his questions, let him make his decision with all the information she could give him.

She enjoyed—appreciated—their friendship. She didn't want to lose it. Maybe he would decide that he wanted to leave this a friendship. That would be okay with her. She'd have him in her life rather than have to say goodbye. The road to something more than a friendship was a road she'd never traveled, and she worried about it ending badly if they went further.

She folded the pillow over again and wrapped her arm around it. She would sleep easier once she knew where this was going. But her heart was telling her this time was different. Sleep was coming later at night as thoughts of him lingered. Paul was more important than any other guy had been in years. Maybe ever.

PART FOUR

JIM
GANNETT

16

Ann leaned back in her chair, comfortably cradling a mug of hot chocolate while she talked with Paul via video. "Sure, my weekend is free, assuming no one calls."

"I've talked to Neva, and she's agreeable to a guest for a couple of days. I can be there Friday around six. We'll go out somewhere for dinner."

"I like the sound of that."

Her phone rang. "Hold on, Paul." She muted the video link and reached for her phone. It was a secure call. She punched in her code and answered. She'd been expecting it.

"Good evening, sir."

She had known him for twelve years, considered him a friend, and no matter how many times he asked her to call him Jim, she still felt most comfortable with sir.

"I've been reading the third volume from beginning to end this week, and I'm pleased, Ann. The final year as vice president, the campaign for president, the defeat, and the years retired from public life—it's all there with good balance and clarity. I know the hours you've spent asking questions in the margins, suggesting words, reordering passages, helping me find that clarity so the book will be readable to all who dip into its pages. Before the crowds begin to read it, I just wanted to say what a pleasure it has been to have your help on this whole project—the current volume along with the prior two. You've done a more than fine job. You've turned my attempts at writing this memoir into editions which will stand the critical test of time."

"Thank you, sir. It's been a pleasure to work with you on them. It's a good legacy you're leaving to your family, and to history."

"How are you doing, Ann? Any second thoughts about chapter twenty-eight?"

"No, sir. It's time. It will be good to have this behind us."

She had known for years this day was coming. Get chapter twenty-eight expert-reviewed and vetted, get the third and final volume of his autobiography released, and then keep her head down as the press swarmed. She could think of better ways to end her year. But at least it would be over.

"I'm thinking about asking Paul Falcon to be the one to investigate and verify the chapter. I think it would be wise to make it a cop you already know, as you'll be the one walking him through the material. And it needs to be federal, given the scope of the investigation to be done."

She wasn't sure what she wanted to say. Paul couldn't investigate the chapter, stay impartial to even the appearance of a conflict of interest, and be dating her at the same time. At a minimum it would push off whatever might be between them until well after the book was released. But if the worst came to pass, she would want it to be Paul—would need it to be him—who investigated the chapter.

She took a deep breath. "He would be my choice, sir," she replied, at peace with her answer.

"Open the door and show him the case. Once he's up to speed, and if you still think he's the guy, bring him to see me. I'll call his director, and then I'll lay out for Paul the contents of the chapter. From that point he'll be running the investigation, and you'll be his guide through the materials. I would imagine the first ten days or so after we tell him will not include much sleep. You should factor that into your plans."

"That sounds about right, sir. He works with two people who have been with him for years. Sam Truebone and Rita Heart. It will move faster with three, and time is going to matter once you open the door."

"I'll make arrangements once he's seen the chapter. I want you to let me know if there is anything I can do for you as this process unfolds."

"I will, sir. I'll be in touch once I've shown him the case, possibly this weekend."

"I'll look forward to your call."

Ann disconnected the secure call and held the phone for a moment, thinking through the implications of what she had agreed to, now needed to do. Of everyone she had thought the vice president might ask to review the chapter, she hadn't considered Paul.

She went back to the video call.

"Everything okay, Ann?"

She forced herself to smile. "Not an MHI case, thankfully. Yes, I would love it if you could come down for the weekend."

"Then I'll see you tomorrow."

"Paul, just in case, pack for an extra couple days."

"Ann?"

"It's the girl scout in me. You assume you're going for a day, it turns into a week."

"I've had those trips as well. I'll see you tomorrow." Paul looked past her on the video link. "Want to say good night, Black?"

The dog thumped his tail but didn't bother to lift his head.

Paul grinned. "I'm getting to him."

Ann laughed. "'Night, Paul."

Ann closed the video connection. She thought for a moment, then ignored the time and placed a secure call to Vicky.

"This is a nice surprise." Ann heard the background noise drop off. "I'm all yours, Ann."

"How seriously am I interrupting you?"

"A secure call comes in from a friend—who cares what you are interrupting. I promise no one's life or property is depending on me being available for the next ten minutes."

"Thanks. I've got news. The VP is considering giving chapter twenty-eight to Paul to investigate."

Vicky was silent. She finally said, "I'm married to Paul's brother Boone, and yet somehow Paul hadn't even crossed my mind as a possibility. Paul's got a solid reputation, and we both know he will do a thorough investigation. What he writes will stand up to scrutiny. He's fair. He'll protect the VP position even if he questions the VP's actions. When the press swarms the issue, his instinct will be to protect his family. That may be important to factor in. So, yes, on the whole I would say it's a good choice. What are you thinking?"

"I'm getting used to the idea. I'll take my share of press, but I plan to duck and hide, let it flow past, and hope the worst of it tails off in a year. The assumption will be, rightfully, that I know who the unnamed individuals are in the chapter. I just worry about the what-ifs. Are you going to tell Boone, just in case?"

"No."

"I'm not going to tell Paul either."

Vicky was quiet again. "It might be good if you could, Ann. Once you see how he reacts to the chapter, you might want to consider telling him."

"It opens too many complications. I plan to take the truth to the grave with me."

"So when does he get the chapter?"

"Possibly this weekend. I'm going to show him the case and see how he reacts to it first, then let the VP break the news."

"You want company? I could get away for a few days."

"Depending on how this unfolds, I wouldn't mind some company when we travel. I assume part of this will end up with us crisscrossing a few states by air. It would be nice to have some company that isn't part of the investigation."

"I'll talk with the VP and arrange a visit. It will be easy enough for me to slide in as extra security once I'm already there. Paul will accept the security—he's going to want Agent Lion focused on answering questions rather than being on the job providing security, and I'm a known quantity."

"Thanks, Vicky."

"I'll tell you, I'm curious enough I would like to be there as this unfolds. Boone has been talking about visiting his parents for a few days of business conversations, so this will dovetail nicely with him and me both traveling at the same time."

———————◢———————

Paul pulled into Mrs. Rawlins's driveway just after five p.m. on Friday. Ann was sitting on the porch swing with Neva, the two ladies sipping from tall glasses of ice tea while Black sprawled across the porch.

Ann came to meet him as he stepped out of the car. "Hi, Paul." She gave him a hug.

"Hi, Ann." He returned the hug and simply held her, enjoying it more than he could put into words. She stepped back. And then he saw her face. His smile faded. "What is it?"

"I'm afraid there's been a change of plans. Let's get you squared away here, and then we'll walk to my place. I'll explain on the way."

He nodded, went and retrieved his bag plus the gift he had brought, and locked his car.

"I appreciate you putting me up for a few nights, Neva."

"It's my pleasure, Paul."

"Your son mentioned it was your birthday this month. You'll forgive me for spotting something you might like and, further, for talking your son into going in on it with me."

She accepted the gift and unwrapped the box, drawing out a porcelain vase. "Oh, my, Paul." The flush that came into her face was matched by a delighted smile. "You found the last piece I didn't have."

"It's a beautiful collection. Even I can tell that."

She carefully set the vase back in the box and rose to give him a hug. "Thank you."

"You're very welcome."

She held out a key ring. "You are no longer a guest. I've put you in the same room as before, and you can come and go as you like. Don't worry if it's late. I'm visiting my sister tonight, as her daughter is getting married, and I plan to stay in town depending on how much needs to be done."

"Thank you." He took his bag inside, wondering at Ann's news as he put it on the guest bed and took time to hang up his suit jacket. His plans for this weekend were changing before it had even begun.

Paul reached for Ann's hand as they walked toward her home. "What's wrong?"

"I need to show you a case. And I need you to get up to speed on it, and to understand it in detail. And to complicate it, I can't explain why. I just need you to work blind for the moment and trust me that there's an important reason behind my request. It's for someone else to explain."

"You've certainly got my interest. Do we need to travel?"

"It's on the murder board at my place." She eased her hand from his. "But before we get there, Paul, I need to release you from the possibility there is going to be something between us. You will need a distance from me." She looked over at him. "I like you, a great deal, so I'm telling you now that I'm going to pull away for your sake. There are legal implications for me with what is coming. When you know the truth, if you want to pick something up again, then you can ask me."

He missed her hand in his. "How serious a legal problem?"

"It will start with a lot of press, and who knows where it goes from there. I'm expecting at least a few depositions before this is all over. I kept a secret. This is the price of it." Her phone rang. She looked at the caller ID. "I'm sorry, this one I have to take."

She entered her security code and answered, "Hello, sir."

She glanced over. "Yes, sir, he's right here. Hold on." She held out the phone. "Paul Falcon, former Vice President Jim Gannett. He would like an update on the lady shooter. He was the FBI director when she first started killing, and knows the case even better than you—if that's possible."

He accepted the phone. "Good evening, sir."

Ann half listened to his side of the conversation as they walked. She didn't particularly care tonight about the latest on the lady shooter case, as fascinating as she would otherwise find it to be. She had prepared for tonight as carefully as she could, and she still didn't know if she'd made the right decision on how to introduce him to what awaited them. She'd felt slightly queasy all day, and Paul's arrival had only intensified that churn.

"Ann . . ." Paul handed back her phone.

She slid it in her pocket, saw his face, and smiled. "He's retired, and he is a nice guy."

"You still call him sir."

"I'm a bit in awe of him in spite of having known him for years. He asks me to call him Jim, but I can't do it. He dominates a room like the state of Texas towers over Delaware. You didn't tell him about the letters or the tapes."

"Eleven people know they are coming in, and that's already too many. Gannett knows about the cash gift you made, so I told him about the one hundred twenty-three interviews under way. It's nice to have your cash. Otherwise I would've had to tell him I'm being stalled by budget concerns."

"I'm glad you told him about the interviews, as he was instrumental in that award transfer, and he likes to be helpful. He's had the lady shooter case as a personal interest for as long as I've known him."

She pushed her hands into her pockets and her smile faded. "I'm known for being able to keep a secret, Paul. It's why I'm trusted as the MHI. It's why I've been working on the VP's autobiography. But sometimes a secret comes with a price. I weighed years ago what keeping this secret was going to cost and concluded I could live with the costs. The legal risks are part of that. It's not going to be a secret much longer. I can tell you this much: in about a week you'll have a good understanding of what is going on. Please trust me that I'm not interested in causing you trouble. And I'm not trying to hide things from you—it's simply not mine to explain."

"The case you need to show me is part of it."

"Yes."

"I'm not comfortable with you pulling away, Ann." He stopped and turned to look at her. "I'd prefer you to trust me, let me make my own decisions."

"In a week, after you know what this is, I'll let you make whatever decision you would like regarding the possibility of us."

Paul thought he could almost feel her sadness. But he didn't know how to untangle her desire to pull away until he understood why she thought it was necessary. He reached for her hand, even though she was reluctant to accept the reassurance. "There's going to be an us, Ann."

"You'll understand soon, Paul, why that may not be the right decision."

They reached her home. She unlocked the front door, let Black enter first. Paul followed as she led the way into her living room. And he stopped. Surprised.

He walked over to the murder board filling the wall. The O'Malley series was gone and in its place was laid out a complex case. Buried skeletal remains, crime-scene photos, missing-person police reports—and a lot of victims. "Ann?"

"Sixteen years ago there was a serial killer who worked the Midwest," she said quietly. "We didn't even know he was out there until he called to confess. We just had missing-person cases that we hadn't put together with a common suspect." She took a deep breath, then let it out slowly. "He called to confess, and at the end of the call shot himself in the head while the cabin he was in burned down around him. We have his DNA, dental work, the locations he gave for his eighteen victims' remains, and no name. He's the John Doe Killer."

"This is a closed case, not an active one?"

"Yes. I'm writing a book about the case."

"Are you trying to identify him? You know the day he died. You know his victims. Even the fact his DNA wasn't in the database will tell you something about him. You can eliminate any suspect in the original missing-persons investigations who's still alive."

"His identity is not a priority for me. The book is mainly profile pieces on the victims—eighteen chapters, one for each victim. I'm working on it with the help of the families, and they will split whatever royalties the book generates."

Paul was surprised at her answer. There was a reason the killer had chosen these eighteen victims. Identifying the killer would turn a good book into a bestseller. A murder cop not wanting to name a serial killer and give him notoriety for his crimes? Yes, that might be reason enough for her not to pursue it.

"I don't understand what it is you want me to do, Ann. Do you want me to fact-check your work? Find a problem in the case? Are there more victims he did not admit he killed? Is one of these victims not his?" He looked over at her.

"I need you to know this case inside and out. That's the best description I can give you of what I need. When you feel like you have the case solid in your mind, tell me. And I will take you to someone who will explain the whys. It's all I can give you now. I know it's not much. But I need you to take it on blind faith that there's a reason behind this, and it's a big deal."

He knew a few things she didn't consider a big deal. If this was a big deal to her, it was something critical. "How long have you been working on the book?"

"I've known about the case and the victims from its earliest days when cops were recovering the remains. I secured written agreement from all the families three years ago, and I've been working on the story since then. It's my first true-crime, nonfiction book, focused more on the victim profiles than the crime itself."

"Can I read what you've written so far?"

"Those soft gray pages on the corner of the table are the latest draft. It's about done. The families have the right to read the chapter about their loved one, ask me to not include it in the book, or add a family-written five-page addition to it. I've verbally heard back from every family that they are comfortable with what I've written, but I've asked that they think about it a few weeks before they sign the final approval paperwork.

"The book covers a lot of the personal information I was able to find out about the victims, the texture of who they were that goes beyond what the missing-person case file includes. I don't know how relevant it will be for what you need, but it does bring the victims alive."

The case files occupied more than twenty boxes. And her manuscript looked to be more than three hundred pages. He'd be reading for hours to get through what was here. Something in this case put her at legal risk—something she had learned about one of the victims?

"Did you work this case?"

"No. What's here is what I've collected from the cops who worked the various missing-person cases, and the cops who worked on the recovery of the remains. I've added to it what the families could provide—letters, photos, calendars, details about the victims before they disappeared."

"I assume time is important on this."

"Very important."

"Then I'd better get started." He began at the start of the timeline and pulled the file for the first missing-person case. He chose a comfortable chair and settled in.

"Thanks for this, Paul."

"Ann, if you don't realize it yet, let me put it in words. I trust you. You need me to know this case. That's a good enough reason for me to do the work."

"I don't deserve that blind trust."

"I think you do."

She didn't know how to reply, and he found that fascinating. She'd never had someone willing to stick before? She needed to realize he would. When a business empire covered the territory his dad's did, legal tangles came up all the time, and often simply because someone carried the Falcon name. Whatever this was about, he knew Ann well enough to know she would have done what she believed to be right. He would figure out what was going on, make a decision about what he thought of her actions, and then probably tug her into going to a movie with him. They still hadn't worked one in, that first choice of a date, and it had been part of his plans for this weekend.

She started to smile. "If pizza is okay with you, I'll order in dinner."

"That works for me."

Paul pulled two slices of pizza from the box and nodded toward the board. "Tell me the story of it, Ann. The day this killer called and announced he was out there."

She balanced her plate on her knees and gave Black a piece of jerky. "This is the first case I've seen where it opened fully developed and didn't move much beyond the initial day's facts."

She reached for a napkin. "According to the police reports, it began when the killer called a man named Ben Harmon. Ben had thirty years with the Secret Service, was retired, was well known in his hometown. The local paper had done a profile piece on him not a week before the call came in. Not a bad choice for whom to call if your goal was to make news. Ben was driving to meet up with a friend, planning to go fishing for the day, when the call came in. It was an older male voice, no accent. 'I've killed eighteen people, and I've chosen you as my confessor.' Ben pulled over to the side of the road. The guy told him to get a pen and paper, and he proceeded to give GPS locations for eighteen victims. Then Ben heard a gunshot. It sounded to him like the phone hit the floor. The line stayed open for about four minutes before it went to a fast off-hook tone.

"Ben turned around and headed to the police station at Petersburg, Georgia. The number for the call he received traced back to a cabin about twelve miles outside of town. Cops swarmed the place. They found the cabin burned to the ground and still smoldering, a body inside, the man shot in the head, a gun and the phone receiver near his body. No car was at the scene, but there was a metal-bottom fishing boat at the pier. It belonged to a business on the other side of the lake, and the security chain had been cut. There were several gas cans recovered at the scene, but no gas purchases were found that might match. No car was found that might be his. The cabin was owned by a businessman in town whose son used it occasionally when he went fishing, but the son had deployed with the military. No one had been at the cabin in months.

"The man's remains were never identified. Victims were found at each of the eighteen locations—the missing-person cases from across seven states and over nine years. The cases had been worked hard, as they were people who just abruptly disappeared from the daily routines of their lives. Foul play was suspected in each case. The recovery of the victims' remains let those cases be closed, but the reasons for why they were taken didn't appear. With the confession, cops knew the cases were related by a common killer, but there didn't seem to be links between the victims otherwise."

"This didn't make the national news?"

"Local papers reported when the individual missing-person cases were closed, but no reporter put together the larger picture. Part of it was the age of the cases, part of it was the time it took for all eighteen locations to be investigated, part of it was the geography and the number of police departments involved. It was several weeks of work before it was clear the killer would not be identified, for the scope of what he had done and who he had killed to become clear. The case got enormous work from the day of the call until the victims were identified, but giving a serial killer press wasn't something any of the cops were interested in doing. They wrapped it up and couldn't identify him and wrote it up as the John Doe Killer."

"Anything in particular strike you about the case?"

"The victims were one moment leading normal lives,

and then they were gone without a trace. All eighteen victims were clean disappearances. Some of the best cops I know worked the missing-person cases when they originally occurred, and worked the task force when the bodies were recovered, trying to figure out who this guy was. But the case didn't move much from the initial day's facts."

Paul studied the board. "Thanks, that helps."

She nodded and took their plates to the kitchen.

He returned to his reading.

He was finishing the police report concerning the eighteenth and final missing-person case when she interrupted.

"Paul."

He put his thumb on the page to mark his place and looked up at her.

"It's almost midnight. I didn't mean for you to read for hours without a break."

"I don't mind—it's what my day job is often like." He gestured to the murder board. "You obviously know more about the reason behind this request than I do. How urgent is this?"

"No one's life is on the line. It's a closed case. Or cases. But when you know the reason, when you find out why you were asked to know this case inside and out, it's going to get very urgent."

"Then I'll work for a bit longer." She was deep into a yellow legal pad of notes and had a cold drink sweating on the coaster beside her. She didn't look sleepy—she looked like she was in the middle of a workday. "Kick me out when you're ready to call it a night," he told her.

"I would normally do a couple more hours."

He finished the initial read-through of the case and the boxes at three a.m. Ann was settled on the couch, her eyes closed. He shifted the legal pad to the table and gently shook her shoulder. "Ann."

She woke with a start. "Sorry, I drifted off."

"One moment I looked over and you were awake and briskly writing, the next you were asleep with the pen in your hand."

"It happens." She looked at the time and her eyes widened. "Three o'clock. Paul, you should have stopped hours ago."

He let her reorient herself and get a bit more alert before he nodded to the board. "I've done the initial review of the boxes. You have a killer, his confession, his victims. The case files appear to be in order and complete. I didn't see any sloppy police work in the history I've read."

She relaxed. "That's my read of the case file as well. The cops did a good job with what was there."

"I'll be back tomorrow whenever I happen to wake up. I want to spend some more time going through the files, now that I've seen the scope of the case. And I want to read what you've written about the victims."

"Okay." She dug keys out of her pocket. "Take my car. House keys are on that ring. Let yourself in if for some reason I'm not here."

Ann was heading out for a walk with Black when he returned the next day. "There's no need to stay," he told her. "Enjoy yourself and make it a long walk. I'm just going to be reading."

"I put coffee on just for you, and there are bagels in the drawer."

"I'll be fine. Go enjoy yourself."

She headed after a still-sleepy Black.

Paul found the bagels, poured his coffee, and settled into the same chair as the day before. He started reading the book she had written about the victims.

An hour later when he heard the front door, he marked his page and set aside his notes.

Black raced into the living room, diving toward the couch to wrestle an old sock from under the end. He lay down to begin chewing it apart. Ann appeared.

Paul smiled at her. "I saw the dog have energy for a brief instant."

"Walks wake him up."

She saw his sketched notes on a legal pad. "You found something?"

Paul handed her the pages. "There's a progression in the victims, not only in complexity of how they disappeared—larger city, more people around, middle of the day—but in who they were. They get more significant, for want of a better word. It starts with the lady who runs the Red Cross chapter and is married to the bank manager, then it's a county judge, a lady reporter, a venture capital CEO, an award-winning economist with a visiting teaching position at Harvard. The victims get harder to reach without leaving a trace, more prominent in their community, their jobs. This wasn't a blue-collar killer. This was someone who could fit into the environment of the victim and take them without someone noticing him."

"I noted that too. He moved up in influence, up in the level of risk."

"He chose them. It doesn't feel random to me. Not with the progression in who he kills. The list looks like his victims were deliberate choices." He got up to pace and loosen stiff muscles.

"It's your turn to take a break and get in a walk."

"In a bit. It's easier to keep reading now. The saturation helps. Little pieces start to click together when I see pages and pages of information."

He settled back in the chair and picked up the police report for victim nine. He was beginning to understand this case. At least to see the questions it presented. *Why these victims?* He could feel the tug of something, and he was trying to put together the idea that was working around in the back of his mind. He read for another two hours, thinking over what he found.

He put his finger on a note in the police report about victim sixteen, flipped open Ann's book and checked victim four. He closed his eyes and mentally went through what he had read about each of the victims.

"Ann, it's political."

She set down her writing pad and gave him her attention.

"Or more to the point—he's political."

She rested her forearms against her knees, studying him. "What did you notice?"

"All of his victims have politics in their history. That's not random, not with eighteen people. A sampling of the general population would never have turned up all eighteen as being active in politics. They are Republican, Democrat, state politics, national politics—the victims aren't linked to each other, but we know they are linked to the killer. All the people who crossed him to the point he wanted to kill them had politics in their life, and that tells me it is politics that is his world. He's a pollster, a fund-raiser, a political campaign operative, some job that comes around every two or four years. And given the variety of states, he was probably working at the national level. The victims were chosen because they intersected with his world, and his is a political world."

He saw her face. "I'm right?"

"I can't comment on the theory. But you did what I asked. You've learned the case and the victims deep enough to see a possible connection. That's what I desperately needed you to do."

She held up a finger. She reached over for the phone and placed a secure call. "Good evening, sir. Yes, sir. He knows the case. It's my recommendation you give him the chapter."

She glanced at the clock. "Yes, sir."

She closed the phone. And then she took a deep breath before she looked over at him. "The VP would like us to come over for coffee."

"A chapter of the VP's autobiography?"

"Yes."

"Does the VP know who the John Doe Killer is?"

"Yes."

"He's going to name him?"

"Yes."

He looked at the book she was writing about the

victims, the profiles she had taken such care to craft. "The victims will get lost in the press focus of who he will name."

"Not with my book releasing alongside the VP's autobiography. It's why he asked me to write it."

"You've read the chapter; you know who it is?"

"That answer is so far above my pay grade, I'm going to pretend you didn't ask the question," she replied. "Would you mind if we wait on dinner until after we speak with him? I've got butterflies."

"I admit to a few myself. I wasn't planning to meet the VP today."

She smiled and offered him her keys. "We'll take my car, as Black is going over with us, but I'd prefer it if you drive. We can stop and pick up your suit jacket if it would make you more comfortable. I'm going as I am. But you look quite dignified in a suit."

He grinned. "Really?"

"I have lots of flaws, but I'm not blind. Black, you want to go see Jasmine?"

He darted away and came back with a rubber-duck chew toy and then pranced around, as they were not quick enough to follow him to the front door.

Ann laughed, then caught up with him and ruffled his ears. "She'll like it too, buddy."

17

The VP's estate was set on forty acres in the rolling hills near the river. "Pull up to the gate. Security will come down to meet us."

Paul pulled to a stop.

Ann saw the guard walking down to meet them and lowered her window. "Good evening, George. I have one guest tonight."

"Good evening, Miss Silver." The dog tried to lean around the headrest to put his head out the open window. "And to you, Midnight." The security guard circled the car, checking the underside of the vehicle with a mirror and stopped at the driver's door. "May I see your identification, sir?" He accepted Paul's credentials, made a call, and returned the items. "Thank you. Please follow the drive, pull around to the north side of the house, and park next to the silver van." The gate slowly opened.

Paul proceeded up the winding drive. Six cars were parked in a side lot. He parked. Ann stepped out of the car and let Black out. The dog got a hold on his rubber toy and led the way to the side door. Ann entered a security code and held open the door. Paul stepped inside with her. They were in a spacious kitchen. Black paused to check the counter, where cookies were cooling, then disappeared down a hallway.

A man joined them from the front of the house. "Welcome, Ann."

"Hi, Reece." She made introductions. "Paul, this is Jim Gannett's lead Secret Service Agent Reece Lion. Reece, FBI Special Agent Paul Falcon."

The two men sized each other up as they shook hands. "It's good to meet you."

"And you."

Reece turned his attention to Ann. He interlaced his fingers with hers as he studied her face. "You look pretty good tonight."

"I'm doing fine. Black came along. He went searching for Jasmine."

Reece grinned. "That's my boy. I was hoping you'd bring him. Head on back. Jim's in the library. I'll join you in a minute."

Ann led the way through the house and knocked lightly on a partially closed door.

"Come in."

"Ann." The former vice president rose from his seat by the fireplace and came over. "You made good time." He greeted her with a hug, studied her face for a moment, and smiled. "I had a private bet with Reece that you would call tonight."

"It looks like you won. I'm not one for delays." She turned. "Sir, I'd like to introduce Paul Falcon. Paul, Vice President Jim Gannett."

The VP offered his hand. "It's good to put a face with a name. I appreciate you coming on such short notice, Paul, and for putting up with this bit of mystery."

"I'm inclined to trust Ann."

"A good answer and one I would endorse. Please, have a seat. May I get you coffee, a drink?"

"I'm fine, sir."

They settled into comfortable chairs, and Reece joined them, standing by the fireplace.

"If you don't mind," the VP began, "I will leave the casual conversation I would like to have with you about the lady shooter, about the Chicago bureau, and many other things which interest me, for another time, and simply get to the reason I asked Ann to bring you over."

"Yes, sir."

Gannett leaned forward in his chair. "I'm about to ask you to do something that will be both a large favor and a significant imposition on your life. I'd like you to hear me out, talk it over with Ann, think about it overnight, then accept or decline my request. Only five people know this information. It's been closely held for a reason. Before I begin, I need your word that what I tell you will remain confidential until the final volume of my autobiography is released at the end of the year, regardless of your decision."

"You have my word."

"Good. Thank you." He leaned back in his chair. "Sixteen years ago there was a serial killer in the Midwest who was active for nine years. Ann has shown you his eighteen victims."

"Yes."

"The John Doe Killer wrote a diary, or rather he dictated it. Who he chose to kill and why, how he snatched them, where he buried their remains. He began his diary with the words 'I have killed twenty people, each more famous than the last.' He had killed just eighteen when he dictated that line.

"I didn't have a boating accident nine years ago. I was abducted. I was to be victim number nineteen, and he was going to kill himself to become victim twenty. He was going to make himself the most famous serial killer in history, the serial killer who killed a vice president."

Gannett reached for his mug. "Ponder that for a moment while I get myself some more coffee."

He walked over to the beverage cart.

Paul suddenly felt overly aware of every sound and motion in the room, including how his chest was feeling as he took his next breath. Surprises went with his job, but this was more than a surprise. The news began to crystallize. The VP had been the near victim of a serial killer, the near victim of a man who had put eighteen people in the ground.

Paul looked over at Ann. She was settled back deep in her chair, relaxed, watching the VP as he stirred sugar into his coffee. If she had any of those butterflies, none were apparent on her face. She wasn't surprised or appalled or even particularly curious. None of this news was news to her. She'd kept a secret. And understated just how big a secret it was. Ann Silver continued to surprise him at every turn.

Paul waited until the VP was again seated and had gestured with his coffee mug for the first question. Paul appreciated the man's wide-open invitation to ask whatever he wished.

"You were abducted by this man."

"Yes. I was at my vacation home in Florida. He snatched me off my own boat. He also abducted a lady to write his diary. She's off-limits by her own request. The rest you can ask."

"You didn't have Secret Service with you?"

"I had dismissed most of the detail after two years of retirement, keeping private security for the house and grounds. I had one agent assigned to my family, and I had asked him to accompany my wife that day as she had a public appearance."

Paul nodded and went for the heart of the problem. "According to the police reports, John Doe called to confess, gave the location of his victims, then shot himself in the head while the cabin burned down around him—that was all a cover-up?"

"Most of it was true. The cabin, the fact he shot himself in the head, the location of his victims—those were the truth. But John Doe never called to confess, and the fire was set in order to destroy fingerprints and hide the fact I had been there, and to help conceal the killer's identity. That was the cover-up.

"There were only two survivors to what the man had done. The lady he abducted to write his diary, and myself. Neither of us wanted to face the press that would descend when the truth was known. We had those eighteen families to think about as well. They needed their loved ones back, time to properly bury their dead and grieve, without the press hounding them. We could do nothing for the victims he had killed, nor could we further punish the man who had committed the crimes, since he was dead, and we were convinced by the diary details that he had acted alone. We decided, as the only two living victims of the man, to make sure we survived how the rest of it would unfold. She was in pretty bad shape after a week in his company.

"So I made the decision to cover up the truth of what occurred. Three people helped me. My Secret Service agent"—he nodded toward Reece Lion—"a retired Secret Service agent, Ben Harmon, who passed away five years ago but who left a detailed video and written interview of his actions regarding this matter, and a person who will remain unnamed, whom I trusted to help the lady who wrote the diary recover and reenter her life.

"We gave the families closure with recovery of their loved ones, made sure the police knew the cases were closed and the right killer identified, and then I made sure the man who committed the crimes was unidentified by DNA, was cremated, and left in the case files as the John Doe Killer."

"Who was he?"

"The John Doe Killer was my former chief of staff, Aaron Crown."

Paul had braced for several names, but that one caught him off guard. "Your chief of staff?"

"That was about my reaction too. He shot himself in the head in my presence and died the same day he abducted me.

"We claimed he was found dead of a heart attack at his vacation home due to the stress of my being missing and presumed dead in a boating accident. We buried an almost empty coffin. What we did put in his casket were the photos of the scene at the cabin, along with a hand-written contemporaneous statement I wrote that day concerning what had occurred, and the cover-up we were going to attempt to keep it from becoming public. When you exhume the coffin, you will find that evidence."

"Why are you revealing this secret now?"

"We didn't keep the secret to protect the man from scandal or to protect me from the negative fallout of his close position. We did it to give us time to recover from what happened, to protect his victims and their families from the press. And we didn't want to give the man the notoriety he craved. So we denied history his name. But the truth was always going to come out. This is the most controlled way I could figure to do it. I've written the account in detail for a chapter of my autobiography."

The VP took a deep breath, then looked directly at Paul for a moment before continuing. "An autobiography is by nature a matter of making decisions about what is included and what is left out. But the account of the day, from the point when the chief of staff on my boat pulled a gun until I was back at my home from the hospital three days later, is complete to the best of my recollection and those who helped me.

"I would like you to choose one or two agents whom you trust and independently verify what I've written. I'll clear whatever time you need with your office. You may use what you learn now and in further investigation after the book is released to write the official FBI report on the matter. Based on what you conclude, you may choose to add a chapter to the book that will be only your words. The book is tentatively scheduled for December of this year, so you have about thirty days to conduct your initial inquiry if you wish to include a statement.

"I'm going to have Ann walk you through the extensive material that has been collected on this matter, give you a copy of the diary text along with the detailed chapter I've written. I'll be available for as many interviews as you wish to have, as will Reece.

"The lady who wrote the diary wishes to remain anonymous. For that reason the diary in her handwriting will not be released, but the text of it will be. Ann has verified the text is word for word identical to the diary. I will in the book mention by name the people who did *not* write the diary so as to avoid the press descending on them when the guessing begins. I am withholding three things: the name of the lady abducted to write the diary, the person I trusted to help her reenter her life, and the handwritten diary itself.

"Paul, when you have looked through what is here and thought about it overnight, let me know your decision. I'll make arrangements based on your answer. If it is not you to conduct this investigation, I would ask for your recommendation for who should do so." Gannett looked over at his agent. "Reece, anything you would like to add?"

"I have a comment about the cover-up after the fact. The official Secret Service logs on this incident do not show the chief of staff was in Florida that day, nor do they show anything other than the VP being involved in a boating accident. Both those facts turn out not to be an active attempt to conceal on my part—I simply didn't correct what other people assumed. For his own purposes, the chief of staff had stayed under the radar about his travel plans, and the boating accident was the working assumption for the VP's disappearance. I used what people presumed had happened to slip the VP back into his life. By confirming their assumptions he'd had a boating accident, both the VP and I covered up the truth. But I didn't have to add new information to try and misdirect people. I would have if required, but it turned out not to be necessary.

"The writer of the diary was missing, the police were investigating, and they had a working assumption of what had happened. She was slipped back into her life in a similar fashion. By agreeing with what other people thought had happened, by confirming their assumptions rather than correcting them, she covered up the truth. But she didn't have to change what people assumed had occurred.

"To the best of my knowledge, neither cover-up caused a problem for an innocent third party. No one was blamed for a crime. This isn't an attempt to excuse what was done; it is simply a statement of the consequences of these events as I was able to assess them.

"There are numerous people who will rightfully be furious they were at a funeral for the chief of staff, not knowing they were witnessing the burial of an empty coffin, and the memorial, if you will, of a serial killer. There will be numerous members of the families of the victims who are going to be furious we knew the truth and did not reveal it. There will be legal fallout of all kinds for the cover-up that was done. But to the best of my knowledge, the harm done is limited to the embarrassment of not knowing the truth, along with the passage of time that has elapsed before this is made public, rather than the silence causing the wrong outcome for someone."

The VP nodded. "Exactly, Reece. This cover-up was

done with the intent of causing less harm than what would have occurred had events become public the day this happened, and I believe that was accomplished. But I did actively seek to deceive and hide the truth, and I have to live with that and its consequences. Reece and the others helped because I asked them to do so. I still consider it the right decision. The cover-up accomplished what I hoped for, and that was time for the matter to be investigated and settled without the press involved." The VP got to his feet. "Paul, I look forward to hearing your decision. I'll leave you with Ann, to show you what we've gathered on this matter. If you would join me for breakfast tomorrow and give me your answer?"

"I'll do that, sir."

"Thank you." Two dogs appeared in the door, a white Samoyed followed by Midnight. They both headed to the VP and crowded against his knees. "I'm going to take these two for a stroll around the grounds, then turn in early for the night with a good book."

Paul watched the former vice president leave the room, and took his first clear breath since meeting him.

"Paul." Ann waited until he turned his attention to her. She gestured toward the door and led the way back through the house. "I'm sorry for putting you in this position without warning."

"Were you the one who suggested the VP should ask me to do this?"

"He came up with your name on his own—my guess from the lady shooter case. But I was glad he suggested you."

"You've kept this secret for years."

"I have. It wasn't my secret to tell. And that has caused

me more than a few difficult nights. From a law-enforcement point of view, the killer was caught and his victims
identified. From a legal point of view, if his name was
known, the victims could sue the estate of the killer. But
the reality is the chief of staff's will still listed the VP as
the executor, the man had no children, and left the dis-
posal of the estate up to the VP's discretion. The estate
took several years to liquidate and settle, as some of it
was in trusts which had come through generations, but
the money was distributed in full to the families of the
victims three years ago. It was called an advance against
the book royalties. From an ethical point of view, they
have a right to know the truth. And the chapter about the
chief of staff does that—it gives them the truth. Justice
came a long time after the fact, but it's happened. I can
live with that fact, as I understand the motivations of
those involved."

"Your legal exposure is the fact you knew the truth."

"Yes. I'm a sworn officer, and the name of the killer
is a material fact. I'm liable for what I didn't do. And I
didn't make the information I had public."

She coded them through a door and into a hallway.

"The archives for the VP's book are kept in this wing
of the house. There are several secured rooms for classified materials." She stopped at the third door. "This
secure room can be accessed by only three people: Gannett, Reece, and myself." She opened the door.

"Aaron Crown murdered some very nice people, Paul.
That's what is so senseless. You've met the people he
killed"—she turned on the lights—"now meet the one
who killed them. In this room is the life of the chief of
staff." The room was large, with two tables in the center,

file cabinets and storage lining three walls. The door closed behind them. He heard the locks click and engage.

"We spent years after the abduction working it as a criminal case, using the diary he gave as a road map and independently confirming what he had said. We collected everything that was out there about the chief of staff and his life going back decades. Personal calendars, receipts, tax documents, financial statements, personal letters—everything we could find. There are also campaign photographs, and interviews with those who worked with him on various campaigns going back to the VP's first election as state attorney general. We wrote the biography of Aaron Crown.

"The materials are organized in the files by date and cross-referenced by subject. The critical documents have been scanned and are searchable. That database of materials will be released to the public along with the VP's autobiography." She pointed to the near table. "I have a copy of the diary and a copy of the VP's chapter printed out for you."

"Ann, do you believe the chapter and these files are an accurate record of what occurred?"

"I'm skeptical by nature. I can say having spent years with these records and investigating the victims, that it feels reasonably complete. The records here are consistent with the diary. The VP chapter matches what I can put my hands on to prove or disprove what he says.

"The VP knows how to manage a cover-up. It has held together for years. He kept the truth of what happened at the cabin to five people. Who knows what else he covered up, if he left it to only himself? The VP is a smart man. Did he never suspect the chief of staff was a murderer? I think he had to suspect something was wrong somewhere along the way.

"I dated Reece Lion, so I'm not exactly an impartial observer, but I consider him to be an honest man. His actions are consistent with what is here. He helped a man he was assigned to protect, a man he trusted, cover up what occurred. The VP would do it with or without his help, and Reece understood why the decision had been made. He did it out of loyalty. I also like Gannett and believe he's a complicated but good man. But ghostwriting his autobiography has shown me the VP will do what he believes is in the best interests of the nation, and he can live with the gray areas if he has to. He would cover up what occurred and sleep well with the decision. So I don't disbelieve what is here. I just don't know if it is everything. If pushed, I would assume it is not, as there is always something that gets tucked away and not said.

"Did the chief of staff murder eighteen people? Yes. Is the diary his words and rationale for why he killed them? Yes. Did he abduct the VP and intend to kill him? Yes. Did the VP cover up what happened at the cabin? Yes. Is this the record of all that happened? Probably not. I know it can be accurate and still not be complete. The skeptic in me always doubts, and I assume I don't know everything that happened."

Paul went to the core question he had. "Did the VP kill the chief of staff?"

"He says no, that the chief of staff pulled the trigger and shot himself in the head during a desperate struggle with the VP and the lady who wrote the diary. I believe that is the truth. It is consistent with the medical examiner's report on the body."

Ann leaned back against the closed door. "Do you want this, Paul? Or would you rather have this dumped on someone else? It's not going to hurt your career or what I think of you for you to wisely say let this be someone else's problem."

Paul smiled. "Do you expect me to decline? Or do you not know me that well?"

"I expect you to take this case, run with it, and relish every minute of it. And that's because I do know you." She ran her hand through her hair in a gesture he had rarely seen before. "This is a bombshell that is going to go off in a few months. You want Sam and Rita? This is going to have to be done quietly and fast, and you trust the two of them."

"It will be like old times. The lady shooter case is quiet until her next letter arrives, and I'm not expecting it for another two or three weeks. Rita's watching for it, but I can shift that to Zane, as he's already read into the case. We can be back in Chicago the same day the letter comes in. It's not the first time we'll have juggled two critical investigations at the same time. When the lady shooter case goes hot again, we're in Chicago, and when it pauses we're back on this. Or I tell the VP now to hand this case to someone else."

"Keep it, Paul. You'll do a good job, and that's what matters. I'll fly your team back and forth to Chicago as needed. I'll get you security codes for this room, a lot of coffee, and dinner. The VP's chapter will take about three hours to read, taking notes. The diary, it's much tougher reading. I'd recommend saving that for tomorrow. Are you still interested in a good steak?"

"Only if you join me."

"There's a good chef here. I'll be back in thirty minutes. I'm now hungry."

He laughed. "I find I am too."

He glanced at the clock as the door closed. And then
he picked up the chapter the VP had written and settled
in to read.

Ann was back in twenty-five minutes and kicked the
door. "Paul, hands."

He pushed open the door and rescued two plates and
carefully balanced silverware. The plates were so hot he
hurried to set them on the table. She disappeared and
came back with two more plates and drinks. "One more
trip." This time she came back with a stacked plate of
brownies. "This day demands chocolate."

"Nicely done, Ann. Two perfect steaks, French fries,
and dessert. I'm impressed."

She looked at the arranged meal. "I forgot the ketchup."
She went out again and came back with ketchup and
steak sauce. "Now that looks right."

She settled in with him at the table. He reached across
for her hands and asked if he could pray. At her quick
nod, he asked God's blessing on the food, and for direction on the important decisions they had to make.

Ann cut into the steak and sighed after the first bite.
"I'm glad I know people who can cook." She glanced at
him. "I have a friend who can fly Sam and Rita here. Or
I can go get them. I wouldn't mind getting out of here
for a few hours."

"Have your friend bring them down."

"You're spoiling my fun." She jotted a name and
number on his pad of paper. "Hangar six, east end of
Victory Airport. He runs a charter with three planes, and

he's working on repairing a plane he just picked up, so he's practically living at the hangar. He'll get in the air as soon as they show up, tonight, tomorrow, whatever you arrange. He's flexible."

"I'm calling them after this meal. It's a good steak."

"It's a wonderful steak. There is a place here on the grounds for guests. I can arrange for the three of you to stay here for the duration of your work. Or if you prefer, there is a hotel about thirty minutes from here that is a comfortable place for an extended stay."

"For security reasons, make arrangements here. I want to spend another hour reading tonight, and then I want to go enjoy a piece of Neva's pie on her front porch swing with you. Tomorrow we'll come back here for breakfast with the VP and get this officially started."

She ate more French fries. "It needs to be thorough-beyond-thorough, and it needs to be fast. And for the VP's sake, it needs to be right. I've done what I can do, but I've got butterflies in my stomach that have me wondering if something was missed. If it was, I need you to find it."

"Eventually every secret comes to the surface. You know that."

"I won't be able to keep my name out of this. The victim profiles' book would be enough to put me in the spotlight, but I know my involvement with the VP's autobiography will eventually be out there. People will assume I have known the truth for a number of years, and they would be right. I'm planning for a pretty ugly six months to a year ahead once the book is released. That's why I want some distance between us, Paul. I've known this day was coming, and now that it has arrived,

I would rather not mess up more lives than I have to with the fallout."

"One day at a time, Ann. Right now I simply want to know this material as well as you do. The idea of the press doesn't bother me. But I agree, the report itself has to be credible and above reproach, or it is not going to do the job that needs done. When you need a lawyer, and you will, you'll let me give you a name?"

"When it gets to that point, I'll ask." She pointed her fork at him. "And before you wonder and ask, money for it is not going to be a problem. I've known this was coming. There's been a legal fund building value for a lot of years. I managed to acquire a sizable amount of silver back when it was trading at four dollars an ounce, and it will more than cover what could come."

"Dave mentioned you had built a fabulous rare-coin business."

"I found an Indian-head penny in a roll of pennies I got from the bank when I was eight years old, and it was worth two dollars. That started a lifelong love affair with coins. My childhood hobby turned into a nice business in the years after I graduated college. I had enough capital to start acquiring coins that ran in the fifty- to five-hundred-dollar range. I sold the business and its inventory a decade ago, but moved most of the proceeds into silver bullion since fiat currencies are an accident waiting to happen over time. It sits there and grows in value year after year without me having to do anything but pay the insurance and storage fees on a good vault. I kept a handful of beautiful coins—silver-capped bust half dollars from 1834 to 1838, the ones I personally love. And I dabble from time to time when I spot a value I can't resist."

"Dad is like that with business. He says he's retired, and he lets my brothers run the day-to-day of the Falcon empire, but he'll dabble again when he spots something he can't resist. He'd be bored if he didn't have his hand in the happenings of a business."

"I like your dad." She gathered up the dinner plates and left him the brownies. "I'll come get you in an hour."

"Thanks."

The next morning, Paul loaded his suitcase in the trunk of his car for the trip back to the VP's estate, wondering if he could get the investigation done before the lady shooter sent her next letter, and wondering what he was going to tell his family to explain his absence.

Ann stepped out of her car and offered the coffee mug she held. "Did you sleep much?"

"Not so much. You?"

"I've known this was coming for a long time. Let's get you settled in at the estate, and then I'll go and pick up Sam and Rita."

Paul nodded but didn't get in his car just yet. "It feels big, Ann. Not just what happened, but what will happen when the news is known. This changes history. Not many cases I investigate have ever truly changed history."

"You have to treat it as a puzzle—the eighteen murders, what did people think the chief of staff was doing, what you can prove he was really doing. You convince yourself he was a serial murderer, then you deal with what the VP says happened to him. It doesn't hang together if the first part isn't true. People will hear the VP's story and that's all they will focus on, but the horrific crime is the eighteen murders."

"Then that's where we'll start. Is there a donut shop around here? My team does better with donuts and coffee."

Ann laughed. "I can find something for you."

18

After breakfast with the VP, and Paul's official decision to accept the task, Ann left to pick up Sam and Rita at the airport. She didn't offer them much commentary on why they had been asked to come, but she saw the look they exchanged when she pulled into the estate. She parked next to Paul's car at the back of the house and led the way to the side door and entered the kitchen. Reece came in to meet them. Ann made the introductions. "Sam Truebone, Rita Heart, may I introduce the VP's lead Secret Service Agent Reece Lion."

"Welcome to the Gannett estate. You made good time."

While they exchanged pleasantries, she unpacked the sack she had brought in, left the smaller box for Reece, and picked up the larger box to take with her. "Paul?"

"The archive room," Reece replied.

"I'll take them back." She nodded to the smaller box. "Save me one of those."

Reece looked at what she had brought and smiled. "Don't delay."

Ann led the way through the house. "I'll give you both a tour later so you can find your way around, and introduce you to the VP. He's a nice guy who will ask you to call him Jim, and you'll find he will enjoy a conversation on just about any subject. I tend to stick to 'sir,' just on principle. Here's Paul." She tapped on the door, then punched in the security code. "Sam, Rita, and one box of donuts, as requested."

Paul looked up from his reading, smiled and took the box she offered. "Thanks, Ann. Hello, guys."

"I'm going to go catch a walk with Black. Call if you need me."

"I will."

She closed the door behind her.

Sam pulled out a chair. "You dragged us from Chicago, to the former VP's estate, into a secure room. This is going to be interesting."

"You don't know the half of it." Paul opened the donut box and approved of the choices Ann had made. He picked up a plain glazed donut. "Help yourself to coffee and a donut and get ready for a roller coaster." He looked at Rita. "Zane's up to speed on what to watch for in the mail?"

She nodded. "We're covered there, boss. I cleared him for our email traffic as well, just in case she changes up her approach. Zane won't miss her offer. I do worry about getting my office back—he looked awfully comfortable at my desk. The official cover is he's doing a statistical review of case results since his retirement as part of the director's review of our team structure. Our guys will treat his presence with kid gloves, and be very nice to him."

Paul laughed. "Nice cover. The day our lady shooter sends a letter, we're on a plane back to Chicago within an hour. We won't miss out on anything good, and here we'll avoid some of the twiddling of our thumbs waiting for her offer to arrive."

Rita set her coffee mug on the table and chose a chocolate-iced donut. Sam tapped his donut against Rita's in their new-case ritual and nodded to Paul. "Okay, boss. We're settled and ready. Why are we here?"

"The VP was abducted by a serial killer, who murdered eighteen people. The serial killer was his chief of staff, Aaron Crown. And the VP covered up what happened."

Sam swallowed his bite of donut. "So . . . nothing too urgent."

"Just another day on the job," Rita offered, licking icing off her thumb.

Paul felt the urge to laugh at their attempted straight-faced reaction to his news. "I've missed the two of you. You should have seen my jaw trying not to drop when the VP gave me that set of facts."

"Is he criminally liable for the cover-up?"

"That's for someone higher up than me to figure out. Gannett is releasing to us a chapter in his autobiography detailing what occurred." Paul tapped the printout of it. "We're on a fact-finding mission. Is this written record of events accurate? Or is it another cover-up? Or . . . ?"

"You don't trust it to be true?" Sam asked.

"I'm staying neutral. We figure out what is here, what we think about it, and we keep this to ourselves. Even the director is in the dark for the time being.

"I would like you both to start by reading the VP's

account of what happened. We'll use that to start planning how we unpeel the layers of this onion. This room holds an archive of the chief of staff's life—his schedules, financial records, letters, et cetera. There is a detailed diary dictated by Aaron Crown of his murders that is grim reading.

"According to the VP, only five people know this information. Reece Lion helped him in the cover-up, as did a retired Secret Service agent named Ben Harmon, now deceased. Aaron Crown dictated the diary to a lady he abducted. She was to be the witness to the murder of the VP. Her name is being withheld, as is the person who helped her return to her life. So it's a very small group."

Sam noted, "They kept it hidden by keeping those who knew to a minimum."

Paul nodded. "Other than the fact this is going to consume our time, I don't know what to tell you to expect. It may be exactly what they are saying, an attempt to tell the world the complete record of what occurred. If it's the partial truth, they have had years to decide what they selectively do not want to reveal. I don't know. Until I do, just stay skeptical along with me."

"I can do skeptical," Sam said.

"And I can do suspicious, which is the cousin of skeptical," Rita offered.

Paul handed over copies of the VP chapter Ann had printed out for him that morning. "It's fascinating reading." He chose another donut and returned his attention to the diary text, which was, as Ann had warned him, grim reading.

Four hours later, there was a tap on the door. "Come in," Paul called.

A click as the door unlocked and then Ann opened it and leaned against the doorpost. "Paul, four things. There's a meal set up in the garden room, end of this hall, back of the house, and you're welcome to break and eat there or bring it back here. I had the murder board on the eighteen victims and case files from my place transferred here. They've been set up in the general conference room two rooms down. The security database did an update roll, and there are now access codes for the three of you to this room." She offered him the cards. "And the VP is going to play bridge with friends this afternoon. Reece is going with him."

"Thanks, Ann."

She nodded and disappeared.

Paul nodded toward the closed door. "Ann wrote a book about the eighteen victims of the chief of staff, profile pieces, and it's a solid read. Her book is going to be released alongside the VP's autobiography. I've read the case files she has on the victims, and it is extensive. Ann also worked on the VP chapter, had a hand in generating this text file of the diary, and organized most of the material in this room. The VP trusts her, and has her in place as a major source of information for us."

"But—" Sam began.

"Just a fact I'm mulling. We'll talk about it later. Do you want to break for food?"

"Let's bring it back here."

While they ate, Sam put in the video of the retired Secret Service agent who had passed away. The video showed him sitting in a comfortable chair in what looked like a family room of a middle-class home. His own, given the family photos on the wall behind him.

"Hello, watchers of my tape. My name is Ben Harmon. I spent thirty years with the Secret Service, and my last seven working in the White House. I was part of VP Jim Gannett's security detail during his presidential campaign. I helped the VP cover up the fact he was abducted on August twelfth, 2003.

"I was contacted on the twelfth at home by Reece Lion. I was aware the former VP was missing, that a boating accident was the media report. Reece said something else had happened, and the VP was personally requesting my help. I was asked to drive immediately to a location near Petersburg, Georgia, and to tell no one this news or the reason I was leaving.

"I arrived to find four people at the scene. VP Jim Gannett, Secret Service Reece Lion, and two women I had not met before. I heard their first names, but was not introduced, and will not reveal those names here.

"The structure was an old cabin, with a dock at the lake, suitable for a hunter or fisherman to shelter from a storm, a reasonably isolated place, rarely in use, with weeds nearby as tall as my waist. I entered the cabin to find four rooms—two small side rooms, a bathroom, and a main commons area. There was power to the cabin and an active phone line.

"Aaron Crown was dead of a gunshot wound to the head in the main room, the gun beside him on the floor. I recognized him visually.

"The VP gave me a brief description of his abduction, laid out a plan to cover up what had occurred, his reasons for doing so, and gave me the choice of whether I wanted to be involved. I made the decision to help, knowing that what I was going to do would corrupt a crime scene.

"As instructed by the VP, I took photos of the scene in detail, including photographs of the VP and his condition, and then gave the camera and film to Reece Lion. I took no photos of the two ladies present. Nor did I photograph any of the vehicles at the scene.

"The VP had copied from a diary a list of locations for the victims' remains. I rewrote the list in my own handwriting, then burned the VP's list.

"I collected and gave to Reece the chief of staff's wallet, keys, and all papers I could find in the cabin and in the chief of staff's car. They were placed in a paper grocery sack, which was sealed shut with duct tape.

"I left the scene in the chief of staff's car, followed by Reece in his car. I destroyed the chief of staff's car at a junkyard, acquired a boat by cutting the lock, parked the boat at the cabin dock, and returned to the cabin with gasoline cans.

"The two ladies had left the scene.

"The VP and Reece Lion now left the scene.

"I used the cabin's phone to place a call to my own phone and set the phone receiver beside the body with the line still open.

"I then burned the cabin down to destroy all finger-prints and traces of who had been present.

"I drove to the police station in Petersburg and pre-sented my Secret Service credentials. I gave the police a statement, indicating a man had called me to confess, given me locations of his victims, and I had heard a gun-shot. They traced the last call to my phone to the cabin. Officers responded to the location, where his remains were discovered in the burned-out cabin, and beside the body a burned phone and a handgun. I stood back and watched as the investigation proceeded under its own course. I repeated my original statement as other officers joined the investigation. I took no further actions to change events as they unfolded.

"DNA tests did not yield a name. He was cremated and buried as a John Doe.

"My handwritten statement on this matter is included with this video and repeats what I have said here. I am making this video at the request of the VP and will give it to him.

"I have told no one what occurred that day. I will take it to my grave. This ends my statement."

"We need those photos of the scene, boss," Sam said when the video ended.

"We do. And apparently those photos, his wallet, and the rest of the evidence from the cabin are buried in the chief of staff's otherwise empty coffin. We can't exhume his grave without attracting interest. We're going to have to figure out a cover story and do it as late into this investigation as we can. If the story leaks, the press gets wind of a piece of this, we may only have a matter of hours to get a preliminary report issued."

"You have got to admire the cover-up they did with only a couple of hours to plan it," Rita said. She pushed back her chair and gathered up empty plates. "Anyone want dessert?"

"Bring back that plate of cookies. It's going to be a long night of reading," Sam replied.

Rita took the next-to-last cookie from the plate. "What are you mulling over, boss? You've been gazing at nothing long enough something serious is on your mind."

Paul rippled the diary text with his thumb. "It took someone a long time to write this diary by hand. The text is over twenty thousand words, so at least a hundred handwritten pages."

"Several days at least."

"The lady he abducted to write the diary doesn't want her name known, and the VP is going to honor that. He made the comment that she was in pretty bad shape when this ended."

"Given the details we know, she likely would have been."

"The VP also said this information was known to only five people. The VP, two Secret Service agents, the diary writer, and one who helped the diary writer return to her life." Paul paused. "Ann knows about it. Either the VP didn't count himself, or Ann is one of the original five."

Sam looked up from what he was reading.

Rita hesitated. "Ann wrote the diary or helped the diary writer return to her life."

"She's a good writer. She would have been known to the chief of staff from her help with the early work on the VP's autobiography. As a cop, her testimony would have extra credibility. She would have been a logical choice for the chief of staff to abduct to write the diary. Equally, the VP and the Secret Service agent knew and trusted Ann. She could have been the one they tapped to help return the diary writer to her life.

"Gannett didn't tell even his family the truth. If Ann wasn't involved, why did he risk asking her to help with this chapter and keep this secret? I don't think he would have. If Ann is one of the original five, it explains why the VP has her helping him. We need to know where Ann was during the time this happened. Is it possible to find that out without tipping our hand that we're asking the question?"

"If she wrote the diary, rather than just helping after the fact, she was gone for several days," Sam said. "That much time missing, someone was looking for her. You need a conversation with someone who knew her well nine years ago. You need to see the archives of the local newspaper. You might need her work files, or her health insurance records. Some of it you don't get without a court order. She's got a security clearance. Her file would have records on something major like an unexplained disappearance. Someone with access to that file could give us a yes or no for the dates in question."

"You could ask her," Rita said quietly.

Paul shook his head. "You don't ask a question like this without already knowing the answer. I ask her, she says no, there are only two options. She just lied to me, or she really wasn't involved. Which is the truth? The VP is protecting the writer of the diary. The VP will agree with whatever Ann says."

"They are not releasing the diary in order to protect the handwriting of the author," Sam offered. "See it, and you would know if it's Ann's handwriting. If they haven't destroyed it, the diary still exists somewhere. It leaves open whether they asked her to help the diary writer recover, that Ann was part of the cover-up after the fact, but it narrows the question."

Paul nodded. "At some point along this investigation

I'm going to ask one of you to get away from this place
and do some looking into that question."

"Boss, do we really want to know who wrote the diary,
and who helped her when it was over?" Rita asked. "Does
the knowledge help us that much? The diary writer was
the only other person there for much of what occurred,
and it would be very useful to have testimony other
than the VP for the events of that day, but a victim deserves privacy. I can understand the reason she wants
to stay unknown. We have the killer's words for what
he did and why. Do we need to know who wrote those
words? We can't put that interview in a report, as every
report is going to be public eventually. And you can't
reveal who helped her without likely revealing who she
is. We can't leave an investigation trail that would lead
to her, as someone else will follow our steps and figure
it out. If we look, we likely cause her name to eventually become public knowledge. Do we want to run that
risk?"

"If it's Ann, we need to know it," Paul said. "She had
access to the material we are looking at, the ability to
bias what we now see. If who it is has had no access to
what is here, it's not as relevant."

"Ann could bias what is here, but do you think she
would?"

"No."

"Then consider not asking the question, boss. We can
be skeptical of what is here without needing to know for
certain if she was involved. We already know the VP and
the Secret Service agent were involved, and they have had
as much access to this material as Ann. If someone wants
to bias this and try to do a cover-up, they've all had the

access and opportunity. The VP is the one we have to be concerned about. The others are following his lead."

"Even if she was one of the original five, I think you let her keep her secret if that's what she has decided she wants to do," Sam agreed.

"Ann has nightmares. Bad ones. And has for years. She wakes to a gunshot."

"Did you really want to tell us that?"

"If I'm dragging you into this, you know what I know. If she wrote the diary, it would explain the nightmares."

"I can find out, boss," Rita offered. "I can do it quietly."

"We need to know. The last thing I want to do is use her as a resource going through this material, talking about this case, only to find out I'm walking a victim back through a major crime, putting her in the position of having to relive it. She's written about this case, she's spent years working with this material, but it is not the same as going back to the cabin remains, or seeing the photos of the scene. Before we get to that point, I want to know if it is necessary to shield her from it."

19

Ann was involved. Everything Paul knew about her, knew about the VP, told him the reason for her help with this chapter was rooted in something big. Ann would have been thirty when this happened. He didn't like the implications of what it meant if Ann had been the one to write the diary.

He walked from the main house to the guesthouse, where Ann had arranged for them to stay. They had been reading materials on the case for the last three days, and he was beginning to feel burned out. Paul entered his suite. He had a bedroom, a bath, and adjoining sitting room to himself. Sam and Rita had similar accommodations upstairs.

Ann had left on an MHI case the day before. He wanted to end the evening talking with her, and a glance at the time showed it just after nine p.m. He made a video call to see if she would answer. The call was picked up and the video flickered to stable.

"Hi, Paul."

She was in a hotel room somewhere. She smiled briefly when she saw him, but it quickly faded. She was writing on a pad of paper, and she set it aside and closed the case folder.

"How's the case going?"

She shook her head. "Three dead. Someone shot a mom and her six-year-old twins."

She didn't offer more. She didn't have to. He could feel the weight of the sadness himself just hearing the news. "I'm sorry, Ann."

"So am I."

"I'll try to distract you for a few minutes if that's okay."

"I'd give you a hug if I could from a distance. Distract away."

"I'll take that hug one day. Business first. It's going well here. You put together a well-documented paper trail for us to work from. We'll need some fieldwork. Would it be possible to do a flyover in a single day of where the eighteen victims' remains were recovered?"

"A long day, but it could be done if weather cooperates."

"I would also like to visit the cabin remains where this happened, and the VP's vacation home."

"Just let me know when you want to travel, and I'll set it up."

"A couple more days. We'll fit it in to when you have some time free. Second question. How does the VP plan to keep the publisher from leaking this chapter of the book early? A leaked copy of this would be worth a fortune."

"There's a tight enough embargo planned, I think it

will hold. The book is printed only at Grifton's Pittsburg plant. The site is highly automated with only a hundred people at the location. They produce fifty thousand copies, and the books remain at the site. The night before the book release, the pallets will load on planes and go nationwide.

"The plant employees are each paid a fifty-thousand-dollar bonus if this does not leak, and it is an all-or-nothing bonus—everyone earns it or no one does. So they are taking steps themselves to make it work. Only one person will actually see the chapter to check the typesetting. They are surrendering all cellphones, turning off phones to the building, and locking themselves in. They are assigning multiple security guards to the warehouse to make sure no book is opened and read. Food and phone messages will be passed in from the outside. They will keep the information tight for five days while the fifty thousand books are printed. Those copies will hit first with reporters, reviewers, and major bookstores. The day after the book is released, the layout files are sent out, and print runs of several million begin to run at major printers worldwide. Within two weeks, the book will be widely available everywhere."

"I see why you think the embargo will hold."

"I think it will."

"That's it for business. Anything I can do for you, Ann?"

"It's nice to have a break. I don't think as well when the emotions run high on a case, and this one is just about all emotions. Kids getting murdered get to me."

"Another topic then." Paul let the silence linger for a bit while he studied her. He decided to turn the conversation toward the questions he'd been mulling over. "Can I ask a semiserious personal question?"

"Sure."

"I know you've said you aren't looking to settle down. Are you too busy to consider it? Being the MHI, writing like you do? Is it inertia? You've stepped aside from the question for so long, you've simply gotten comfortable being single?"

She blinked. "You came out of left field with that question. Let me think about it."

"Not so out of the blue—I've been thinking about it for a few days."

She found a candy bar and tore open the wrapper. "Okay, I'll give you that it's an interesting question. You want the long answer or the short answer, given I haven't really sorted out what my answer is yet?"

"Go with long. We both need a break from work for a few minutes."

She thought about it. "There are probably a lot of reasons why. I don't mind the idea of being married—I write about it in all my books, and I've got a boatload of happily married friends. I'd want a good marriage, not one that is somewhat right or tolerated or snippy from the day of the I do's. That takes the right choice, a lot of energy to build, and decisions about the job and my time that would help rather than hurt a marriage. How many guys really want a cop as a wife? When it comes down to that question, it's a surprisingly small world." She settled back in her chair.

"I can do this job now because there doesn't have to be much of me left when I get home," she added. "I can hibernate and recuperate and take whatever time I need to absorb what the case brought with it. If I were coming home to a husband and needing to have something left for him, I'd try my best, I'd juggle the roles, but I don't know where the energy would come from over the course of a few years. There is margin in my life right now, but add a marriage and that margin is gone. In my twenties I could burn the candle at both ends and not pay much of a price. I'm not twenty anymore.

"And personally, I don't have a desire to have children, which is another caution about getting married. Most marriages, at least one of the two wants to be a parent. I'd hate to end up in that Gordian knot—marrying knowing my husband wants children, I say yes because I love him, and my child finds out she's got a mother who does the job the best she can but doesn't have the confidence for it. When you dream of something from the time you're a kid, all the work that it takes to come true is just part of the dream. When it's a choice for someone else, you can do it, but it's always a struggle to get it right. You're trying your best, but it's just harder to be a good parent, or at least feel successful at being one, when you haven't been acquiring the skills for that role during your whole life.

"I don't want to get married for the sake of not being single, only to make a mess of it. It's a permanent one-time decision. I won't get divorced. I might get charged with murder because I kill the guy out of frustration, but I wouldn't walk away from a marriage. So my choice is to stay single or get married, and so far stay single has been the wise decision the few times I've gotten close to considering it."

Paul had been listening carefully. "Thanks. It's a useful

answer. If it was a successful marriage, do you think you'd enjoy it more than being single?"

She smiled. "I know I would. I love watching marriages that work. You only have to hang out with Lisa and Quinn for a few days, or Vicky and Boone, Dave and Kate, to realize what a good marriage can be like. They are a unit. They are incredibly good together. I'd like to know I made someone that happy. I'd love being married. I'm just cautious enough to know wanting something and having it are different things. From single to a good marriage—there are a lot of decisions to get right, with a lot of risks if I get it wrong. I'm not young anymore, ready to assume it will work out."

"How much risk does it feel like you're taking right now, talking about this?"

"I'm giving you the reasons you should leave this a friendship, Paul. There's not a lot of risk when I'm basically throwing cold water. You want to get married. You've as much as stated that as your goal. So I already know my job is to put as much reality into what you know about me, and what I know about you, as I can.

"I like you. Enough I'm sharing my evenings, and while you may not realize how big a deal that is, I do. You've got a chunk of my time and attention. I just don't know where this goes, and I'm hoping you figure that answer out before I have to. If you want to leave this a friendship, I won't have to make a decision. Not having to make a decision is fine with me. I can give you time and honest answers and hope you have your eyes open. I like the fact you're interested. I like you and what I know about you. But I'm the least pushy lady you've probably ever met. It's not how I'm wired. I'm not looking to change the present into something else."

"You like the comfort of now, the knowing what you've got."

She nodded. "Nothing is in crisis. If tomorrow looks like today, I can live with that." She studied him. "Would it be easier on you if I was looking for a guy? If I was pursuing you?"

"My ego would enjoy it." He smiled. "I've never met someone like you, Ann. On so many levels, this being just one of them, you are unlike anyone else I've ever met. Your calm willingness to stay with what is now makes this an interesting relationship."

"You don't have to move forward or back in a relationship; you can be content with what is. But I know you're looking for a change. You have made a decision that you don't want to be single. You're just trying to figure out the who."

"I told Dave I don't want to be the single guy coming to dinner when I'm fifty."

"You and I both know it's more than that. You want to be a good example when you're head of the Falcon family." She smiled. "You might not have put it into those words, but that's one of the reasons you want to be married. You want to be like your dad, good at the role of leading the family that is the Falcons. I like the fact that role matters to you. You've been preparing for it for years. You'll be a good leader. And you should be married, if you find the right lady. You've got lots of family looking up to you and wanting your time and attention and approval. You can love and lead a family better with a wife to share that role."

It was after eleven when they ended the call, and Paul did so because he knew she still had hours of work ahead of her on the case. He turned in for the night, thinking about their conversation. She didn't want children and a family of her own.

He would enjoy being a dad, he was certain of that. He appreciated his extended family, and he liked watching kids grow up. Did he want his own family? There had always been the assumption it would be part of being married, that he'd end up with a family, with children. Could he go into marriage knowing he wouldn't have a family? Could he live with that? He decided he could live with anything if he went into it with his eyes open to the choice. But would he be happy with that reality as the years went by?

She wasn't saying, I would rather adopt than have my own children at my age, with the stress a pregnancy would be. She was saying she didn't have a desire to be a mom. If she fell in love, she could be talked into changing her mind, and she didn't want to be put in that position.

He'd wondered if he would hit a wall with her and where it would be, and he realized he just had. Should he simply not pursue Ann? She fascinated him at every level. If it came to the balance of Ann as his wife or having a family, he could almost feel the decision already leaning toward Ann. But children aside, was marriage itself a good option for her? Maybe she was right—she was single because that was what worked for her life. Would the things that fascinated him about her, that gave her the balance she had now, survive in a marriage?

Or would marriage harm the very things that attracted him to her?

She'd be easy to love. She would be a delight to have as a wife.

She never spoke about attraction, about passion, but he knew it would be there and flare hot with ease. It was hard to take his eyes off her now, and he'd never even kissed her yet. It was an awareness that was growing stronger. He'd enjoy having her as a wife, with God's blessing on taking her to bed with him. A good marriage would be so much better than being single.

Ann would thrive being in a good marriage. Marriage was ideal for someone who formed such deep relationships. She just didn't want to make a mistake, to the point she was simply standing still, waiting. She wouldn't pursue him. She wouldn't look at his family wealth, at who he was, and think, good catch, and try to win him over. She wasn't wired that way, but she also wouldn't even think of it. She wouldn't get married for money or position.

Why *would* she get married?

He knew what he wanted in a marriage. A partner. A lover. A friend. He wanted someone sharing his world and sharing his life. He wanted the joy of being involved with the same someone for the next fifty years. He wanted husband as his role; he wanted to no longer be single. He didn't know what Ann wanted in a marriage. He knew a lot about her, but not that. He needed that answer.

Three days later, Paul entered the secure room. He pulled out a chair beside Sam. "Did Rita call?"

"She's leaving Chicago now. She said to tell you the office is quiet and that Zane has added a fish tank to her office. She stopped at your place and packed another few days of clothes for you. And she said she has what you asked her to research."

"Any indication what she found?"

"She just said you should pick her up at the airport around six p.m."

"So . . . she found something."

"Sorry, boss."

"It's why I sent her. Where are you at?"

"Victim nine. You have to admire the work they did." Sam held up a receipt. "The official schedule has the chief of staff in Chicago. They found a receipt signed by the chief of staff for a restaurant in Ashville, Ohio, the day of the disappearance."

"He wanted the proof to stick around, otherwise he wouldn't have kept his receipts."

"Oh, the chief of staff wanted them to be able to prove he was the killer, that's clear. He kept paper on everything. There were six hundred forty-two disorganized boxes of it in his basement. They worked it down to this organized assortment of facts. They put it together as if they were going to have to take the case to trial. And they did the job without a dozen people to help them do it. I have to admire the fact they knew this was going to come public one day, and they were willing to make as organized a presentation as they could. Those six hundred forty-two boxes of paper—less what is in this room—are over in what Reece called the long-term secure storage room. You want me to go over and start looking through what is there?"

"After you get through victim eighteen."

"I'll be there by tomorrow." Sam shifted in his chair. "I don't know about you, but I could use a run later. I've been sitting way too many hours."

"I'll join you and be glad for it."

"You're interviewing the VP today?"

"I'll sit down with him in an hour. Any other questions come to mind?"

"Your list seems complete."

"Want to come along?"

Sam leaned over to pull open a file drawer and rifle a stack of folders. "My excuse for why I'm busy, and you should accept a no-thanks."

Paul laughed. "I'll have a tape of the interview for you to listen to."

"Thanks. It can't be easy, trying to figure out how to ask the questions when it's the VP on the other side of the conversation."

"He's only going to tell me what he's decided to say, and he's had years to think about his answers. I'm not expecting much; I'm just curious to see what he's going to want to say."

"I wonder sometimes if he misses the spotlight. He could have released this information after his death, rather than do it now, knowing he's going to have months of media interest. He's setting himself up to be the center of attention again."

Paul nodded. "I believe part of it is clearing his conscience—he wants to take responsibility for what he did rather than leave it for others. And part of it is the media. He's going to be in the spotlight, and he thinks he can handle it. He's trying to unfold this according to a script he's written so he can control events. It won't last past first contact with the news media of today, but that appears to be his goal."

Sam reached over to the file cabinet and got out a second recorder. "It's going to be a famous tape. You should sound as professional as you can. And you should have a backup recorder."

Paul smiled. "Thanks for the reminder."

Paul had several pages of questions for the interview, and he worked down the list systematically, occasionally jotting down the time to remind himself when they had reached various topics. They were in the library where they had first met. The VP seemed relieved to be having the conversation, and he was trying to be helpful, answering the questions in an expansive way. Paul let Gannett talk, making a point not to interrupt him, guiding the conversation with his questions. He had changed the tapes at the two-hour mark.

"Did you ever suspect the chief of staff was lying to you?"

"It's hard to separate what I know of the man now from what I knew then. He was my chief of staff, he was a man who got things done, and in government and politics that often meant he played hardball and even played dirty at times. He would use whatever information he had to get the obstacle in front of him to move aside. So I knew even during the early years that he was often not telling me things for my sake—better that I didn't know. He would get done what had to be done. Back then I trusted him not to cross the line, even if I knew he would press that line hard. I knew him to be loyal, committed to the task we were focused on. He was a goal-driven man, and we shared common objectives. I rose through government because he was my chief of staff, and I trusted him.

"I never had a moment where I thought, He just lied to me. I never had that sense of outrage. I want to believe I would have seen what was going on, but he killed eighteen people while he was working for me. I look back and can't understand why I didn't sense at least something off about him. I'm ashamed of that. There had to be signs I missed, and I don't understand how I overlooked them over so many years."

"Do you know of any incident where he got in trouble with the law or had personal legal troubles, where he used his position to get out of the trouble, or where someone decided to look the other way because of the fact he was your chief of staff?"

"It's a very good question. No, I know of no such situation that ever arose. But I don't know either that I would have caught wind of it if he was covering something up. I haven't looked, and I realize I should have."

They had been talking for over three hours now, and the questions were prompting more color about the chief of staff, but not more facts. Paul was comfortable the VP had put into the chapter what he intended to say.

Paul turned a page in his notes and settled into the next area of questions he had. "Tell me about the other individuals on your staff who were with you for several years. Who else would you say knew the chief of staff well?"

Paul drove to the airport to meet Rita, exhausted after the four-hour conversation with the VP. On its surface this wasn't a hard case to review, but it was difficult to look back so far in time and catch the nuances, the emotions, the unspoken. Gannett was a smart man. Was it loyalty to a friend that had blinded him to what was going on? Had the VP ever suspected something else was there? Paul knew what the VP had said, and still he couldn't settle that core question in his mind.

He arrived at the airport, parked, and went to meet Rita's flight. She was fifth off the plane. She crossed to join him. "Hey, boss. How did the interview go?"

"Sam told you."

"He said you looked nervous." She laughed at the face he made.

"It was four hours of conversation that you're welcome to listen to. It's done, that's the best thing I can say for it, although there will probably be another conversation once we're further along. I didn't hear anything new in what he said, but there were impressions of people that you might find useful."

He carried the bag she had packed for him back to the car and stored it in the trunk. Paul held out the keys. "Drive while I read, Rita." He opened the door and got in the passenger seat. She handed him a thick file from her briefcase.

"The articles are from Ann's local newspaper archives. I used my phone to take photos of the pages that applied to Ann, and I printed articles that matched what I was officially there to research. I signed in under a false name. No one is going to put together I was looking."

"Bottom line?"

"Ann wrote the diary, boss."

Paul felt a sudden chill. He had been hoping he was wrong. "You're sure."

"Yes."

"Talk me through it."

"Ann disappeared on August five, 2003. Police were conducting an aggressive search to find her. A confidential informant who was seen with her the day she disappeared was their top suspect. He was a known schizophrenic who could get violent. He was found six states over on a rural road, dead in his car of a self-inflicted gunshot. The ME put his death at August twelve. There was evidence Ann had been in the passenger seat of the car, but she was nowhere to be found. She reappeared on August fourteen when she called her boss. She was on medical leave for sixteen weeks before returning to work. She spent that medical leave somewhere else, and didn't return to her home until just before she returned to work.

"The official story: the confidential informant had been suicidal, had a passenger with him, had a gun, and she had entered his car in order to convince him to let the passenger out. She eventually succeeded. The CI wanted to go home, meaning his parents' farm. He drove into the country but was lost in his mind, thinking they were in a foreign country. She stopped him. They got out of the car. He panicked, it turned into a violent fight, and during the struggle she was struck in the face. She woke to find herself tied up and locked in an abandoned farmhouse cellar. She had to break out, and when she finally did so, she found she was in the middle of nowhere. She was fighting a concussion and stayed put for the first couple of days until her vision

FULL DISCLOSURE

cleared. She hopped a train to the nearest town to make a call. Not a bad cover story. She used what the police already thought. She eliminated their ability to find the farmhouse and check her story. Sixteen weeks of medical leave suggests she was in pretty bad shape. Someone paid those medical bills. There will be records if you want to go deeper."

"That she was the diary writer, rather than the one called to help after the fact, tells me enough for now. We're going to have to work out something regarding the cabin and the coffin photos. I don't want to walk her back through them."

"If you cut her out of the investigation, she'll know something's up. She'll know we know."

"I don't mind keeping her in the loop. The VP was part of it, along with Reece, and we're keeping them informed of our progress. I just don't want to be causing her more harm by refreshing the details of what happened—letting her see the photos or taking her to the cabin location. You read the diary. You can imagine as well as I can what those days between August five and twelve were like for her."

"The memories alone would explain the nightmares," Rita agreed. "I'd rather let her tell us if she wants to than reveal the fact we know. It's minor, boss, but I like her. It would be ripping the scab off a nasty wound when she wants to keep it private."

"Even if we never say a word, she'll know we've figured it out. Ann doesn't miss the obvious. She'll wonder why we aren't looking for who wrote the diary."

"Then maybe you should tell her now, if only to let her know we're not going to pursue it."

"I'm thinking about it. Thanks for making the trip and finding out the facts."

"If I could find them out this easily, reporters are going to figure it out when the book is released. Every newspaper in the country will be going back to look at their archives for the week of August 2003. How many people went missing during that week? Ann will stand out like a sore thumb, given her connection to the book about the victims."

"I know. Ann has to know that too. And yet she's keeping this quiet. That's what bothers me. I understand a victim not wanting to go public about what happened. But this is beginning to feel like more than that. She's staying quiet for a reason, and I don't think we know the full reason why."

20

This way, Black." The dog came back from a tangent to check out a rose bush, then followed Paul through the gap in the evergreens. They both needed a long walk tonight, and Paul took them toward the back of the estate grounds. He needed the time to sort out his thoughts.

Ann had accepted she would live with whatever came as a result of her decision to remain silent and keep the VP's secret. She was prepared to deal with the press scrutiny, the legal costs, and the legal risks. Paul worried about what was going to unfold. He wondered if she was prepared for it to cost her job, and he feared, in the worst outcome, she might face that possibility.

She needed to state on the record that she was the writer of the diary. Her legal risk ended with the statement she was the writer and a victim of this crime. But if she couldn't come forward, if she maintained her silence because she couldn't speak of what had happened, he would do everything he could to protect her. But he didn't know if he could save her job.

As a law-enforcement officer, she had a legal obligation to report a crime. If all Ann admitted to in public was helping the VP write his autobiography, she was in legal trouble. She had known about the VP abduction, the chief of staff's death, the cover-up at the cabin, and had not reported it. The best she could hope for before a police disciplinary panel was a long suspension. The duty to report a crime was a legal obligation of her job, not one on her as an individual, so her legal risk would end with the disciplinary panel. But losing her job would be a devastating price for her to pay.

As a victim she had a right to privacy. That right was enshrined both in legal statute and in the police code of conduct. She could report, or not report, the crime against herself and the law would support her decision. To report she knew a crime had been covered up, she would have to report she had been present and been a victim of the crime. Her silence about the cover-up at the cabin stemmed directly from her own right to privacy as a victim. Her right to privacy trumped any legal obligation she had to report. She was a victim first, and a law-enforcement officer second.

But Ann couldn't assert that right to privacy unless she went public that she had been a victim. There would be no way to quietly inform the police disciplinary board she was in fact the victim of the chief of staff, that a failure-to-report charge should not be brought against her, and expect it to not be leaked to the press. This was too high-profile a case.

She could stay silent and hope the police disciplinary board suspended her rather than fired her. Or she could make public what happened, mitigate all her legal risks, but give up her privacy.

Paul didn't know if she could take that step. She was staying quiet for a reason. She knew the law as well as he did. She knew the possible outcomes. And she was choosing to stay quiet. She wouldn't have made that decision unless she saw no other way to survive.

He could force her hand, send Rita back to do the investigation on the record, and make Ann's name public in the FBI report as the writer of the diary. He could save her job at the cost of their relationship. Even thinking of that path left him certain he would never take it. This was Ann's decision. He'd support and help her however he could, but he wouldn't force her hand.

Based on what Rita had told him, Ann had also given false statements regarding her injuries. She had misled the investigating officers by confirming the confidential informant who had died had caused her injuries. That would have to be handled as a separate matter between Ann and her boss at the time who investigated her disappearance. She was speaking as a victim, not as a law-enforcement officer, when she gave her statement, and Paul doubted a complaint would be brought by the investigating officers.

Reece Lion was the one with the most legal exposure. This was, at a minimum, going to cost him his job and his pension. A good lawyer would argue mitigating facts in the case. The death itself had been investigated the day it occurred. An autopsy had been performed, and it confirmed the man died of a self-inflicted gunshot. The cover-up's only legal ramification had been that the case file didn't have a name to record for the body, and a false death certificate had been issued for the chief of staff. The actions at the cabin were taken to protect the privacy rights of the two victims, for the VP had a right to privacy as well as the writer of the diary. The facts would be enough for a good lawyer to get a negotiated plea on the charges of tampering with a crime scene and making false statements.

The VP had put those around him in legal jeopardy in order to keep quiet what his chief of staff had done. His motives were more complex than that, but that was the bottom line. And of the people facing legal jeopardy, the one person Paul didn't know how the law would treat was the VP himself. He too was a victim of the crime. He had a reputation that would forever be tainted by the fact a serial killer had worked for him for decades. He put in motion what occurred with the cover-up. If charges were ever brought related to the cover-up, which seemed doubtful at best, the VP would die of old age before the matter was ever settled in the courts.

Paul returned to his core problem. Ann. He didn't know if she would find the courage to tell him she had written the diary. He could pray she did. If she could trust him enough to tell him she wrote it, he could help her through the legal options. But if she couldn't tell him, if her only way of surviving this was silence, then he had to figure out a way to prepare her for what it would mean if she faced a failure-to-report disciplinary charge.

He had time. That was the only good thing he could see. Until the FBI investigation concluded, until the VP's autobiography became public, there was time to prepare. But he had to somehow get Ann to trust him enough to tell him she had written the diary.

She'd been dealing with this for years. He had been dealing with this for days. Paul forced himself to mentally step back from the worry. If there was one thing he knew about high-profile public cases, it was that the outcome always had unexpected turns. For all Paul knew, the VP had quietly arranged a pardon for the actions of everyone who had helped him keep quiet about what had happened. There was no way to know which way this would play out legally for those involved.

Ann would have a good lawyer, and if events unfolded so she might lose her job, Paul would somehow talk her into stating she was the writer of the diary. That was the one bright spot to all of this. The truth would defend Ann against any legal concern. She just had to have the strength to say it on the record if it came down to that outcome—her job or her privacy.

He hoped he didn't make things worse for her by how he handled this. She'd agreed with the VP's decision to ask him to investigate what happened. She wanted him to be the agent in this position. But it was playing havoc with his ability to decide how to handle matters with her, both on the legal side and the personal.

His phone rang. He pulled it from his pocket and was relieved to see it was Ann. "I was hoping you would call tonight. How are you?"

"Feeling beat up. The funeral for the mom and her six-year-old twins was today. There was an arrest made this afternoon. The case came down to a divorce. The mom got custody of the kids, and the father decided none of them should live. The man was a state court judge. I'm not sure how much I helped my cop beyond buying the food and listening, but at least he's finally going to get a decent night's sleep. I'm on the way to the airport. A question: do you want to do the flyover of the burial sites and visit the cabin tomorrow? The weather is good. It may not be later in the week. A front will be moving through."

"Sure, but you would benefit from a day off."

"Flying is my way to relax. I wouldn't offer if it wasn't something I wanted to do."

"Then the answer is yes. The timing dovetails well with where we are at in the review."

"We'll need to be in the air by seven a.m., if you could let Sam and Rita know. How's Black?"

He held the phone down. "Black, say hi to mom." The dog barked once, and his tail slapped Paul's leg.

"He misses you. We both do." More emotion than he had intended went into those words.

She hesitated before responding, and her words when they came were a soft echo of his. "I appreciate the sentiment."

"Fly safe, Ann."

"I always do. I'll see you bright and early tomorrow."

Paul walked through the VP's home to the sunroom just before six a.m. to see if Ann had arrived. He stopped short. His sister-in-law was having breakfast with the VP.

"Paul, please, get a plate and join us."

"Glad to, sir. Vicky, this is a pleasant surprise."

"The VP asked if I would go along as security for this trip. He said Reece was helping you on a case and would be otherwise occupied, and someone needed to watch that your trip attracted no particular attention.

That's the definition of my specialty. I'm going to hang out with Ann and watch your back."

"I'll be glad to have you." Paul glanced at the VP, wondering if any of that reason was true or if the VP had simply found a reason for Ann to have the company of a friend on the trip. Either way, Paul was glad for the outcome.

He joined them at the table with a breakfast plate.

"Ann has already come and gone," Vicky said. "She arrived, stacked three bacon sandwiches, said good morning to Black, and left for the airport. She said to join her at hangar four."

Paul nodded, regretting that he'd missed her.

―――――▼―――――

Paul was beginning to appreciate airports and private hangars and the coordinated activity going on around the flight line. He walked with Sam and Rita, following Reece and Vicky to the hangar Ann had specified. Ann was circling a stunning plane painted deep blue. The name Grant Summer was painted in crisp white script near the open passenger cabin door and stairs. She tucked her clipboard under her arm when she saw them. "Good morning. We've got beautiful weather to fly. Settle in and get comfortable. I'll be ready to go in about ten minutes."

The cabin was configured to seat eight, all captain's chairs in a deep plush leather. Paul chose a seat in the middle of the cabin, and the others spread out around him. Ann boarded the plane fifteen minutes later and pulled the door closed. "Everyone comfortable?"

"It's a nice ride, Ann," Reece remarked, speaking for all of them.

"It is that." She scanned the group. "I'm going to give a one-minute safety drill, so listen up. Emergency exits are those windows marked with orange squares. The top two levers, pulled together and turned ninety degrees, will pop the window out. They will also yield to a hard kick. Smoke is a problem in this cabin configuration. If oxygen masks come down, use them. If this plane is going down, your best defense is to tighten your seat belts, brace your feet against the closest seat, and lock your arms around your neck. Better a broken arm than a broken neck. Turbulence can bounce this plane around the sky, so if I turn on the yellow caution lights in the cabin, find a seat and a seat belt. The highest risk on a clear day like this is a bird strike on takeoff. You hear a thump, you yell bird, and you brace as fast as you can. The airports we are using today aren't forgiving about an immediate stall. I'll be picking grass out of my teeth thirty seconds after we lift off if we strike a bunch of blackbirds."

"You know how to set the stage, Ann," Paul said.

"Now you'll be glad when I get you safely in the air. On a lighter note, the snacks and beverages on this flight are top drawer and fair game, so help yourself. The purpose of this flight is a visual survey of the grave sites, so I will be flying at a low altitude for most of the flight. I will give a two-minute alert as we come to each location. There are two planned stops today, the first one in about six hours. I hope you enjoy the flight. I know I'm going to have a nice day flying this gorgeous plane."

Ann walked forward and settled into the cockpit.

Minutes later the engines were started. The plane pulled slowly from the hangar and turned toward the taxiway. After a pause and when they were cleared for takeoff, Ann turned onto the runway and began to pick up speed. Paul saw Sam and Rita both at windows, scanning the sky looking for birds, while Vicky and Reece relaxed in their chairs, conversing quietly about a mutual friend. The flight lifted off so smoothly, Paul didn't feel them leave the ground.

Paul spread out the map of the Midwest, marked with the victims' burial sites. Ann had added small numbered Post-it notes to show the order they would pass over the sites.

Forty minutes after the flight began, Vicky's phone vibrated with a message, and she walked forward to join Ann in the cockpit. She returned and announced, "Out the east windows, coming up in two minutes, will be the burial site for victim six."

They flew over the area, and Paul got his first look at what this killer defined as a proper dumping ground. Thick, mature trees, a country road, isolated, not a house within sight even from the air. He hadn't stumbled on a place like this just by pulling off the highway and driving into the countryside. He had spent some time to locate this area. Paul made notes on the burial site.

Ten minutes later they passed over another one. More trees, and isolated, hard-to-reach terrain. A hunter would wander those woods, wildlife, but it was isolated ground. The victims had been buried too deep to have an animal disturb the remains, or a heavy rain dislodge the body.

The day passed in a grim progression of burial sites, each one more remarkable than the last for how similar they looked from the air. The chief of staff had been a planner. He had wanted his victims to remain secure until he chose to reveal their locations. None of the eighteen had been found before he wished them to be found. The sites were yet another taste of the control he had wanted to exert over his victims.

Vicky came back from the cockpit. "Ann says we'll be landing at Columbus in ten minutes. It will be a half-hour stop, depending on the refueling time, but enough time to walk around. Any changes you need her to make to the flight plan, this is the time to say so."

"Her plan is fine. We're getting what we need," Paul assured Vicky after a quick glance around at the team.

The second leg of the trip took them across more grave locations and then toward the cabin site. Late in the day, Vicky came back from the cockpit carrying a hand-sketched map. "The cabin is about ten minutes ahead. Ann will fly over the site, then circle to the airport, and we will drive to the cabin." She held up the map. "Here's the lake. The cabin is on the north side of this inlet, back from the shore about fifty feet. Watch for where the water and shoreline start to look like the letter Y, and you'll have the area."

Ann brought the flight in low enough that Paul could clearly see the leaves on the treetops and the water shining bright below them. They flew toward the inlet. The area of the cabin was remarkable for what it was. Isolated, heavily wooded, with only one access road coming to a dead end. Ann banked and turned toward the airport. Paul saw only two fishing boats visible on the water.

Ann landed the aircraft with such skill he didn't feel the wheels touch down. She taxied to a private area of the airport, turned the plane in a tight circle, and came to a stop lined up along the taxi ramp.

Paul was thinking about how to suggest that Ann stay with the plane rather than join them for the drive to the cabin. But when Reece came back with keys for two rental cars, Ann walked with Vicky to the second car. Paul hesitated, but decided it was best she make her own decision.

Reece drove, making the trip from memory and not even needing to glance at a map. Paul watched him, aware of the tension in the man. They hadn't sat down for an interview yet—Paul intentionally keeping it for a later date. The VP had been a victim, and Paul understood the man's instincts to hide what had happened. Reece was the man who had decided not to push back against the idea of a cover-up. Paul wasn't sure yet that he fully understood Reece's thinking, or his motives.

The dirt road leading to the site wandered through heavy trees, in places nearly impassable from washouts over the years. Reece slowed and pointed. "There's the cabin site, up ahead near that cluster of white pines."

Reece scanned the road and chose a place to park where he could turn around later. Vicky pulled in and parked beside him. Paul could see the lake now, the sunlight flickering off the water. The dock on the lake still stood. They all got out of the vehicles.

Paul glanced at Ann. She was talking with Vicky, all but ignoring the scene. He was relieved when Ann stayed leaning against the car while they walked to the grown-over remains of the cabin.

Paul stood at what would have been the cabin's front door, and he listened. There was only the faint sound of a motor on the water. He could hear no traffic. There were few indications of civilization. The chief of staff had not been one to take chances. He had fully believed he could leave the diary writer here for two days while he went to get the VP.

This place had been carefully scouted out and selected. Though isolated, it was on a lake where people came and went. He hadn't chosen a farmhouse in the middle of nowhere. A car being seen here would not attract attention. Maybe that was enough of a reason. A too-remote area would mean a car parked over a week would draw attention, but here a car coming and going would not be noteworthy.

"Let's go down to the dock and see the lake," Paul said.

─────────── ▼ ───────────

Ann leaned against the car, waiting with Vicky and watching as the others walked down to the lake. She glanced over to her friend once she was sure they were out of earshot. "Paul knows, or he suspects. I'm the only one the VP told in nine years? Paul's asked the question. He's too good an investigator not to have asked. The question is, why hasn't he asked me?"

"He doesn't want to put you in a position of having to answer," Vicky guessed, her voice soft.

"Maybe. Probably."

"What will you say if he does ask?"

Ann shrugged. "There are a lot of shades of not answering. I can simply not answer and still confirm whatever he wants to know."

"However you answer, you'll confirm what he already knows."

"Yes. But the whole truth is going to go to my grave."

"He's strong enough to know the truth, Ann."

"I'm not strong enough to tell him." The silence stretched between them. "I'm glad you came along."

"So am I. You want to talk about it?"

"There's nothing new to say."

"You would have been better off if you had accepted the VP's offer to write a chapter of your own. If everyone knows, you wouldn't need to look at someone and wonder."

"The only thing the truth does is give people more to gossip about. I still wish the VP had let this go to his grave. It's another crime. The world already knows plenty of crimes."

"You know it's not that simple."

"It could be that simple. Gannett doesn't want to see God with a lie on his conscience."

"Would you?"

"Depends on how many people I had to tell in order to clear my conscience. There's telling one person, and there's telling millions. The public is going to be fascinated with the story, and the families of the victims are going to have to deal with the press, and the money the book brings in for them is going to only partially offset the staggering impact they will have to absorb. The victims were in the way of the chief of staff's master plan to have the VP one day become president. They were killed because the chief of staff blamed them for what they did or didn't do during a campaign. These were senseless murders done for stupid reasons, and the diary just shows how twisted the chief of staff really was inside. The details of the truth serve little purpose, Vicky. That's the sad part of this. It ends a cover-up, but the truth doesn't benefit anyone. It's just another crime."

"I know. The sad thing is Gannett would have been a good president. Had he never met his chief of staff, maybe that would have been what he achieved eventually."

"When it comes down to it, the outcome of most people's lives hinges on only a few decisions. The VP will be remembered in large part for his wrong choice of a friend and employee."

Ann saw the group returning and reached over to open the passenger door. "When we fly back, would you come join me up front? I'd rather not have Paul come forward to carry on a conversation about flying or whatever else he chooses to bring up. I'm moody today, and it shows."

"Sure. And I don't mind moody."

Ann tried a smile. "You're too good a friend to say so if you did."

Paul stretched his legs out, grateful the plane didn't crowd them together like a commercial flight. The day had been long and was still an hour from being over. They had accomplished what he had hoped—they'd seen the eighteen burial sites and the cabin. He looked over to Sam and Rita. "What did you notice about all the burial sites?"

"Rural terrain, mature, thick trees, a winding country road passing near the site," Sam said without a pause. "He had a destination in mind before he grabbed his victim. He didn't find those sites by chance. He planned them out."

"Looking at his schedule, can we figure out when he had time to do that? Was he choosing the sites in the days just before the abductions, or was he doing that kind of planning weeks or months before the abduction?"

"We can look at that. The diary suggests a familiarity with their lives. But the chief of staff is a known person. He couldn't have been in an area very often and not have been noticed and remembered. Same with the burial sites."

"Are the two of you up to visiting the VP's vacation home tomorrow? Ann said we could fly out early in the morning and be there by midafternoon. I'd like to get this done."

Rita smiled. "A trip to Florida is no hardship, boss."

21

The VP's vacation home in Florida was on the water, a residence kept private by a tall, white stone wall and a break wall protecting a private cove from the open ocean. The Atlantic waters rolled with chop farther out, but the cove was a perfect place to swim and large enough even to sail. Ann flew over the property so they could see it from the air, then turned toward the nearby airport. They arrived back at the estate by car just after three p.m. Reece introduced them to the private security protecting the estate.

Paul sent Sam and Rita to walk through the house and get overview photos of the layout while he walked with Reece toward the boat dock and the water. It was a beautiful cove, with sandy shores and calm waters rippling under a nice breeze, which helped to cool the heat of the sun.

"The VP said he was heading toward the open water but had not yet passed the break wall when the chief of staff pulled a gun, turned them back to shore, and abducted him."

"Right. The chief of staff put them ashore on the far side of the cove"—Reece pointed—"there, by that lone tree. He had parked his car in the turnaround area."

"Where did the boat end up?"

"The chief of staff put the boat on autopilot and sent it back through the break wall and into the open waters. Once it cleared the break wall, the boat was taken by the current almost two miles out where it was found drifting."

A boat was moored at the floating dock. "Is that the same boat?"

"A newer model, but the size and cabin layout are close to being the same."

Paul walked down to check it out. "Tell me, Reece, about that day, about what you thought when you realized the VP was missing."

"I was with his wife attending a flower show, where she was making a few public remarks. We returned to the house, and the VP wasn't there to meet her. He made it a point to be on hand when she got back from a public event, to ask how it had gone, to thank her for attending. I had known them both for years. It was a mainstay of their relationship, that small courtesy of his to be there for his wife. He knew she wasn't comfortable with public events, and it was the reason he had sent me to travel with her that day. I immediately knew when we walked in the door and the VP wasn't there to meet her that something was wrong.

"The boat had GPS on it, and it showed the boat moving slowly in the area he normally fished. He didn't answer a radio call. We went out by another boat to see if he was having problems. Before long we found his boat, drifting and empty. The fishing gear was out. The public was told it was a boating accident, but we were working it as several things: a foreign agency had snatched him, a kidnapping for ransom, a heart attack that caused him to fall into the water and drown.

"When the VP called me from the cabin, the ocean search had been under way for seven hours. By the time I got him from the cabin back to Florida, it was three o'clock in the morning. We used the drifting tides to create a story that put him in the water and had him drift into shore about four miles north of the house. The story we used was he had seen debris in the water, thought it was from a capsized vessel, and had been retrieving a piece that had writing on it when he'd gotten into trouble and had fallen into the water. The current had pushed him into shore, but the surf had beaten him up on the rocks as he came ashore.

"I knew that area was isolated. I thought we could make it work. The story would be, the VP got ashore, no one was at the nearest home, but he had lived in the area long enough that he recognized the property. He broke into the home and called me to say where he was. I arrived, confirmed he was secure, and called in a helo to pick us up from there. The story held because the VP sold it as true. The VP had plunged into the ocean and drifted for thirty minutes, so he was cold and saltwater-saturated, while I broke the glass in the back door and called my own phone. If I hadn't known the truth, I would have believed the story."

Reece stood looking out over the water, then shook his head. "Paul, the only thing I really thought that day was, I'm glad he's alive. The rest was simply details. I'd spent a lifetime ready to take a bullet for him. Jim's a friend, as was his wife. I could deal with about anything as long as I didn't have to attend his funeral. And as sad as I am at his wife's passing, I guess I'm glad she isn't here to see this day. It would have broken her heart to realize who the chief of staff really was. The VP never did tell her the truth."

"This will cost you your job with the Secret Service."

"I know. If they take the pension and benefits along with it, Jim has already insisted I let him make it good, and I'll probably let him. I broke every duty I had to the country by keeping this quiet, but I can still live with the decision. It wasn't just the VP; it was the lady abducted to write the diary. I would have been destroying her life too had this become public that day. I couldn't protect her and leave that scene intact."

Paul considered asking if Reece wanted to say that lady was Ann, but he didn't. This was the man who had known the truth and had helped Ann in the years since. Ann trusted him. Ann had dated him. And Paul thought he understood why. The man was a solid guy, and Paul liked him even more now.

"Ann mentioned that you've recently gotten engaged. Have you told your fiancée about this?"

"Not yet."

"You should tell her."

"I will, a couple weeks before the book is released. I think Ann has already warned her something is there. They were friends long before I met either of them."

"You used to go out with Ann."

"We spent about four years together," Reece replied, assessing him. "I've heard you're dating her now."

"Trying to."

Reece's smile was both sympathetic and amused. "I remember that feeling. Ann and I have history, and a friendship, and somewhere along the way we realized it was going to be a lifelong friendship rather than end up with us married. A few years later, Ann introduced me to Cindy, and the next thing I know I'm buying a ring. I don't regret what is now, nor do I regret those years with Ann. Of everyone I've ever known, Ann still leads the list of people I enjoy spending time with." He looked a long moment at Paul. "You mind some advice?"

"Sure."

"Don't let her stall. There's something back there that keeps her from getting married that I never figured out. I didn't realize I'd hit that wall until later when I looked back on it. It worries me, what it is. She's good at relationships, and yet she's still single and seems content to stay that way. It's one thing for that to be a decision; it's another when there's a reason for it."

"Have you asked her?"

"Ann is more skilled at sliding around a question than anyone I've ever known."

"I've noticed. I appreciate the counsel." Paul thought about it and what it said about Ann, then put it away to ponder later. He turned the conversation back to why they were here. "Can you show me the map again, of the route from here to the cabin and how you and the VP came back that night?"

"Sure." They walked back to the house, and Reece laid out the map on the dining room table. He traced the way the chief of staff had traveled, and the way he had returned. Paul then took Sam and Rita on a walk of the property, replaying the events of that day to see if there were any holes in the story detailed in the chapter.

"The security is one problem, boss," Rita said. "The VP and the chief of staff went fishing together, the chief of staff abducts the VP, and security isn't in a place to know what happened, or to even know the chief of staff was here on the estate. That's where the press will focus."

"Talk me through it again."

"The wife left with Secret Service—Reece—for a public event, the VP went down to the dock to go fishing, the three security officers on-site locked down the two gates with padlocks, and begin a long-planned upgrade of the security system and cameras on the grounds. The chief of staff timed his abduction to the day and hour they began that security upgrade. He had scripted what would be done during the upgrade and what order it would happen, so he knew exactly where the security staff would be. He made sure they were blind and they were busy. Their priority was getting the system swapped out and the cameras back on within forty-five minutes. For those forty-five minutes, no one was watching the back of the house.

"The chief of staff came to the south gate, cut the padlock, drove to the turnaround, and parked. The VP pulled the boat alongside that floating platform and picked up the chief of staff. After the abduction, the chief of staff drives out the same way, puts on a new padlock, and heads to the cabin with the VP. The chief of staff even had arranged for the new padlock key to be on the peg where the others were. It isn't until the diary was read that it's known the padlock wasn't the one security had put on the gate. It was perfect, boss. How many abduction plans go perfectly?" Rita shook her head.

Sam added another concern. "The chief of staff planned getting onto this estate and getting out without being seen. My question is why didn't the VP tell anyone the chief of staff was coming? Why not mention it to his Secret Service or his house security staff that the chief of staff is coming to go fishing with him?"

Rita nodded. "That's a key question. Maybe the VP didn't want to distract his wife with the idea of company coming that day. Maybe the chief of staff had downplayed the idea he might be able to come—I'm probably going to be tied up and unable to get away—such that the VP wasn't expecting him unless he called."

Paul thought about it and shook his head. "The security upgrade that the chief of staff had arranged gave a window for him to come and go unseen. We've seen bigger breakdowns in security before, and this one is large, but it actually makes sense. It was part of the abduction plan, diverting the security, and the chief of staff had a solid plan. Part of that plan had to be somehow keeping the VP from mentioning the chief of staff's possible arrival to go fishing. It's going to be messy for reporters to believe, but that's the story the VP is telling. Does it time out?"

"We've timed it, and it does play out as possible."

"All right. What else is catching your attention?"

"The cover-up held once he was back. That the VP was in the water for hours, that his injuries were from the surf knocking him around on the rocks," Rita said.

Sam nodded. "That's not such a problem. He's wet, cold, half in shock, and says with a laugh, I fell off my

boat. They're going to take his word for it. Even if a
doctor suspects there is more to an abrasion than what
he's told, the suspicion is doctor-patient privilege. The
VP says he's got a rope burn on his wrist because he
tried to pull himself back up onto his boat and the wet
rope abraded his skin, it's a plausible explanation. He
says he's got a bruised rib because a wave tossed him
into a boulder, it's going to be accepted. The cover-up
held because it was a plausible story."

"What else?" Paul asked.

"There's not much else to pull apart. It could have
happened as the chapter outlines. It's simply a near-
perfect abduction and cover-up, and that is rare. The
chapter is well written and accurate for what is here, but
there is no way to know if it is the truth."

"Go ahead and wrap it down, finish your notes, then
enjoy the beach and some of that food they've put out.
I'm going to take a walk, think about all this a bit."

"Sure, boss."

The two headed back to the house, and Paul went to
the beach. For the first time, this was feeling just a bit
too perfect. The chief of staff could have done this, but
it all worked because the VP also didn't say anything,
didn't tell anyone the chief of staff was coming to join
him fishing. It wasn't like the chief of staff was someplace
just down the road. He'd been in Illinois and made a
long trip to come. The VP should have mentioned to
someone—the housekeeper, the chef—that his chief of
staff was going to be visiting. It felt like a hole, and Paul
couldn't explain it. Maybe Rita was right, the VP hadn't
wanted to distract his wife before her public appearance.

Maybe the chief of staff had been vague about it, or simply said he couldn't come.

"Paul."

He turned, and there was Ann coming toward him. He held out his hand as she joined him.

"If you've seen what you need to see, I can have us back home tonight if we get ourselves to the airport now."

He heard something in her voice he'd never heard before, and he studied her thoughtfully. "We could. Or we could spend the night and have a few hours to walk on the beach while we're here. It seems a pity to let the sand go to waste."

"How about a walk on the beach now, then we go home?"

"You in a hurry?"

"After this you're going to dig up a coffin, get the photos, and finish your investigation. I'm looking forward to putting this case into the forever-closed column."

He'd become accustomed to the cool distance in her voice when she spoke about the case. This was the first sign of impatience—maybe under it a touch of dread. She wanted desperately to get this over with and be done. Because he understood that, he merely nodded. "Beach first. Then you can fly us home."

She promptly sat down and tugged off her tennis shoes, rolled the socks up to stuff inside, and turned up the cuffs of her jeans. He had to smile as he watched her. So much determined energy on getting him to move in the direction she wanted. He reached for her hand to help her up. "You really want to be back in the air."

"I dislike wasting time when there's a case to finish."

"I'll remember that." He nodded toward the break wall. "To the break wall and back. While we walk, tell me about as many times as you can remember when you have been on a beach."

"It's not a long enough walk for that," she protested, and began with a trip she had taken with Kate and Shari.

Paul listened to her, studied her, and made a decision that they would exhume the coffin as soon as they were back in Illinois and could make the short flight to the cemetery. In forty-eight hours this could be over. They had enough figured out now that if the press somehow caught wind of the truth, they'd all be ready to deal with it. He would simply have to make sure no one saw inside the casket and realized the chief of staff had not been buried in the grave marked with his tombstone. Ann was right. It was time to get this case finished.

A military honor guard stood present as they exhumed the chief of staff's grave. Paul stood at respectful attention, Ann beside him. Sam, Rita, Reece, and Vicky were watching from the opposite side of the burial plot. The cover story—the transfer of the deceased at the VP's request to lie at rest beside friends and fellow soldiers—was holding. They exhumed the entire grave, lifting the coffin inside the casing vault intact and securing it, after appropriate ceremony and draping of the flag, onto a flatbed truck for transport. They followed the casket to the army base, where a temporary resting place in the armory had been arranged before transfer in the morning to its assumed final resting place. They would, in fact, rebury it in an unmarked grave.

When they were alone, Paul nodded to Sam. Under the flag, the vault containing the coffin was caked in dirt and scraped by the hoist, but seemed otherwise undamaged. Rita took photos while Sam opened the vault lid. Paul caught the faint smell of stale air and polishing oil. The coffin rested securely inside, its burnished wood still gleaming.

"Open it in place," Paul said. "There's no need to remove the coffin from the vault."

Sam leaned inside and turned the clasp, lifted the coffin's lid.

Knowing it was empty of a body and seeing it empty were two different emotions. A long box made of hard plastic rested inside, sealed tight against any air. Sam lifted it out and carried it to the table. He used his knife to slit the tape and caulked seam. And then he removed the box lid.

They looked in at the collected evidence of the crime. The paper sack with the chief of staff's collected belongings still looked as if it had been rolled up yesterday. The duct tape had pulled away and opened with age. A camera rested securely on a bed of foam. Negatives in protective sleeves, and photos curling at the corners but still sharp with color, rested beside the camera. The VP's handwritten account was in a box, each page protected by an evidence sleeve and carefully marked into evidence by Reece Lion.

"Reece, anything you want to add or remember now that you see this evidence?"

"No."

Paul picked up the photos and spread them across the table.

They saw for the first time the cabin as it had been.

The fight was there in the broken and overturned furniture, smashed television, mauled rugs.

They saw the chief of staff with a fatal gunshot wound to the head.

The VP had bruises on his face, a split and bleeding lip, swollen wrists from tight restraints, a badly bruised rib cage, and shock still present in his eyes.

It was the blood on the cabin floor, unrelated to where the chief of staff lay dead, that held Paul's attention.

He looked from the photos to find Ann. She had come no farther into the armory than where the vehicles had been parked. From there she was looking at what was on the table. She was sheet white and fighting nausea so bad he could see it in her face, but she hadn't left. She hadn't asked Vicky to step outside with her. "Anything you would like to see?" he asked quietly, making no effort to encourage or discourage her decision.

"No."

He swept the photos together and gave them to Rita.

"Sam, seal up the coffin and vault. Let's get this finished."

On the plane back to the VP's estate, Paul read the hand-written account of events Gannett had written the day of abduction and found it remarkably organized for the stress the man had been under. The account matched what was in the chapter, the cover-up plan less detailed and a bit different for what had actually been done, a fact that only added to the authenticity. These pages had been written before the cabin burned, for there were photographs of the VP holding this handwritten document with the cabin behind him.

Sam and Rita finished work on the trip report. "Tell me what you think of this." Paul handed over the VP's report on the abduction. "Let me see those photos again, Rita." He held out his hand, and she put them in it. Vicky had moved forward to the cockpit to sit with Ann an hour ago. Paul caught Reece's attention and held up the photos. Reece shook his head.

Paul slowly flipped through the photos. He stopped on the one he suspected marked Ann's private nightmare, the floor of the cabin overlaid with crisscrossing splatters of blood.

He would eventually need to have a conversation with her. He knew, and she suspected he knew. She still couldn't put it in words. He understood a victim surviving by silence, dealing with what had happened by not giving it room to breathe and live. It was carefully packed and locked closed to keep it in the past. She hadn't found the courage to risk telling him.

Ann's reaction to what was happening with all this worried him. When the coffin had been opened, when she had seen the recovered evidence, she had felt it as a living thing. He was concerned about those nightmares, about what they would be like tonight and for the next many nights. What might all this trigger? But he couldn't help her unless she would let him.

He slid the photos into a manila envelope and sealed it in an evidence bag.

An hour later, Paul watched the small airport appear and the runway lights grow brighter. Ann landed the plane smoothly, taxied as directed, and brought the aircraft inside the hangar before shutting down the engines.

Reece opened the cabin door and lowered the steps. Sam took the first evidence case with him while Rita carried the second one. Vicky followed them. Paul waited at the cabin door for Ann to step from the cockpit. "Ride back to the VP estate with us."

She shook her head. "Vicky's taking me home."

"Ann—"

"Don't push. Please."

He settled for wrapping her in a hug. "Sleep in, then come find me. Okay?"

She simply hugged him and stepped back. "Go get this finished."

Paul joined Sam and Rita the next morning in the secure conference room. He hadn't slept much, and the coffee was barely cutting the fatigue. The photos were spread across the table. "Where are we at?"

"His written account matches the chapter. The photos back it up," Rita replied. "The evidence in this room, these photos, the written accounts, it all lines up to be what it is—proof the VP's chapter is correct. They have proven the chief of staff killed eighteen people and abducted the VP. It may not be a complete account, but what is here fits with this evidence."

"Have we found anything indicating there's something else out there?"

"There were only five people there. What we have is what they were willing to share, and what we can see in these photos. There is a solid line of evidence that what they did say is in fact true. But it leaves an open question. There were probably things said that day that the VP chose to not include in his account. We can't answer that question," Rita concluded.

Sam added, "The chief of staff wanted to be famous for what he did, and he gave a detailed account in the diary. There may be more murders he did that were not part of his confession. I don't know how we answer that question after this amount of time either."

"Okay." Paul had reached the same conclusions. "I want the two of you to finish writing up the FBI report that will be released to the public when the VP's book comes out. While you're doing that, I'm going to put together what I need and take this to the director. Let's get this tied into a bow and go home."

Sam nodded. "We can get it finished today, tomorrow at the latest."

───────◆───────

Paul had hoped Ann would join them, but as the morning wore on, she didn't appear. Paul tried calling her occasionally throughout the morning but only got her voice mail. Reece came to find him when they broke for lunch. "Paul, for you." He held out a folded piece of paper.

"Thanks, Reece." He opened the note.

Paul, I'm taking Vicky home and staying a few days with her. I'll be in touch when I get back. Ann

That explained the unanswered calls—she was in the air. He thoughtfully tucked the note in his pocket. She'd been smart enough to go stay with a friend. He'd hold on to that bit of comfort until he could find out for himself how she was doing. Ann was the one paying the highest price for this. It wouldn't be over for her when the book came out. It would only be the beginning. He wanted to stand in front of that storm and stop it from hitting her, but he knew he couldn't prevent it. The best he could do was to try and minimize the damage. He had time, a limited amount of time, to figure it out before the book came out.

The next step in front of him was to tell the director what was coming.

———————▼———————

Paul set his suitcase and briefcase down on the second hotel bed, out of habit turned on the TV to hear the news, and found the temperature dial to kick on the air-conditioning. He'd been able to get a room in Washington, D.C. on short notice, but it was next to the vending machines and across from the stairs. He was tired enough tonight it probably wouldn't matter. He was tired of the travel, of the weeks of investigation, of how things had been left with Ann.

He had an appointment with the FBI director first thing in the morning. His boss was flying in from Chicago to meet them. Paul opened his briefcase and retrieved Sam and Rita's report. He'd begun reading it on the plane trip. He sat on the couch and finished his review. It was a good, solid piece of work. That left only his conversation with the director, and his work on this would be wrapped up until the book released.

He considered the time change and tried again to

reach Ann. Her phone didn't go to voice mail this time. She answered on the fourth ring. "Ann, it's Paul. How are you?"

"I'm fine. Sorry to duck out on you so abruptly."

"You don't sound fine."

"It's relative. I've got a headache, and I need some more sleep, but it's nothing time won't help cure. How's it going with you? Where are you?"

"I'm in D.C. I have a meeting with the FBI director in the morning. We're confirming the contents of the VP chapter. Sam and Rita have written the official report. After the meeting tomorrow we will be on hold, waiting for the VP to release his book."

"I'm glad. Thank you, Paul. For all of this."

He felt uneasy at what he heard in her voice, a kind of stress shimmering just under the words. "Take it easy on yourself the next few days, okay? When you get home, call me. I'll be down to see you the first chance I get. You still owe me a movie."

"I would like a movie." He was relieved to hear a bit of a smile in her answer.

"Then it's a date. I hope you sleep well tonight."

"So do I. Good night, Paul."

"Good night, Ann." He hung up and set the phone on the nightstand.

He hoped she found the courage to tell him before he had to ask. When the VP's book came out, they were going to be dealing with this all over again. He had to help her get prepared for that, for the reporters who would be calling her at all hours, wanting the rest of the story. He couldn't do that unless they had a conversation about what really happened in that cabin.

Paul had walked the upper floors of Washington's FBI office often enough to not need more than a few minutes of cushion time for his appointment. His credentials were checked by the executive assistant coordinating the director's schedule, and he was escorted right in.

The FBI director rose to greet him. "Paul, it's good to have you in D.C." They shook hands, and the director waved him to a seat next to Arthur. "Jim Gannett called last night and apologized for the fact he was about to give me a stressful day. I'm going to assume that's why you are here."

"It is, sir."

"If you didn't know it, the VP and I go back several years. He was influential in my becoming the director."

"He speaks highly of you, sir."

"You look tired, Paul."

"An understatement, Arthur."

Paul opened his case and removed the letter Gannett had written. He handed them each a copy. "I'm instructed by the VP to burn these pages after our conversation." The VP had done him the favor of laying out in a two-page letter the core of what had happened.

The director read the letter twice, looked at Paul, then got up and carried it to the window and read it again.

Arthur read it, and half smiled. "At least it's not going to be a boring day." He got up to cross to the drink cabinet. "What'll you have, Paul?"

"Coffee, sir."

Arthur poured coffee for all three of them.

"You believe this is true."

Paul turned to the director. "Yes, sir. The chief of staff murdered eighteen people and planned to murder the former VP. It's probably not the entire story, but what is there is supported by the evidence. The book becomes public in December, along with a release of the diary text."

"How many know?"

"Five at the time of the incident, but now my investigators and security make it nine. This meeting brings the total to eleven. We keep it at that, there's a chance it stays under wraps until the book is released."

"There's no upside to us breaking this news before then. The fact the chief of staff got away with eighteen murders puts into question our security clearance review of the man," the director said dryly. "The Secret Service is going to have a black eye. At a minimum we're looking at a congressional inquiry. Where else is this going to bite us, besides the obvious that it happened under our noses and we didn't know it?"

"It's a bombshell, but so far it is contained to what is here," Paul said. "The case files are complete, the evidence solid, the questions left open very few. The VP withheld the names of the one who wrote the diary and who helped that person recover. We have an idea who may have written the diary, but no idea who helped her return to her life. I haven't pursued those questions, and don't see a need to do so. I wouldn't put the answers in any public document, even if I were certain of them.

"There will be numerous questions for who knew what, when, and why it wasn't all put together before the climactic abduction and confession. You need to find out if the chief of staff was ever suspected of a serious crime, and if he was allowed to slide underneath the radar because of his position. I can't investigate that question without raising questions about why I am asking. That's the biggest risk I can see, but it's hard to mitigate it until the book is released. It's not worth raising a flag by looking now."

Neither of the two men seemed to question that conclusion.

"The book's being embargoed under conditions I think will hold," Paul continued. "There is time to prepare. I would recommend the report Sam Truebone and Rita Heart have written be released once the book is public. What worries me, though, is the unknown. If you can keep a secret of this magnitude for this long, you can keep just about anything secret. I haven't seen a copy of the VP's full autobiography, just this chapter of it."

The director nodded. "You've finished your investigation of this matter?"

"I'm done, sir, unless questions arise you need me to cover. I have some catching up to do with my family, and then I plan to head to Chicago and dig out my desk. The less it appears there is something out there to be worried about, the less likely there is to be a leak. Staff in my office believe I'm taking some vacation time to visit a girlfriend. Sam and Rita are believed to be traveling for a few days to cover interviews for me. We go back to work and let this become public at its own time."

"He's seeing Ann Silver, Edward," Arthur put in.

"Annie? I'm inclined to think more highly of you than I already do, Paul. Good choice."

"Thank you, sir."

"It's nice to know I've got some gossip my wife is

going to love to hear." The director took a seat behind his desk and tapped the letter. "Best case, Paul?"

"The VP does several interviews with the press the day the book is released, he comes across as sympathetic, and nothing else comes out that will change the chapter or the report we've put together. The Secret Service decides to be kind to its own, Congress wants to keep their Christmas vacation, and a heavy snowstorm takes the lead in the news cycle. Reporters will dig, television hour specials on the crime will air in prime time. Best case this is six weeks of a firestorm, and six months of depositions and hearings and reports, and it dies out as news. If the full story is out there on day one and never materially changes after that point, this will be survivable."

"I'm going to want you in front of the press when it's time for those interviews," the director said. "Truebone and Heart as well. The public will want the inside story on the investigation. We should plan to give those interviews the first week."

"Yes, sir. We'll be prepared."

"For now, my main concern is keeping this from leaking. This is the VP's story to break. So while we'll mull this over and decide what other steps need to be taken to get ready for this, let's do it quietly and not bring anyone else in." The director rose, struck a match, and burned the two copies of the letter. "If I don't tell you this later, Paul, thanks for saying yes when the VP handed you this chapter. It's going to matter, having your name on the investigation."

"Let's hope that's still true after this becomes public."

"I don't suppose we've heard anything more from the lady shooter?"

"Zane is watching the mail, but there has been no word from her. She's still sitting on twenty tapes. My guess is she'll deliver them in two or three more lots, as she takes a lot of risk retrieving these agreements. The way this is timing out, we'll be making the thirty arrests a few weeks before the VP autobiography is released."

"You've got a green light to make the arrests as soon as we have all the tapes. I'll just hope for a couple of weeks' gap either way of the book release or else it will look to the press like we're using one case to divert attention from the other. Paul, you are welcome to stay or head on back to Chicago. I'm going to get Jim Gannett on the phone, and Arthur and I are going to start talking through the details of the book release with him."

"I'll head on back, sir, if you don't mind."

Paul rose and shook hands, thanked Arthur, and headed out.

22

Ann accepted the hot chocolate Vicky handed her with a quiet thanks. She was curled up on her favorite seat, the kitchen bench where the sun came in and warmed her back. She hadn't slept much, and Vicky was kind about not mentioning the fact her guest had been up pacing in the middle of the night.

"What am I going to do, Vicky?"

"Tell him. You aren't comfortable going forward with him if you're hiding something this big. It will bother you forever. Paul is coming out to see Boone on Saturday for some family matters. Stay a few more days and talk to him. He already suspects, you know."

"What he suspects versus the truth is a long bridge to cross." She sipped at the hot chocolate. "Either way, will you be okay with Boone?"

"Don't worry about Boone. He already accepts there's a lot I've never told him."

"I don't think I want to tell Paul. He's a friend, Vicky. A good one, but still only a friend."

Vicky pulled out a chair and turned it so she could sit and prop her feet on the bench beside Ann. "He'll never be anything more than that if you don't step off the ledge and take a risk with him. You can trust him, Ann. If you don't believe your own assessment of him, believe mine. Paul's a protector, and he'll instinctively do everything he can to help you."

"That's my read of him too." Ann rubbed her eyes.

"You'll need his help. When the book is released, I give it three days before the reporters are publishing your name and photo and the dates you were missing and asking your former boss for comments about the accuracy of their police report on your disappearance."

"I figured two days max." Ann warmed her hands around the mug. "I've already written the press release. I don't mind if they are going to think I wrote the diary, Vicky. As long as that's all they think."

"Why not confirm it? You'll be asked by everyone who meets you if you're the one."

"I helped write the VP's autobiography, and I wrote the book on the John Doe Killer victims. I knew the truth of the abduction years before the public did. That's where the line will always stay. The rest I can simply leave as no comment." She sat quietly, thinking about that reality and feeling like a train was heading toward her. She shook her head and pushed to her feet. "I need to walk. Thanks for the hot chocolate."

"Wander to your heart's content. Here, I'll put the rest of your chocolate in a thermal cup to take with you. We're having spaghetti for dinner, and it will be ready whenever you get back."

Ann walked because she didn't know what else to do. She craved the time to think and hoped for a decision that could give her peace.

Vicky said to trust Paul and tell him.

The thought made her feel slightly nauseous.

She would be opening a door she had never opened for anyone else.

She trusted Paul. He would listen to what she told him and not use the information to hurt her. But the news would change how he saw her.

If they were ever going to be anything more than friends, she had to tell him. She didn't want to make this decision, but she had no choice. Life events had forced the point. Her secrets were either going to stay hers alone or were going to belong to both of them, but either way their relationship would change, for better or for worse. It would never go back to what it was before.

She could make the decision for them both by leaving to see Rachel—and this would stay only a friendship. Or she could give him the information, give him time, and let him make the decision for the two of them. A friendship only was probably where this was still going to end up, but she could make that decision or let Paul do so.

She wanted to avoid the pain. But she wouldn't take the easy way out and leave. She would tell him. And this relationship was going to go somewhere she could not predict.

Paul was glad to have the trip over. He parked in front of the new garage, smiling at the memory of the novel and

Ann's description of why it had to be rebuilt. It would be good to see Boone and Vicky. It had been too long since he'd last been here. He'd gone from D.C. to New York to see his father, back to Chicago, then decided to drive out to Colorado rather than fly to give himself time to think and unwind.

His brother came out to meet him as he pulled his bag from the back seat. "You made good time."

"Hey, Boone. I did. Traffic stayed light." He reached for a box, a gift for Vicky—half a dozen jars of Nick's Spaghetti Sauce.

Boone grinned when he saw it. "She'll appreciate it." Boone took the box and tucked it under one arm. "Ann's still here."

Paul stilled. She'd been leaving for home two days ago, planning to make a stop to see her friend Rachel on the way. He'd been relieved to hear the more normal tone in her voice when she'd told him her plans, relieved enough he hadn't asked her to stay until he arrived. "How is she?"

"Looking rough enough around the edges that Vicky didn't have to push very hard to get her to stay a few more days. Sorry, man. I don't know what's going on, but I'm truly sorry for what it's doing to her."

"So am I."

Paul walked with Boone to the house and set his bag in the entryway. Boone nodded toward the kitchen. Paul headed that way.

Ann was sitting at the kitchen table with Vicky, eating a piece of pie. He could almost feel Ann's exhaustion, could see it in her hollow eyes, and face tinged gray. So much for hoping she'd been able to get some sleep. She offered a tentative smile. "Hi, Paul."

"Hi." He made an effort to put some warmth in his smile, for he really was glad she had stayed.

She relaxed just a fraction. "I need to talk to you."

He pulled out a seat at the table. He glanced at Vicky, who looked worried, her attention on Ann. Vicky caught his look and shook her head slightly to stop his question.

Ann pushed away the pie. "Did you have a good drive?"

"It was fine."

Ann picked up her flight bag from the floor beside her chair. She hesitated, then opened it and pulled out a cardboard box. She slid the box across the table.

"I wrote the diary, and Vicky helped me return to my life."

He looked at his sister-in-law, caught by surprise at the second part of what Ann said. He looked back at Ann. "You've been protecting Vicky."

"Among other things." Ann looked sick rather than relieved to have told him. "Vicky, you and Boone go for a walk. You've lived through this nightmare enough to not have to listen to it again."

"I can handle it."

"I can't. Go and tell Boone. Tell him I'm sorry."

Vicky hugged her, and did as instructed.

Ann waited until Vicky left. "My blood is on the diary pages, that is why the VP had no choice but to conceal it in order to protect my name."

Paul closed his eyes. "Okay." He reached over for her hands. "Tell me." He didn't want the images in his head that her statement prompted, but he had only one thing he could give her now, and that was a willingness to live with the images too. He couldn't help without knowing.

She struggled to start, but then she told it with quiet words she had obviously carefully thought out. "The chief of staff chose me because I was a young, good cop; he chose me because I was a writer. He wanted a cop so the details would be remembered accurately, he wanted a young cop who would be around for decades and able to tell his story to those who asked, and he wanted a writer who would one day write a personal account of what had happened.

"I knew him as the chief of staff, as someone careful about the details, as someone protective of the VP. I found him a hard man to get to know, but I respected the position he held, even if I wasn't sure I liked him. He was a cold man, holding on to a great bitterness that the VP had lost the presidential election.

"That last day he came to my home. I wasn't expecting him. He said the VP had found some documents he needed to show me before leaving for Florida. I went with him out to the car. He caught me in the back of the shoulder with a syringe as I was getting in.

"I woke up tied to a chair in a small, plain room—rough floor and rough walls, and it smelled of humid earth. I could hear birds and hear branches rubbing together in the wind and see thick foliage out a window with a broken pane across the room. From the cobwebs and the dead insects, the place hadn't been occupied in months.

"He put a composition book on the table in front of me and told me to write what he dictated. He confessed to being a serial killer. He took five days describing the people he had killed and why.

"When I refused to write, he'd deliver a backhand

to the face. When I wrote anything other than what he said, he'd kick the legs of the chair and topple it, and I'd slam onto the floor. When he occasionally left, he'd leave me shackled in the bathroom. When he returned, he'd open the door and hit me with a dart of that drug again. I'd wake up tied to the chair. And we'd repeat the process. He finally left. He didn't come back. I thought he'd left me there to die.

"Two days later he reappeared, bringing a bound VP with him. He had me read the diary to the VP, and then he started dictating again, describing what he was going to do. Kill the VP, then himself, and become the most famous serial killer to ever exist. I was to be his witness to what happened.

"The VP tried for the chief of staff in a desperate attempt to stop him. The fight ended with the chief of staff dead, Gannett looking like he was having a heart attack, and my left arm broken. I don't think the chief of staff planned to kill himself at that moment—he simply didn't want to give ground on the gun. I was on his back using my weight and the chair to force him off-balance, the VP was under us both, and the chief of staff was trying to shoot me. He'd twisted the gun around aimed at my face to try and shoot me off his back. I caught his elbow with mine, and the next second he was dead of a gunshot to the head.

"The VP helped me out of the room and outside the cabin, where I could sit on the steps of the porch and get some fresh air. The VP went out to the car the chief of staff had driven, brought up the dashboard map, and called Reece. He gave the agent directions on how to find the cabin, told him the only two people he should bring with him, then came back to sit beside me. And for the next twenty minutes we didn't say much.

"Then the VP started to talk. We were the only two survivors, he said. There were eighteen victims and their families to think about. And I wasn't holding up very well. We could let it play out, or we could manage what was going to happen next. He asked if I could live with the full truth being known only to the two of us.

"He thought it could be contained with three people to help us. One to deal with the chief of staff and the cabin, one to slip the VP back into his life, and one to help me get back into mine. He said Reece had told him the public thought he had suffered a boating accident, and a search was under way for him at sea.

"I didn't want the truth to become public. I had a broken nose, broken arm, badly damaged left shoulder, raw skin infections on my ankles and wrist, a moderate fever, a mild concussion, and trouble breathing from all the drugs I'd been hit with. I knew my department was searching for me, and my injuries would support about any story I wanted to put together on my disappearance, including one where I didn't remember much about what had happened.

"We sat on the porch and we planned the cover-up. The VP knew the chief of staff had arranged removal of fingerprints and DNA from the federal databases for both of them when he retired, and we could use that fact to our advantage. We could burn the cabin and body to cover evidence of who had been there. We settled on a called-in confession as a way to put the locations of the victims into the hands of the cops, and as a way to lead the cops to the cabin location. The best cover-up would be one that let most things flow out as they normally would.

"Reece, Ben, and Vicky arrived. The VP laid out what was going to happen and why. The VP introduced me to Vicky, helped me to her car, and told Vicky to go. He called hours later to tell me what had been done, and that it had gone as we mapped out. That day was the first time I had met Vicky. I don't know how she handled it as well as she did. It was my decision that we drive all the way back to this area before we stopped. I wouldn't let her get me medical help, since it had to appear whatever I'd patched together I'd done on my own. I gave myself forty-eight hours while I got a story figured out that could hold, figuring the pain wouldn't kill me if it hadn't already.

"Cops searching for me were working under the assumption my confidential informant had pushed me out of the car somewhere along the drive, and they assumed I was likely dead. Vicky took me to within fifty miles of where they were focusing their search. I called into my department from a rail hub and asked them to arrange for someone to come get me. I said I'd hopped a train to reach a town and find a phone. The local cops showed up and took me to the hospital. My boss and several cops from my department were there within an hour, and I gave my statement confirming their CI assumption. I'm not proud of any of that, but it was the cleanest way to approach the problem. I've gone back over it many times, and I don't know I would do anything different if I had all the time in the world to plan.

"I checked myself out of the hospital three days later with Vicky's assistance, telling my boss I wanted to get away from the press. I stayed with her for a few months before I returned to work. She's a good friend to have. She made it possible to get through that recovery with some sanity intact. I healed, I returned to my life, and I went on with the job."

"Is this what you are hiding, Ann? Is this what's tearing you apart?"

She shook her head.

"What is it then? If you've trusted me with this, trust me with the rest of it."

The pain reflected in her eyes made Paul want to flinch. Ann found the courage and forced the words out. "I might have been able to stop murders sixteen, seventeen, and eighteen. The chief of staff was killing people when I knew him. I saw him the week before and after he killed victim fifteen. I was picking up inconsistencies. I knew he was lying to the VP. I knew he was in Cedar Rapids, Iowa, on April eighth, 1999. I didn't act on what I saw, and three more people are dead because of it."

He closed his eyes. He took a hard breath. "You don't do easy secrets, do you?"

"No. Nothing is ever easy with me."

"Tell me, please, if you can."

"I was working on the first volume of the VP's autobiography, helping with some of the research. It was January 2002, and I was about three years in as a cop, intensely busy, but I was honored the VP had asked me to help him on it. I saw the chief of staff frequently along with the VP, for they spent a couple of hours together every day, organizing materials for the autobiography.

"The chief of staff asked me to find a copy of a funeral eulogy he had given in 1999 for a man who had been key to the VP's first election win for state attorney general. I found the document in a box of miscellaneous memos, notes, and letters. I picked up a receipt signed by the chief of staff at the Master Grill Restaurant in Cedar Rapids, Iowa, on April eighth, 1999. It was such a detailed kind of record to have kept, I remember thinking at the time, This is interesting. The date stuck because remembering numbers happens without me trying.

"Two days later, searching the official record on another matter, I put in that date and found the official government log—the chief of staff had been in Chicago on April eighth, 1999. Those places are hundreds of miles apart. One was true and one had to be false. The signature on the receipt was the chief of staff's, so the official record was wrong.

"In the most colorful answer I could come up with, I thought the chief of staff might have been having an affair, or had lied to keep the VP out of some political deal he was making. But to save myself having the conversation, I let it go, and I didn't mention the discrepancy with either the chief of staff or the VP. I would later learn that was the location and date victim seven disappeared.

"A month later I was in the room when the chief of staff told the VP he would be spending the upcoming Valentine's Day weekend in St. Louis, Missouri. The VP joked with him the next week about how good a mood he was in after his weekend away. Two months later, while getting tax-return information that the chief of staff asked me to bring over from his office, I opened the wrong box and found receipts that put the chief of staff in Brownsville, Indiana, on that Valentine's Day weekend.

"The chief of staff had lied in the past, was lying now,

and still I didn't ask questions. He had killed Heather Thomas that weekend. Had I asked a question, asked what the chief of staff was doing in Brownsville, it might have changed history, Paul.

"I'm not saying I could have discovered·then that the chief of staff was a murderer. But I might have asked questions that would have led to him changing his actions. He might not have killed victims sixteen, seventeen, and eighteen if I had been asking questions. Instead, I said nothing. He killed again on July sixteenth, 2002, and on October seventh, 2002, and on February eighteenth, 2003.

"And on August fifth, 2003, the man showed up at my home, said the VP needed to see me for a few minutes before he left for Florida, and abducted me to write the diary. There are three deaths on my conscience that never leave. When in my dreams I write those pages of the diary, their blood is dripping on the pages. I could have prevented their deaths."

Paul could hear the pain in her words tearing her apart. He struggled to find something he could say to get her to see it the way he did. "The VP knew the chief of staff while he murdered eighteen people. You knew him while he murdered four people. It's a nasty and horrific problem, Ann. I don't minimize it. You're a cop and you had threads that might have gone somewhere. I can list the qualifiers you already know. You didn't know there was a crime. They were slivers of knowledge in days filled with a river of information. But I know those qualifiers don't help the emotions, or the regret. I don't know how you live with what happened beyond the fact you do live with it.

"While those two dates are important looking back at them from the knowledge of today, at the time they were merely lies, Ann. The inevitable lies people tell for all kinds of reasons. You were being polite, and letting the lie go, because there was a social cost to challenging the lie. Whatever the chief of staff's reasons, there didn't appear to be a compelling case for challenging the lies.

"In the first case, it was old data, a historical artifact. In the second case, it was a personal matter, and if the chief of staff wanted to be somewhere other than where he said for Valentine's Day weekend, there was probably a lady involved and he didn't want the VP to know. Probably a lie to cover a romance. You learned it was a lie two months after the fact, and it would embarrass the chief of staff if you mentioned it. So you let it go. The decision to not say something was in both cases the courteous thing to do, and given what you knew at the time, probably the right thing. It's not your job to reveal every lie you come across. You speak up when a lie is hurting someone. But none of us can call out every lie we come across. And if you had decided to pursue it, you would have likely soon been another victim, long before you could have discovered enough to stop him."

"I've thought through all of that, Paul. But I can't walk away from three more people being dead because I didn't follow a lie to the reason behind it. He was killing people. It was a small thread, but it was there."

"You have to stop tearing yourself apart about it, Ann. You would do differently if you could go back and change it, but you can't. You have to let it go."

She nodded, but the sadness was stark on her face. "It's not so easy to wish away." She nodded at the diary.

"Please ask your questions now while I have the courage to answer. I don't know if I can ever talk about this again."

"I really have only one core question. Is this your nightmare?"

"Yes."

"I know the nightmare is coming more often now. I can see its damage just by looking at you. Has the dream changed compared to what it was a month ago?"

"It's the same dream."

"Okay." He rubbed her cold hands. "Okay. Thank you for trusting me."

"I don't know what, if anything, this will change."

"What changes is the fact you were willing to trust me." He brushed her hair back from her face. "I'm falling in love with you, Ann. I'm falling in love with the lady I am meeting in conversations like this one."

She turned even paler. He smiled. "You don't have to say anything. I'm just laying out the landscape for you on the off chance you're slow at realizing the obvious."

"I'm beginning to realize," she whispered.

"When you get home, I'm planning to visit and take you to a movie. That's all you have to consider for now as to what comes next. Get some rest, Ann, however you can. Let go of this and what's happened. We'll turn a page and start over from here."

She gave a shaky nod and let out a breath. "Okay."

"Thank you for protecting Vicky. For having that part of your decision to stay unnamed."

"She's a friend, one I would do anything for that I could."

"All right, one last question. What do you want me to do with the handwritten diary?"

"Burn it. If you can't do that, then put it in a personal safe and tell your estate to leave it untouched as well. You can protect that diary better than I can. Once the VP's book is out, I don't put it past a reporter to break into my place for a little search while I'm away."

"It will never see the light of day."

She pushed over her plate of pie and offered her fork. "Vicky made an exceptional pie."

He tried it. "I would stay a couple more days just for the pie. You being here is nice too." He got up to get another fork. "I'll share these last bites.

"It's over, Ann, but for the press and the reporters. And those you can deal with. I'm going to help you deal with them."

"I'll take your help." She rested her head on her hands. "I'm so tired, Paul. Tired of what this has been. A decade with it sitting there, and I turn the page and now it's going public. It never goes away. He's dead, and I keep paying the price."

"It will end. A year from now, the worst of this will be over. No matter what people think or speculate, the worst of it will be over. Just close your eyes and plan to make it to that day. Your friends will be here. I will. One day at a time. You know how to do that."

"It's not exactly what you thought you were getting into when you decided to get to know me."

He carefully took her hands again and waited until she met his gaze. "I see it differently. I wanted to get to know you. You're letting me, and I admire that. You know the VP, Ann. You gave away half a million dollars. You write incredible books. You are all of this, including August five to twelve, and a nightmare most people could never comprehend. I asked to get to know you. Had you not been able to share this, I would have understood the pain that left it unsaid, but I would have been blind to part of who you are. I asked you to trust me, and you have. I'm grateful for that. This is what I want, to know you."

"There are other secrets I haven't told you. Some I don't know if I will ever be able to tell you."

He weighed the way she had said it and nodded. "Okay."

"Just okay?"

"Your secrets are safe with me, Ann. A year from now, when you know how I've handled this one, maybe you can trust me with another. I'm under no illusions this is easy for you. I'm not asking you not to be cautious or careful with what you entrust to me. How many people knew this secret? Three people? The VP, Reece, and Vicky? And they only knew because they were there?" She nodded.

"I know the risk you took to tell me this. If there are secrets so intense and private you can't share them, then I'll adapt to that. It's part of who you are. But I really believe most of the answer is simply time. It will get easier when you *know* you can trust me. You've already extended a lot of trust. You'll do more with time."

"I don't suppose you've got a secret like this out there, so we could kind of even things up."

He couldn't help his chuckle. "Nothing even close, I'm afraid. Mine's a reasonably boring kind of life."

"That's what I'm afraid of. I haven't. And most of them are things like this, events that just happened."

"You've already given me part of those secrets. You've told me they are out there."

She blinked as she realized he was right.

He asked the question he had to ask. "Can I talk to Vicky? About what those first weeks were like when you came back from the cabin? Or do you want to tell me about those weeks yourself?"

"Vicky is probably the better one to tell you. I found the heaviest painkillers I could tolerate and did my best to get through the first ten weeks by not thinking or feeling anything. I remember reading when I was awake, and being awake at very odd times, and sweating with a cold chill for no reason. The nightmares didn't start until a year later.

"I was glad to have the cast off, and I was glad to get back to work. I think it took that first year for the numbness to wear off. The rest of this unfolded slowly. I started helping Reece on the investigation of the diary two years later as a way to sort out what in the nightmare was based in fact. It has always felt like a distant event to me. That still hasn't changed. I wrote the diary, I can look at the pages and remember writing them, but it feels like I'm detached from it. My mind really has put most of this event in the past.

"The nightmare is different. It's driven by the regret, and that still lingers. I can see myself writing the diary, I can see those last three victims, each in turn standing beside me as I write. I can see their blood dripping on the pages. I can't change what I'm writing, and I desperately want to change what I'm writing."

"It looks like you feel the gunshot."

"At the end I know I am fighting for my life. I can feel my racing heartbeat and the physical struggle I am losing, the desperate fear. And then the shot goes off and the shock wave goes through my mind like it is being

shaken apart, and I stop thinking the pain is so intense.
Then I'm awake, gasping for air. It literally takes a moment to realize I'm alive and that I was dreaming. That
disorientation, that moment of pure panic, is worse than
anything I have ever been able to describe."

"Have you let anyone try to help you?"

"There's a team of doctors who have worked together
to help. There are some very good psychiatrists among
my friends. They don't know the nightmare's source, but
they know enough to realize some of what my mind is
working through. This nightmare isn't lending itself to
being tamed. At best it fades at times in frequency but
not in intensity. The dream itself, the shot in particular, is
a living memory. It gets touched off by a smell, a sound,
a thought. It replays in vivid detail.

"Normally the doctors would reshape a repeating
nightmare, would help identify different details to remember, add new elements, construct a new ending, so
that eventually what was a nightmare would be changed
to a less stressful dream. But that doesn't seem to work
for this one.

"One of the doctors watching it play out said it's like
my mind dies. I can't get a different outcome because
my mind realizes the shock wave of the gunshot is death
moving through my brain, and my memory freezes. My
thoughts can't get past that point because there's nothing more there. My mind believes it is dead. I wake up
gasping, startled to be alive, because my mind skips out
of that memory and back to the present."

"Do you ever experience it when you're awake?"

"It's only a dream. And maybe because it never
changes, it is something I've learned to live with. I as-

sume I will have it. I've learned how to shake off the aftereffects. It's an injury, just as if I had been shot and lost a kidney, or been shot and lost an arm. It's an injury that simply is there. It's a scar of what happened."

"Vicky knows about the nightmare."

"There's not a friend of mine who doesn't know about the nightmare, though only Vicky knows the images. Jack is probably the best at it, and the one I link up to by video the most often when the nightmare jolts me awake and I need to fill some time. He teaches me stupid card tricks."

The soft tone and her smile tipped him off. "Jack—the fireman. His wife is Cassie?" he guessed, remembering the book.

"That's Jack. He's at the fire station in the middle of the night, waiting on call-outs. He taught Cassie the card tricks to help her with her hand coordination. Now he tries to teach me. He's good for a laugh."

"You're smiling just remembering."

"I've got good friends."

"Very good friends."

"I live with it, Paul. And I hope it's going to ease off and go back to being an occasional thing. It's rare to dream it twice or more a night, and that's been going on this last week." She slid her hands from his and offered an attempt at a smile. "You came to see Boone about family business, and Vicky and I were going shopping today. I'd like to keep those plans."

"Life goes on."

"Yes. It's the only way to handle this."

"Then I hope you have a good day shopping. Do you like to shop?"

"I like to get what I need and get out. Vicky is more flexible. She'll shop, and I'll be amused with her choices and her rejects, and then I'll buy her food and listen to what else she wants to find."

"I imagine you'll buy a book."

"And probably a present for Midnight."

"I plan to stay a day or two, then head back to Chicago. I could drive you home if you like."

"Thank you, but I'm going to keep my plans to meet up with Rachel for a few days. She's like Vicky, good for me when it's a bad week." She got to her feet. "I may have Vicky drop me off at the airport, so if I don't see you later today, I hope you have a good visit with Boone."

"I will. Fly safe, Ann."

"Don't worry, I'm catching a lift with a friend rather than flying myself, and she's got more hours as a pilot than I do."

He wanted to hug her, to tell her again it would be okay, but she took a step away that was a deliberate request for distance. She was holding her emotions together by a thread, however much she tried to present that she had patched them together. Paul gave her the distance because it was all he could do. "I'll call you, Ann. And be down to see you."

She nodded and disappeared out the back door. Paul took a careful breath. It felt like a boulder had landed on his chest. He knew the details now, she had trusted him, and if she felt a bit of relief to have the conversation over, in contrast he now felt a bit sick. She'd been right to describe it as an injury and a scar.

He ran his hand across his face and got up to get himself a drink. It explained why she could write the books she did. She had to put the emotions somewhere, and she had learned to cope by letting those emotions flow onto the page. She would cope, because she had no choice. He'd have to learn to do the same.

The door opened, and Paul glanced over at Boone. Paul dug out a second soda. "Sorry for it, Boone."

His brother shrugged. "Vicky has a lifetime of secrets, and most of them I will never hear. It's not a surprise to learn there was one shared with Ann. I'm sorry for what it is, but I can't say I'm surprised. Those two ladies didn't get to be the kind of friends they are by just sharing tea and shopping. The VP is probably an idiot to wait this long to tell it or, conversely, an idiot to feel like he needs to say anything at all."

Paul sat down again at the table. "It will be public soon enough, and we'll have an answer to which it is. Reporters will quickly speculate it is Ann for the diary, but getting to Vicky will take some doing. She's not one to leave a paper trail with her true name on it, even inside the U.S."

"The hospital records were long ago scrubbed for any sign she had been the one Ann left the hospital with," Boone confirmed. "They won't get to Vicky directly, but people know they are friends. Vicky was in the States that fall on a rare leave. A few will speculate, but I doubt it goes further than that. The few who could put it together as more than speculation aren't the kind to talk."

"You'll handle it if they do."

Boone just glanced at him as if surprised he'd bothered to put it into words.

Paul didn't want to talk about the last forty minutes with Ann, and he didn't particularly want to talk about work, or about the family business. There were four pieces of pie left. Paul chose another one. Boone got a plate and fork and joined him.

"I like Ann."

Paul smiled. "What do you want to know, Boone?"

"How long before you do something about it?"

"She doesn't shift easily from being friends to being something more."

Boone considered him, and then just nodded. "You'll figure it out."

"No advice?"

"Women are a mystery best handled with care."

"You're right about that one. Anything you've noticed about Ann that might help me out?"

"She plays Dad at chess online and beats him."

"Really?"

"She doesn't realize it's him. He's playing under the old KM9 log-in. It probably wouldn't matter to her if she did know who it is, but he's enjoying the games too much to let me tell her. Did you realize she knows Luke and Caroline?"

"No."

Boone walked into the next room and returned with a book. He set it on the table.

Paul realized he'd just hit another air pocket of information about Ann he didn't know. "There are two of Ann's books I have yet to read. She wrote their story?"

"She did. It's a good read."

"Does it ever surprise you, Boone, the number of things you stumble into with Ann?"

"I think she's just made that way. What others would tell you in the first five minutes of conversation, to brag a bit, to present who they are, with Ann you find out by accident in a few years if you happen on to the information. It says more about who she is than the facts you learn. I like her for it."

"So do I, but it's hard to know when you've found all those pieces."

"With Vicky I just assume most of them are going to stay out there unfound. She keeps getting more interesting the longer we're married as they keep turning up."

"I don't understand Ann not saying, I wrote Luke and Caroline's story."

"She doesn't talk about friends. First rule of Ann in her personal list of rules. Friends are private."

"It would be nice to know if that would change if we were more than friends."

Boone half smiled. "Only one way you're going to find that out."

"I'm working on the problem. She likes what she has now and isn't in a hurry to change. I can't afford to get it wrong. I may only get one chance with her."

"You need to figure it out before the VP's book is released. Ann's world is going to get a lot more complex once it does. If you think she isn't in a hurry to make a decision now, once that arrives, she won't make a decision for a good year or more."

Paul nodded. "I can feel the clock running."

PART FIVE

LINDA SMYTHE

23

Paul stood in the doorway of his office. Twenty-two days since he'd last been here, and his chair had acquired a stack of binders, with Post-it notes tacked onto Post-it notes. At least most of the mail was still on Rita's desk. He piled the heap from his chair to his desk and sat down with a sigh. It was going to be a long day.

"I brought you good coffee." Rita stood in his doorway holding a mug. "Margaret was sympathetic and sent a carryout."

"Thanks, Rita." Paul accepted the mug. "Did Zane take his fish home?"

"He's offering to let me adopt them. I think he just doesn't want to figure out how to get the aquarium out of there. They're kind of cute. I may let them stay. It's good to be home, boss."

"I was getting used to not being able to be found."

She laughed and headed to the door.

"Rita."

She turned.

"Get out of here for a few hours this afternoon, come in late in the morning. Your priority is to watch the mail for the lady shooter's next letter. The rest of the catch-up can wait. You and Sam have earned as much vacation time as you want. Go shopping, see a movie, whatever appeals. It's going to get hectic in a few months when the book is released and when the arrests are made. Take some half days and enjoy the time off while you can."

"I'll take you up on that, boss."

"Pass the news to Sam. I'll be upstairs to make the rounds with the team in about half an hour, get up to speed on what's on the board. We'll have the briefings at noon for the next couple of weeks, as I want to live up in the conference room for a while to get back into the flow of things."

Rita grinned. "I like it, boss. It will put people back on their toes." She left to find Sam.

Paul looked at the monitor and wondered if Ann would answer a brief call. He wasn't under any illusions about her next few weeks. She needed some rest that went deep enough to matter, and a lot of it. He wanted to see how she was doing.

A tap on the door had him glancing back. He grinned. "Dave."

"I thought I'd come welcome the prodigal home. I heard you were south seeing Ann."

Paul leaned back in his chair and folded his hands across his chest, but it was hard to keep the smile in check. "Where'd you hear that?"

Dave dropped into a chair with a laugh. "As if you think our girls don't talk. Kate's pleased, as if it was entirely her idea. You two want to come over for dinner next time Ann's in town for a few days?"

"Need to check with her, but sure, we'd love to."

Dave's smile faded. "Kate deserted me for breakfast with Ann and Rachel, so I know some of what is going on. Ann might not talk about the past, but you don't have to be that wise to see nightmares crawling out her skin. She hasn't looked this bad in years. You're going to fix that, I assume."

"Not that easy to fix, I'm afraid." Paul didn't try either to avoid the question or expand on it. Dave might not *know*, but he *knew*. It didn't take information about the cabin to put together the truth that Ann carried her own version of a very bad day as a cop. "Stuff got stirred up. She just needs some time."

"Did you do the stirring?"

"The VP did."

Dave scowled. "I never did like the guy."

Paul laughed. "I wish I had your quick assessments on people, Dave. I haven't figured him out yet. To begin with, it's kind of intimidating to have Ann pull up to the VP's estate and tell security, 'I have a guest with me tonight.' She's comfortable there in a way that's hard to get used to."

"She's just Ann. She's comfortable about everywhere. She's going to borrow the plane and run a bunch of cops over to South Carolina this afternoon. Part of the search-and-rescue crew has a chance to train with the National Guard. So if you're at loose ends tonight, a bunch of us are getting together for a basketball game. You're welcome to join us."

Paul wasn't sure if it was a peace offering or a way to make sure he ended up with a few bruises. "Which gym?"

"Ellis Street. We'll be starting about seven p.m. Bring Sam along."

"I'll be there, and I'll ask him. Thanks." Paul tugged out two sodas and handed Dave one so his friend would stay put a few more minutes. "You want to know the reason Ann's not married?" he asked abruptly, going back to their long-ago conversation. He'd been mulling over that problem on the drive back to Chicago.

"You think you know?"

"Dave, she's scared to fail. That's why she isn't married. Read her books again. She's the author offstage, but she's the author. It's there between the lines—what she puts in, what she leaves out, where she pauses, and where she pivots. Ann is in the books she writes. To Ann, a failed marriage is a failed life. It won't matter that the rest of life was good. She's scared to fail, so she won't try."

"Being scared to fail is like shadowboxing with a shadow. If you're right, what can you do with that?"

"Make it so she can't fail. That's what it is going to take to close the sale."

"How do you plan—?" Dave's phone interrupted. He glanced at it and winced. "Sorry, buddy. That's L.A., and they're not happy since I arrested one of their witnesses last night. If I avoid this call, they are going to fly out and complain in person."

Paul laughed. "Been there with them myself. Go, make peace with the enemy in our West Coast office."

Dave left with his question unfinished.

Paul wasn't sure how he would have answered. He

was going to have to figure it out. He knew where Ann's resistance was at, he had discovered why she was cautious, but he didn't have an answer yet to solving it. And he was very aware time was going to push his hand. The release of the VP's autobiography was a ticking clock for both of them.

She might think she was ready for the firestorm of press that would come, but there was no way to fully comprehend what that would be like in advance. He'd been in enough high-profile cases where the press pushed in to know something of what was coming. He wanted her to be able to make a decision in the calm before that arrived, to decide while she wasn't dealing with those crosscurrents. But he also knew he might be better off to wait, to be her friend through the worst of it, give her more time. He didn't know if another year would help or hurt the relationship. Reece's warning not to let her stall was sitting there as advice from someone who knew Ann well, and it was factoring into this equation.

The only thing he was certain about right now was they needed a quiet couple of weeks. He knew how much the nightmare was eroding her quality of life, and she needed time to get that back under control. It would be good for them both to have life return to normal for a few weeks, for her to have time at home, to take the occasional MHI call, for them to spend evenings together on video. She needed to read a few books, sleep in regularly, take walks with Black, and get back a sense of order. The wise thing to do right now was to help that happen however he could.

He looked at the piles on his desk and sighed. Getting

back to his routine meant clearing the backlog. He picked up the first document and got started.

------◆------

He was too old to play basketball like it was a college scrimmage game. Two days later, Paul was still nursing a bruised ankle and silently replaying Dave's jumper that had taken the game away in the last minute. Two years ago, even a year ago, he would have blocked the shot rather than watch it skim by his fingertips. Sam, on the other hand, had dominated the boards the entire game. Paul flexed the ankle. It was hard to be in charge and get old. It undermined his authority.

Sam stuck his head in the office door. "Boss, a letter in today's mail. Rita's office."

Paul walked into Rita's office two steps behind Sam. It was the same light green stationery, and Rita was gingerly unfolding it. She laid it flat and held it open with her pencil holder and her coffee mug at opposite corners. Paul offered Rita his phone. She took a picture of the letter and passed the phone back.

Agent Falcon—

My offer—I will send you twelve tapes if you can get the states to agree to leave it a federal case.

I want a different lawyer writing this agreement. I will let you choose the lawyer who represents my interests from the list of names below. Have him send two signed client representation letters and two signed copies of the deal agreement to the address below. I will send the twelve tapes and signed copies of the documents back to the lawyer.

L.S.

There were fifteen lawyer names, many Paul recognized as top defense attorneys in the country, a few were media darlings, and halfway down the list were three former state attorneys general all now running for political office. At the bottom of the list the name Jim Gannett had been handwritten in—a small smiley face beside the name, along with the words *It can be like old times.* Paul had to give her points for boldness. The guy who began the chase to catch her now acting as her lawyer.

Sam read the letter over Rita's shoulder. "Is it even possible to get the states to waive the right to prosecute the murders, and do so without us telling them why we are asking?"

"We're going to find out. Twelve tapes is a huge step forward." Paul read the letter again, thinking about the lawyer problem. "Rita, take everything for prints. I'm going to head upstairs and show this to Arthur. Sam, work the address she gives for this reply, see what you can find out. The decision-makers are going to have to assemble to figure out an answer on this one."

Early the next morning, Paul took the stairs up to Suite 906. Margaret smiled when he appeared and nodded toward Arthur's office. "Go right in. They're expecting you, Paul."

"Thanks, Margaret."

Paul entered Arthur's office. "Good morning, Arthur. Director."

He was surprised to see the VP sitting on the couch drinking a cup of coffee. "Sir." Reece Lion was standing near the door, and Paul exchanged a nod with him.

"Tori will be joining us in a couple minutes. I felt we needed a few minutes to clear the air first," the director said, and looked to the VP to explain.

"A polite way to put it, Edward," the VP said. "I was in town to talk about the book, and this arrived." The VP held up a sheet of paper. "I got emailed a letter, a duplicate of yours, I've now learned. Reece is tracing its origin. So far no other lawyer she lists has called to say they also received one." He gave a wry smile. "I feel so special."

The VP set aside his coffee. "Agent Falcon—Paul—I understand and appreciate why you didn't tell me what was going on when I asked you about the lady shooter case. You kept your mouth shut about the tapes and the letters, and I admire that. It makes me even more glad I asked you to be the one to look into my autobiography. This is your case. If you want me to leave this matter, leave this email with you, and go away, I'll do so."

"I'm trying to figure out the reason she would have sent you a copy, sir."

"The case began when I was the FBI director. She wants me to know what kind of deal she's going to get since I didn't catch her when I had the chance. My guess, it was a bit of a joke to put my name on the list, it caught her fancy, and she decided to send me a copy. The fact Reece can't trace it says she knew there was very little risk in sending it."

"Some variation of that is probably right," Paul agreed. "She's asking for another lawyer, so we're going to have to give her someone off that list if we choose to honor her request. And twelve tapes makes me think we should honor her request."

"How good were the tapes she has sent so far?"

"They were worth the deals she asked."

The VP nodded. "So ask me to be her lawyer. She can hardly refuse since she put my name on the list, even if it was done tongue-in-cheek. I can represent her for the purposes of drafting a legal agreement that codifies the offer conveyed in this letter. It's not an open-ended attorney/client relationship. It's for the document only. I can make that clear with the client-representation agreement. I am her lawyer only for the purposes of turning a written offer she presents into a legal agreement with the Department of Justice. The most I'll do as her advocate is try to convince you it is in your interests to accept her offer. But I won't be negotiating on her behalf as her lawyer trying to cut a deal for her."

Paul could tell he had thought this through and was making his pitch. What he wasn't sure of was why.

"What she will get is an airtight agreement," the VP continued. "She'll get my best work, and I'm probably a better lawyer than some on her list. So take that into consideration if you choose me, but I'm not going to jam you up. I won't be a media problem, leaking a rumor of this to the press. I won't be using the case as a stepping-stone to my career. You will see the document I send her, and decide when and how I send it.

"Any lawyer you select is going to have his own agenda. I'll tell you mine. I want her caught, or convinced to turn herself in. I want all the murders solved and prosecuted, and I want to stay involved with the case. That agenda will dictate my actions.

"I'll require an agreement between myself and the Department of Justice that accepts that agenda, and just so nothing gets later tossed in court, I will state that agenda to her in writing in the client-representation agreement. I'm her attorney for the paper only."

Paul broke in before the director could speak. "You won't go rogue and contact her on your own initiative if you think we're taking a wrong tack?"

"My word. You'll control every contact I make with her."

Paul looked at Arthur, then the director. "It's better for us if this stays in-house. Security is already a problem. If the VP wants to be her lawyer, I suggest we let him."

The director nodded. "Agreed. I appreciate this, Jim. I may need your help when it's time to sell this to the attorney general."

"You'll have it. I'll stay at my Chicago home for the next few weeks while this unfolds. Paul, you are welcome to set up in my office there. Or I will work here, as the documents are put together."

"Your home, sir, if you don't mind. It is lower profile than the Secret Service being here."

The director poured himself more coffee. "Arthur, give Tori a call and ask her to join us. Let's figure out how we deal with the fact our lady shooter wants the states to leave this a federal matter."

Paul joined Sam and Rita in the small war room. "We've got two developments. Linda Smythe emailed a copy of her letter to the VP. He was in town to discuss his book with Arthur and the director. Since he's now aware of what is going on, it's been agreed that the VP will act as her lawyer for this offer. They're still debating how to do it, but they will try to get the states to agree to leave this a federal case. They want the twelve tapes." Paul grabbed a pen and added a note to the whiteboard. *How did she know the VP's email address?*

"Any thoughts?"

"She wants her offers accepted. Who better for her to nudge toward being her lawyer than a former director of the FBI? She's trying to guide where this is going," Rita guessed.

"I know there must be a downside, but I don't see it," Sam said. "She wants her offers accepted, so she's getting someone with clout involved. None of the other lawyers on that list could swing a decision, but the VP, the former director of the FBI, he might be able to influence getting her the deal she wants. It makes sense in its own way. My guess on the email address, we're going to find she crossed with someone the VP knows and got access to the address."

Paul hadn't thought of it that way, but their instincts about why she had tried to involve the VP made sense. "I buy that logic," he agreed. Linda Smythe wasn't one to do something by accident. "She's been planning the details. She would try to orchestrate the lawyer she wanted. One with influence in the agency to get this kind of deal. It makes you wonder what kind of deals she will seek with the remaining tapes.

"Assuming the states cooperate, we should have a signed agreement to deliver tomorrow. Let's talk about the address where this package goes, and how we want to stage for it."

Paul closed the door to his office. Ann didn't answer a video call. He tried a secure call to her phone. "Paul, hi." The line was filled with static and the background sound of traffic rushing by.

"Where are you, Ann?"

"Ohio." She covered the phone and the words became muffled. "I'll catch up with you." Her voice firmed. "What's the news, Paul?"

"She's offering twelve tapes if the states will agree to leave the cases to be tried in federal court."

"Twelve tapes." He heard the smile in her voice. "That's big."

"It's huge. They're working to get the states to agree to make the deal without revealing it is the lady shooter case they are waiving rights to prosecute. The politics of it are tricky."

"They'll get it done."

"I'm hoping they do. The agreement is being sent to a company that forwards mail, so she's changing up her game a bit. Sam's on the road to put his eyes on the current forwarding address, but I'm guessing she'll change that address once or twice before the package is actually delivered."

"A good guess."

"What's happening in Ohio, Ann?"

"Someone shot the Grange County sheriff in the back."

"Please tell me you're wearing a bulletproof vest."

"Not an officer in the county without one on. There's a rumor this was payback for an arrest the sheriff made last week, a highway traffic stop that turned into a human smuggling case. There's an entire task force on that one. I'm on family detail, backtracking to help find his grandson who is hiking with friends. I've got them traced to a rest stop, and I'm about four hours behind them now. I'm just getting ready to take a hike and intercept them."

"Please be careful."

"The deputy with me is carrying a shotgun, and he's got two dogs with him who would make Black howl for joy. I'll be fine. They just needed another cop to give a hand as everyone is on more urgent tasks. The family isn't going to rest easy until the grandson is back in town. So we'll go get him. Cell-tower service fades out once you start hiking."

"Call me when you can."

"I will."

"This one's an interesting drop-off point, boss." Sam was driving, and his audio was briefly cutting in and out. "It's a farm, with the mailbox one of those that sits out at the road. The postman pulls up to it and reaches out to put the mail inside. I'm going to have to camp out in order to watch the box, so my plan is to simply install a camera in a tree focused on the box and spend my time in town. The road doesn't give a lot of options for coming and going. If we know when she takes the package, we can locate her vehicle from the air."

"Set it up, Sam. Although I'm beginning to wonder if she will let this package even get close to that mailbox. She's using a forwarding company for this one and may simply hack their system and change the address to where the package is being sent."

"I wouldn't put it past her," Sam agreed. "This right now is almost too easy."

———————◆———————

Paul walked into the war room carrying a bacon-and-egg sandwich for a late breakfast. "Good morning, Sam," he said, knowing the microphone picked up anything said anywhere in the room. He looked at the video of the mailbox. Yesterday he had seen a hawk briefly perch on the mailbox, scanning the surrounding field for prey.

"Morning, boss."

Paul pulled out a chair and read the line of Post-it notes Rita had left for him. Nothing urgent needed his attention. "Any change?"

"I saw a chipmunk on the mailbox this morning. Seriously, it's been three days. Our agreement should be here. The fact it's not says she's already got it."

"I tend to agree with you."

"Do you want me to come on back?"

"Until her twelve tapes arrive, there's a slim chance something happened and she doesn't have the agreement. You'd best stay put until we know for certain."

"It's not a hardship. I'm partway through the restaurant menu, and they do a really good pork chop."

"I'll be around if you notice anything." Paul settled in to pick up reading the files where he had left off the day before.

Paul called Sam back later that afternoon. "Sam, Zane just called. The twelve tapes have arrived by courier. Come on home."

Paul watched Rita add another name to the list on the board and smiled. "Nice."

"Give me another couple days and there will be twelve new names. The tapes were worth the deal, boss."

"I'm inclined to agree with you." They would have twenty-two out of the thirty murders solved when she was done. The fact they happened years ago didn't reduce the satisfaction by much. "Anything I can get for you?"

"I'm good, boss. I'm finding voice comparisons for Nathan to use, and he's working through the tapes one by one. It's not every day I get to solve a stack of old murders. I'm enjoying this."

"Sam?"

"Our files have decent background information for the names Rita is listing. But until we can serve warrants and start using this information, there's not much else to do. I doubt we hear from our lady shooter again until she thinks there's been time for us to look at all twelve tapes."

"It's going to be a few days," Paul said. "I want to ask a favor of you both. I want to make a fast trip south to see Ann. I'll be back Sunday evening. Can you two manage this for the weekend?"

Rita smiled. "Got it covered, boss."

Ann had found the grandson, then stayed to help the task force. There were three dead cops now, and while she promised she was working only on the analysis and was not out in the field, he could hear the weight of it in her voice when they talked. Paul thought it would be over soon, for most law-enforcement agencies at the federal and state levels were working the case now. If it ended, and Ann was able to return home this weekend, he wanted to be there to meet her.

"Appreciate it, guys. You can reach me by cell if something serious comes up."

24

That's her call sign. She'll be descending through the clouds in about a minute," Jason noted, pocketing his radio and picking up the blocks he used to secure the plane. "She made good time."

Paul nodded his thanks for the news and straightened from where he leaned against his car. He watched the small plane land at the private airstrip outside her hometown. She set down center line of the runway and taxied toward the hangar.

Jason walked over to meet her. When she came to a stop, he put blocks under the wheels. A few minutes later she stepped out. "I've got it for you, Ann," Jason offered.

"You sure?"

"I've got time."

"Thanks. Logs are on the clipboard and fuel goes on my bill." She pulled a bag and a satchel from the plane.

She hadn't seen him yet. "Ann."

She looked up and stopped, surprise crossing her face, then pleasure. "You're a long way from home, Falcon."

"Missed you enough it seemed like a good idea to travel, and Neva was agreeable to a guest for the weekend." He took her bags. "How about pizza and cold soda at your place, and we'll share it with Black."

"Okay."

"Ride with me. We'll pick your car up tomorrow."

"Even better."

He put her bags in the back seat and held the passenger door for her. He could tell she had not slept well on the road. There was a hollow look around her eyes. He was glad the case was over.

He left the airport and turned onto the highway. "Where do I pick up Black?"

She stirred. "He's still at the house. Friends stopped in to get the mail and let him outside. He probably slept the entire time I was away, so expect him to want to play."

"I'll enjoy that."

She visibly relaxed as he turned down the road to her home.

They ate pizza on her back patio, enjoying the evening breeze and watching the sun drift low in the sky. The case had drained her and left her bone tired; he could see it in the way she only partially engaged even with Black, her thoughts lingering on what she had left behind. There was a price for being the MHI, and she had paid it in full this week.

He tossed the ball for Black again, then took both plates inside, stored the remaining pizza in the fridge, and returned with the wrapped peppermints that had

DEE HENDERSON

come with the delivery. She unwrapped hers with a quiet thanks. "I'm glad you came."

"Not a hardship on my part. Sam and Rita have the case covered, and I had a desire to see you."

She half smiled. "Can't figure why, when you see me so often already."

"Can't do this over a link," he said as he slid his hand behind her neck and drew her toward him. He kissed her and caught the taste of pizza and peppermint. He lingered with the kiss, feeling her smile and sharing it. When he eased back he ran his thumb across her bottom lip. "I've wanted to do that for a long time."

"Thought you had. Shared the sentiment," she murmured. Her hands resting against his chest flexed in the fabric of his shirt, and she leaned forward to kiss him back. "It's a very nice way to return home."

They took a walk together the next afternoon, enjoying the sunny day, following Black. Paul glanced down when Ann slid her hand into his, smiled. He interlaced their fingers. He'd been trying not to crowd her today, to give her space, and he liked the fact she'd made the decision to close it.

"Lovely is a very private name for God," she said quietly, breaking the companionable silence. "But had we lived a lifetime together, I would never have mentioned that name to you. It bothers me that I did."

He stopped walking, understanding instantly the significance of what she had said, and the trust she was giving him. He thought about it and then smiled as he started walking again. "What a perfect name for God."

"Names are important to me. I spend weeks with a new story searching to find the right names for characters, to hear their voice, to find who they are. There's a point in writing a story where I finally have the right name, and the book in my mind begins to sound different. It sounds richer. It begins to read in the voice of the character, and it sounds alive.

"I was a child when I met God. God the Father was an easy concept for me to grasp, and Jesus the Son, being God who died to save my life, I often thought of as the wonderful older brother I wanted to have. When I got to God, the Holy Spirit, and realized the Bible said He lived with me, I instinctively thought of Him as being a best friend.

"I wanted to get to know Him, and the only way I knew to do so was to have a conversation with Him. It was hard to say 'Holy Spirit' and not feel like it was a formal conversation. So sometimes I'd call Him Ancient, Wise, Wonderful, Eternal. I was trying to get to know Him by reminding myself who He was.

"I'd say, 'You're showing off tonight,' when the sunset and clouds were an incredible display of color, or I'd say, 'It's hot, I miss the breeze you sent yesterday,' or I'd tell Him about my day and what I was working on. I was just talking, trying to get to know this person I was living with. And like a book, the name was right, but it wasn't a conversational name. Jesus had names like Alpha, Omega, Good Shepherd. So I asked the Holy Spirit if He had another name I could use. He said, 'Call me Lovely.'

"I thought it was kind of a girl's name and corny and stupid of me to have asked. But I think He knew. In a week or so, He couldn't shut me up. I had a name for the person I was sharing my life with. 'Lovely, you painted a great sunset.' 'Lovely, Black just went chasing a rabbit.' 'Lovely, I've lost my keys.' It was still the same simple comments, but they suddenly turned into God and I having a conversation. And in a few more weeks, it was 'Lovely, I'm lost on how to help in this situation,' and 'Lovely, why did I say that?' I started to trust Him with the emotions behind my actions. And now it's 'Lovely, where should this story go next?' And 'Lovely, what am I going to do about this guy that just showed up in my life?'" She smiled.

"He listens to all that stuff. He smiles at me a lot. God said call me Lovely, and I fell more in love with Him that day. I had this huge open hole inside that so desperately wanted love, and God filled it up with himself. His name was reminding me He loved me. Every conversation just adds another certainty to that.

"Lovely is His character. And Lovely is His company. And Lovely is how He treats me. Lovely is God."

Paul understood in a way he didn't know how to put into words. "I often call Him Dad—when God and I are talking together. That's how I think of Him and it's a natural title to offer Him."

He tightened his hand on hers. "Did you think I wouldn't understand why you have a private name for God? Tell you God is there with you, God is in you, living with your spirit, and He wants a relationship with you—Ann, you would rush toward that relationship with everything in you. You would throw your arms around God and say welcome, do everything possible to make Him comfortable as an honored guest.

"And since for you a name, the flow of words—the sound of a conversation, the tempo and the pace of it—matters, you looked for the right name. Just like you give your characters in the books a shortened special nickname between those in love, you did the same for Him. You gave God a special name. You went from formal with God to intimate with God. You call Him Lovely. I bet God's heart goes absolutely soft with pleasure when you call Him that. God wants to be loved, and with you God got what He most desires."

"I hope so." She stopped walking. "Sometimes when I'm flying, Lovely will give me a nudge to notice something or to hear something and He'll make it safer flying. Or I'll be on the job, and Lovely will point out something in the room to notice that will help me understand the person I'm talking with. Or Lovely will whisper 'Turn around,' and I'll see someone I need to help. Or Lovely will prompt me to go to bed early, and I'll get some sleep before I get called out at four a.m. He doesn't live life for me. He lives life with me." Black nudged her for attention, and Ann tossed another stick for him.

"God will let me put to Him what I'm feeling and thinking and doing, and He'll take the burden of it and the complications of it, and He'll hand me back something that I can do okay at. He'll sort out the knots. Sometimes He sends someone to help me. Sometimes He helps with the sequence of what to do when. Sometimes with the wisdom to figure out what's important and the courage to drop the rest. Lovely spends His life with me. And I am learning to spend mine with Him. I trust Him. And we're becoming pretty good friends. An eternity is a long time to live with someone, and it matters to me that I get this relationship right."

Paul knew the kind of hug that was God loving him. His friendship with God was good and solid and the most important priority in his life. And he realized Ann knew God better than he had ever envisioned was possible. "I'm glad you have that intimate relationship."

He wanted to laugh as he grasped what he was feeling. "I'm jealous of God, in a way. I'd like that for myself, Ann. That inner Ann that loves so completely and trusts so absolutely. No wonder you hesitate to share your life with someone else. You would be taking what you are giving to God and sharing it with God and someone else. You want to give it all to God."

"It's not that exactly, Paul. I don't know how to love God well and love a guy well and do both at the same time. One gets the leftovers. That's probably the main reason why I'm still single. I haven't figured out how to do it. It's not that I don't want to get married. What is easy for other people to do seems very difficult for me. I'm too introverted and inside my head. Lovely rather gets me by default, because I'm never particularly quiet with Him. I'm sure there are times He would like me to be quiet for a while. He hears about everything."

"I think you don't realize how much what you have with Lovely flows out to everyone around you," Paul replied. "That's why you are such a good friend. That's why people trust you like they do. Part of what you are giving back to them is God loving them through you. Everyone around you would lose out if you didn't have such a strong relationship with God."

"I'm still bothered at the fact I told you Lovely's name.

Of everything I have that is private, that was the jewel at the center."

He rested his arm around her shoulders and hugged her. "I know more about you because of that mistake than everything else you've told me combined. I can't be sorry it happened. But I do understand just how intimate and private that name is between you and God."

▼

Paul drove back to Chicago in a thoughtful mood.

She had trusted him with Lovely. She was taking big risks with him. She was trying to see if this could work. And he knew she wasn't yet anywhere near the same place he was.

He still faced the very possible risk that she would decide she simply didn't want to get married. He wanted them both to end up at the right decision, and he was worried he'd be at a yes, and she'd come to no. She deserved to be treasured. That was the one thought that came to mind and felt right to him. Treasured, loved.

This relationship was beginning to matter more than any cost he might have to pay to see where it could go. He was falling in love with her. And he thought he had found his future wife, if she would have him.

▼

Ann hugged the bed pillow with one arm, but she didn't try to close her eyes and find sleep. Her emotions and her heart were too full. Paul had kissed her goodbye before he left for Chicago. The memory still lingered like a soft touch against her heart.

He is falling in love with me. She had thought when

he first told her that, sitting at Vicky's kitchen table, that the words had come in part out of a very emotional conversation. She had returned home, and Paul had given her back the calm of what they had before, the conversations, the casual friendship, the reasons to smile. He'd given her space so she could settle and rest. It had been good to get back out on MHI calls, to have her work.

And then he had come to meet her flight, sat with her on her back porch, and he'd kissed her for the first time. She had enjoyed kissing him back. He'd kissed her four times over the course of this weekend, each one bright in her memory, and while it had been a light touch on his part, there had been nothing casual about the change in their relationship. Her heart was so full of emotions. Paul was falling in love with her. When he crossed that line to *I love you*, he would want much more than a friendship.

He was going to ask her what she wanted. And she didn't know how to answer that question. She was overwhelmed with the emotions of it. For the first time in years she wanted to pull the covers up over her head and hide. Her joy was welling up alongside pure fear. He had her emotions so tangled that if she let her feelings decide tonight, she would either run toward him or run away, and she couldn't guess which it would be.

She was single, content being single. She'd come into the year with no inkling she might be asked to consider a change. She admired good marriages. She'd just never let herself dream about one happening for her. She had risked with Paul, every step along the way, sharing secrets, giving him the most precious private facts she had. She'd found him a man she could trust at every level. It wasn't that she hadn't known this day was a possibility;

she just hadn't expected for it to be here this weekend. She wanted a slow shift from where she was comfortable to where Paul was taking them. This wasn't going to move slowly anymore. Paul was doing the shifting now, to something a lot more solid, permanent, than a friendship.

Could she be a good wife? For the first time in years she asked herself the question knowing it was more than speculation, and one she might have to answer soon.

The physical intimacy would be new ground for her. She still blushed at the thought of what it would be like. The idea of being with Paul every night for the rest of her life was an intoxicating thought. She'd enjoy being his wife and love the intimacy of being with him.

She'd like his family, like having relatives again. The conversations, the inside family jokes, the holiday gatherings—she'd be absorbed into his large family and have a place again.

Paul wouldn't have a casual marriage. It would be a lifetime, an *everything* decision on his part. She wanted that kind of connection to someone who knew her secrets and loved her.

She just didn't want to fail.

She owed it to him to say no rather than let him walk into a marriage that would fail. She was the weak link when it came to a marriage. Paul would be a good husband, comfortable in the role. He'd step into it with the same assured confidence with which he would one day step into the role of being head of the Falcon family.

But she was deeply uncomfortable at the idea of being a wife. Even the mere thought exhausted her. She could ruin her life and his by assuming she could do this, be a wife, only to find out she couldn't handle it. It would mean a new place, new people, new expectations, the transition of her job, her writing—all of her life would be different. Change drained her. Time would help, but it would be a constant struggle to adapt to the role. He didn't realize what it would take for her to say yes.

Did she want to say yes? None of her doubts were about Paul. All of them were about her. She didn't want to find out two months into the marriage that they were both disappointed. She had to live in reality, not in wishful thinking. She couldn't afford a marriage which failed.

What did she need so she wouldn't fail? How did she say yes and not fail? She pondered those questions as sleep eluded her.

She needed Paul to give her more time. She needed to be able to dial back the pace at which this was moving. She felt like she was being pulled forward into a decision before she was ready to make one. He'd want to hear "I love you," and she couldn't even identify her emotions right now. Paul had her twisted into knots with wonder, and deeply afraid at the same time. She smiled, then groaned in the darkness. That wasn't what he had intended when he came for the weekend. There were no easy choices in front of her.

25

Paul walked into the war room Monday morning, opened his briefcase, and retrieved the long list he had written the night before. "Where are we at, Sam?"

The man nodded toward the board. "Rita has names identified for the recent twelve tapes. That makes twenty-two out of the thirty murders solved. It sure feels good, looking at those cases and knowing the truth of what happened."

Paul handed over the pad of paper. "Look over that list and give me your impressions. I've been sketching out how we best make these arrests."

Sam settled back in his chair and began to read. "I can tell you I'm looking forward to it, boss."

"So am I. Any questions from our guys?"

"They're curious about what has us occupied in the war room, and they've guessed there is a lead on the lady shooter case, but I don't think anyone's picked up the rumor we've got all the cases potentially solved. No one has whispered 'audiotapes.' The guys will be eager

to help once it's time to fill them in on the developments." Sam read the list. "You want our guys to do
the interviews."

"Yes. We're going to get one opportunity to use those
tapes to our advantage, and that moment is the interview when we present the deal we're prepared to offer in
return for a guilty plea. We divide the thirty cases, two
or three murder suspects per team, and let our guys use
their knowledge of this case to their advantage."

"Do we play the tapes, as brief as they are?"

"I think we have to. That tape is the risk to them. They
either believe we can turn that audio into a guilty murder
conviction, or they don't. I think more than a few will
be caught off guard by the fact we have it on tape, and
they will take the deal rather than run the risk of a trial."

Paul pulled over the files Sam had been building for
the twenty-two listed names. He settled in to catch up
on the reading.

Paul's phone rang just after lunch. He pulled it out of
his pocket, nodded at Sam, and answered, putting the
phone on speaker so Sam could listen in. "Hello, sir."

"Her letter arrived in today's mail. Should I open it?"

"Yes, sir." They heard some paper rustling.

"She is offering eight tapes—all high-profile names—
to get medium security in the state of Wisconsin," the
VP said. "This is the last of the thirty tapes. You knew
there was going to be a difficult-to-swallow offer, and
she just made it. She wants to do her time at a medium-
security federal prison in Wisconsin. The question is,
how valuable are eight tapes with high-profile names?"

"The last four were worth it."

"Medium security for thirty murders—it's asking for a lot. Let me know if Arthur wants me there when this offer is discussed, or if you want to bring me the decision on what to reply."

"I will, sir. If I don't have an opportunity later to say it, thanks for the help you've provided. I am eight tapes away from having thirty murders solved. That wouldn't have happened as smoothly without your help as her lawyer, sir."

"I've wanted this case solved ever since it first came to my attention when I was the director, so I echo your sentiments. It's good to have the truth known."

Paul went to update Arthur with the news. When he returned to the war room an hour later, Sam was pulling cable for an additional monitor. "What do you have, Sam?"

"This final answer goes to a post-office box. I've got a tap into the security cameras at that post-office branch." Sam finished securing the cable and then spoke into the phone he held. "Wave, Tim." The man on the video feed waved. "The back of a postbox is just an open slot where they can put the mail. You open the box on the lobby side with a key and get your mail." Sam switched to the phone. "Put the package in her slot, Tim." The man on the video ran his fingers along a line of numbers, stopped, and put a blue-and-white mailer into a slot. "Thanks."

Sam stuck a Post-it note to the monitor. "We can hand-deliver our reply to the post office and put it in the box ourselves, and you can tell it's there. That size and shape and blue and white stands out. Since the cameras are stationary, we mark on the monitor which box is hers. We can see the package sitting there.

"Short of putting a cop standing beside the box with his hand on the mailer, this is good coverage. If there's any concern, we lock down the building. It's a small branch, ten employees, with another thirty who come in and sort mail and go out on deliveries."

"It sounds like I need to make the popcorn. I like it, Sam. Choose guys you trust from the local office to watch the building and be ready to lock it down if necessary."

"You think she's still going to lift the package."

"I think she knows exactly what you do, and she's figured something out. If she wants to get caught, she's going to open the post-office box, take out the agreement, sign in, and surrender. She won't run. She'll either slip that package out from under our noses or she will pick it up and surrender."

Sam blinked. "I actually hadn't thought of that possibility."

Paul smiled. "We're so used to chasing people who run, it seems odd to consider someone might stop running. If she gave us her real name, there's a chance she's also decided to end this after thirty tapes and a decent deal and turn herself in. We still don't know what changed, what caused her to send those first tapes to us. She was out there and unknown, and something changed that she wanted a deal ready if we caught her. We may have been closer than we realized.

"She has to know that once we start to make arrests, there will be thirty people with considerable financial means who will have an incentive to kill her before she can testify. I'd lay fifty-fifty odds she's going to pick up the package herself, sign the document, have the tapes on her, and turn herself in."

"You want to come with me? Rita? We should be there, all of us, if she's going to surrender."

"Take Rita with you. If our lady shooter turns herself in, keep it low profile, and drive her back to here. Chat if she's inclined to chat. Put anything she says onto tape. Both you and Rita should be wearing microphones and have a couple turned on in the car. Redundancy will be your friend. If she turns herself in, I'll buy the dinner when you get back. If she somehow slips this package out from under us for a final time, you're buying the dinner."

Sam smiled. "I'll take that deal. What's upstairs going to decide about the deal she wants?"

"I have no idea on this one. They're meeting later today."

"Rita and I will get on the road just as soon as they have the reply on paper."

* * *

"We'll take a hit for giving medium security for thirty murders, but I can live with it." The director finally called the debate closed after two hours of hashing out how to respond. "It's not worth losing the tapes. Not when they are this valuable." He turned to the VP. "Write up the offer, Jim, and let's get those last tapes. Given the ones on the last four high-profile tapes, I need to know the names on these next eight tapes regardless of the cost to get them.

"If she continues to elude us, this deal is just a piece of paper. If we catch her several years from now, she's going to be in her sixties and the thirty arrests are going to be history. This gets interesting if we pick her up when she retrieves this package. But if we do, the press is going to have thirty murders to take some of their attention. We can ride out the news cycle of it."

"I'll have the agreement written up by this evening," the VP agreed.

———————▼———————

"Ann."

"Hi, Paul." She smiled when she saw him appear on the screen. "Say hi, Black."

The dog barked once and stood up with his feet on the table to better see the video. Paul chuckled at the dog, who looked wide awake and wanting to play. "Hello, Black."

Ann hugged the animal and nudged him back down. "You're up late."

Paul glanced at the clock and realized it was nearing midnight. "The last agreement for the last of the tapes is ready to go. Sam will deliver it tomorrow. We're at the endgame."

"Nice." She settled into her favorite chair and picked up a book to show him the cover. "Thanks for the book. I just started it. It's a good read."

"I thought you might enjoy it."

"Neva sent a lemon-meringue pie home with me. I wish you were here to share it."

Paul smiled. "Same here. I didn't need anything in particular; I'm just calling to say I'm heading home, and to say good night."

"Glad you did. Good night, Paul."

"Good night, beautiful."

The post-office stakeout wore into days of boredom. No one approached the postbox, no one moved the package. Sam and Rita would at times begin games of I-spy to fill in an hour. They began counting people with red shirts, and then yellow hats. On the morning of the fourth day they began to compare the number of sprinkles on the donuts to select the best one. Paul, listening in on the audio feed, smiled and read files, glad he had not gone with them.

Paul interrupted their animal alphabet quiz shortly after one p.m. on the fourth day. "Guys, Zane just called. The eight tapes just arrived along with a Post-it note that says 'Thanks.'"

"The package hasn't moved in the last three days. I can see it, and it's our package, our label," Sam protested. "You're watching the same picture I am, boss. It's right there."

"Go retrieve the package. Find out if she looped the security feed on us."

Paul heard a door slam as Sam left to check out what had happened. "Rita, you might want to give him room to blow off steam when he gets back."

"After four days of sitting here, I'm liable to kick something too. It never left our sight, boss. We've been stuck on this image like bees on honey."

"Speaking as someone who has that monitor image practically tattooed to the inside of my eyeballs, I didn't see it either. Maybe something middle of the night, when we only had security lighting to work with to see the box?"

"Maybe. Sam's coming back."

Sam slammed the door. "It's been steamed open and replaced with a bunch of white paper. She had to have done a swap with one blue-and-white package for another, retrieved the documents, and swapped the package back so that when Tim walked by and glanced at the label for us he would see the same handwriting as what he had put into the box. The view of the package is rarely blocked on the video, maybe half a minute when someone tall stops to have a conversation at the end of the aisle. Someone on the post-office staff was helping her. They were at the box at least twice and not challenged by staff as not supposed to be there. We can pursue it. We have the security feed. She had inside help, boss."

"I agree. But we don't have time to pursue it today. We have all thirty tapes. We don't have her. Come home, Sam. I need Rita identifying the names for these tapes, and you and I have thirty arrests to plan. We'll come back to this and ask questions later about who helped her."

"I feel like an idiot."

Paul smiled. "She's good at this. She probably had someone watching the same video you did, so don't worry about it. Just remember, you're buying dinner."

Sam laughed. "Yeah, rub salt in the wound, boss. We're coming home."

* * *

Paul took the eight tapes to Nathan in the audio lab himself. "The same as the last tapes, I need copies carefully made, we will listen to the tapes and bring you a list of names, and we need you to find an audio match and tell us who is on each tape."

"Got it."

"One new reality. You find a match and find a name, you tell that name to no one but me. Not Sam, not Rita, not Arthur, not even the director."

"Knowing the names from some of the earlier tapes, I can imagine who these might be. I'll tell only you. I would prefer to duck the politics of this and not write anything down until you give me the green light to make the names official." Nathan made copies of the tapes and handed them to Paul.

"I'll be back with the names shortly. It's not much, but order dinner on me. Something good."

Nathan smiled. "Appreciate it."

Paul entered Arthur's office shortly after eleven p.m. the next evening and closed the door. "We have names for the last eight high-profile tapes. It would be worth interrupting the director's evening to put him on a secure conference call."

"That bad?"

"Worse."

Paul drove home, trying to reach Ann on her phone but getting only her recording. She must be in the air. It was going on one a.m. and he hoped she would be on the ground soon. He left a message for her, that they had the thirty names, and for her to call him when she could.

They had thirty tapes, they had thirty names. Now it was arrests, interviews, a press conference, arraignments, and then passing the thirty murder cases off to the U.S.

attorney general's office. The list of names was enough to make the anger run deep. People with money and power paying for murder. He needed the arrests just to be able to sleep at night. He needed the justice.

———————▼———————

Paul found Sam and Rita in the war room early the next morning, comparing notes over a box of donuts. "Where are we at, boss?"

Paul found himself a glazed donut from the box while he waited for the locks to engage. After the click, he nodded to the board. The list of thirty were neatly written in Rita's handwriting. "I've got the green light for arrests," he told them. "The U.S. attorney general is sending a task force of lawyers. We lock them in the room to keep from leaking word of this, and we brief them on what is going to happen. We plan the deal we are going to offer for each of the murders. We don't have the lady shooter to testify, so we hope we can get some of these people to take a deal and offer a guilty plea. And we hope our lawyers are good.

"Sam, assemble our full team in the conference room. Let's brief them in. Then let's decide who we want to conduct each interview. We'll put our guys into the field in the next twenty-four hours to the nearest FBI office based on where their arrests are going to be made. I want to have the interviews happen within hours of the arrest. Have you decided the ones you want?"

"Henry Green and Lilly Delta."

"Rita?"

"Nichole Sims and Frank Teller. Who are you going to take, boss?"

"I'm going to stick to roving between cases based on who needs help. And I'm going to take responsibility for herding those lawyers to make sure they are helping us rather than slowing us down."

Sam pushed the box of donuts over. "That's a two-donut problem."

Paul laughed and took a second one.

Paul walked to the front of the conference room, onto the platform, and turned on his microphone. "Ladies and gentlemen, please find a seat at one of the tables and give me your attention. I am about to tell you why your boss had you surrender your phones and electronic devices on the way in, and why you have now been locked in this room."

The lawyers and paralegals in the room found chairs and the room grew quiet.

"My name is Paul Falcon, I'm FBI based here in Chicago." He turned on the projector and began to click through thirty murder-scene photos. "One lady shooter murdered all these people. She was paid, and paid well, to kill them. She began in 1989, and her thirtieth murder was in 2003. She's been silent the last nine years. That changed a few months ago."

Paul changed the photo on the screen to tapes spread out on his desk. "These are thirty tape recordings of the murders for hire. Who to kill, how much they would pay, and why they wanted it done. She's offered the tapes in return for a deal for when she is caught. We have identified the voices on the tapes.

"Tomorrow we are going to be arresting"—he looked

at a list on a sheet in his hand—"four congressmen, three CEOs, two CFOs, one professional football coach, two State Department officials, two cops, three DEA agents, a former governor, a mob boss, three mob-family enforcers, a banker, two arms dealers, and five rich ex-wives." Paul started displaying the photos of the arrest targets on the screen while he waited for the burst of conversation to die down.

He finally gave a whistle and the mike amplified it enough he got the silence he wanted. "Yes, we are very certain on the audio matches and the authenticity of the tapes. Your immediate task is to put together a package of search warrants for financial and phone records, and to craft the deals we will offer to each individual in return for a guilty plea for murder for hire. We plan to look hard at each of these individuals, and for whatever else they might have done to break the law in the years since.

"Each murder will be assigned a legal team and a lead prosecutor. Your boss is making those assignments. I need the best work of your career because you can bet each one of these individuals is going to have the best defense attorney money can buy on retainer. The clock is running. We begin the arrests in twenty-four hours."

"Ready to go make some arrests?"

Paul paused from digging out his keys. Ann was waiting at his car with two cups of coffee. He grinned because he couldn't help it. "It's five a.m."

"I hate this early-morning start of a job, but I hear you—for some reason—like it."

Paul took one of the coffees. "Thirty arrests need an early start."

"I thought I would offer to chauffeur today, and I'm good at keeping the coffee coming. I know about Margaret's secret stash."

Paul leaned forward and kissed her. "Thanks. You don't like coffee."

"These are both for you. I figured you couldn't have too much caffeine on a day like this. Do we need to go get donuts for Sam and Rita?"

"They're already in the field, but I can use a box. I know a place on the way."

"Then let's go to work, Agent Falcon."

The arrests began at six a.m. and rolled through the day, the last of the thirty being made shortly after two p.m. Paul paced the main conference room, glad to have his full team working on the case now, shifting off between several phones, listening to updates. Agents were acting across two dozen different cities, serving warrants and making the arrests.

"Here." Ann put a soda into his hand.

He turned, startled, and she smiled. "You're growing hoarse."

"Thanks."

Ann rejoined the intern, who was working the grid on the board, checking off when an arrest was made, when the interview began, when the offer was made for a deal, when warrants were served, when phone and financial evidence began to be gathered.

Paul had enough agents that even thirty arrests were

unfolding in an orderly way. Half of the interviews had already begun, and all of the warrants had been served. What Paul didn't have yet, what he was hoping to find, was someone with more information about the lady shooter willing to trade it for a better deal.

Paul saw a check mark go onto the board in the column with the heading Deal Accepted. He looked at the name on the board of the agent doing the interview and smiled. "Way to go, Franklin," he said softly, wishing he was there in person to congratulate the man.

Moments later another check mark went on the board. Rita had a deal accepted. Paul mentally raised his expectations from three people accepting a deal to eight. An audiotape could shake the most confident person.

The head of the legal task force passed him, circling the room in the opposite direction. Paul had decided he liked the man. The director had been by earlier, and Arthur was a regular. Paul was a bit surprised not to see the VP here to watch the arrests unfold.

Paul scanned the muted televisions they were monitoring to see how this case was breaking in the news cycle. Reporters had most of the thirty murders. The connection to a common, single lady shooter had just been made. Paul thought in an hour the news of the audiotapes would be out there.

He crossed the room to join Ann. He didn't care who was in the room or who was watching. He wrapped his arms around her to give her a hug. "See where your middleman wreck eventually went? You pushed to crack the day-planner codes, we found the house, we did interviews, she reacted, and now we have thirty murders solved. This all began with you."

She smiled. "Ice cream works as a nice thank-you."

"Whenever this case finally ends," Paul promised. "Do you think she is out there watching the breaking news as arrests are made?"

"I think she's watching, and she's wondering how close you are to knocking on her front door."

"Let's hope that day arrives. In case you get an MHI call and need to leave, let me tell you now how much I appreciate you being here."

"You're very welcome."

"Boss, I've got Sam for you."

Paul walked over to take the phone.

Paul switched to decaf during the three weeks after the arrests in order to survive the pace of the job. Margaret already had a mug poured for him as he walked into Suite 906. She put it in his hand with a smile. "He's expecting you."

Paul took a deep breath and drank half the coffee. "Can I bargain for one of those ten-minute interruptions of yours?"

"I'll interrupt in ten minutes."

Paul headed into the office. "Boss."

Arthur set down his phone and waved him in. "Have you had time to catch your breath yet?"

The question caught Paul off guard enough that he had to laugh. "No, sir. It's been a busy few weeks. I think I've met myself coming and going a few times."

Arthur pointed to a chair. He came around to lean against the front of the desk. "The U.S. attorney is pleased. His legal teams are up and running for the thirty murder cases. We've got nine guilty pleas, and six more angling to give a guilty plea on better terms. Even the press is positive. Where are you at with the lady shooter?"

"Sam, Rita, and I just finished a detailed review of what the interviews provided us in new info about her. The bottom line, there's little new to work. A search of the Boston area for someone who recognized her old picture has come up dry. We'll keep looking, but I'm not optimistic. Unless she makes a mistake, we may never catch her."

"She's had time to plan this out in detail. She gave us the tapes, and I can live with the deal we made with her. We'll catch her eventually. Just think of where this case was a year ago and you've got to appreciate the progress."

"I can live with the deal as well. I didn't think all thirty murders could be solved. At least now we know the truth of what happened."

"Will you take some advice?"

"Of course, sir."

"Take a long vacation. When the VP autobiography is released, you will be back in the middle of it. Take the time while you can. You've earned it. Sam and Rita have proven to me they're ready for a significant promotion. Leave them in charge so they get a taste of what it's like if they say yes."

"I appreciate that, Arthur. They can handle the work. But I don't want to lose them; we work well together."

"My word you won't. I'll just put more on your plate, and you'll need them carrying what you've got now. Your public profile leaped with these thirty arrests, and that press is nothing compared to what's coming when the autobiography comes out. You're going to be the personal favorite of the media, and I can guarantee the director is going to take advantage of that. Besides, you've got so much vacation time on the books, HR complains about it regularly. Use up some of that time and enjoy it."

"Thanks, Arthur. I'll seriously consider it."

Paul took the stairs down to the conference room. He had spoken with Ann a few times in the last weeks, but they had been hurried conversations between other meetings, updating her on how this massive case was going, keeping tabs on where she was at with MHI calls. He hadn't been home much, and she'd been pushing him to spend time with his family and to get some sleep when he did finally get home. There hadn't been much casual time together. A vacation would be a smart step. His personal life needed attention.

"Sam."

"Right here, boss." Sam stepped out of the war room, an audio cable being coiled around his arm to store away. Rita walked out a step behind him, carrying the extra chairs that had accumulated in the small room.

"The boss has practically ordered me to take a vacation."

Sam grinned. "What are you still doing here then?"

"Leaving you and Rita working while I go be slothful seems like a lousy idea."

Rita laughed. "Boss, we're famous. I haven't had to buy a breakfast, lunch, or dinner since the arrests began. I'm having too much fun to want to take a vacation right now."

"How did the meeting go with the legal task force chief?" Paul asked her.

"He'd love it if we caught the lady shooter so she

could testify at the trials. Otherwise, his most interesting comment was a thank-you for having the case files organized and indexed. I like the guy, Paul. He's got a practical streak to go along with that legal degree."

"Sam?"

"I'm as popular as Rita. I'll take the time once the snow begins to fall and I can get in some skiing."

Rita returned the chairs to where they normally belonged. "There's no reason for you to stay, boss. The other cases on the board are being managed, and I'll keep an eye on them. Besides, when the boss is away, people relax, as they aren't trying to impress you. If you take a vacation, everyone will get a subtle version of a vacation too. You need to go see Ann."

"That's what I was thinking. If you two want to do my job while I'm gone, I'll take more than a few weeks off."

"We'll enjoy running this place. We've got your number if an emergency comes up."

Sam nodded. "I'm with Rita. Go see Ann. Take a long vacation. You can come back rested and ready to handle the press for the VP's book, and we'll gladly take our vacations then and abandon you without a qualm."

Paul grinned. "Thanks, both of you, I think."

PART SIX

CHOICES

26

Paul thought about Ann and where they were at while he fixed himself dinner. He knew the issues. She was very quiet. It took steady effort to get from her what was on her mind. She would find the social side of being a Falcon a major stress and an energy drain. She was very much an introvert, more so than he had thought. She wouldn't be comfortable having a family. He'd have to accept that. She was awake at night, and he'd have to figure out how to handle her ten p.m. to two a.m. fight against that nightmare.

But he was content with her. He liked her personality. He liked who she was. She loved God. People trusted her. She had earned that trust.

He carried his plate into the den. He called up the video and the pictures of Ann he had collected, scrolling through his favorites. He hadn't planned to make the decision today, but he realized he had made it. He knew her. He knew her secrets, he knew who she was. And he loved her. If Ann was going to be his wife, it was time to find out. It was time to press this to an answer. Waiting would not materially change the outcome.

He couldn't guess what Ann's decision would be. The reality was she hadn't decided. He'd have to bring her to the point of making a decision and hope it came out in his favor. The big risk was a no, and as painful as it would be for him to hear, the larger risk was what it would be for her. She had put so much at stake with him. She had left the place of being single and content with it, to exploring the idea of marriage because he'd ask her to make that step. To say no would break her heart—and his. "God, don't let me make a mistake in how I handle this. Don't let me hurt her. However this ends, please don't let me hurt her." He looked through the pictures, and he planned out how to proceed over the next few days.

"Hi, Ann." He was pleased to catch her at home the next morning, working at her desk.

She turned to the screen and flashed a smile. "Hi." Her expression turned puzzled. "You're not at your office? It's ten o'clock."

"A vacation day."

She stopped what she was working on to rest her chin in her hands. "I love that word. You need it. That sounds like a very smart move."

"I'm going to the gym, then stopping at Falcons to let Jackie feed me. Then I thought I might come back home and spend part of my day interrupting yours."

She grinned. "I like that plan."

"I'll see you in about four hours then."

"I'll be right here."

Paul found a soda and settled in the den. He called Ann. The video came up and he had to grin. She'd been napping on the couch—he could see the pillow line on her cheek. "Hey, sleepy eyes."

She covered a yawn and half laughed. "I crashed about an hour ago. It was a late night." She ran her hand through her hair, messing it more than straightening it. Black was sound asleep in front of the couch. "The gym looks like it agreed with you."

"It was nice to shake off a bunch of cobwebs. I like the job, but I could do without a repeat of the last few weeks. Lunch was wonderful. It was good to catch up with family, and I'm woefully behind on all the family news. Jackie said to say hi."

Ann smiled. "I like your sister."

"Go get something to drink, Ann, catch a shower, whatever you normally do to wake up. I'd like to have a conversation if you're interested."

"I'd like that. I'll be back in about twenty minutes."

She disappeared from the video. A few minutes later, Black rolled to his feet, shook his head to wake up, and went to find her. Paul smiled.

Ann returned in half an hour, towel-drying her hair and carrying a cold soda. "That's better. I'm awake."

"Would you be willing to have a hypothetical conversation about the future?"

She lowered the towel, hesitating. "Could we put it off for a few weeks?"

"No."

She cautiously sat down in her favorite chair and nodded. "Okay."

"The assumption is we're married."

She took a deep breath. "All right."

"Where would you be comfortable living?"

"Wherever you are."

"You could handle Chicago or New York?"

"I didn't say they would be my choice. I could be comfortable living there. There's a difference."

"Would you still want to be the MHI?"

"No."

He blinked. "No?"

"I'm not bringing murder into a marriage."

"When did you decide that?"

"When you asked the question."

"Change the job you have or give up being a cop entirely?"

"I wouldn't be a cop."

"Ann, a pause, please. What just changed? You love being a cop."

"If I'm married, something has to give. I can stop being a cop. I don't know how to stop being a writer. I wouldn't be able to shut off the story ideas. So I stop being a cop. Trying to have a marriage, be a cop, and write would kill me in a period of a few years. The wise thing to do is to not put myself into a situation I know I couldn't carry long term. You seem surprised at my answer. Why? You see the same thing I do. Did you think marriage wouldn't carry a cost for me?"

"I hadn't put it in that stark of terms."

"You were thinking maybe it works if she doesn't travel as much. If she works homicide for the Chicago PD again, works with Kate again, it could fit. That simply moves around the pieces on the board, but it doesn't change the problem. There is only so much of me to go around. I won't make the decision to get married only to make a bad choice that puts the marriage under stress from the beginning. You don't need my income. I'm not indispensable as the MHI. You ever talk me into marriage, I retire as a cop." She paused. "Want to stop your hypothetical conversation now?"

"No, not when I realize you're making that level of decision about this territory. I would offer that you're more than welcome to work for the FBI as a consultant and be curious about any murder on my desk."

"I'd thought of that."

"You would continue to write?"

"I would probably write more of my own fiction rather than do books about friends. Your family gets a fair amount of press interest, and it would become public knowledge I was writing books about friends. That would defeat the reason I have done the stories."

"What do you think about having a family?"

"I think before we got married there would need to be an agreement we would not have children. It's beyond what I could do. I think you've got a large family that is getting larger with every passing year, and there are enough children to care about, interact with, that the hole of not having our own could be partially filled. Being a mom is outside what I can stretch to do. You don't look surprised."

"I had read you correctly."

"I'm sorry for it, Paul, having to put you to the fact

that I come without a family of your own. I know it's huge. It's not easy to say I can't do it. But I can't."

"I'm sorry for it, but I do understand where you are at." A moment of silence passed. "An easier one. How do we deal with the fact you're a committed night owl and I'm a very morning person?"

"You get your own breakfast and be reasonably nice about not waking me up in the morning. You want a pleasant wife, you let me sleep in. What's that smile?"

"The way you said it. Do we keep a schedule of events and make plans to attend or host gatherings?"

"You give me four months a year where you don't put anything at all on the schedule. The other eight I struggle through."

"What else?"

"I get four hours a day and one week a month of solitude. You don't call me. I ignore the doorbell. I don't see another person."

He blinked. "That's steep."

She waited.

"You want to spend that solitude in our home or do you want a place you go to? Which of us leaves?"

"I'm flexible."

"Okay."

"No pushback?"

"You know what you need. I can accommodate it. If I have to, I'll buy another floor in the building and give you an apartment to go hide in."

It was her turn to look stunned. And then she paled. "You really want me to say yes. You're not going to change your mind about this."

"Breathe, Ann." It was settling in with her that he really was going to ask her to marry him one day soon.

"Okay. I'm okay."

"You're not, but it's adorable and another reason I love you, Ann."

She paled even more. She wasn't at the point she was ready to say the words back, but she might be getting there.

"I'll call you tonight. I think you should go talk to Lovely."

"Okay," she whispered. "I think so too."

He called her shortly after seven p.m. and watched as the video flickered and then stabilized, the audio bar turning green. "Hi, Ann."

"Hi." He heard a shyness in her voice he hadn't heard since their first conversations, and her smile was tentative. He wished he was there to give her a hug. Black pushed in beside her to see him. Ann wrapped her arm around the animal and laughed when he tried to lick the monitor.

"Hey, Black. No need to ask if he had a good time walking. Is that part of an evergreen tree plastered in his fur?"

"I'll be picking pine needles out of his coat for the next week. He went chasing a rabbit at full speed, and it could go under the tree and Black could not." She held up a handful of pine needles. "He yelps when I pull them out of his fur. It's going to be an ice cream night at the pace it's going."

She let the dog go, and Black retreated to his chew bone and attacked it with a vigorous shake of the head.

"You might have to cut his hair."

"I may resort to it. We'll see. I needed something to keep me occupied, so I'm not sure if the rabbit wasn't Lovely's idea of a distraction."

Paul smiled, suspecting she might be right. "I would like to have one more hypothetical conversation and get it finished."

She took a deep breath and nodded. "Thought you might."

"If we ever get married, what kind of wedding do you want?"

"You aren't going to like my answer. I'd elope or the equivalent."

"Really? You wouldn't want your friends, Kate and Lisa and Vicky, at your wedding?"

"If it was my choice, I wouldn't have a wedding, just a visit to the church and the minister without invitations announcing the event."

He blinked. "This is more than just not wanting to be the center of attention."

"I don't like ceremonies. I know it says something awful about me. Weddings. Funerals. Graduations. I don't like attending them, and I dislike even more being part of one. Birthdays are kind of okay. I know that is unrealistic, but a wedding is not something I will anticipate. All that goes into making the event happen is all stress and no upside. I won't enjoy the ceremony. So whatever the plan is, my best hope is simply to survive it."

"Why?"

"If I could answer that, I would. I don't know. I just

get sicker than a dog and will take any out I'm offered not to be there. Vicky asked me to rescue a friend of hers in a domestic dispute, and I about kissed her for giving me an excuse to not stay at her wedding. It's not rational, or explainable, it just is. On the bright side, at least you'll know I really want to marry you if I'm willing to go through with a wedding." She pushed her hand through her hair. "I know it's not realistic. It's your wedding too. You need a wedding your family attends, wedding pictures you have on your desk, and all the rest of it."

"Ann, it's our wedding. It can be anything we want it to be. I'm looking at the marriage. If I have to compromise completely on how I get there, it's part of the deal. Marie had a very private wedding. Immediate family only. Dad gave her away. They invited friends to a party a month after they returned from their honeymoon. My family will survive whatever we decide. Do you want the wedding dress and the cake?"

"I like cake."

"You want to be married—you just don't want to get married."

"I could sign the piece of paper. Everything else gets a little shaky."

"Would you wear my ring?"

"If you wear mine. And I don't want a stone—a nice gold band is good."

"What about an engagement ring?"

"Please, no."

"Would you take my name?"

"Yes."

"Where do you want to go for a honeymoon?"

"Anywhere there isn't a bunch of people. I want a long honeymoon, not rushed, and not somewhere I'm expected to go, like sand, or water, or snow. Home sounds nice."

He started to smile. "In your world, a marriage is supposed to reduce stress, not add to it."

"You're beginning to think like me."

"We're not twenty, Ann. If you want a very simple private wedding and a long honeymoon somewhere no one can find us, I can figure out how to make that happen. I'd like a good marriage. I'd like a wife to survive the experience. And I can accommodate a whole lot to get those things."

"You're doing all the giving. You'll regret it one day."

"Will I? Ann, I haven't moved at all. You're the one moving from the unthinkable toward being able to say yes."

She paled, then blushed.

He smiled. "You are so endearing when you blush."

"We should finish this another day when I remember what I should have asked."

"Okay. Go find a book and read for a while."

"Paul, I have to say this. You're making a mistake thinking about marrying me."

"How much of that is simply scared, and how much of that is something I should know that I don't?"

"You're optimistic this can work. I'm terrified it won't."

"One of us will be right. Is there anything else you need to tell me, Ann? Anything that bothers you that you wish had been dealt with?"

"You know me better than anyone alive. You're just optimistic I'm easier to live with than I really am."

"I'm optimistic that you love well. You say yes, I won't have to worry about your very best effort to work on making it a good, strong marriage. Ann, we've got Lovely on our side. What else do we need?"

"Ask me that again later, please. I'm going to go read a book now."

"A very good idea. Have a good night, Ann. I'll call you tomorrow."

"Good night, Paul."

"Ann?"

She paused before she dropped the link. "Yeah, Falcon?"

"I love you."

Her smile that started before she clicked the link off was beautiful to see. Paul saved the video and printed that last image.

Paul chose a favorite shirt and a sport coat he was comfortable with. He'd go as the FBI agent he was, with no pretense one way or another. He would be at her home by midday. He had given her five days to consider what they had discussed. It was time. There was no benefit to waiting even a few more days.

He picked up the present he had bought for Black, and a book about stars he had spent some time finding for Ann. However this day turned out, it would mark the best few months of his life. He had met Ann Silver. And his life was richer than it had ever been before.

He just hoped he handled this day as well as he possibly could. She knew he was coming. He hadn't said, she hadn't asked, but she knew. He'd arrive, and he would ask her, and both their lives would be forever changed.

———————▼———————

He chose to ask her on the back patio where he had first kissed her, where the sun warmed the day and the breeze rippled her hair, where flowers burst with color and birds sang, and Black roamed, hunting for small animals he could chase. This was her home, and this was where he had come to know her.

She was beautiful, and so very scared. He wrapped his arms around her in a comfortable hug. "I love you, Ann Silver."

"I wish you wouldn't ask."

"I know. You would rather have things stay the same. It's safer. Do you need more time? Are there things about me you don't know, that you wish you knew?"

"I know you. I just don't want you to ask me to make the decision. Because I haven't made it. And I don't know what that answer is going to be if you require me to make it today. I don't know why."

"I think I do. You trust God to always love you. You don't trust me to always love you." He rested his head against hers. "You want to trust me. You want to be confident that I'll always love you. But you are afraid there will be a day it will change. You are afraid there will be a day I won't love you anymore. And you are afraid of the risk. You wouldn't survive the pain if that day came. You're afraid that the love won't last."

She didn't say anything.

"How did I do?"

"Probably got me right."

"I can't take away that fear you feel. I can tell you two things you can count on. I value God's opinion of me and my relationship with Him. It matters to Him that I love you and that I keep loving you as the years go by. He's even said how He handles my prayers will be directly tied to how I treat you. I'm not taking this lightly. I will love you the best I know how for as long as I live. I'm never going to divorce you. I will put what you need ahead of what my family needs. I will put what you need ahead of what my job needs. I won't let you have second place."

"I just don't understand—why me?" she whispered. "You don't get a family of your own. You don't get someone comfortable with the social demands of the Falcon family. You don't even get much help with your family."

"I get someone who loves God. I get a wonderfully deep, imaginative thinker and reader and writer. I get someone who keeps a quiet life, who values friends, who can fly a plane and talk business with ease. Who can work a murder. How many husbands get that?" He smiled.

He continued, "I get someone who takes relationships seriously but doesn't take life too seriously. When you say I love you, I don't worry about it ever ending. You give your heart when you say I love you. I get a good wife, something very rare and hard to find. I get you, Ann."

"What happens if I say no?"

"I survive. So do you." He rubbed her arms. "If that's the decision you make, we will both survive it. We've given this the best we have, and if the decision is no, I'll accept it. You aren't going to lose a friend. You're too important to me. If I can't have you as my wife, I'm keeping you as my best friend."

"Ask. Then give me a day. No, two days."

He settled his arms more comfortably around her. "Ann, I know your secrets and who you are and the things that matter to you. I have the blessing of your friends who know you best. I don't make this decision lightly or without thought and prayer. I love you. I know you, and I love you. Ann Silver, would you do me the honor of becoming my wife?" He lifted her chin to see her face and wiped her eyes, and very softly kissed her. "You have two days to decide."

27

She went flying. She left at dawn, soaring into the cool morning air as the sunrise began to lighten the sky. The clouds, puffy and drifting, floated across in front of her as she headed north. "It's a beautiful morning, Lovely."

She didn't need to ask for His advice. She already had it. She knew Paul, had met him, knew his heart, and how he handled stress and joy. Lovely had helped her see who he was and what was before her to decide.

And Lovely was leaving the decision to be hers.

Her emotions quivered at the choice, the fear that something would go wrong. She was the weak link in this decision. She didn't know if she could be the wife he needed. Her heart would break if she failed at this, her life would never recover, and she'd be taking a good man down with her, one who had a large extended family depending on him. She'd ruin the best thing that had ever entered her life if she got this wrong.

He loved her. He wanted to marry her. He was offering

her a priceless gift. She wanted that lifetime connection to someone who knew her secrets and loved her. And she was scared to reach for it.

She went back in her mind to the first time she had met him and let herself remember the conversations, the risks she had taken with him, and the man she had found him to be. *Paul is a good man. The kind of man who will make my future so much better than my present.*

He'd love her, and keep loving her, even when life got hard. She could trust him to be what she needed. But she wasn't sure she could be what he needed.

She went to see Kate. She arrived at the Chicago Police Department headquarters shortly after noon. Kate's office was empty. Ann found her assistant. "Is Kate in the building or out in the field?"

"She's in the building somewhere. Want me to find her for you?"

"I don't mind the wait. She'll be back eventually."

Ann stretched out on Kate's couch and out of habit closed her eyes for a catnap. Within minutes she could feel herself drifting to sleep.

"Hey, sleepy girl."

Ann opened her eyes just enough to see Kate. "I can nap awhile longer if you've got something to do."

"I'm taking the excuse to not do something for the next half hour." Kate held out the second mug. "Hot chocolate. Thank Tabitha. She had it waiting for me as I passed her desk."

Ann sat up and accepted the mug. Chocolate helped. "Paul asked me to marry him."

Kate grinned. "And you got on a plane to come nap on my couch."

DEE HENDERSON   485

"It seemed like the thing to do."

"What did you say?"

"That I would tell him tomorrow."

"Want a girls' night out? We can pick up Rachel and be with Lisa and Vicky by evening."

She thought about it and then accepted reality. "Not if I'm the pilot. I haven't had enough sleep to want to be responsible for passengers."

"Dave can fly us out. He owes me."

"Then a girls' night out sounds nice. I need courage. I'll borrow it."

Kate softly laughed. "Since Lisa had to talk me into saying yes to Dave's proposal, I'm in your corner on this one."

———————◆———————

Paul's kitchen was crowded with his three brothers occupying the territory. He still felt like pacing, but there wasn't room. The nice thing about family was a wait didn't happen alone. Harper took the offered soda. "You asked her to marry you."

"Yes."

"What did she say?"

"She hasn't answered me yet."

Boone leaned against the counter, nursing his own soda. "You didn't mess up the asking? Didn't forget the ring, or forget the love-you part?"

"She didn't want an engagement ring, and I got the love-you part just right."

Joseph raised an eyebrow. "Something else going on?"

"She's so scared to death the marriage will fail she's not willing to make the decision."

"What are you going to do if she says no?"

Paul had been weighing that every hour of this wait. "Give her time, ask her again."

Joseph laughed. "She doesn't have a chance—she just doesn't know it yet."

Harper tipped his soda toward Joseph. "I'll start the pool for how many times he has to ask before he gets a yes. Five bucks a number? Winner buys the wedding gift?"

"I'm in."

Paul smiled.

Boone slung his arm around Paul's shoulder and pushed him toward the elevator. "Come on, big brother. We're going to go play ball and take your mind off it."

"She might call."

"She's with Vicky. For your sake, she's in the best place she could be. If four married friends can't get her off the indecision, you've got a definite challenge on your hands. Dave flew them out and stayed. He'll call if Ann wants to find you."

———————◆———————

Vicky hosted the ladies' night, and the five of them ended up in her living room with carryout Chinese.

Ann finished an egg roll. "Why is marriage worth it?" she asked, then immediately felt herself blush.

Lisa laughed, shook her head, then turned serious. "Belonging. I'm Quinn's and he's mine. I like spending my days and nights with him, and he likes spending his with me."

"With Cole it's the hug after a very long day. He makes life better," Rachel offered.

"Boone excels at easing that knot that shows up at the base of my neck," Vicky agreed.

"Laughter. Love. Holly," Kate replied.

Ann shared an amused smile with Kate. She set aside her plate and settled deeper into the couch. She pulled over a pillow.

"We know Paul. He's a good man, Ann," Vicky offered.

"I know that. I don't know why I can't decide. I don't know why I'm waiting. I know him. I know myself. We've talked about every subject I can think of that will matter to a good marriage. And still I can't settle on what is the right decision."

"Do you trust him with your secrets?"

"Yes."

"There's friendship. Is there chemistry?"

"Good chemistry. My heart does this flutter flop and a smile takes over anytime he's around."

"Do you love him?"

"Yes. I wasn't sure, but I am now. I love him." They waited for her to find the words. "We match at the core. Same intensity of beliefs. Same values. Same work ethic. Same respect for marriage being forever. And he asked me, and I froze. I just froze."

"Can you see yourself as married?"

"No."

"Maybe you're asking yourself the wrong question. Marriage is not better than single. It's just different. The right question is, do you want to spend your life with Paul?"

"The idea of saying I do makes me freeze. Maybe he asked the question before I was ready for it. But I'm afraid I'm hesitating because I know the answer should be no, and I don't want to disappoint him."

"Ann, you're deliberate. So is Paul. He's been thinking about getting married for a long time, and you just started to seriously consider it. You might simply need more time. There's no reason not to take more time. If you and Paul are a good fit, it's not going to change if you get married this year or next year. You've got fifty years ahead of you. Take more time."

"And if he decides he doesn't want to wait?"

"If he's too impatient to wait for you, he's an idiot. Take the time if you want more time."

"I don't know what more time will change."

"You're waiting for someone to promise you it will work out. No one can."

"I've got cold feet."

"I'd say you've got ice blocks."

Vicky passed over the plate of brownies.

"It's sad that I'm this indecisive."

"Ann, you might never be comfortable saying I do. You might just have to take a deep breath and do what you want, regardless of how you feel about the decision."

"Close my eyes and jump."

"Paul is willing to catch you. He's a good man. You can trust our opinion on that as well as your own."

Paul heard the elevator chime, glanced at the security board, and saw Boone had keyed in to come up. He poured an extra cup of coffee and walked through to meet him. He was heading to Ann's within the hour and having Boone to make the drive with him was going to help.

The elevator opened.

Ann was standing there. She held up Boone's key. "Hi."

"Hi."

He set the coffee on the side table and wiped his hands on his slacks. "Sorry, you surprised me. Come in, Ann."

She caught his sleeve as she walked past him and tugged him to come along. She headed toward his den. She pointed him toward his favorite chair and perched herself on the arm of the couch. "You know why I have friends?"

He smiled. She looked punchy tired. "To keep you up all hours of the night?"

"With four friends to tell me stories about being married? It was like an adult slumber party without the slumber. They like to hold up a mirror and tell you what you already know."

"And what do you know?"

"I'm scared. And somewhere along the way I fell deeply in love with you. They pretty much concurred I should take a deep breath and do what I want."

"And?"

She looked at the clock. "I've still got eight hours. You owe me a movie. And I need a nap. And I've got a couple more questions for you. So I'm taking a nap on your couch, then you can take me to a late lunch at Falcons and find us a movie. Somewhere along the way I'll make a decision."

He smiled. "I can handle all of that. I'll leave you to get a nap and give Jackie a call so she can set aside a quiet table for us."

"I want to try whatever is her latest favorite creation. And have some more of that apple cobbler."

"Have a preference on the movie?"

"Funny would be nice."

———————▼———————

She was tired enough she was asleep minutes after her eyes closed. Paul glanced into the den a couple of times until he was certain she was deeply asleep, then quietly retook his seat. He wanted a lifetime of being able to share his home with her.

He touched her hand when the nightmare started, and she jerked awake. "Just a dream," he said quietly. She ran her hands across her face. The pallor began to fade, even though her eyes still looked bruised. She needed more sleep, but it wouldn't easily come. She blew her breath out, then visibly relaxed. "Something else we're going to have to deal with."

"Nothing you can do about them. Not much I can do either. You won't have to wake up alone."

She slid her hand into his. "Worth more than you realize." She swung around to sit up. "Give me a minute, then let's go to lunch."

He dropped a kiss on her hair. "I'll go get the movie ads so you can see the funny choices."

———————▼———————

They walked from Falcons to the theater. Paul talked her into ice cream on the way, and she stayed with a vanilla cone, content with her old favorites.

"If I give you power of attorney, would you sell my grandparents' place for me so I don't have to deal with it?"

"You don't want to keep it? It would be a nice place to get away to."

"If I keep it, I'm going to be feeling like this is your place and that is mine. Unless you want to move to a neutral new place, then all my stuff lands in yours and we have to deal with it."

"I can handle that for you. What else?"

"Midnight."

He reached over and took her hand.

"He doesn't deserve a city."

"You aren't giving up Black. He's too important to everything you are."

"I'm going to send him on vacation every once in a while. Quinn offered he could come visit for a few weeks. Black loves that ranch. He comes back muddy and tired and happy. Dave's got a nice place with grass, and he wants a dog to guard the cat and the kid. He offered Black could visit. We give the dog a place to be himself a few weeks every other month. He can sleep when he's with us and recuperate."

Paul smiled. "Okay."

"You have to give him a morning walk before you go to work. And he complains about being woken up early, so you have to bribe him with food to get him to move."

"Are you going to fuss if I share my breakfast with him?"

"Given how much he mooches off me, I'll let you get away with it too. I walk him late, and you have to let me go out in the middle of the night and not feel like you have to stay up to walk him with me."

"You'll carry your side arm."

"Always do. Fact of the security clearance. I'm required to carry even after I'm retired."

He waited to see if she had another concern.

"Did we reach the last question?"

"Maybe. Ask me after the movie."

She enjoyed the movie and the story line. He knew her expressions well enough to recognize it. He took it as a good sign when she slid her hand in his as they left the crowd of the theater behind. "Jackie said she'd keep a table free for us after the movie," he offered.

"How about your place. You can fix me some hot chocolate."

He took her home and fixed them both her favorite hot chocolate. He forced himself to relax as she took a seat at the counter and he joined her. She tugged over the glass jar full of ginger snaps. "We're going to have bad days, when the words get hot or icy and the emotions get raw."

"It's inevitable."

"I need to know how we're going to handle them."

"I don't know. You get quiet when you get hurt. I tend to get cool and cautious. It's going to be a problem."

"We need a standing time on the calendar when we clear the air. I don't want Saturday morning, it's when we can both sleep in, and I don't want it on a Sunday. If it's evening, you're tired. And if it's morning, I'm tired."

"Fridays at five. You come join me at the office, we can go get dinner, even if it's just a vendor hot dog, and we walk as long as it takes until the concerns are on the table, even if we need more conversations to figure out the answer."

"Okay."

"You'll bury the hurt, that's what I worry about. Jackie throws things, you bury them. You'll have to risk talking with me about what's causing the wounds. If you can't find the words, if it's really bad, you write it down for me. It's probably a good idea that you give me a letter every month, good or bad—just put down as much as you can of what's right and what's wrong and what we need to talk about. It's the small things that keep getting larger that will need addressing."

"Will you tell me what I'm getting wrong with this marriage? I don't want you to settle for who I am rather than ask me to change to be what you need."

"I won't ambush you with what I want to say, but I'll be honest. There are things both of us will simply have to live with."

She pulled two ginger snaps from the jar and handed him one. "When could we get married?"

"Next Friday."

"Do I have to do anything?"

"I've got arranging the license, Harper is handling the place, Dad's got the minister, Marie is bringing you some dresses to consider, and Jackie insisted she's doing the cake. I told Mom you'd walk around a flower shop and help her choose the flowers, but your job is really to keep her from buying everything she sees. We'll go shopping for rings together. I'm borrowing a place from a friend where we can take Black and enjoy a very long honeymoon. I already told my boss I'm taking six weeks of vacation. I figured if you said no, no one would want to work with me, so I'd need the time either way. What do you think?"

She slid off the stool and wrapped her arms around him. "Could you deal with a rather weepy yes?"

He planted his feet and picked her up. "Yes?"

She settled her hands on either side of his face. "Yes. I would be honored to marry you, Paul Tudor Falcon." She leaned in to him for a long kiss. He felt a wall of tension that had knotted his stomach fall away, his heart leap in his chest.

His smile matched hers. "You've been talking to my mom."

"She wanted to add her reasons why I should marry you. She said you were a good man. She said you would protect me, and provide for me, and defend me, and love me, and if I didn't marry you I'd miss out on fifty years of being treasured." She held his gaze with hers. "I love you. You don't have to worry. I'm slow at decisions, but I won't change my mind once it's made, and I won't look back. Let's get married next Friday."

The wedding would happen at Paul's parents' home, and no matter how much Ann wanted to get nervous, there was too much laughter to give her time. She stayed at Kate's the night before with Rachel, Vicky, and Lisa joining her there for breakfast. Paul had clearly decided piling on her friends was the right way to get her through the ceremony. Marie brought half a dozen dresses on loan from a designer for her to try, and they spent the morning with lace and trains and beautiful wedding dresses. Ann chose a simple design that she felt she could turn in without tripping. By noon she was walking into Paul's parents' home, where flowers burst from vases lining the tables, and his mom was waiting for her.

"Oh, you look gorgeous," Karen said and hugged her. "I'm to take you to the sitting room and ask if you would like a drink or some crackers."

Ann laughed, but nodded. "I need them both." The nerves had been building since she had stepped into the car.

She entered the sitting room and carefully sat down, accepted what Karen brought her. And then the door opened behind her, and Paul came in, wonderful in a tux.

"Ladies." He grinned as he spotted Ann. "Very, very nice. Would you mind giving us the room for a moment, please?" He waited for the ladies to exit and closed the door.

He took a seat beside her and grasped her hand. "You have a few minutes. Lean your head back, close your eyes, and catch your breath. I'm walking you the few steps that constitute the aisle so you don't bolt on me."

She gratefully did just that. "I can't believe how panicked I feel."

"I can tell. You're turning very pale. It's a ten-minute ceremony, long enough for you to look devastatingly beautiful, and for Mom to start crying for the joy of it. All you have to do is say I do. Both rings are in my pocket, and I'll make double sure you can't drop mine."

"Are you nervous?"

"I won't be in about twenty minutes."

She laughed. "I hope you never regret this, Paul."

"I love you. With time you'll realize just how deeply I mean that. We're going to have a brief ceremony, cut the cake, and then Vicky is going to help you change, and twenty minutes later we are going to be in the car on the way to the airport. We're taking part of the wedding cake with us. Harper is handling Black and the luggage, and Dave is providing the flight. Once you say I do, it all gets easier from there."

"Don't let go of my hand."

"I won't let go." He squeezed her hand. "You ready?"

"I love you."

He smiled. "Come marry me."

28

The borrowed vacation home in Montana was defined by an open vista of land where sunsets and sunrises dominated the horizon without being marred by buildings. Paul was growing comfortable with the silence. They had been here three weeks. Ann returned, carrying a soda they could share, and the swing shifted with her weight. He settled his arms around her, content to hold her. She smelled of horse and hay and dust, for they had spent the morning riding together. The wind was still steady from the west. He collected her hair in one hand and gathered it behind her, and used the opportunity to rub the tension out of her neck. "Any regrets?"

"That extra half hour of the ride is going to catch up with me. My tailbone hurts."

"Didn't mean the morning."

She smiled. "I know." She drank the first part of the soda and companionably offered him the rest. She rested her head against his shoulder. "I used to wonder, what in the world will we do living in each other's space all the time. But now I miss you when you're not there. I don't have any regrets. A few minutes of the morning where it still feels very odd not being alone. But I'm getting more comfortable."

She wore the ring he had given her. He turned it with his finger and was reassured just to have it on her hand. "You know how Black follows you around? You get up and leave the room, and a few moments later he'll lumber to his feet and go see where you've gone? He wants to be where you are."

She lifted her head to look at him.

"You do that with me. Look around to figure out where I just went. It's nice." He ran a thumb across her blush. "If you ever stop doing that, I'm going to miss it more than I can put into words."

"I didn't mean to cling so tight."

"You're not. I like to look around and find you there. I might have to tug you out of a book or a story to get your attention, but you're there. I was tired of being alone. I've had a lifetime of being alone."

"I need that connection. To reassure myself I'm part of a couple. I still feel single sometimes."

"Stay as close as you need and want. I mean it when I say I like it." He set the swing to moving again. "I have a question for you."

"Okay."

"I was thinking we should go to New York next week. We can see family and friends and then leave everyone behind and not mention where we are heading from there. I'd like to show you Washington, D.C. You've never been, I like the Smithsonian, and there's a Mexican restaurant Jackie opened years ago that a friend still runs."

"Whatever you would like is fine with me."

"You're sure?"

She nodded. "I'm content. Three weeks away does that. You can dump me in the middle of a family party, and I could swim for a while. I'd like to meet everyone."

He dropped a kiss on her hair. "We'll do that then. There was a message from the director that he'd like to see me when I'm back from vacation. I thought I'd take care of that meeting while we're there."

"He's going to promote your boss, and he'll want you to take the Chicago office."

"I know." He hadn't settled on what he would say if it was offered. "I'm hoping you have an opinion."

"Lots of people would like you to say yes. If you're the boss, they get continuity and someone who will let them do their job without extra hassle. You'd hate the paperwork and being in the office so much. Do you want to be the FBI director one day? If you do, say yes. If you don't, then suggest another name you know can do the job well. You'll enjoy the challenge whatever you decide."

"You can pray about that decision with me."

"I can do that."

He finished the soda as the porch swing rocked, and he wondered if he had ever spent a more enjoyable few weeks in his life. She felt right, and being married felt right. The stillness stretched to ten minutes between them, and he didn't try to break the silence. He felt content, for the first time in years, that life was finally beginning to fit as is should, and as it would for the future. He was married to someone he loved, who was just right for him. And it was more than he had ever hoped.

She interlaced her fingers with his. "Could I ask you something?"

He angled his head to see her face. "Sure."

"We need a Friday five p.m. conversation, but I would rather have it while my courage is intact. Could we do that now?"

He could feel himself shift to alert mode and tensed at what she needed to say. He willed himself to relax, to take a deep breath. She wasn't going to give him many opportunities to create a first impression in this marriage, and this was a major had-to-get-it-right moment. He reached across her with a casualness he didn't feel to enclose her in his arms. "Advance the clock to Friday at five and pretend we're on a long walk. What would you like me to hear?"

"You have to stop trying to save me from the nightmares."

He jolted at the topic and his arms tightened just a fraction around her.

"I'm keeping you awake at night. Just the fear that I might have a nightmare has you watching me, hoping to intervene. You have to stop doing that. You need to let yourself deeply sleep."

"I'm there. I can wake you up and save you from that last bit of pure terror."

"If I kick you and wake you up, by all means stop my nightmare. I'm glad when you do. But you're staying half awake trying to anticipate my nightmare. You're tired, and getting more tired every day." She rested her hand on his.

"When I have a nightmare and it wakes me up, I'll get up and go read for a while and shake it off, just like I've done for the last many years. You can't fix them. You need to let me cope. We're going to be home soon, and you'll be going back to work for a long day, so being up with me isn't a viable option."

He shifted to see her face. "My presence is making the nightmares worse."

She bit her lip.

"Don't bother trying to say it's not. I'm not blind, Ann." She'd been alone so long, slept alone for so many years that her subconscious was sensing his presence as a danger. And given the memories crowding her past, her mind was throwing her back into a fight for her life. She'd jerk awake gasping for breath, fighting to not be sick, her eyes glassy and for an instant full of terror.

"I'm not giving up sharing a bed with you just because part of my mind is still skittish about a guy being near."

"Well, asking me not to try to help is not a workable answer either."

She sighed and tried to find words and then went silent.

"What?"

"The fact you're watching me is part of the problem. I know you're watching me."

He closed his eyes as he felt pain slice inside. His arms tightened, she flinched, and he forced himself to relax. "Sit still and let me kick myself for a minute," he whispered, shifting his hold on her. He was watching because her nightmares could be vicious around four a.m., and because he was watching, she was sensing it and tumbling into a fear-driven panic of a nightmare. He couldn't win for trying to help her. He sighed and rubbed his cheek against her hair. "Well, isn't this a nice pickle."

Her hand curled into his shirt. "I'll get used to you being there, I know I will. But telling my mind that and having it be true are two very different things."

He kissed her hair. "Not your fault. You want to blame someone for this, direct the emotion where it belongs, to the guy now where he belongs." He shifted her away to face him on the swing. "There is no way I am going to let you sleep alone, so mark off that option. Give me others."

"You have to let them happen, let me wake up and talk my mind into not being afraid. And the next night when it happens again, I have to do the same thing, and the night after that, for as long as it takes. When my mind finally grasps I've been here before and it's the same as before, it will calm down. I know the nightmares will calm down. They used to be triggered by a case I was working, by a sight or a smell that would bring back the memories of what happened in that cabin. They weren't rare, but they weren't as frequent as this."

"Now it's not the MHI job triggering them; it's someone being there when you are asleep. It's my presence you are sensing that is new and dangerous to you."

She reluctantly nodded.

He realized the next problem. "Our home is going to do the same thing. A new place, new sounds, your mind won't know it is a safe place. You'll have to deal with learning how to sleep there without having a nightmare too."

"Yes."

How had he missed this? He had been trying so hard to know her, understand her, and he had absolutely missed this. He had thought having someone with her would ease the nightmares, not make them worse. "Did you suspect this would happen?"

"I hoped that leaving the MHI would be enough to compensate for the new things I would have to adapt to. I hoped my brain wouldn't register everything different as a threat. That was rather a stupid wish."

"Don't say that." He was a contributing factor to the nightmares. He couldn't figure out a way through the problem. "If it's time that helps, it hasn't helped yet."

"I need you to trust me, Paul. You have to tell yourself to go to sleep and not to worry about me. I promise you, if I need your help, I will wake you up. I promise I will crowd in beside you and hug you hard when I'm back, reassure you I'm okay. And if I'm gone from our bed for a long period of time, you are welcome to come find me. But you can't stay awake trying to protect me. I can't handle you tired, not when I know I'm the cause of it. You have to sleep. I don't want to see you tired and crabby."

He tried to smile at her choice of crabby. He handled tired with lots of coffee and conserving energy any way he could. He didn't have the energy to even get annoyed when he got truly tired. "This is rather awful, Ann."

She solemnly nodded.

He settled his arms around her and nodded toward the door of the house. "We're going to go take a nap on the couch. Because we both need it, and I want to figure out if we sleep well together anywhere."

She half smiled. "Okay."

"Just okay? No wise insights?"

"I like sleeping with you."

He picked her up because he was in the mood to carry her. "Do scents trigger nice dreams? The smell of vanilla in the room, or the smell of flowers? There's got to be something that could give you a better chance of dreaming something other than that nightmare."

"I hadn't thought of that. Maybe."

"Hold the door."

She held it open and he maneuvered them inside, waiting for Black.

He settled her on the couch and leaned down to kiss her. "We'll find it. And for the record, that was a very useful Friday-at-five conversation."

He tugged off her boots, then his, and shifted on the couch so he could stretch out with her. "Give me a guess, how long before you sleep through the night with me without a nightmare."

"Eight weeks."

"Yeah?"

"What were you thinking?"

"I was hoping we'd be there by Christmas."

"If I've had a nightmare every night between now and Christmas, you are going to have a problem on your hands. I don't handle being tired. I can fake it okay for a few weeks, but I get snippy and sharp and teary and unreasonable, and you're going to get every bit of it."

"Snippy?"

"You haven't been miserable until you've been around me when I'm snippy. If I ever get to that point, lock me somewhere alone for a month and let me sleep it off. It's your only hope."

"Let's hope we never get there." He nudged her head onto his shoulder. "For right now, just catch a nap with me. We'll see if you can do two hours without a dream."

Ann was curious about history, and she was a tourist's tourist, wanting to listen to the tour guide, read all the exhibit signs, stand and gawk at things both magnificent and ordinary. She was enjoying Washington, D.C., and Paul was enjoying immensely showing it to her. But he had made a mistake suggesting they come here before heading home. They had left Black with Dave and Kate, gone to New York, and then come here for a week. They should have returned home.

Ann was asleep on the hotel bed, facedown, one arm wrapped around a pillow, as the clock moved toward eight p.m. They had come to change before an evening meal, and he had encouraged her to stretch out for half an hour. That had been two hours ago.

He watched her sleep, knowing it was exhaustion that had put her down so quickly. He prayed she stayed asleep. All of it was piling up on her. The change in her routine, the marriage, the nightmares. He didn't know how to get her through it. The reality of being married was pulling energy out of her that she hadn't been able to replenish.

She took a couple of walks on her own, she read for a while, and often up during the night she would spend another hour or two reading or writing. She'd asked for four hours a day of solitude, and she was carving it out. It was probably helping more than he realized, but it just wasn't enough. The idea of her being gone for a week was something he didn't want to think about, but he'd have to honor that request when they were home.

He hadn't really understood before. He'd thought her wish was because she was comfortable being single and used to being alone, and she wanted assurance of some space to be alone even while married. He was seeing now why she had put it out there so bluntly. She needed the solitude to survive. She had to sleep without interruption, and the only way she knew to find it was to be alone where nothing could trigger that dream.

He reached for her hand as the nightmare ripped through her. "Easy." She jerked awake. And she started to cry.

Paul keyed the elevator to the fourth floor. Ann had grown quieter the closer they got to the building, and he could almost feel her nerves. The weeks so far had been a honeymoon and a vacation, and now it was the forever of a new home and a new life as his wife. He wrapped an arm around her shoulders and quietly hugged her as the elevator doors opened. "Welcome home."

She smiled, but it faded. Black, not used to the elevator, darted around him, glad to be free, and disappeared toward one room and then the next. He found one of his toys and the bear growled. Ann smiled when she heard it. Paul carried their luggage inside, turning on lights as he went.

Lisa and Kate had been busy. He could see small signs of Ann's things about the place—the photos on the wall, the dog-treat jar on the counter, her jacket hung next to his, the books on the table beside the couch, and the stack of yellow writing pads and pens within easy reach. They had messaged that they had unpacked her clothes and done their best to recreate her work space.

"I asked them to set up your office in with mine. Your

table fits, with some rearranging of the furniture. I'd really like you to share the space with me. I can learn when not to interrupt your train of thought."

She simply nodded. He carried their luggage through to his bedroom, their bedroom. He should have asked Lisa to do some shopping for him, to get more neutral colors in here so it wasn't so much his. He turned to find Ann standing in the doorway watching him, and of all the emotions and expressions he had seen on her face in the last weeks, this was new and the most troubling. "What's wrong?"

She rubbed her arms. "I should feel married. And I don't. That same queasy uncertainty just sits there, like I'm going to wake up and this is an unreal dream. Why don't I feel married? What's wrong with me?"

He smiled. "Not a thing."

"Do you feel married?"

He crossed over to join her and slid his arms around her waist. "Very married." He rested his head against hers. "Don't worry so much. You will eventually feel married. I promise you that. I'll keep reminding you until you do. You can unpack more of your things tomorrow, and put in better places what Lisa and Kate unpacked for you. It will feel more like your place when you see your things around here."

"What are we going to do tonight? Tomorrow night? The night after that?"

He smiled, but chose to take the question as she had intended. "For tonight, you are going to find a book to read, or pick up a pad of paper and write for a while, and I am going to fix us something to eat and then watch whatever ball game I can find on TV. If you want to share the couch with me, I could probably be talked into sharing. In about four hours we will figure out which side of the bed you're going to prefer to sleep on and sort out who gets to shut off the alarm clock in the morning. For the rest of it, we've got a week before I return to work to figure that out. I know it feels like the world just shifted on you, but it will find its footing again very soon. This won't feel so strange a month from now."

"I'm really scared I'm going to get this wrong."

He stroked her shoulders, her arms. "There's no test, nothing to pass or fail. Relax. The days will be different, but you'll find a new rhythm soon." Black crashed into her and about threw them both off-balance. "He'll help."

She steadied the dog as she laughed. And she relaxed. "Paul, I love you." She reached up and kissed him. "Take Black for a walk for me. You know the neighborhood. He's going to want to smell everything. Let me unpack without him underfoot."

He smiled. "I can do that. But one thing first. I've got a wedding present for you." He nodded to the hall. "Beyond that door."

"What?"

He gave her a hug. "I know you're tired, Ann, the kind of worn-out-inside kind of tired that makes that smile an effort, and your energy feel like it's never returning. You need a place of your own to use as a retreat, to find some solitude if you're ever going to rebuild, somewhere to let you get away for a week every month where you can find some real rest. So I've arranged some options."

He opened the door.

The construction had come out better than he hoped.

"There's a bedroom and sitting room on this level, and up that flight of stairs you'll find a studio." It would take a few days for the new carpet and new paint smell to dissipate, but otherwise it looked ready to move in.

"The lady upstairs has been a friend of the family for years. Her husband painted for a living, and had a separate studio created to keep the oil paint and fumes out of their home. It's been dormant since his death a decade ago. She hasn't wanted to sell the space and have someone new coming in and out of the building, but she liked the idea of adding it to our place. Come up and see it. It looks just like it did the day before he passed away, a half-finished painting on the easel and his paint supplies still on the worktable." He took her hand and led the way upstairs.

He was watching her when she got the first look and caught her instant smile of delight.

"What a wonderful life he must have spent here in this room. You can see it in what he had around him. It's a good space."

"I know you've been painting, and you could continue without an interruption this way."

She wandered around the room and looked out the windows, and then turned to smile at him. "It's really nice, Paul."

"I surprised you."

"Knock-me-over-with-a-feather surprised me."

"I think it could work, Ann."

"I think so too."

He joined her near the windows. "I also have a second option arranged." He pointed to the building across the street. "There's an apartment in that building, fifth floor, the fourth window from the corner. It's a two-bedroom place, with a nice-sized living room and a small kitchen. I'd rather not have overnight guests in our home if there are other options, so I like the idea of having the place. It can be for family and friends to stay when they visit, or for you to use if you prefer. We'll keep it at least for a year as a fallback plan."

She rested her head against his chest. "You're flooring me here, Paul. And I didn't get you anything."

He laughed. "You're sharing the dog. That will do for now."

She slid her hands into his and interlaced their fingers. "I have something I need to tell you. I think it counts as another secret, as it is kind of big. About why I've been painting."

"I'd like to hear it. Do you want to tell me tonight or have the conversation another night?"

"I'll let you decide. I was working on a book for friends that I stopped when I married you. It was a price I paid when I married you, my choice, and one my friends supported and understood. But it was a big price. That book was why I've been painting. It's not right that you not know that or why."

He had thought there might be a book in the works from what Dave had mentioned, but he hadn't realized there was another secret out there related to her writing. "Let's go downstairs, and you can tell me." He led her to the kitchen and got them both sodas.

He nodded to the stool and leaned against the counter facing her as she sat and opened her soda. He wondered how many conversations in a lifetime it would take to really grasp the layers in this lady he had married. She was hesitating, even now, to risk this with him. "Trust me, Ann. Just start somewhere."

"This falls into the gray area of almost being a se-curity-clearance-level secret rather than just a personal secret, and I wasn't comfortable talking about it before I was married. It is a big-deal kind of secret. No one knows, not Kate, not Vicky, no one knows about this couple except for Marcus, and he knows them through his role as head of the U.S. Marshals."

She had friends in witness protection. That fact had his full attention. "When did you meet them?"

"I was hoping you wouldn't ask that." She toyed with the soda, watching the moisture bead on the countertop and then rubbing it away with her palm. "I promise I'm not going to do this again, so don't flinch when you hear. Marcus needed a favor, a fast one, and I was the clos-est pilot he could put his hands on who was willing to land on a private airstrip during a serious thunderstorm. There were rumors deemed credible that a sniper after the couple was in the area, and it had to be done. Given his history with Shari, Marcus is not one to dismiss a threat like that. I've been in more danger at times, but never taken a more intentional risk."

"What happened to the flight?"

"What always happens when you put metal into a thunderstorm. I got hit by lightning and about scorched the plane. I limped us out of the area, feeling like I was flying a rock through a mud puddle. It was an unforget-table night. I wouldn't even fly near a dark cloud for the next few months. The marshals shot a sniper that night, so the threat was real."

"It tells me something profound about you, that you

said yes when Marcus called. Promise me, over the next year, you will tell me what stories you can that fall in this gray area."

"I'll try. And it says more about who I was than it says about my good judgment. I was single, I was a cop, and I knew the risk, but I didn't fully appreciate it. I was a brave idiot."

He smiled. "Tell me about your friends. Tell me about the book you set aside."

"She's an artist. On her way to worldwide fame. Ambitious, genius, driven, brilliant. She was twenty-six when she witnessed a murder."

Ann paused and for a time disappeared in her own thoughts. "It's a sad story, Paul. The kind as a cop you hurt just hearing. She saw the murder, she told the police what she witnessed, and she drew a portrait of the man from memory. She told the DA she would testify. They arrested him. He's Irish mob, politically connected—a mean streak in him that goes with a violent temper. Within days there was a contract out on her life. They put her in witness protection.

"The man set out to destroy her art. He wanted to pull her out of the shadows so she could be killed, and he put his thumb down on the one thing she treasured. Every piece of her life's work on public display or known to be with specific collectors was suddenly at risk. Paintings were slashed, acid was thrown, some were stolen and burned. She lost a lifetime of work. The pieces she could retrieve from collectors were stored away to safety in art vaults—three vaults around the country—and he found one of the vaults. She lost another thirty pieces in one day.

"It was six months before he came to trial. She testified against him. The jury deliberated four hours and came back with a guilty verdict. He was sentenced to life without parole. It didn't stop him. He had connections, and family, and it was now a point of honor. Museum exhibits, galley exhibits, anywhere one of her works was displayed, were sprayed with bullets, people were hurt. Her work was too distinctive for her to show a painting, even unnamed.

"It about destroyed her. She retreated, and for a time she simply stopped painting. She tried photography, as she had a good eye and had to earn a living. She created a name for herself in her new field of marketing. She built a good business around her camera and her marketing images, while she died some more inside.

"She had been in witness protection for five years when she went for a pizza and met a guy. She didn't know him, he didn't know her, but he was as famous in his own field as she had been in hers. He had a similar history, of fame and money and a forced retirement, and like her he was a driven businessman. He had bought a pizza business with three locations and turned it into a national chain.

"He liked her, he liked her photographs, and he talked her into doing the marketing work for his pizza business. And he pursued her. As he puts it, he tumbled after her like a high school boy with a sweetheart crush. And she puzzled him to no end because she refused his invitations and wasn't interested in being seen with him.

"He's a smart man, and he can be relentless when he decides it matters. He eventually discovered who she was. He gave her back her art, in a very private studio and a very private vault. He convinced her it was safe to paint again. It took him another two years, but he convinced her it was safe to love him, and he convinced her to marry him. They've been married for ten years now." Ann, remembering, smiled. "She thrives with him. They are a power couple, in the best meaning of that word.

"She's been painting every day of their marriage. She's had no critic to comment, no observer to comment, no collector to respond to her work, she's only had herself. And she has turned painting into something extraordinary. I have to go back centuries to find such an intense talent of genius in her field.

"He loves her, and he wants very much to give her back at least a slice of who she was before this happened. Her husband wants to release a book telling her story, and alongside it he wants to produce a coffee-table book showcasing her art. He asked me to write their story. He asked me because I had written Sara and Adam's story, because I was the MHI, because I was a good cop with a security clearance and resources and friends who could help me watch for signs of trouble brewing.

"When I agreed to write Sara and Adam's story, to write *Danger in the Shadows*, the man who'd gone after Sara was already dead. The reason she had been in witness protection was over, the threat was past. But this book is different. The man who wants to destroy her has a powerful family. They are still actively searching for her.

"My writing sounds like me. For the same reason she can't change her style of painting so it's not recognized as one of hers, I can't change my style of writing to not have the book be recognized as mine. Even published under another name, eventually it could be figured out. The assumption will correctly be that I know her, know the name she now has, and have an idea where she lives. Those after her would go through me to get to her.

"When I was single, that risk could be managed. It changes now. I told them if I married you, I would end work on the book. And they were in complete agreement with that decision. Even published under another name, the risk is too great now. He is going to go ahead with the art book, but not her story. It was a very special case of someone who could write the book and have a reasonable chance of staying free of trouble. Her story is not going to get told, even if her art will get shared."

Paul said, "You can't do the book because it will sound like you, and someone could recognize that you are the writer, and if they did, the Falcon family and businesses are at risk."

"Yes."

"You made the right decision, but I'm sorry, Ann. It would have been an incredible story for you to write."

"I'm simply glad you hadn't met me after the book had been released. Marriage would have been a much more difficult decision for me to make if I knew this book was out there."

"Who are they?"

"The retired shortstop for the Atlanta Braves, Kevin Copper, now the Pizza King, and his wife, Kimberly. Her real name is Paulette Sunfrey. She is never seen in public with her husband. She's had plastic surgery, but if you wondered, you would look at her and say maybe."

He walked around to take the stool beside her and just considered his wife. "Sunfrey. Whose works already were legendary in her twenties before she disappeared. Whose work titled *The Coming Dawn* sold for just under two million when she was twenty-two. I keep postcards of her works in my desk drawers just so I can enjoy them."

"If she were able to sell the paintings she now has in her private vault, she would be able to feed a country or two. They are extraordinary works."

"Your friendship with them—you travel occasionally to see them?"

"They would keep a guest bedroom with my name on it when I was in the area. He travels a lot, and since I'm one of a handful of people his wife can be herself with, he encouraged the friendship from the first days we met. Now they are both simply good friends. They were some of the first people I called to tell I was getting married."

"You need to keep seeing them, along with your other friends tucked around the nation. I know you've got a long list of them, many I haven't heard about yet. It's important you keep those friendships, Ann."

"You'll hear about them now that we're married, and meet them too. I won't keep a friendship from you, even if I might be a bit cautious about when I happen to make the introduction."

"I'm glad you told me."

She studied his face and smiled. "I'd like the studio space upstairs, even if I'm just going to paint occasionally. I enjoy it, even if I don't have much talent, and I need the time alone. I wish I'd understood how tired I would be, so I could have warned you before we were married. I spent most of my working life traveling, in the air, sleeping in different motels, away from home, but I didn't see this coming, this fatigue that is sitting on me."

"Time, Ann. You'll adapt and start resting again. You've got all the time you need." He ran his hand across her back. "Let me go take Black for a walk while you unpack. Tomorrow I'll show you the nearest bookstore and the best place for Black to stretch his legs, and I'll introduce you to a few neighbors. We can have lunch at Falcons and try whatever Jackie considers to be her newest favorite dish."

"That sounds perfect."

After three days, the sounds in the house at night were beginning to seem familiar, and Ann was no longer surprised to hear the faint noise of traffic at all hours. The bedroom was quiet. She was wide awake as she often was near midnight, and she was accustomed to lying quietly, using the time to think. Paul was drifting to sleep beside her. His arm was firmly anchoring her to his side. "I love you," she whispered.

"I like hearing it," he murmured, smiling even as he slid further toward sleep.

She was beginning to form ideas for a new book. She thought again about putting Paul in it, the idea of him, and writing her own love story. She smiled as she thought it and watched him sleep. She'd get up soon and go work for a while. But for now this was the place she most wanted to be, watching her husband and enjoying how much she loved him. She wanted to write their story, and have it for his family, so they would see this man who would be head of the Falcon dynasty like she did. She turned the ring on her finger, not feeling married yet, but getting used to the idea and the fact that she was. She'd made a good decision.

"I can feel you thinking, even with my eyes closed."

He opened them enough to see her and offered a sleepy smile.

"I'm going to go work for a bit."

"Okay." He reluctantly moved his arm to let her get up. "I'll miss you."

She leaned over to kiss him. "Hold that thought. I'll be back."

PART SEVEN

SECRETS

29

Paul walked into his office, set his briefcase down, and shrugged off his coat. Rita had been kind to him. His desk was clear. "Where do you need me first?" She set coffee on his desk and, as today was his birthday, added a cupcake with a candle. He grinned—she'd gone with purple icing this year.

"The legal task force putting together the murder cases wants you all day tomorrow. It took me five reams of paper just to print the latest iteration of their trial case plans. Sam and I can talk you through them person by person faster than you can do the reading, but you'll have to get through the binders this week just to say you did."

"Anything major?"

"Nothing Sam and I couldn't handle. They want more of a case than we have. But after this amount of time, well, you know, what we've got is what is there. Your mail is on my desk, sorted by what I think is high priority first. I'll bring you the top inch, let you get started on it."

"Thanks, Rita." He held up a hand to delay her long

enough to be sure he'd seen the particulars of her neck-lace. "Did Sam finally stop being an idiot?"

She fingered the necklace and the stones as she smiled. "His birthday gift."

"About time."

"Yours wasn't so shabby either. How did you know I was learning to play the guitar?"

"I have a wife who notices things. She spotted the picks and the calluses."

"I'm hoping weddings are contagious."

"Sam couldn't do better. You want me to give him a shove, just let me know."

"Thanks, boss."

"I'm going to go walk the conference room and say hello to the troops, stop in to briefly see Arthur, then I'll get at the mail. Are you ready for that vacation to make up for the last weeks of double duty?"

"I wouldn't turn it down, but it was a surprisingly light few weeks. Either that or I'm getting better at being bossy and everyone was too terrified to complain."

Paul laughed. "Whichever it was, I'm glad I left you in charge."

———————▼———————

The work pulled him in, and within an hour of being back at his desk he was catching the rhythm of it again. He'd missed it, the flow of cases.

Rita tapped on his door. "Paul, the VP is on his way. Said it's urgent. He didn't give a reason."

"Meet him in the lobby and bring him straight up. I'll let Arthur know he's on the way in. Sam upstairs?"

"Yes."

Paul made the calls and was just hanging up the phone when the VP arrived. Paul stood to greet him.

"Congratulations, Paul. I'm so pleased for you and Ann."

"Thank you, sir."

Paul's boss walked into the office with Sam behind him. The VP pulled an envelope from his pocket. "This came in this morning's mail. I wasn't looking for another correspondence from her. I opened the letter before I realized what it was." He laid it on the desk.

Paul snapped a picture of it, encoded the image, and passed his phone to Arthur. He read the letter. "Rita." Paul stepped back to let her take his place, read the letter, and put it into an evidence bag.

Sam read the letter and passed Paul back the phone.

Agent Falcon—

I have one more tape more valuable than all the others combined—I come in, and I get witness protection for the rest of my life with house arrest for the first thirty years at my own expense. If the money runs out, I do the rest of the thirty years in medium security at a federal prison of my choosing under a name of my choosing. If you wish my attorney to know the name on the tape, have him send me a client attorney representation letter for purposes of knowing the name and advocating for the acceptance of my offer.

L.S.

It was the quiet in the room that told Paul more than what they might say. No one knew quite what to make of this. "What do you think, sir?"

The VP shook his head. "She's got financial means,

she's free, and she's deciding she wants to come in? I'm not sure what to think. Do I ask her to tell me the name?"

Paul looked at his boss, then at the VP. "Ask her for the name. Sam will go with you. Get it out in the mail today if you can, Sam."

"Did we miss a murder? Something even higher profile?" Rita asked.

Paul read the letter again. "She's certainly implying we did. We need to look for someone shot in the head, high enough profile the murder made the national newspapers, from the present back to when she first began to kill in '89. Someone else might have been convicted of the crime, so we look for the essential fact, the shot to the head from a distance, not the outcome of the case. It's got to be she didn't leave a signature, she did the murder and we missed the signature, or she was paid to do it, she has the tape, and she didn't take the shot—she disappeared instead."

"I'll get the guys in the conference room looking," Rita said. "If everyone takes a different year, we can come up with a list of cases by end of day."

Paul nodded. "Go."

He looked at Arthur. "We need to convene decision-makers because this is going to be a Gordian knot."

"Agreed. Tomorrow, noon. I'll get the director here. Find the case, Paul." Arthur headed out.

Paul turned to the VP. "Thank you, sir. For the speed of bringing this in."

"I wish I had more to give you. We'll get the request for the name into the mail today."

Paul spent until six p.m. in the conference room, watching possible cases being added to the board, then marked off as further investigation showed it was not a match for their lady shooter profile. In the past he would have stayed here until midnight, searching for the case the letter implied was out there. He looked at the time. He was married, it was his birthday, his wife likely had something planned, and his family certainly would. He had to go. "Sam, I'm leaving this to you to monitor. Call if something really interesting shows up."

Sam smiled. "Go, married guy. Rita and I have got this covered."

The elevator doors opened. The dog wasn't waiting for him, looking desperate to escape. Nothing smelt burnt, so Ann hadn't crashed and burned on a birthday meal. Paul relaxed and stepped off the elevator. Now that they were home, she was trying too hard to be a good wife, and he was waiting it out, figuring she'd relax if given enough time. Ann's flight bag was resting on the floor by the statue, and Black's leash was draped over the horn of the saddle. That was reassuring. She'd been out today, had taken her book with her. He heard music.

He walked through the kitchen on the way to find her and got them both sodas. Black showed up wagging his tail and looking for his attention. Paul rubbed the dog's head and scratched behind his ears. The dog was more content in the city than either one of them had figured. He seemed to think the thousands of scents crowding every block were all there just for him.

Paul found Ann hauling around another box of the

books she was still unpacking and mixing in with his. He scanned the shelves and smiled. "You've made progress."

Ann leaned into his hug. "Hi, birthday guy."

He rubbed her back. "I'm feeling old."

She grinned. "Jackie came through with your birthday cake. White cake, chocolate icing, lots of sprinkles. It's the box in the fridge. She said this one is just for us. We are to stop by the restaurant for the family-sized one. Your parents are entertaining the grandkids, and the party for the adults isn't really getting started until the restaurant closes. I told her we'd be there late."

"Thanks."

"I bought you a present yesterday."

"Did you?" He smiled as he brushed her hair back from her face just to have a reason to touch her.

"I even put a bow on it. Would you like your present now or when we get home?"

"I like the anticipation of it. I'll wait till we're home."

"How was the first day back at work?"

"I've got something to show you."

"This can wait." She pushed aside the box of books. "What do you have?"

He decrypted the photo on his phone and showed her the latest letter from the lady shooter. "She's really going to come in?" Ann sank down on the couch and patted a place beside her.

Black took the invitation as for him and landed on the couch. Paul laughed and pushed the dog to the far end, not minding his foray onto the couch but not inclined to share Ann. He scanned the letter again. "I don't see how they can take the deal. We need her testimony to help with the thirty murder cases. But offer her witness protection and house arrest, the defense attorneys attack the sweetheart deal she got, and the political firestorm is intense. The decision-makers are gathering at noon. I'd like you to come."

"Sure, I'll come if you want me to. Any ideas on the case she is referencing?"

"We're looking for a high-profile murder we missed, or a case that sounds like hers but someone else has been wrongly convicted of the crime. Nothing looks like a match so far. The VP is asking her for the name. I'm hopeful he can give us some direction without revealing what she said."

"She has interesting timing."

"You noticed that too. The legal task force has dug deep enough into the murder cases that they know her testimony would be helpful. I'm guessing, despite the politics of it, that they'll be advocating for some kind of deal to be struck. They need her testimony." Black laid his head on Paul's knee, and he absently stroked the dog's back.

"I had accepted the fact she was going to be out there, and we had probably lost the chance to ever catch her. I'm inclined to think I could even live with witness protection and house arrest if only to get her somewhere we can talk with her. If she's really got something as significant as she describes, we need the tape. I'm worried she's dead if she stays out there. There are thirty people with resources who want her dead right now. But I'm surprised at her offer to turn herself in. She's got money, she's got her freedom. She could stay hidden. Something about this doesn't make sense."

"Maybe she doesn't think she's as safe and hidden

out there as we do. House arrest wouldn't be a bad alternative if she thought someone who would kill her was close to finding her."

"Maybe." He leaned over and kissed her. "What do you say we take a walk before we go to Falcons?"

"Black, want to walk?" The dog hit the floor and headed to the elevator. Ann laughed. "I think that was a definite yes for both of us. Go change into something more comfortable, and we'll take a wandering walk before we celebrate how much older you've become."

Dawn slid across the bedroom, and Paul could see the dog now, stretched on his back with four feet in the air. As Paul was often up before five o'clock trying not to wake Ann, and the dog loved the bathroom doorway, they had all too often encountered each other with yelps and limps in the dark room.

Ann had her arm flung around a pillow hugging it, facedown, deep asleep. She rarely moved once she finally went down. Her dreams had been quieter the last few days. He traced a hand lightly across her back and softly kissed her hair before sliding out of bed. He could feel the contentment of being married grow stronger with every morning. The dog opened one eye as Paul stepped over him, and Paul obligingly scratched his tummy.

He found his toothbrush and dug around in her basket on the counter to find where she had put the toothpaste. The bathroom down the hall worked for his morning shower, to shave and to later dress for work, but for the next few hours of breakfast and a dog walk and handling family business, he could use the master bath quietly enough to dress casually and not wake Ann.

Ann was good at birthdays. She had bought him a yo-yo and showed him how to properly "walk the dog" with it, and she had bought him a high-speed game station and told him he'd have to connect it without her help, as she was impossible with electronics—the kids had told her what to get. Then she'd cautiously told him they were hosting a houseful of kids the next weekend, all of them under twelve. She had said it solemnly as if she wasn't quite sure how he'd take the news. He'd instantly grinned. She'd put out word to the family, and the kids had poured in with pleas for the opportunity to come see the cowboy in the entryway and play with Black.

He couldn't think of better birthday gifts for what it told him about her. He'd set her up with her own account on the family website, and she had settled in with such alacrity it felt like she'd been part of the family forever. The kids loved her. So they were hosting a houseful of kids. If their marriage survived this event, it would be a good milestone. He looked over at Black. He thought he'd better find a second dog to borrow for the weekend so Black didn't take the full brunt of all the attention.

He put away his toothbrush. "You want to share my bacon for breakfast?"

The dog rolled over, shook his head to wake up, and lumbered to his feet. The dog was much more a morning animal than Ann had realized. Paul found he liked the company for breakfast. They were rapidly settling into a habit of the newspaper and breakfast and a walk.

After breakfast, handling family business, and walking the dog, Paul quietly walked back to the bedroom for a last check. Ann hadn't moved. He was relieved she looked more rested than she had a couple of weeks ago. He slid a note under her phone and softly kissed her, then headed to work.

———————▼———————

Paul finished the morning update meeting, along with a review of the cases they had found, considered, and rejected, then returned to his office to get ready to see Arthur and the director about the letter. Ann was sitting in the visitor's chair in his office, reading a paperback and drinking a root beer. He ran a hand across her shoulder as he passed her, unloaded what he carried onto his desk, and got himself a soda. He leaned against the desk and just enjoyed looking at her.

She put her book down. "You've got that amused expression on your face again. Did I get the outfit wrong?"

"If the director has a problem with jeans and teal, he's an idiot. I love those jeans."

"I was at Falcons talking with Jackie, and I didn't have time to get home to change." She tucked her book into her bag.

"Let's go flying tonight. You haven't been in the air much at all for the last two months. We should fix that."

She looked over, interested. "Have a destination in mind?"

"Wherever a plane needs to go where there's one to bring us back."

"I got asked to ferry a bird to St. Louis, if you don't mind a few hours for a round trip."

"I'm game. I'd like to watch a sunset with you."

"I'll set it up. What's the plan for upstairs?"

"I don't have one. I want the tape, and I want her to come in. The deal she wants to make is more than they will be able to accept. So it's probably three hours of going in circles, trying to figure out an answer that is a no without it being a hard no."

"Has the VP heard back on a name?"

"Not yet. We know she has his letter requesting it. We still don't know how or even when she intercepted the letter this time, but it got lifted in transit again."

"Are Rita and Sam joining us?"

"They asked to wave off so they can stay looking for the case the letter is referring to. So far they haven't found what looks like a good match." Paul looked at the time. "We'd better go up."

Paul caught her hand, and they went upstairs to Suite 906 where Arthur, Tori, and the director were waiting. The VP had not yet arrived. Paul got himself coffee as he listened to Ann and the director chat. Ann was comfortable with Edward in a way that told him it was an old friendship. A few minutes later it became obvious Tori and Ann had mutual friends as well. Paul settled into a chair beside Ann.

The VP walked in, followed by Reece Lion. "Sorry I'm late, gentlemen. Hello, Ann. And congratulations to both of you." He nodded at Paul and pulled an envelope from his pocket. "Her answer came in this morning's mail. Should I open it? Or do you wish to check it first?"

"Open it."

The VP stepped over to the desk. He slit open the envelope and removed a single sheet of light green paper. He read it, paled, and pulled a lighter from his pocket. He slid over an empty candy dish and burned the page. "Give me twenty minutes. I'm going to take a walk around the roof and think about this." He left with Reece.

"The name spooked him."

"I'd say." The director looked at the pile of ash. "Paul, there's no case that looks like a good match for her reference?"

"A few are long-distance head shots, but none hold up as being her once you read the case file. We haven't found it yet. And nothing matches a name that would be this high-profile."

The VP finally returned with Reece right behind him. "One more minute. Arthur, may I use your desk?"

"Of course."

The VP pulled out the chair, picked up a pad of paper and wrote quickly. "I can't tell you what she said, but I can tell you the name she gave me is a retired person on this list." He handed the page to the director.

Edward scanned it, frowned, grew angry, and read the list aloud. "Supreme Court justice, Speaker of the House, majority leader of the Senate, CIA director, FBI director, U.S. attorney general, vice president, president." He looked up from the page. "You're serious, Jim. She's got a tape of someone on this list, retired, hiring her to commit a murder?"

"That's the statement she's making. You need to solve what case she's talking about, or you need to give her the deal she wants."

"It's an old tape she's going to turn in. She can hide a forgery in bad recording equipment. These people give speeches all the time. Enough time, you can make me say anything you want. We give her the deal, and it proves to be a hoax or an elaborate forgery."

"We can make any deal contingent on the tape not being a forgery. No, I think she believes the tape is real. She's asking for witness protection for thirty murders. It's an astounding request. She thinks she's got information that warrants that kind of deal."

"Paul, what are you thinking?" Arthur asked.

"How many names total does that list of retired individuals include? Fifty? A few more than that? These are well-known people, in the news when they held the job and still newsworthy after they retire. We cover the time period from her first shooting until now, and we look for people connected to them who are dead. They aren't going to hire someone to kill a stranger. So we look for disputes on record, any court papers, civil disputes. Who on that list of disputes is dead? Who on that list of dead died by a gunshot? If there's something out there, it's going to have at least a rumor somewhere."

Arthur nodded. "Start that search. We need to have at least a possibility of what we are dealing with."

"We should convene again tomorrow," Tori suggested. "We aren't in a position to make a decision."

The director nodded. "Agreed. Can you imagine what this is going to be like if it is true? We're prosecuting thirty murders. We're about to be hit with the release of your autobiography and the boating accident being an abduction. Now we add a high-profile hired hit? The agency is never going to get out of the news cycle at this rate."

———▼———

"Paul." Ann handed him a sandwich.

"Thanks."

She had brought in a meal for everyone on his team. The clock showed it was after ten p.m. and they were still trying to find a case that fit. "You might as well go home, Ann. This is going to be another few hours before we finish checking the possible names." Based on the VP's definition of who was on the tape, they had a list of forty-eight names to consider.

"I'm okay for another hour," she said. "These people have been sued, threatened, suffered personal tragedies, but no one close to them, or in a dispute with them, has died of a gunshot."

"Do you see another way to do this search?"

"Maybe broaden the question. Someone on this list hired a hit, a very expensive hit. It still makes sense that it was done to protect someone. Maybe not to protect themselves, but to protect someone in their family. I'd guess the children or the grandchildren rather than something more distant like a cousin. Maybe look for a police report on a child. If family were the victim of a crime, if the law didn't get them justice, then maybe hire a professional shooter to get their justice."

Paul nodded, liking the idea. "Do you think the tape is real?"

"I think the lady shooter planned for witness protection before she ever sent you the first tape. She has something big. The other thirty tapes, they were incidental. They were simply to get you to recognize why you needed to say yes to something so off the scale as witness protection and house arrest for thirty murders."

"It will be quite a conversation tomorrow."

30

can't give a hired shooter witness protection and house arrest for thirty murders, even in exchange for a tape of an individual on that list. It would never make it through trial to a successful prosecution," the director said, rubbing his face with his hands. The conversation had been going on for two hours, and that was still the core problem. She was asking for too much.

"You hand me a tape of a retired Supreme Court justice asking the lady shooter to kill his brother, and I don't know if I can make the case. We don't know how old the case is, if there is any supporting evidence. The body could have been cremated, and we can't even prove a murder occurred. The lady shooter would have to appear in court and back up the tape and confess to the shooting and the money received—all of it. And I would still likely not get a conviction. The credibility factor would be too much to overcome, not to mention the argument that the tape could be a fabrication. We need a lot more information before we could accept this offer." He looked at Arthur, and then to Paul. "Can we figure out the contract murder without the tape?"

"It's not an easy list of people to investigate, even if it is a limited number of names," Paul answered. "We haven't found anything so far with a dozen agents and a dozen hours. It's likely out there, but I don't know if we will find it, and I don't know how we would prove it if we didn't have the tape." Sam and Rita had joined them for this conversation, and Paul looked at them to see if there was anything they wished to add. They, like Ann, had been quiet since the meeting began.

"Give her a contingent deal. There has to be a guilty plea or a successful conviction to get witness protection," the VP recommended.

The director turned. "Say that again, Jim."

"She's asking for too much. But there might be a combination of facts that would get you to the point you would agree to her offer. Give her a contingent deal." The VP leaned forward in his chair. "Take her offer but with terms. It takes a confession and a guilty plea from the person on the tape, or it takes a successful prosecution, to get her the long-term deal for witness protection and house arrest. You decide not to go to trial, you go to trial and lose, she spends the rest of her life in medium security at the prison of her choosing and under the name of her choosing. But that's not much better than the deal she has now, and she's presently living free and apparently has substantial financial resources. You have to give her an incentive to come in and roll the dice on the trial outcome."

The VP looked around the room before continuing. "So give her an incentive. She agrees to cooperate and testify at every murder trial you bring for the thirty murders. During the time between when she turns herself in and the last murder trial is brought, she gets witness protection and house arrest. It raises the likelihood you get convictions on the murders, it gets her to turn herself in, it gets her protection from the thirty people who have reason to want her dead, and it gets you the last tape she's talking about. You simply say no, she stays out there and free. An offer with terms is worth the try. At least it keeps the conversation open."

"Yes, that's the best way," Tori agreed. "We don't know what this tape is, but if it proves valuable enough to enable a conviction, even witness protection is not an unreasonable outcome."

The director reluctantly nodded. "Write it up. We watch the package every step of the way. If she hasn't opened the reply when we catch her, we can argue the only deal she has is the prior one."

The VP nodded. "I'll get a new phone solely for this. I'll request that she call me on that number to make arrangements to turn herself in. You can't put a trace on the line or listen to the call, as it risks everything she gives you being tossed out in court, but you can know the moment she has the letter and learns the number to call. Put tracing and recording on my other phones. If she calls on one of those lines, I don't accept her as a client and you can use the information. Paul, what do I suggest for how and when she turns herself in?"

"I'm sure she'll have a suggestion on where and when. We need these core pieces. She comes alone. It's in a location without civilians around, who could get hurt if there's trouble. It's daylight. I'll assume she is going to want you there, and you don't go anywhere without Secret Service and cops. You can sit in a bulletproof vehicle and talk to her on the phone until she's in handcuffs. My preference would be a bankrupt building with a big parking lot, she arrives in a vehicle and parks, we pull into the parking lot, she calls you and you talk her through getting out of the car, walking away from it, putting her hands behind her head, and we get out and put cuffs on her."

"That's good, but we need less open," Sam said, speaking for the first time. "We've arrested thirty people who have reason to want her dead so she can't testify against them. There's a serious risk that someone takes a shot at her. They have to assume if you caught them, you can get to the lady shooter, and they want her dead if they can find her first."

"What do you suggest?" Paul asked.

"I don't know. An underground parking garage solves part of it but adds a lot more problems."

"Rita, have an idea?"

"I want to hear Ann's."

Ann looked uncomfortable with the attention, but looked at Paul. "All you need is for her to be unarmed, alone, and at a specific place. You want her to stay alive. So use a big office building, something that has shopping on the lower levels and multiple businesses on the floors above. The Hanson Building would work. Gregg Tripp has his offices there. Tell her to turn herself in on Sunday afternoon. The business floors will be empty. She takes the elevator or the stairs to the fifteenth floor. She walks to Tripp's office. She comes into the room and puts her hands on her head. You open the door, step into the room, and handcuff her. You have security cameras in the elevator, stairs, hallway, and office. You keep her away from windows. You give her lots of places to hide, and a lot of time to get into the building by the avenue of her choice. She comes to you. You can even make the time Sunday afternoon at her discretion, she just calls the VP to say she's coming to the agreed upon office before she enters the stairs or elevator. My guess, she'll have tucked herself away on a higher-level floor the day before and come down to the meeting place. If it all goes wrong, you can close the floors above where the public is at and possibly contain her by blocking stairs and locking down the elevators."

The VP nodded. "If you can identify such a building to use in a few key cities, I can work with that. Let her choose the location, but have it be that simple. She comes to you. If she wants her own plan, she'll have to give it to me in detail, and then call me back for what you want to reply."

Arthur nodded. "Let's find a building that suits us in five cities—Los Angeles, Chicago, Atlanta, New York, and Denver, something with an attached parking garage, easy public access, and at least fifteen stories."

Paul could work with it. "Sam, as soon as the letter is in the mail, I want you and Rita to stay with the VP and on that phone. We have to assume she's going to lift this reply as she's done all the others. I need you there to monitor the phone. I'll stay on the package and try to monitor its delivery. The call is the most important point."

Three days later, Paul took Sam's call. "Yes, Sam."

"The phone is ringing."

Paul looked at the monitor. "The package hasn't been picked up."

"If it's not a wrong number, she's got it."

"Tell the VP to answer the phone, and go with the plan."

Sam muted the phone. He came back on moments later.

"It's her. The VP answered the call, nodded to me, and walked into his office to have the conversation."

"I'm heading upstairs to Suite 906. I'll put together a conference call. Put the VP on it as soon as he's done talking with her."

"Will do, boss."

The VP joined the conference call twenty minutes later. "It was an interesting call. She's proposing her own when and where. This Friday three a.m., at the Chicago Mercy Hospital cafeteria. It's closed at one a.m. and opens again at six a.m. The doors are electronically locked and unlocked from the security office. She wants you to unlock the staff kitchen entrance door by the cancer institute elevators ten minutes before three and relock them ten minutes after. She'll walk in alone and take a seat. You come in and handcuff her there. The tape will be in the hospital somewhere. She wants a brief conversation with me, she will tell me where the tape is, and she wants me in the room when she says who is on the tape and I give that tape to you. I would suggest I pick up the tape while you safely transfer her to this building, and we have that conversation about the tape and who she names in a secure conference room here."

Paul looked at Arthur, who nodded. Paul agreed. "We can arrest her, leave the hospital by ambulance, and move her to this building in a very short time with minimal risk."

"When is she calling back?"

"Six hours."

"Let's go check out the hospital layout. We'll get back to you, sir."

The hospital looked more promising than Paul had first thought. There were no patient rooms nearby. In the middle of the night, the offices along the hallways leading to the cafeteria would be closed. The cafeteria itself was large with more than fifty tables.

"Let's keep this simple. We set up in the security office to watch her arrive. Once she's inside, we put two guys outside every door. I walk in with Sam behind me, cuff her, and based on what it looks like we have a short conversation here before we move her."

It was a simple plan, but they still went over it so many times that when the clock finally began to tick toward Friday, three a.m., the need to have it over was adding to the layer of nervous energy. Paul put Rita in the security office and waited with Sam in the office nearest the cafeteria doors. "We're ready, Rita."

"Unlocking the doors, boss."

Paul leaned his shoulder against the wall and waited, knowing it would be twenty minutes before the doors locked again. The time ticked by.

"A lady just entered the cafeteria. She's looking down, wearing a wide-brim hat. Her hands are open and empty."

Paul felt his heart rate pick up and shared a brief smile with Sam. Maybe. Maybe this was going to go as planned. Paul forced himself not to look at the clock, to simply wait for Rita's word.

"The doors have locked."

Paul stood. She had been inside for several minutes. "Sam, with me."

Paul walked to the door she had entered. "Rita."

The locks clicked open. Paul stepped inside the cafeteria, making the choice to leave his side arm holstered, let Sam provide the cover.

She had chosen a table near the center aisle. She was facing him, her hands resting on the table.

"Hello, Linda."

"Agent Falcon."

She was nervous, but not moving.

The years had not been kind. Sometime in the past she had been shot in the head. The scars were unmistakable—a blown-out jaw and rebuilt face. Old scars, faded white with years. One eye didn't focus on him and was only a well-crafted shell behind the glasses. Her hair was long and swept to cover most of the damage.

"We'll be talking for several hours. Why don't you make it Paul," he offered quietly. "Would you stand up, please?"

He secured a cuff on her right wrist first, moved behind her and secured her left. "Did you bring a purse or a bag?"

"No. There's a photo in my back pocket. My cash

and car keys are in the hat over on the table by the door I entered." Her voice was low, slightly hoarse.

"Have a seat again."

He eased her back into the chair, scanning the floor and chairs around her. "You asked to speak with the VP regarding the tape. Is it here?"

"In the hospital, yes."

"Sam."

Sam radioed for the VP. He entered the cafeteria with Reece.

"A minute alone, please, Paul." Gannett pulled out a chair but sat well back from the table. "Hello, Linda."

Paul retrieved the car keys and cash and waited with Sam by the cafeteria door.

A minute later the VP walked over to join him. "The tape is in the surgical floor waiting room. Rita and I will go get it and meet you back at the FBI office. Linda's waiving counsel if you wish to speak with her regarding the tapes she has already provided. Leave this last one until I'm present."

"We'll meet you there. We'll use the secure conference room for the interview."

Paul considered the lady at the table and how the next several days of conversation were going to unfold. "Sam," he said quietly, "I want ten to twenty minutes of conversation here first. Tell folks to settle in where they are at."

He crossed over to the table and rested his hand on the back of the chair the VP had used. "May I ask you a question, Linda?"

She nodded.

"How close did I ever get?"

She gave a small smile. "We shook hands once, when you were investigating Brett Larson's murder. I'd heard rumors you were looking for a woman, and I was curious how much you knew about me. I was afraid I had been seen and you might have a good sketch, but you only had a general description. I was introduced as a witness who had seen someone coming down the outside stairs and getting into a dark blue or black sedan parked at the corner. I gave you good information, pointed out the shooting perch, pointed out where I had parked, gave a general description that was accurate as far as it went. You said thank you, and I breathed a sigh of relief that I wasn't in cuffs right then. That was the day I began to think about retiring."

He pulled the chair toward the table and sat down. He tried to get accustomed to looking at her face, so damaged and yet put back together. In the end, he simply held her gaze. "Why did you come in?"

"It was time for the truth to come out. The murders are done, I can't change that. But some of the secrets I carry around need to be told."

"Will you help with the trials and testify to what you did?"

"Yes. There are file boxes in my car for you. I followed the person who I had been hired to kill, I took photos, and I made sketches of my plans. And I took photos of the person who had hired me. I wanted to know the true motive for the murder, not just what they said on the tape. So I would watch, and follow, and in most cases I would see what they were really hiding. People with power kill for a lot of reasons, but money and sex and eliminating business competitors were common grounds."

"Thank you for keeping that evidence."

"It was my protection and insurance, just like the tapes."

"Your weapon?"

"Destroyed, in pieces in several different rivers."

"Why did you stop?"

"This final tape, this final request, convinced me to retire."

"Is there any medication you take regularly that I can arrange for you?"

"Thank you for asking. Tylenol. I could use a couple in another hour. I tried very hard to kill myself. I flinched."

"I'm glad you lived."

"I didn't plan to." She straightened up in the chair, just a bit. "I have a daughter now, and a husband—the surgeon who put my face back together. I would like to be able to speak with them every few months, to see them once or twice a year."

"If the tape is what you've described, you'll find witness protection and house arrest is tight but not a prison. They'll be able to visit you."

"That was the hardest part of the decision. Knowing I might never see them again."

"Do they know you are here?"

"No. I told him who I was before we were married. I told him I would turn myself in when I found the courage to do so. And I told him last Christmas this was the year I would find the courage to do so. We've spent the year saying goodbye. The death of Gordon Whitcliff, your interviews, was simply a reason to begin seeing what might be possible in a deal, and the arrests you

made provided a reason to conclude it. I know people
want me dead before I can testify. I didn't want to put
my daughter, my husband, at risk. I left them before I
sent you the first tapes."

"When we get to the FBI office," Paul told her, "we
will talk about this last tape. Then you'll be taken to a
secure house within the city to settle in. You'll be fitted
with an ankle bracelet and allowed to move around the
house as you like. We'll talk for a few hours every day
and go through the material you have, that I have, until
the record for these murders is complete."

"My memory was not affected by this trauma," she
said, motioning toward her face. "As much as I wish the
memories were no longer in my mind, they are sharp and
clear. I'll take you through what I know. I'm aware I'm
getting what I don't deserve in exchange for the truth.
I know justice would be life in prison or death row."

"We were prepared to have you remain a shadow
out there, never caught. We accept that the deal you
arranged was a necessary fact, and we'll honor it. The
trials for the thirty people arrested will begin in roughly
six months and likely stretch out over five to seven years,
depending on the appeals. You'll be moved to a new safe
house every six months or so, depending on the risks
observed. Tonight we are going to walk out of here, take
the elevator to the lower level, and leave the hospital in
an ambulance."

"My rental car is in lot B, slot thirty-nine. The boxes
for you are in the trunk."

"I'll have them brought in." Paul rose. "Sam."

He gave word they were moving.

"This way, Linda."

------------▼------------

They gathered in the secure conference room.

Paul removed the cuffs once Linda was seated at the center table and brought over a bottle of water, along with a couple of Tylenol. He pulled out a chair across from her.

The VP took a chair at the table.

Arthur, the director, Tori, Sam, Rita, and Ann took seats behind them, with Reece standing to one side. Paul wanted the people who knew the case to be present. He wanted the decision-makers to get their own perspectives firsthand.

Paul turned on a recorder, gave the place and time and names of those present. "This interview with Linda Smythe is regarding tape thirty-one. Sir, you have the floor."

"The legal matters are in order," the VP began. "If there is a confession and a guilty plea from the person on the tape, or a successful prosecution, Linda receives witness protection for life and house arrest for thirty years. I have a signed copy of the agreement, plus the tape in question. For the record, it's labeled thirty-one and I am giving it to Agent Falcon."

Paul took it and saw it was different than the thirty tapes he had received from her so far. The middleman hadn't made this one. He set it beside the tape recorder he had brought in, keeping his attention on Linda. She was trying hard to keep her courage together. "Why don't you tell me, Linda, what I'm going to hear on this tape."

She met his gaze, and held it. "The vice president hired me to kill his chief of staff."

Paul heard a chair crash behind him but ignored the chaos that erupted in the room. He kept his gaze on Linda. She had been carrying a secret so heavy it made her risk capture just to be free of it. *The VP had hired her to kill his chief of staff.* Paul felt a muscle in his jaw spasm. Ann's heart must be breaking right now.

Paul looked over at the VP. Gannett laid another piece of paper on the table, took out his pen, and signed it. "Her deal requires a confession and a guilty plea from the person on the tape. I offer that signed confession. I hired Linda Smythe to kill my chief of staff."

"Sam, throw out anyone in this room that can't shut up, then get me a couple of those Tylenol." Paul felt the tick start around his left eye. "You need legal counsel, sir. Before I take your statement, and before this proceeds."

"I waive legal counsel. I wish to put a statement on the record at this time."

Paul leaned back in his chair, considering the man, the office he had held, and made a decision. "Ann?"

"The only two people who know what happened are sitting at the table. From his view of a greater good, he could probably kill if it was necessary. Based on what I see, he's not lying." Ann had found her composure, but he'd never heard that kind of ice in her voice before.

"I'll take your statement for the record, sir."

"I discovered while writing my autobiography that people associated with my campaign were dead, and I traced their deaths to my chief of staff. He was my friend, working for and with me, while he was murdering eighteen people. I saw him on the days before and after his murders, and I did not put it together in time to save their lives. I figured it out on July twenty-second,

2003. I couldn't prove he was the murderer in a court of law, but I knew it.

"I decided to confront him with what I knew and what I suspected while we were boating together out at sea. If he was a serial killer, I was not going to return to land with him. I was going to kill him myself and dump him at sea. But I knew it would be too easy for it to go wrong. So I hired someone with a solid reputation for killing their target. I hired Linda. I'll tell you later how I found her.

"I would take the chief of staff boating with me. I would confront him. If he was the killer, I would sail for the open sea. If we went past the break wall, she would kill him and it would look like an attempted assassination of me that had hit the wrong person. If I confronted him, and he convinced me it wasn't him, I would stay in the cove and return to land, and she would walk away and retire.

"I had followed the lady shooter case, and I knew someone was arranging the murders. The middleman was one of the possible connections to her. I sent a note for him to deliver, and the lady shooter called me back. I met with Linda and laid out what I wanted her to do and why. I paid her in full in advance. Whatever happened that day, whichever way it came out, she would walk away and retire. I arranged my security so I would be boating with the chief of staff alone. I arranged for security to be occupied so Linda could come and go after the shot was fired without being seen.

"My chief of staff had his own plans, and he used the change in security as an opportunity to abduct me. Before I could sail past the break wall and have him shot, he had pulled a gun, turned us back to shore, and abducted me. He drove me to the cabin. He would kill me, then kill himself, and become the most famous serial killer in the world.

"The chapter in the autobiography on the abduction is accurate in every detail from the point he pulled a gun on me in the boat. What you do not have is the chapter I'm now prepared to give you for my decision and arrangements made before that to kill the chief of staff.

"The chapter regarding hiring Linda is my full confession and detailed account of what I did. I kept the evidence—the bank account withdrawals for the money I paid her, my tape of our meeting, for we agreed to both tape the conversation—another three tapes I made at the time, recording what I was going to do and why. All of it is in my second office safe, the one in the floor under my desk."

"Why didn't you turn him in?"

"I was too infuriated at him not to kill him myself. I felt both duped as well as complicit in the deaths, because I hadn't put together the pieces and seen who he was. He had murdered people, and I had called him my friend. I was guilty of being stupid. Pride and anger and fury were enough to decide I was going to kill him myself. I never had a second thought about that decision."

"Did you kill him, at the cabin?"

"No. I wanted to. But his hand was on the gun, and he was trying to shoot the diary writer off his back. She caught his elbow, and he shot himself in the head. I was at the bottom of the pile with one hand on his throat and another gripping his hair, and the shot drove a piece of his skull bone into my hand." He held up his hand to show the scar on his palm. "That's my statement at this time."

"Who else knows what you did?"

"No one. I told no one what I had discovered, what I suspected, what I was going to do. These were solely my actions, my decision."

"Linda, what do you have to add?"

"I have it on videotape. The abduction at least."

The VP turned to her, surprised.

"I saw the chief of staff pull a gun and turn the boat back to shore. I saw the VP get hit with something that put him on the ground. I saw the car they left in. There was a search for the VP and news there had been a boating accident. There was a tip line. I called in on the tip hotline to state I had seen the VP forced into a car, and I gave a partial license plate number. I don't know if it was ever checked out. When the VP returned after the 'boating accident,' and the chief of staff was buried having died of a heart attack, I thought the VP had been able to overwhelm and kill him. We never spoke about it, never saw each other. My only contact with the VP was the one meeting when he hired me, and you will hear it on that tape."

"Why the video?"

"I was using a wide-angle lens to capture the cove and the break wall. I wouldn't be able to tell if I hit my target when it was bobbing around at sea. I'd practiced and it was simply impossible to be a hundred percent sure of a shot when I couldn't predict the waves. The wide-angle video solved that. I would take the best shot I could, then run the tape back and look at what I'd actually hit, see if I needed to take a second shot. If necessary I was prepared to sabotage the boat and sink it and pick the chief of staff off in the water. I'd never taken a contract and not finished it, and it was a point of pride that the last job wouldn't be my first failure."

"Where is the videotape?"

"I mailed it to you today. It will arrive by courier in the morning."

"Did you plan your surrender with the VP?"

"The VP contacted me six weeks after the middleman died. He said there was an opportunity if I would like to come in and stop running, and he would do what he could to help me get some kind of deal. We had arranged a contact method years before. He placed a different ad in three newspapers, I combined the numbers, and I had a phone number to call. We spoke only once. He laid out how it could be done, laid out the steps to turn in the tapes, what my letters should offer. He told me the date the book would be released and that I was not part of it, but he had written the chapter about hiring me, and it would be found at his death. He left it up to me if I wished to come in. If I was going to do so, I should email him a copy of one of the letters I sent you, and he would do what he could to help me. That was my sole contact with the VP—the phone call, and emailing him a copy of the letter. The decision to come in and when to do so was mine."

"Director?"

"It's your case."

"Sir," Paul said, turning to the VP, "I am going to listen to the tape, and then I am going to place you under arrest for conspiracy to murder. I will retrieve the chapter and the evidence you have in your safe. We will have another conversation after I see those materials. For numerous security reasons, you are going to be held at your home tonight. In the morning you will inform your staff of your plans to take a vacation for a week, have them clear your schedule. You will then call an attorney and tell him everything."

"I waive legal counsel."

"Call an attorney. If there is a deal to be found for what you have done, it will not be negotiated by you."

"I wish no deal. This goes before a judge for sentencing."

"For the sake of the office you once held, the ending is not going to be your decision. It's heading for a judge, but the route it takes is going to be decided by others."

"Then a compromise. I will ask Michael Yates to act as my attorney. I will cooperate on whatever you wish, in return for one agreement. You permit this final chapter to be published. Let me accept public guilt for what I've done. No matter how else this ends, that truth needs to be known."

"Cooperate on everything I need, at every step along the way, and it can be published when I give you clearance for it to be released."

"Agreed." The VP looked past him. "Ann, I am sorry for letting you down. I emailed you an encrypted copy of this chapter before I left the hospital tonight. The encryption key is the first ten-digit code we used. Add a chapter of your own, write the end of my autobiography in your own words. When Paul gives you the clearance, give the chapters to the publisher. Do it because it needs to be done. I trust you to get it right."

"I will, sir."

Paul listened to the tape, the room deathly silent as it played. Then he rose and formally placed the vice president under arrest.

"We keep what the VP has confessed to the people in this room," the director said, pacing the small war room. "We get a deal worked out. Tori, that's your headache. We put him before a judge to accept the guilty plea and schedule sentencing. We time it to coordinate with release of the autobiography. We put him under house arrest while we work this out with his lawyer, and we keep this out of the news until we're ready for it to break."

Arthur nodded. "We can announce the capture of the lady shooter and her upcoming testimony at the various murder trials without making any reference to the VP's confession. It will buy us time. We can keep this contained."

The director looked to Paul, then Ann. "I can't imagine how much a punch in the gut this is. But I need to ask you, Ann. Can you write that final chapter? We publish the chapter on the abduction, the chapter of him hiring the lady shooter, and you write a final chapter. We need his confession out there and public, so we release that confession he just signed, and a transcript of this interview."

"Give me ten days. I can have his chapter and mine ready for the printer."

"Will the embargo with the publisher hold?"

"If we raise the bonus for everyone at the plant, I think it will."

"Get it arranged." The director looked into the other

room at the table, where the VP and the lady shooter were having a quiet conversation. "This is going to be a nightmare. We get ready for it. We put copies of the book out the night before to prep what is coming. The VP is arraigned, then a press conference, then we have the VP sit down for interviews if he's still willing to accept responsibility for what he did. Once this is public, the VP reassigns royalties for the third volume of the autobiography to the families of the victims, as he cannot profit from this.

"I want daily conference calls while we work out the details. Paul, put Sam and Rita on handling his house arrest, and give them as many people as they request on the rotation. Use a cover story that there was a credible threat and we're assisting the Secret Service. I'm comfortable trusting the lady shooter's safety to Marcus and the marshals he assigned. Get her tucked away for tonight, start debriefing her tomorrow."

"We'll be able to handle it, sir."

The director nodded. "There's no choice but to handle it."

Paul took the next hour to get security arrangements made for the VP and confirmed the lady shooter had an airtight security configuration waiting for her. After he finally saw both on their way, he went looking for Ann. She had disappeared shortly after the discussion with the director. He thought she would be somewhere reading the chapter the VP had sent her, or sketching out on a pad her notes for the events of tonight. She wasn't in the conference room. He headed down to his office. She wasn't there either. He pulled out his phone to call her, then saw the office light that was on. He leaned against the doorframe to Rita's office. "Hi."

"Rita said I could use her system since she has the double monitors."

"No problem." Ann was playing back the hospital security tapes. Every camera feed for the hours before and after the lady shooter's arrest had been put to disk for them. "What are you looking for?"

"I thought I would go tell her husband she's okay." He pulled out a chair beside her.

"She was comfortable in that hospital. You don't miss noticing someone with those facial injuries. Staff knew her and thought nothing of her being there in the middle of the night. She was on the surgical floor to leave that tape. Her husband is a surgeon who saved her life."

"You think her husband works at the hospital."

Ann found the moment she wanted, of the lady shooter on her way into the hospital. The lady stopped on the walkway from the parking garage to the hospital's main building, stood for a moment looking over and up, then turned and went into the hospital. Ann ran the same camera forward to the middle of the night. She pointed to a lit window in an otherwise dark floor. "There he is, watching, hoping to see you leave with her. Do you want to go tell him she's okay? I'd like to do something nice tonight."

The odds were good Ann was right. "She's got witness protection and house arrest. He'll be able to see her once this settles down. Let's go find his name, find him, and tell him she's okay."

PART EIGHT

HOME

31

Ann was growing comfortable in this home that was no longer just Paul's but hers as well. She picked up the yellow legal pad and the letter she had written for her husband and went to find him. She found him in the kitchen, fixing dinner for them both.

"Hi." She slid her arms around him and rested her head against his back. She loved being able to hug him.

He shifted so he could kiss her. "Welcome home."

She'd spent the last week in the solitude of her private quarters. She'd slept, read a stack of books, and painted in her studio. She felt more relaxed than she had in more than a year.

Paul brushed back her hair. "You look more rested."

"I needed the week."

"I know you did." He kissed her again. "I missed you."

She leaned into him, loving him. "Can you read my writing?"

He looked at the pad of paper and smiled. "I can probably work through it."

"How did Black survive?"

"He slept outside your door for the first three days, then conceded he'd come sleep in the master bedroom. I think he's now crashed in the den watching that animal video you got him." They heard a clatter and a thump. "Change that. He's heard you. He's coming."

The dog skidded around the corner into the kitchen, his tail slapping everything he passed.

"Hey, gorgeous." Ann knelt to hug him. She laughed and glanced up at Paul. "He's not being annoyed with me this time."

"He's just glad to have you around again." Paul turned down the heat and reached behind him for a spoon. "Try this and tell me what you think."

She accepted the spoon and sampled the sauce. "It's good."

"It's Jackie's new pineapple sauce to go over ice cream. She also sent over her roast beef dish and some kind of corn dish she's experimenting with. I promised her your opinion."

"I'll be glad to give it."

Ann slid onto a stool to watch him finish putting together the meal. "I'd offer to help, but, well, you know."

Paul smiled. "First night back is on me," he reassured her. "Tomorrow night you can choose which restaurant we call for delivery."

Tomorrow night. A lifetime of events from now. Tomorrow it would begin.

The VP autobiography was shipping tonight, and sometime in the next couple of hours copies would be delivered to their door. By morning the media would have the biggest story of their year, and tonight no one out there knew it was coming.

Every hour of tomorrow had been scheduled with attention to every detail. The VP would be arraigned at noon and plead guilty, with a deal for a five-year prison sentence. The expectation of a pardon to commute his sentence to house arrest was likely, but it wouldn't come before sentencing, a month away. The lady shooter had agreed to sit for an interview in a location carefully designed to keep her secure. Ann would join Paul for two interviews and a press conference. Sam and Rita would sit with Paul for a series of interviews over the coming week as reporters got their hands around all the elements of what had occurred.

"Don't look so sad."

Ann glanced up and offered a half smile. "It's more relief, and a desire to be past this. I'm not really worried. So many secrets will be released that speculation about who wrote the diary is going to get buried under more interesting facts for the reporters to concentrate on."

"You have this place to hide in, and if necessary a plane trip to anywhere you wish to go. I won't let the press be a problem for you."

"I know. Vicky is coming?"

"Vicky and Boone will be here when we get home tomorrow night."

Ann was grateful. "I need to tell Kate, before she hears it on the news."

"Call her after the book arrives and read her the chapters."

"When do you want to tell your family?"

"I arranged a family call for very early in the morning. Whoever is around will be on it, and I'll post an audio of the call so others in the family can listen to the news." Paul set a plate before her. "Eat while this is hot."

Paul fixed himself a plate and slid onto a stool beside her. They ate occasionally at the dining room table, but both preferred the simplicity of this.

"You can tell Jackie it's wonderful."

Paul smiled. "She's nervous about food in a way I wouldn't have expected. You look really good in my shirt, by the way."

"I rather like this one."

"Did you and Lovely get a chance to talk?"

"We did. I needed that kind of week even more than I did the sleep. There was a lot to catch up on, and a lot to prepare for. He told me not to fear what was coming, that He was with me."

Paul squeezed her hand. "So am I."

"I know."

"I'm glad you had that time." Paul pulled the pad of paper over. "What did you write me in your letter?"

She smiled and let him read. She was coming to like these monthly letters to her husband. She saw him wince and figured he had reached her list of minor things that had to be mentioned. He wanted to know, and she was doing her best to be honest and tell him. Next he laughed. She relaxed. She'd planned what she wanted to sneak into the letter, and it sounded like she was going to get her wish.

She got up to fix a bowl of ice cream with pineapple sauce and brought back two spoons. "I'll share."

He considered her over a spoonful of ice cream.

"You really want another honeymoon?"

She smiled. "I'll be better at it the second time around.

You'll need a reason to get away from the weight of the job for a couple weeks once this settles down. It will be something to look forward to."

"Where do you want to go?"

"I wouldn't mind a repeat of last time."

"I can arrange something for when this is over." He studied her face. "Are you going to be able to sleep tonight?"

"I expect it's going to be choppy. I'm nervous about the interviews. I'm glad you're going to be doing them with me."

"You won't have to do any of the interviews alone. I was thinking for tonight you might want to see an old movie. We'll share the couch for a few hours."

"My favorite way to pass an evening."

He caught her hand as she slid off the stool. "I'm glad you married me before this day arrived. You could have asked to wait, and you didn't."

She linked her fingers with his. "I made the right decision. I love you."

"I figured that out when you agreed to the wedding." He leaned forward to kiss her. "You want popcorn for the movie?"

"I do, if only because Black likes to mooch."

"I'll fix it while you choose the movie. Tomorrow, when the day is getting chaotic, remember the peace of tonight. We'll have more quiet evenings like this one eventually."

"It's what I'm counting on."

"Ann?"

She stopped tugging away from him and smiled at him. "Yes, Paul?"

"If you're going to be up reading tonight, I might join you. You still owe me Tom and Jennifer's story. Print me out a copy?"

"It's just a background piece, not a story, but I'll make you a copy."

"I like your love stories. When you finish writing ours, I'd like to read it first."

She blushed. "How did you know I was working on our story?"

"You smile when you're writing on that pad of paper, and you often get lost in thought looking at me. I know your expressions. You're remembering this last year together."

"You are the best part of this year."

"I'd agree with that. You are the best part of mine."

"You need to let go of my hand."

"In a minute. I love you, Ann. I know your secrets, I know what the next few days are going to bring. I'm going to protect you, have a non-answer ready when the questions get posed I don't want you to deal with. You'll let me protect you and speak for you tomorrow when necessary."

She thoughtfully nodded. "I'm going to let you handle as much of it as possible. I don't want to be famous, or known, or be the center of attention. I'll gladly let you speak for me."

He kissed her palm and released her hand.

He watched his wife and his dog disappear into the den. Tomorrow he got to be a husband when it mattered the most, when the world came tossing questions at his wife. She'd handle the VP story, she'd handle the questions about the chapter she had written, and he would get her through the chaos of the day. He had wanted the role of husband, and he had it now. He'd make sure she was carrying her duty weapon, he'd make sure she was in comfortable shoes, and he'd make sure there was a good book tossed in her flight bag so he could carve out thirty minutes of sanity for her whenever he could.

He fixed popcorn and thought about a year ago. He decided God had answered most of his hopes and most of his dreams. He'd found a good wife. The details were still unfolding for what that meant, but it was a change he'd wanted, needed. He liked being a husband. And sometime after this was over he was going to have to tell her the director had formally asked him to take over the Chicago office. He'd let her decide if he should take it. He'd had enough of the politics of being in charge during the last few months to last for a lifetime. He thought he'd enjoy going back to being just a murder cop.

"Black, I get the couch tonight, buddy."

The dog dropped from the couch back to the floor, and spotted the bowl of popcorn. He came over with a wagging tail and upturned face. Paul had brought a paper plate for him and dumped two handfuls on it. The dog had to step on the plate to keep it from sliding around the room. Paul settled on the couch with Ann.

"We both spoil him."

Paul smiled. "We do. I like spoiling my family." He leaned over to kiss her again because she was near, because he could. "I think we should spend part of a honeymoon being tourists again. You can fly us to all the interesting spots for taking pictures, the Grand Canyon, the Tetons, the beauty of the Great Plains. I'd like a few hours in the air with you, where no one can interrupt a long conversation."

"What do you want to talk about?"

"I'll come up with something. I've missed you, Ann. It's been too much work and not enough time hanging out with you."

She laid her hand against the side of his face. "We'll get it balanced again. I think spending some time being tourists sounds perfect. And there is nothing I like better than to fly for a few hours for pleasure. I would love spending that time with you."

"It's a date then. We haven't had enough of them."

She smiled. "I'll put it on my calendar."

"I found your calendar in my briefcase the other day. That tells me how much you missed it. It's probably been there for about a month."

"I'm like Black. My schedule is to see where you are and follow you."

He laughed. "I do like that about you, Ann. You keep your priorities straight."

The dog pushed at him for more popcorn. He refilled Black's plate.

Ann started the movie. "If I could define what I most want in life, it's this, an evening with you."

He dropped a kiss on her hair. "There will be more of them. That's a promise. We're in this together, forever."

Dee Henderson is the author of numerous novels, including *Threads of Suspicion*, *Traces of Guilt*, *Taken*, *Undetected*, *Jennifer: An O'Malley Love Story*, and the acclaimed O'MALLEY series. Her books have won or been nominated for several prestigious industry awards, such as the RITA Award, the Christy Award, and the ECPA Gold Medallion. Dee is a lifelong resident of Illinois. Learn more at DeeHenderson.com or facebook.com/DeeHendersonBooks.

More from Dee Henderson

Visit deehenderson.com for a full list of her books.

State Police Detective Evie Blackwell is part of a new task force dedicated to reexamining unsolved crimes in Illinois. While looking at old evidence for a couple of missing-persons cases in Carin County, she pulls out a few tenuous leads—with startling implications.

Traces of Guilt
AN EVIE BLACKWELL COLD CASE

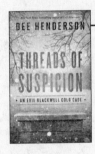

While Detective Evie Blackwell and her new partner, David, investigate two missing-persons cases in Chicago—a student and a private investigator—their conviction that "justice for all" is truly possible will be tested to the limit.

Threads of Suspicion
AN EVIE BLACKWELL COLD CASE

BETHANY HOUSE

You May Also Like . . .

Attorney Kate Sullivan has been appointed lead counsel to take on Mason Pharmaceutical in a claim involving an allegedly dangerous new drug. She hires a handsome private investigator to do some digging, but when a whistleblower is found dead, it's clear the stakes are higher than ever. Will this case prove deadly for Kate?

Deadly Proof by Rachel Dylan
ATLANTA JUSTICE
racheldylan.com

In this collection of gripping novellas from three beloved masters of romantic suspense, sins of the past lead to danger in the present. The collection includes Dee Henderson's "Missing," Dani Pettrey's "Shadowed," and Lynette Eason's "Blackout."

Sins of the Past by Dee Henderson, Dani Pettrey, and Lynette Eason

◆ BETHANYHOUSE